ISLAND *Magic*

Books by Elizabeth Goudge
from Hendrickson Publishers

Island Magic (1934)

Towers in the Mist (1938)

Green Dolphin Street (1944)

The Rosemary Tree (1956)

The White Witch (1958)

The Dean's Watch (1960)

The Scent of Water (1963)

The Child from the Sea (1970)

The Eliot Family Trilogy

The Bird in the Tree (1940)

Pilgrim's Inn (1948)

The Heart of the Family (1953)

ISLAND *Magic*

ELIZABETH GOUDGE

Island Magic

Hendrickson Publishers Marketing, LLC
P. O. Box 3473
Peabody, Massachusetts 01961-3473

ISBN 978-1-61970-772-6

First Hendrickson Edition Printing — June 2016

Library of Congress Cataloging-in-Publication Data

Names: Goudge, Elizabeth, 1900-1984 author.
Title: Island magic / Elizabeth Goudge.
Description: First Hendrickson edition. | Peabody, Massachusetts : Hendrickson Publishers Marketing, LLC, [2016] | ?1934
Identifiers: LCCN 2015040206 | ISBN 9781619707726 (alk. paper)
Classification: LCC PR6013.O74 I85 2016 | DDC 823/.914--dc23
LC record available at http://lccn.loc.gov/2015040206

Dedicated to

my Mother

The author's thanks are due to the compilers of "Guernsey Folk Lore" from which the Island songs have been taken.

Only the Island which we sow
  (A world without the world) so far
From present wounds, it cannot show
  An ancient scar.

White peace, the beautifull'st of things,
  Seems here her everlasting rest
To fix, and spreads her downy wings
  Over the nest.

As when great Jove's usurping reign
  From the great plagued world did her exile,
And tied her with a golden chain
  To one blest isle;

Which in a sea of plenty swam
  And turtles sang on every bough;
A safe retreat to all that came
  As ours is now.

Sir Richard Fanshawe.

Chapter 1

I

THE little fishing boat rounded the buoy and came in sight of the Island. She was a fat little white-winged boat, resembling an overfed baby seagull as she came skimming along, coquetting with the little waves, dipping up and down with an air of gay contentment.

She had reason for her gaiety. It was fine summer weather and the sea had been kind to her, it was evening and a harbour bright with the sunset was waiting to welcome her home. She had reason, too, for looking fat, for her interior was full to bursting with fishing tackle, fish, three men, one small boy, and a dog.

The small boy had caught nothing, but he did not care. Sufficient for him that Hélier Falliot, Guilbert Herode, and Jacquemin Gossilin had let him come with them in their boat for a whole blissful Saturday afternoon; had let him pretend, for four glorious hours, that he was one of their company, a fisherman of the Island, rich in strange oaths and tarry smells. Every rise and dip of the boat, every spurt of foam as she cleaved her way through the clear green water, carried him nearer to awkward explanations with parents who disapproved of Hélier, Guilbert, and Jacquemin, but he did not care; for four blessed hours he had run away, he had been free, a man and a sailor. With deep happiness he spat over the edge of the boat in imitation of Guilbert, and noted with satisfaction that he could spit quite a yard farther than this time last week. Under his breath he practised the new oaths he had learnt from Hélier, and felt within him that glow of delight that comes with the acquisition of knowledge.

He was a nice small boy, this Colin du Frocq, and, when clean, good to look upon. He was small for his eight years, exquisitely lithe and slender, dark-haired and brown-eyed, with a fair skin tanned by the sun to a warm golden brown, the colour, so said his eldest sister, who loved him, of the nicest kind of brown boiled egg. To add to his other attractions he had little pointed white teeth like a squirrel's, a very red tongue, whose tip was always to be seen peeping out at the side of his mouth when he was engaged in thought, small ears with the faintest suggestion of a fawn in their shape, and a dimple. He was now curled up in the stern of the boat, sleepy and happy and smelling abominably of fish. Beside him, scratching its underneath, sat his dog, Maximilian, a plumy-tailed, jet black animal of no known breed.

Now they were slipping along beside the Island. It lay on the sea like a sleeping animal, the rocks at its northern end stretched out like claws. Then gradually, as it emerged from the sunset mist, trees, houses, churches and forts became faintly visible. In the half light it took on the semblance of a faerie land, a withdrawn, unreal country, a mirage in the midst of the sea, showing a little and no more of its beauty, holding the rest jealously locked away. Leaning his head on his arm, sleepily dabbling one lean brown hand in the water, Colin watched as the Island permitted the beauties of its coastline to appear one by one, held them for a moment of time before his eyes, and then, as the boat sped on, drew them back once more into the mist.

First came the long, low levels of the northern sands, golden as a ripe cornfield, edged with the silver and lilac of sea-poppy and sea-lavender, melting imperceptibly into rolling wind-swept stretches of common. Here and there, peeping from behind the shelter of grey-green hillocks, were cottages, their walls washed with white or rose colour, roofed with grey slate. On the highest point of the common were the stark, upstanding cromlechs, built, some said, by the men of old as tombs for their dead, though the Island peasants vowed they were raised by the fairies as storehouses for their gold. In either case they were as old as time and as haunted—no Island-born peasant would go near them after dark.

After the common civilization began. The long sea-wall stood grimly fronting the waves, while behind its rampart were heaped the houses of St. Pierre, the Town of the Island. These were higgledy-piggledy houses, some high, some low, built of weather-stained grey granite, their uneven roofs rose-red against the sky. In the midst of them, like a hen amongst her brood, towered the tower of the Town Church. Beyond the town the country began again, but it was a very different country from the wild waste at the northern end of the Island. Here, beyond St. Pierre, were little rocky bays and above them rounded hills tree-covered and parting, now and again, to show green meadows and prosperous farms hid in their hollows. But Colin gave but a glance towards these woods and hills, for Hélier had swung the boat round and they were entering the Harbour.

The three men had been chattering hard in the Island patois, gesticulating with scarred hands, dark eyes flashing in their weather-beaten faces, but as they entered the Harbour they fell silent, the Island dominating them, the Harbour gathering them in. This Harbour of St. Pierre was not strictly beautiful, but it was perhaps the dearest part of the Island to the Islanders. It stood to them for home after tedious journeyings to inferior islands, for refuge after nights of storm. On one side was the grey mass of the fort, on the other the pier. These two were stretched out like arms, and within their shelter were security and calm water.

Hélier brought the boat round beside a flight of stone steps carpeted with green seaweed, shouted, flung a rope, sprang lightly out, his bare toes squelching on the wet seaweed. Jacquemin and Guilbert, the spell broken, continued their argument where it had left off, the while they hauled down their sail, disentangled the boy and the dog from the fish and ejected them kindly but swiftly by the scruffs of their necks. Colin stumbled up the steps, slipping and sprawling on their slimy surface, then turned courteously to thank his hosts for their hospitality, for Colin, like all the Islanders, had a beautiful dignified politeness, as natural and unstudied as the song of a bird or the bending of the corn. The three men paused to smile at him, their teeth flashing in their dark faces, their gesticulating hands expressing the amiability of their feelings towards him, then with a final grin and flicker of the fingers they dismissed him into the sunset and became garrulously absorbed in fish. Their talk, rapid, dramatic, rising and falling with a soft musical inflection, drifted after Colin as he skipped and hopped along the Harbour wall with Maximilian at his heels. It would drift through his dreams all night like a purling stream, and the memory of it, when in after years he became a wanderer on the face of the earth, would catch at his heart and make him sick with longing for the sound of the sea lapping against the Harbour wall, for the smell of the boats and the seaweed, and the sight of St. Pierre in the summer dusk. But Colin the boy, running along the wall, knew nothing of the memories of fugitive beauty that would haunt Colin the man; he only knew, as he paused suddenly on one leg and looked at the loveliness around him, that the Harbour looked jolly and that though he felt happy he had a curious pain in his stomach. He had so recently joined the suffering and joyous company of those who comprehend beauty that he did not connect these three facts. This initiatory pang confused him; gazing round him at the familiar scene he wondered why it hurt. There were the Town and the Harbour just as usual, but yet not just as usual. He had not seen them before at just this hour of sunset. The grey granite walls were flushed with a strange golden light, the roofs were shadowed, dim, the protectors of queer mysteries. Little lights twinkled up and down the streets in the shop windows, and the woods against the sky were black. The masts of the ships, black too in the evening light, were etched like the bare trunks of winter trees against a sky of palest translucent green barred with apricot and pearl grey. The waters of the Harbour, holding a bright remembrance of sunlight on the crest of each little ripple, reflected the pale colours of the sky and the dipping wings of the seagulls. Salt and tar and seaweed gave a delicious tang to the air, and the sounds of the Harbour, subdued by the evening hush, seemed to come from very far away. . . . A world of colour and light, transparent and unreal. . . . A world at the bottom of the sea. . . . A beauty so fragile that it would shiver into nothingness at a touch. . . . Somewhere a door banged and a man shouted. . . . It shivered into a thousand splintered rainbow fragments round Colin and his dog, and the two of them went careering towards the town, that queer momentary pang forgotten.

II

Past the Town Church Colin took a short cut up a steep, cobbled street that went twisting up the hill like an intoxicated corkscrew. He adored La Rue Clubin and went up it at every possible opportunity; partly because he was forbidden to go near it and partly because its noise and colour fascinated him. Maximilian, too, considered it a delectable spot. Nowhere else on the Island were the smells so rich and so varied, nowhere else was there so large an assortment of mangy cats. On a Saturday evening La Rue Clubin was particularly attractive, for the whole length of it was lined with booths, lit after dark by flaring gas jets and laden with unimaginable glories; great sticks of striped peppermint rock, boiled sweets of all colours of the rainbow, piles of live lobsters and crabs, fish of every possible variety, vegetables, scarlet petticoats, yellow sunbonnets, more crabs, more sugar sweets, all piled along the gutters in a wealth of smell and colour.

Over the stalls the top storeys of the old tumbledown houses jutted out so far that they nearly met overhead, making La Rue Clubin almost like a tunnel, and confining the noise as though in an echoing cavern. And what a noise! The inhabitants of the tumbledown houses, the very poorest inhabitants of the Island, all issued forth of a Saturday night to buy and sell, to cheat and shout and sing and swear. The women, with green and yellow handkerchiefs tied over their heads and blue aprons over their rags, clattered up and down the cobbles, pouring out conversation. Their men-folk, in blue jerseys and baggy trousers patched in all conceivable colours, shouted themselves hoarse as they brandished crabs aloft or weighed out haricot beans and pink and purple sweets. Sailors from all parts of the globe strolled up and down, pipes in their mouths, gold rings in their ears, their eyes, keen from so much gazing on sun and sea, darting here and there in search of a pretty face or a cheap drink. Every language under the sun was talked in La Rue Clubin, but the Island French preponderated, rising and falling, echoing and swelling like the sea against the enclosing walls. Now, in this drab twentieth century, La Rue Clubin has been condemned as a disgrace, rebuilt, cleaned and turned into a respectable thoroughfare, but on the twentieth of August, 1888, when Colin du Frocq was eight years old, it was neither respectable nor clean, it was merely a wonder and a glory.

Colin threaded his way slowly through the jostling crowd, his mouth and eyes wide open, an expression of beatific delight on his face, absorbing the joys of La Rue Clubin through every pore. One hand was in his pocket clutching his eight doubles. The Island double was equivalent to one-eighth of a penny in English money, and two of them were presented to Colin every Saturday morning by his father; it was all the wealth he ever had and he saved them up until he had a pennyworth to spend on his beloved mother. Last time he had purchased her a white sugar mouse with pink eyes and a string tail, and she had told him she considered it too beautiful to eat just yet, she would keep it for a little while longer on her mantelpiece, where she could see it as she lay in bed. To her husband she said, "I can't eat the thing. It is like the cup of water that was brought to David at the cave of Adullam. Perhaps a little later on you could manage it, darling, your teeth are better than mine. . . ." But the mouse was still there. This Saturday Colin purposed to buy her some sweets from the stall at the far end of La Rue Clubin, one of each colour, purple, red, cream, lemon, green, and rose colour, and the rest the striped pepperminty sort that made your mouth feel lovely and cold, as though you had been eating frozen snow. If she asked him where he had bought them he would say "From Le Manouri in La Rue Grand Mielles," and she would smile and say "Le Manouri's sweets are so wholesome. One knows they are clean. Not like those disgusting things from La Rue Clubin." Then she would pick out a lemon-coloured globule from the bag, pop it in her pretty mouth, crunch, and say, "Yes, Le Manouri's special flavour, I'd know it anywhere." And her son would smile at her like an angel straight from heaven.

Colin had not at this period of his life, nor at any other, the smallest objection to telling lies. He liked things to be pleasant and agreeable all round, and he had found from painful experience that the giving of truthful answers to direct questions bearing on his recent whereabouts and behaviour invariably led to unpleasantness. Therefore in conversation he aimed always at giving pleasure rather than accurate information, and was throughout his life universally beloved.

Mère Tangrouille, seated behind her piles of sweets at the far end of La Rue Clubin, surveyed the small boy who stood planted in front of her, his legs wide apart, his head thrown back, the light of battle in his eye, rather as though he were confronting some wild beast. And, indeed, Mère Tangrouille needed some confronting. She was enormous. She was so large that she was completely circular. She had no neck and no waist and was literally as broad as she was long. She always wore dark green with a black bonnet perched on top of her head, and was for ever knitting a large red woollen muffler. Whether it was the same muffler and like Penelope she undid her work each night and started again the next morning, or whether she knitted hundreds of different mufflers, it was impossible to say. Mère Tangrouille's temper was uncertain. If she had drunk just a little she smiled benignly on Colin, her little black eyes twinkling in her scarlet face, added an extra lemon drop to his pennyworth and called him a little angel on his way to heaven; but if her potations had been heavy she stormed and raved at him, relegated his everlasting soul to a destination in the contrary direction and, did he dare so much as to touch a boiled sweet with the tip of his finger, her great arms shot out like the claws of a crab and dealt him such a box on the ear that stars leaped and danced all up and down La Rue Clubin. But Colin was not afraid of her. He was never afraid of anything. His very wish to have things pleasant and agreeable made him able to twist people and things and places with their pleasant side outward. He had done this to Mère Tangrouille. When she was possessed of a demoniacal temper he confronted it, beat it down by sheer courage, pushed it away, and was left with just Mère Tangrouille, a very fine figure of a woman indeed, and his friend. But to-night there was no need for courage, Mère Tangrouille was butter and honey. She beamed at him, all her chins trembled with welcome, her eyes snapped with delight and she uttered soft crooning noises with her head cocked slightly to one side. Colin relaxed his tense attitude. The light of battle died from his eyes and its place was taken by the particular twinkle which he kept for Mère Tangrouille. He brought his feet together and made her a little bow. He inquired politely after the health of Mère Tangrouille—after the health of her cat—after the health of her various disreputable relations. He commented upon the state of the weather and the state of trade, and finally he produced his doubles from the recesses of his pocket and indicated his choice in the matter of boiled sweets.

"Ah, the little cabbage! Ah, the little cherub!" crooned Mère Tangrouille. Her dirty fat fingers hovered over the sweets and she picked out one purple, one red, one cream, one green, one rose, and four striped balls, then, looking up to wink at Colin, she added two reds and a green as a gift of love. She placed the treasures in a pink bag, handed them to Colin and then, bending sideways with a little chuckle, held out her arms. This was a part of the proceedings that Colin did not relish, but he had got two reds and a green for nothing, and he had already discovered that in life all delight must be paid for in one way or another, and that the wise pay without flinching. Running round the stall he suffered himself to be gathered to Mère Tangrouille's bosom, to be enveloped by her large person, with its aroma of beer and peppermint, and finally to be kissed upon the mouth. . . . If his mother had seen him she would have died of shock. . . . Colin returned the kiss, grinned at the old lady, withdrew a little hastily so that the performance could not be repeated, and pursued his way.

As Mère Tangrouille watched his slender little figure darting in and out through the crowd, his sleek dark head so beautifully and fearlessly poised, his brown legs twinkling, tears filled her eyes.

Sweets, crabs, stalls, cobbles, crooked houses, all became blurred to her, a rainbow background for that little creature, who was hers only for one short second once a week. She sighed gustily and wiped her eyes with the red woollen muffler. She wondered if his mother fed him right. A child like that needed a lobster to his tea, and a glass of stout now and again wouldn't do him any harm. . . . Someone barged into the stall and sent a few sweets flying. . . . Mère Tangrouille swore volubly and felt better.

La Rue Clubin ended abruptly in a flight of steps. The town of St. Pierre was built upon sheer rock, and so steep were the precipices that every now and then the streets found it impossible to climb them, gave up the struggle and turned into steps. There were only three streets in the whole town which were possible for a carriage, and even then it went up pushed by the whole populace and came down with the horse sitting on his tail.

The steps at the end of La Rue Clubin had steep, grey, granite walls on each side, and on top of the walls were the back gardens of more tumbledown houses. Every Islander was a passionate gardener and these gardens, full though they were of old tin cans and brickbats, yet had a wealth of flowers as well. Colin, as he climbed the steps, looked up to see madonna lilies shining through the gloom. The smell of honeysuckle mingled with the smell of fish from the street below, and scarlet nasturtiums hung down the grey walls like little hanging lamps. At the top of the steps Colin sat down to wait for Maximilian. He knew it was no use hurrying him. Though normally an obedient dog Maximilian in La Rue Clubin became completely demoralized. When every cat had been chased, and every smell had been smelt, he would condescend to return to his duties, but until that moment of repletion arrived Maximilian was as a creature let loose in the primeval jungle.

While he waited Colin took the little pink bag from his pocket, opened it and surveyed the sweets. . . . His mouth watered. . . . They were for his mother, but was he entitled to eat the two reds and the green which were extra, not purchased by his penny but by his courage in winning the friendship of Mère Tangrouille?

Colin's conscience was a curious organ. In most directions it entirely failed to function at all, in other directions it was abnormally sensitive. It was so in all things relating to property. Colin had a very strong sense of what was his and what was not his. Now he pondered long and deeply. Were the three sweets his or his mother's? He gazed inside the bag and his mouth watered so violently that he had to swallow three times. Suddenly, abandoning the argument, he seized a red sweet and popped it into his mouth. As he sucked it he gazed upwards at the strip of sky framed by the old red roofs. It was a lovely shade of green, the colour of a robin's egg and clear as sea water in a pool. Three lilies nodded against it, and in its cool depths burnt a silver star. Again he felt a little stirring of pain, and quite suddenly it seemed to him that his mother was looking down at him from the strip of sky, his pretty mother with her white skin like the lilies, night-black hair and twinkling starlike smile. A rush of love surged up in him. He put his finger in his mouth, disentangled the red sweet from a back tooth, wiped it carefully on his knickerbockers and put it back in the bag. His darling, darling mother, she should have everything he had to give her, always and always. . . . The little star twinkled with approbation, the lilies bent gently towards him, and Maximilian came charging up the steps.

Maximilian's ear was torn and bleeding, his nose was scratched, and portions of garbage adhered to his paws, but he was happy, though fearful of the heavy hand of justice. He sat down, hung out his tongue in a way that was meant to suggest pathos, and wagged his tail fast and furiously to create that atmosphere of happiness in which punishment would seem out of place. He was successful. Colin, disarmed, wiped his bloody face tenderly and assisted his ascent up the steps with the very gentlest of kicks.

III

For the next twenty minutes the boy and the dog climbed upwards through steep cobbled alleys and up flights of worn stone steps, twisting and turning between grey, old, red-roofed houses and lichened garden walls. The orange glow from lighted doorways shone out on them as they climbed. In and out of the light and the dusk they went, emerging suddenly into the lamplight like little moths and disappearing in the shadows again like forgotten dreams. Once out of the town, with the steep climb over and more level ground reached, Colin took to his heels and ran, Maximilian lolloping after. He had three miles to go and night was coming.

Colin was a magnificent runner. His habit of being late for everything kept him in excellent practice. On and on he padded, through deep dark lanes scented with honeysuckle, past meadows still smelling of hay, past cottage gardens whose wealth of colour burned in the dusk against whitewashed walls, past lonely farms with their green treacherous ponds waiting for the moon and the dancing feet of the water fairies.

He rounded a corner guarded by a battalion of foxgloves and entered a little lane that plunged downhill like a round green tunnel. On either side of it were stone walls covered with green ferns and crowned with tall bushes of escallonia, their little pink sticky flowers shining against dark green, glossy leaves. Behind the hedge of escallonia nut trees grew, stretching out their branches to make a roof over the lane and guard its secrets. For this lane was no ordinary one, it was a water-lane, and therefore fairy haunted. Hidden by the foxgloves was a little well of very clear water, and down one side of the lane a little stream, fed by the well, ran tinkling and gurgling on its way to the sea. Somewhere down below the lane, out of sight, was the sea itself. The low murmur of waves dragging lazily over shingle was a background to the song of the stream. The little lane was the meeting place of these two voices, even as the running stream linked the mysteries of the waters that lie in the dark of the earth to the greater mysteries of the sea.

When he came into the lane Colin stopped. He never entered that leafy tunnel without a shiver of expectancy, but he felt no fear. He was not afraid of the Things that lived in the depth of the earth or of the Things that lived in the sea. Whenever he entered a water-lane at dusk he trod softly and forbore to sing and whistle lest he should disturb the Things in Their journeyings backwards and forwards, but he was not afraid of Them and he longed passionately to see Them. They did not frighten him any more than did the evil spirit that sometimes possessed Mère Tangrouille. He confronted Them with the same cheerful courage and both let him by unharmed. Now he knelt down, parted the foxgloves, and looked at the water that welled up framed by forget-me-nots and hart's-tongue ferns. It was very clear, very cold, and came from who knew what unimaginable depths. It was a wishing well, one of the most powerful on the Island, and held in great veneration by the Islanders. Colin shut his eyes very reverently and had three wishes, one that he might lick de Putron minor next time he fought him, two that he might one day be able to give his mother a pearl necklace, and three, that he might become a sailor. This last was more in the nature of a prayer than a wish, the most fervent he ever prayed. It floated out from Colin's soul and went with the stream down the lane, across the beach and into the sea, and there it was hidden away in a seashell for safety until the time came for it to be taken out and granted.

He got up and walked down the lane very slowly. Maximilian, with the hair on his back slightly raised and his tail lowered, padded after, puffing and blowing like a steam-engine and looking wistfully at the stream. But though the tip of his tail twitched with desire he did not drink. He knew better than to lap from the stream that linked the waters of the earth to the waters of the sea—they were sacred.

The hot sweet smell of the escallonia was like incense swung into the air in welcome, and the nut trees whispered to Those who passed beneath their branches, but yet Colin, silent and attentive as he was, could not see Them. He could feel Their passing, but yet he could not see so much as the shadow of a wraith glide up the stream, not even poor Undine, though she alone of all the water spirits possessed a suffering human soul.

Halfway down the water-lane another one, waterless, sloped steeply to the right. Turning up it Colin broke immediately into song of the most vulgar type and Maximilian, following him, became another dog. The hairs on his head sank into place, his tail was erected once more like the plume on a skittish horse, and he sprang from side to side snapping light-heartedly at flies. This lane was identical with the other, but yet completely different. The trees talked of quite everyday things and the scent of the escallonia suggested no mystery but that of the budding and unfolding of the flowers of the earth.

This second lane led out into a wider one lined with the stunted Island oaks, all of them twisted one way by the winter gales and covered with lichen on the side nearest the sea. It was much darker now, the road was dim white and the trunks of the trees a ghostly grey. A fog was floating in from the coast, trailing scarves of mist in and out of the branches and lying like a soft white blanket on the fields beyond. Far out at sea a foghorn sounded very softly. Colin ceased singing about his mother-in-law, stood still and listened, every sailor's instinct in him wide awake. It would be a bad night at sea. Sudden August fogs were more dreaded by ships than lightning and tempest. With its jagged coast and "banques" of treacherous rocks veiled by fog the Island was a death trap. That afternoon, as Guilbert's boat came in sight of it, the Island had looked like a sleeping animal crouched on the water, to-night it would be awake with claws unsheathed. Listening, Colin heard the foghorn again and a faint sucking sound which was the sea surging round Les Barbées, a reef of dangerous rocks only half a mile from where he stood. Yes, it would be bad to-night.

Faintly visible down the road was a pile of farm buildings. An orange square of light patched their darkness, and as Colin looked a second and third sprang out. . . . Father was lighting the lamps at Bon Repos. . . . A fourth light challenged the dusk. . . . That was the kitchen. . . . For supper there would be bowls of bread and milk with crunchy brown sugar on the top, eggs laid by his own bantam hens and baked apples with cream. . . . Colin kicked up his heels and raced down the road towards his home.

IV

The farmhouse of Bon Repos was separated from the road by a high grey wall, immensely thick, built to withstand the onslaughts of gales and enemies. Lichen and yellow stonecrop flushed its hoary old surface with warm colour, and on its summit scarlet snapdragons nodded defiance to intruders and welcome to friends. A wide doorway was set in the wall, crowned by an immense lintel of solid stone, but the door had long since disappeared. Within was the cobbled courtyard, used long ago as a sanctuary where in times of trouble peasants and cattle could be gathered for safety, now a parade ground for Mrs. du Frocq's pigeons and a sun parlour for the cat.

Coming through the door the farmhouse was on the right, taking up the whole of one side of the square. It was built of grey granite, with small diamond-paned windows and an arched doorway with the date 1560 on the central stone of the arch. Let into the wall above the door was a stone of much later date, bearing the inscription in French "Harbour and good rest to those who enter here, courage to those who go forth. Let those who go and those who stay forget not God."

The roof, that had originally been thatched, was now covered with old red tiles stained by sea wind, fog, and rain.

At right angles to the house, opposite the entrance from the road, was a great barn converted now into stables and storerooms, old as the house and built, too, of granite. Behind it, but out of sight, were the more modern farm buildings, the pigsties, cow byres and outhouses. Another wall separated the courtyard from the flower garden and a little orchard of stunted fruit trees. Beyond that again a great rampart of earth and stones, covered with turf and crowned with old storm-twisted oak trees, had been raised by some long-dead determined farmer as a protection for the house and garden; for beyond the rampart were the cliff and the fury of the sea.

But no winds that ever blew could shake Bon Repos. Very old and very grim, low and solid, like a grey rock, it squatted on the ground as though it were part of it. But though its structure was unshaken its surface was scarred and ravaged by time and storm, and Rachell du Frocq, Colin's mother, in pity for tarnished beauty, had trained a passion flower over the windows and planted scarlet fuchsias on either side of the door.

So small were the windows that the interior of Bon Repos was very dark, but that did not worry Islanders like the du Frocqs. Out of doors was their natural habitation. Their house was not so much a place to live in as a place to take refuge in. They went to it, as the cave men went to their caves, when storm and darkness were upon them; for the rest they liked to be out in the sun and the wind. Even Mrs. du Frocq and her maid Sophie, whose work kept them more or less tethered to the house, peeled the potatoes in the courtyard, and did the washing in the vegetable garden at the back.

The front door gave entrance to the stone-floored hall, always, even on the hottest days, cool and dark as a sea-cavern. An oak table, so old that it had become black as ebony, had stood in the centre of the hall as long as anyone could remember. On its polished surface, black and shining like a mountain tarn, Rachell kept a bowl of old French china, patterned in red and scarlet and gold, and always full of fresh flowers. Primroses, cowslips, mignonette, roses, clove carnations, asters, and Michaelmas daisies followed each other in succession as the changing seasons spread their glowing tapestries, each in such a hurry that spring had barely time to draw back her cream and blue and gold before summer's weave of scarlet and rose pink was flung over the garden. The scent of the flowers floating out into the dim coolness of the hall was the first thing to welcome visitors to Bon Repos. Rachell believed passionately in the value of beauty. If she was pressed for time she considered the filling of her bowl with flowers more important for her family's welfare than the making of a cake for tea. On this point her family entirely disagreed with her.

To the left of the hall was the kitchen and living room, a large raftered room, whitewashed, with a red tiled floor. The huge chimney had carved upon it the du Frocq arms, an ermine with the motto

"Plutôt la morte que la souille." The original low hearthstone, with its fire of vraic,[1] had been replaced by a more modern grate, but the old stone seats were still inside the chimney enclosure, with the bread oven built in the thickness of the wall and the hook whereon to hang the "cräset" lamp. The "jonquière," stuffed with dried fern and covered with chintz, stood under the window; a species of day-bed wide enough and long enough to accommodate the whole family sitting together in a heap. The great oak table, with chairs to match, stood in the centre of the room, and against the wall stood an eight-day clock by Lenfestey, and a dresser bright with willow-pattern china. On the walls were copper warming-pans and sporting prints, the delight of Colin's soul, depicting stout gentlemen in red coats being thrown into ponds by triumphantly prancing steeds. A door from the kitchen led to the modern sculleries and dairies.

On the other side of the hall was the parlour. Rachell's female neighbours, revelling at that period in fruit under glass cases, wool antimacassars and albums full of whiskered male relations, considered this parlour shamefully and disgracefully old-fashioned, but to Rachell it was as the inmost shrine of her being. There was a French carpet on the floor, so old that its pinks and blues had faded to the soft colours of a dove's breast. At the windows with their deep window-seats—there were two, looking south and east, so that the room was brighter than the kitchen—were primrose-coloured brocade curtains with a pattern of gillyflowers and forget-me-nots embroidered by Rachell's grandmother. The stiff-backed chairs, covered with brocade that was fraying a little, had been a wedding gift to this same grandmother from her grandfather. It was a marvel that their delicate frailty had succeeded in supporting the hoops and panniers and silken petticoats of this same lady and her wedding callers. Over the mantelpiece hung little miniatures of departed du Frocqs, painted on ivory and framed in oval gilt frames. Below them a fire of driftwood was often burning, for the room was damp, and even in summer Rachell, fearful for her treasures,

[1]Seaweed.

would set green and orange flames flowering in the grate. Against one wall stood an inlaid cabinet with glass doors containing Rachell's two best tea-sets, one of French china matching the bowl in the hall, richly patterned in scarlet and blue and gold, and the other of delicate fluted white Worcester with handleless cups. On the other wall hung a lovely French gilt mirror, with slender columns on each side, and a panel of dancing cupids above. On either side of it exquisite strips of Chinese embroidery, sent home by a sailor du Frocq, splashed a perfect riot of blue butterflies and golden dragons with crimson tongues against the pale blue wallpaper. There was one rosewood table with a bowl of flowers and pots of pot-pourri upon it, but there was not a single whatnot, knick-knack, album, or occasional table. The whole room, according to the neighbours, was in execrable taste, and marked Rachell as being clearly no lady. Good taste or no, this room with its soft colours, its sweet musty smell of pot-pourri, damp, and burning logs, its dancing shadows and sliding sunbeams touching here a piece of glowing china, there a gilt frame, remained with Rachell's children all their lives as one of the most vivid of their memories.

At the far end of the hall, opposite the front door, a flight of winding stone steps, built in a curve beyond the straight wall of the house, led to what was originally a "ch'nas" or loft. This had now been partitioned off into bedrooms. The rooms were whitewashed, with sloping ceilings and dormer windows and odd nooks and crannies, difficult to keep clean, that delighted the children and broke the heart of Sophie, the maid. The big front bedroom, the property of Rachell and her husband, André, contained a four-poster with crimson curtains, a mahogany chest of drawers with a bow front, a dressing table with a petticoat of flowered chintz, a terrifying French print of the Day of Judgment, and similar glories. The children's rooms had nothing in them but little beds covered with patchwork quilts, and wooden washstands and chests of drawers painted a startling shade of magenta.

All the rooms in Bon Repos were soaked in peace. The sun, slipping round the house from east to west, sent long shafts of light through the little old windows and painted the whitewashed walls pink and amber and then pink again. The leaves of the passion flowers, creeping round the windows, set shadows dancing from floor to ceiling, and under the eaves birds twittered. The scent of flowers was everywhere, and always, night and day, the rooms were filled with the murmur of the sea.

V

Colin ran across the courtyard to the house, his nose twitching a little as the smell of baked apples floated out into the misty air. At the front door he stopped, for his mother was standing between the fuchsias watching for him.

Rachell du Frocq, standing with the glow of orange lamplight behind her and the scarlet fuchsias on either side, was a sight to make anyone stop and look, and look again. She was a beautiful woman, slender and straight as a stalk of lavender, tall and stately as a pine tree in a sheltered valley. She wore her masses of dark hair plaited and twisted like a great crown, and carried her head proudly poised as though aware of sovereignty. Her white skin was tanned by the sun and her eyes, under the strongly marked eyebrows of an artist with a sense of humour, were dark, flashing sometimes with vivacity, sometimes with laughter, sometimes with anger, but always with beauty and warmth. No one, looking at her, could have guessed that for sixteen years she had been the wife of an unsuccessful farmer, battling day after day with poverty, struggling with her husband to wrest for their children living and happiness from the earth and life. She had had eight children and had seen death take three of them from her. Yet, so strong did the flame of beauty burn in her, only the observant noticed the scars left by those sixteen years. Her lips were a little hard, as though they had been compressed too often in the bearing of pain, her hands, though they had not lost their shapeliness, had lost their beauty of texture, and her lids were faintly shadowed with purple, as though grief that had been denied expression had stained them. Perhaps she owed her unshaken loveliness to the spirit of independence that possessed her. Although she gave herself in love to her husband and children, although she claimed delighted kinship with the beauty and humour that she met in her way, yet at the same time in her innermost being she held herself aloof. There was a part of her, deeply withdrawn, that was wrapped in a great tranquillity, and this she defended fiercely from all violation. It was her very essence, independent of time or place or person, and all that threatened its peace, all outcry, anger or clamour, she hated and thrust away from her. It might be that this inmost core of quietness, stronger in its influence than the blows of fate, had preserved her beauty. However that might be, beauty dwelt in her like the lamp in a saint's shrine and radiated from her like light. Everything she touched and lived with was lit by her beauty and glowed with her warmth. She was always dressed in black—she said it was so handy for funerals and therefore economical. She stressed the economy of it. She looked superb in black; had she not there would have been less said about economy and Rachell would have worn colours. In her shapely ears she wore little gold ear-rings shaped like shells, and in summer she wore tucked into her belt a maiden's blush rose from the bush by the garden gate.

Colin stopped and looked at her. He smiled sadly. He loved her. She hurt him with her beauty.

"Colin, where have you been?"

The sadness in Colin's smile melted away and cheek took its place. He loved prevarication and the exercise of his imagination.

"There's a fog coming up, mother. It'll be dirty weather at sea to-night. Did you hear the foghorn?"

Rachell waved this meteorological digression contemptuously aside.

"Where have you been, Colin? It's very late."

Colin came to her and turned his dirty face up to hers. His eyes, candid and beautiful, gazed unwaveringly straight into her eyes.

"I went to tea with the de Putrons, mother, and there was crab for tea and goche,[2] and afterwards Mr. de Putron took Denys and me out in the boat . . . Denys was sick . . . I wasn't. . . . Mr. de Putron sent you his kind regards and is sorry we were back so late, but his watch had gone wrong. He took it in his bath. Mrs. de Putron said—"

"That will do, Colin," Rachell interrupted sharply. The de Putrons, she knew, were spending the day on a neighbouring island. Seeing he was making very little impression Colin tried a new tack. He produced the pink bag of sweets.

"For you, mother darling. No one is to eat them but you, not even father. They are from Le Manouri's."

Rachell was touched.

"Oh, Colin, you bad boy, you shouldn't. All your pocket money gone!"

She looked at him. What was one to do with a child like this? So generous and yet such a shocking little liar, so courageous and yet so shameless. She ought to punish him of course. She ought to whip him. But the evening, the day's work ended, was so peaceful. She could not shatter its peace with violence and sorrow. Then, too, he was like her and she understood him to the very core. He wanted independence and he wanted serenity, and to get the two together he would go to any lengths. How was she to teach him that independence was a thing of the spirit, and never gained at the expense of integrity? She gave it up and led the way into the house.

At the kitchen door Colin was confronted with his father and his spirits rose. He loved romancing to his father. André du Frocq, good easy man, believed every word that was said to him, provided it was reasonably probable. Colin began to etch a few more details into the vivid picture of the de Putron tea party already existing in his mind.

André, small and thin, and bent with toil, his fair hair and beard already flecked with grey, his kind, light-brown eyes peering

[2]Cake.

short-sightedly from behind glasses, stood at the door with his pipe in one hand and his newspaper in the other. His look of puzzled bewilderment was habitual to him, and not occasioned by his son's behaviour only. A thinker and dreamer, forced by fate into the rôle of a practical man of affairs, a role he filled but poorly, he seemed always bewildered by his own inadequacy. Now, cruelly aware of his own inability to deal with the situation, he looked severely at his son and forced a hard note into his musical voice.

"Colin, where have you been? Your mother has been very anxious."

Colin grinned.

"I've been with the de Putrons, father, and out in Mr. de Putron's boat afterwards. We had a squiffing tea. Crab and goche, and apricot jam and tarts. The de Putron's aunt was there . . . the one with the lovely ivory teeth made in Paris . . . they fell out . . . Mr. de Putron sent his kind regards . . . Denys was sick in the boat—" He paused, wondering what to select next from the wealth of imaginary detail that thronged his mind. His father, believing the de Putron legend, nevertheless filled the pause with reproof.

"You should not have gone to the de Putron's without telling us. I have already forbidden you to be out so late alone. Your poor mother has been exceedingly anxious. You are never to go anywhere without asking permission first. Do you hear?"

Sudden anger surged up in Colin. Oh, these parents! What business of theirs was it where he went? He *must* be free, he must, he must. He would not be guarded and watched and caged. The fury of a trapped wild animal raged in him. He wanted to hurt his father. He would. He would tell him he had been out with Guilbert, Hélier, and Jacquemin. Then his father would know he had deceived him. Nothing hurt his father more than to find himself deceived. Colin flung back his head, opened his mouth—then stopped. His mother, standing behind him, was speechlessly crying out to him not to tell. The bond between Colin and Rachell was at all times very close. So strong were the filaments of sympathy between them that unspoken messages could slide from one to the other down the unseen threads. They came to Colin now, thick and fast, confused but compelling. She understood his rage. . . . She felt the same herself. . . . Not to be free was worse than anything. . . . But he was all wrong. . . . He did not know what freedom meant . . . not yet . . . one day she would teach him that only the bound are free . . . a paradox . . . a new word that he must learn if he would live rightly. . . . And he must not hurt his father. . . . Above all, he must not hurt his father.

"I'm sorry, father." Colin, smelling horribly of fish, embraced his relieved parent, pushed past him into the kitchen and precipitated himself into the midst of his three elder sisters, Michelle, Peronelle, and Jacqueline, who were preparing bowls of bread and milk by the fire.

"Wash him, one of you girls," cried Rachell, "he's filthy. Get him clean before we have supper."

Peronelle, the second of the family, aged fourteen, seized Colin by the slack of his jersey and haled him into the scullery. Peronelle, the most practical of the family, was always the one to answer any urgent call for action, and to answer it, too, with a shattering energy. She was thin, small, vital, with fair, curly hair that sprayed round her face as though each separate curl had a vivid life of its own. Her tawny eyes and pale pointed little face were the animated sparkling mirrors of every emotion that possessed her. Courageous, quick-tempered, generous, truthful, intolerant and passionately loving, she was a perfect whirlpool of emotion. Just now she was in a towering passion with Colin. She adored her father and she loathed lies. Dirty little coward! He was afraid of being whipped, that's what it was. She'd teach him! She slammed the scullery door, poured water into a bowl, soaped the flannel and fell upon her erring brother. Colin, his fishy jersey torn off his back and his sister's hand twisting in his hair, submitted. Useless to try to make Peronelle understand his point of view; she did not understand nuances of temperament. Useless to fight her—when possessed by rage her physical energy was immense. Nothing to be done but give in and wait for an opportunity to get in a good hard kick on the shin.

"The de Putrons indeed!" stormed Peronelle as she scrubbed, "everyone knows they've gone off for the day with the Bailiff. Lying to a sweet innocent like father who believes every word you say! All that vulgar nonsense about the aunt's teeth! Keep your mouth shut, you dirty little tike, or I'll put soap in it!"

She turned to reach the towel. Colin delivered well and truly a good hard kick on the shin. Peronelle swayed. Though her energy and vitality gave her an appearance of strength she was in reality delicate. The kick hurt horribly. Waves of pain went up her legs into her back. She felt sick, but not a sound came from her. She set her mouth like a trap, swung her arms, and dealt Colin a terrific box on the ears. Colin, too, made no sound, and for a moment they swayed together, seeing stars. Then Peronelle seized the towel and dried him. Three minutes later, honours being even, they kissed lovingly and re-entered the kitchen glowing with affection.

"Now, children."

Rachell lifted the saucepan of boiling milk from the fire and poured it on the cubes of bread in the children's bowls. For herself and André there was home-cured ham and a jug of steaming coffee. Sophie, the maid, went home every evening, so the supper was Rachell's province.

Peronelle and Colin slipped into chairs one on each side of their father, the one filled with protective, the other with contrite affection.

Michelle, the eldest, aged fifteen, sat on her mother's right and stared into vacancy with dark eyes bright with thought. Her straight black hair was strained unbecomingly back from a face very like her father's. She, like Peronelle, was small and thin, but whereas Peronelle was thin like a fairy, Michelle was thin like a scarecrow. Her clothes, which were usually torn, always seemed too big for her and whenever possible she put them on back to front. She was the despair of Rachell and Peronelle, for if she had cared to put them the right way round she would have been pretty. Her eyes were beautiful, and her shapely head, and her beautiful slender hands and feet. But Michelle did not care. What were clothes to her? She lived in a world of the intellect and the imagination, a world more real to her than that of Bon Repos and the Island, inhabited by people more visible to her eyes than her own exasperating relations. Later on in her life she was revered as an intellectual and a saint, but now she was voted a shocking, untidy little prig. . . . Only her father understood her.

But no one, not even her father, understood Jacqueline. Outwardly she was the perfect picture of a good, normal little twelve-year-old, pretty in an unexciting way, black-haired, blue-eyed, rosy-cheeked; but inwardly she was a whirlpool of queer unchildish desires, nightmare terrors, tormenting anxieties. Longing to be clever she could never learn anything, and the others laughed at her for her stupidity. Longing for friendship she was too agonizedly shy to claim it, and her awkward self-consciousness only repelled the admiration stirred by her pretty looks. Peronelle, gay, friendly and utterly unself-conscious, had love and admiration poured out at her little feet in heartsfull, but Jacqueline, starving, lived in outer darkness. When she had been in the making a little brother had been dangerously ill. He had died a few weeks before her birth. Anxiety, fear, sorrow, heartsick railing at fate, were woven into the very tissue of her being.

There was yet another female du Frocq, Colette, aged five, upstairs asleep in the cot in Michelle's room.

Supper began happily. The du Frocqs all had a wonderful capacity for forgetting past unpleasantness. Colin's doings had already passed from their minds and would not be alluded to again. Sufficient unto the day were the escapades thereof.

Rachell, seeing her husband tired and dispirited, thrust her own tiredness from her and entered into a gay description of a visit to Miss Marguerite Falaise, an interfering spinster who lived down the road. Rachell was a marvellous raconteur. Though she did not, like her son Colin, rely entirely upon imagination in recounting the day's doings, her memory was sufficiently constructive to hang a gay embroidered border upon the sober garment of truth. She was unaware of her embroidery; she thought she only did good plain hemming. As she talked her black eyes sparkled and amusement rippled over her face like sunlight on water. Every now and then she laid down her knife and fork to gesticulate with both hands. As he listened the years rolled off André one by one. He forgot his cows and pigs and diseased tomatoes. He straightened his bent back and his eyes behind their glasses twinkled back at her. For the moment they were both young again, the children sitting between them forgotten.

Peronelle and Colin, usually fluent conversationalists, were completely silent, absorbed in food. They ate three times as much as anyone else; bread and milk, baked apples and cream, slice after slice of bread and dripping. Every now and then they heaved great sighs of utter repletion.

Jacqueline ate some of her bread and milk and then hid the rest under her spoon, anxiously hoping her mother would not notice. How could she eat when she knew herself to be dying? The knowledge made her feel sick and she couldn't swallow. She had fallen down that afternoon and grazed her knee and now, under her black stocking, she felt quite sure she could feel the knee swelling. She had tetanus. She was going to die. Perhaps when she was dead the others would be sorry they had not loved her more. Perhaps they would cry. Yes, they would go to her funeral all dressed in black and crying dreadfully into pocket handkerchiefs with black borders. This was a pleasant thought and for a moment the band of iron that seemed clamped round Jacqueline's throat loosened a bit; she even took another spoonful of bread and milk and swallowed it down. But then, quick as lightning, came another thought, a terrible one. *She* wouldn't be crying into a black-bordered handkerchief in the sunshine, she would be in a wooden box nailed down tight so that she couldn't get out, and they would put the box in the earth and bury it deep down, and perhaps she wouldn't be dead after all, and would scream and shriek inside the box, and there would be so much earth on top that no one would hear her. . . . The perspiration was trickling down her back and she put up her hands to her throat where the iron band was clamped tight, tight. It seemed to her that she was screaming now. . . . She looked round at her family, at her father and mother talking to each other and oblivious of her suffering, at Michelle gazing out of the window, at Colin shovelling bread and milk into his mouth as though he were Sophie stoking the fire, at Peronelle feeding herself daintily but with great rapidity and thoroughness. No, they none of them cared. Selfish beasts. She would be dead soon and perhaps, after all, they wouldn't cry at her funeral. Cautiously she felt her knee and even as she felt it it swelled horribly under her fingers. If only she could tell someone about it, but she was so constituted that she could never express herself properly. What she said was never what she had meant to say. She could never think of the right words to express her fears. When she tried people just thought she was being funny and laughed. Sometimes she tried to tell things to Peronelle, but Peronelle, though her love was always warm and comforting, was too much a child of the daylight to see very far into nightmare. If Jacqueline told her, for instance, that she was frightened of being buried alive Peronelle would simply say in her downright way, "You won't be, darling, *I'll* see to it," entirely disregarding the fact that being a year older than Jacqueline it was probable that she would be buried alive first. . . . Should she tell her mother about the tetanus? She glanced at Rachell's sparkling face and decided that she couldn't. Rachell would simply laugh, bathe the knee and say "Don't be silly, darling," and Jacqueline would feel a fool, and anything, simply anything, was better than feeling a fool. . . . Deep down in Jacqueline, hidden away, was the knowledge that other people thought her a fool, and she simply dared not face that knowledge. She wanted above all things to be admired, and with infinite care she had built up for herself a picture of herself as she would like to be, a creature beautiful and charming and very, very clever; from all self-knowledge that disturbed this picture she fled like a hare. . . . No, there was no one that she could tell. Anyhow, she would look lovely dead. Jacqueline du Frocq, the beautiful, charming, clever Jacqueline, dead . . . white and wasted. . . . But did one look beautiful after dying of tetanus? Did one, perhaps, swell? Oh, it was terrible! She wished she could be like Michelle, who was never frightened of anything that could happen to her body, never, in fact, gave it a thought.

Jacqueline looked enviously at Michelle eating slowly and thoughtfully whatever was placed before her, quite unconscious of what it was. There was a smut on the side of her nose, and her frock had come undone at the neck, so that her underclothes showed. She did not hear a word that anyone said and her dark, shining eyes, gazing out of the window, saw not the sea fog pressing up against it like a muffling pall but a little town built of white marble, pillared and beautiful, its slender columns fluted against a sky of deep dazzling blue. A wine-dark sea lay on one side of the little town, its waves slapping gently against white marble steps. On the other side was a forest of dark cypress trees, purple-black against the sky. The little town was completely empty, not a soul was in it. The stillness was deep and cool like a sea cavern, the emptiness thrilled with a sense of space and freedom. . . . This was one of the greatest days of Michelle's life . . . she had discovered Keats. Lovely phrases had lit candles in her mind, one after the other, till she felt intoxicated with the brightness. "And, little town, thy streets for evermore will silent be; and not a soul to tell why thou art desolate, can e'er return" . . . "She stood in tears amid the alien corn" . . . "Cooled a long age in the deep-delved earth" . . . "Beauty is truth, truth beauty. . . ."

"Michelle," roared Colin, "pass the cream, you greedy pig!" It was the first remark he had made since the meal started, but then it was the first time he had been unable to reach the cream.

Michelle started and found that she was gripping the cream jug in her right hand.

"Michelle," said Rachell, "if you want some cream take it, but don't sit there holding it like that."

"Your frock's undone," said Peronelle, wrinkling her nose with disgust, for she hated slovenliness, "I can see your combies."

The blood rushed in a wave to Michelle's forehead. She felt hot with fury. Their remarks, forcing themselves in on her exaltation, were like a horde of stinging insects. She gave the cream jug an angry push and it emptied itself across the tablecloth into

Peronelle's lap, making a nasty slimy river all down the front of her dainty pink cotton frock. Peronelle, always exquisitely fastidious, leaped to her feet in a rage, her cheeks as pink as her frock, every single curl standing straight up on end with exasperation.

"You pig! You pig!" she stormed, stamping her feet, "you've ruined my frock! I hate you! I hate you!"

Rachell rose to her feet, her eyes blazing, looking like Mrs. Siddons as the tragic muse.

"If there are any children on this Island worse behaved than mine I've yet to meet them," she thundered.

Jacqueline, the tension of her misery broken by the sudden storm, burst into floods of tears, and for a few moments the du Frocq temper was in full blast, rolling backwards and forwards, an unseen force, from wall to wall. Then as quickly as the tumult had arisen it subsided, and the habitual peace of Bon Repos flowed back. The cream was wiped off the tablecloth and Peronelle, the tears off Jacqueline. Everybody kissed everybody else. Michelle apologized to Peronelle, Peronelle apologized to Michelle. Colin finished what was left of the cream while they both apologized to Rachell.

But the storm had left its mark. The years, one by one, had rolled back on top of André. His worries returned too, the pigs, the cows, the diseased tomatoes, his five children, his fear that he would not be able to start them properly in life. His shoulders bent again beneath the weight. . . . And outside the window the little town had suffered earthquake and fallen into ruins. Michelle could not see it any more. Tears pricked her eyelids and she felt suddenly forlorn and outcast. How hateful was this world of everyday things that was always impinging itself upon the world of her lovely dreams, always blotting out the interior vision.

"What a fuss it all is," she said suddenly.

"It's you that started the fuss, upsetting the cream jug," Peronelle reminded her.

"I didn't mean that, I meant life. I wish there wasn't so much eating and drinking in it."

Her father looked at her with his sudden smile. "Magic casements, opening on the foam of perilous seas, in faery lands forlorn," he said, "they are dangerous to cream jugs, Michelle. Keep a hold of practicality. To be a well balanced woman you must eat and drink at the proper times."

Michelle looked at him long and lovingly. "You're a thought-reader, Daddie. How did you know I'd just found Keats?"

"Your idiotic expression as you looked at a vision beyond the window, and your equally idiotic lack of interest in your supper," he smiled back.

"Which reminds me," said Peronelle, "no one's fed the cat."

Maximilian and Marmalade the yellow cat were fed, supper cleared away and the dishes piled in the scullery ready for Sophie to wash next morning. Then André went out of doors to inspect the fog while Rachell coaxed her family up to bed.

VI

Peronelle and Jacqueline shared a room, Michelle and little Colette. Colin had a minute apartment to himself, so tiny that there was no room to swing a cat in it; but, as he said, having no wish to swing Marmalade it didn't matter.

Rachell deposited her daughters with kisses in their rooms, bent for a moment over the cot where slept the fat yellow-headed Colette, and then went to Colin. She loved all her children, but Colin seemed as much a part of her as though he still lay beneath her heart. She would cheerfully have sent all the rest of her family to the bottom of the sea to insure a perfect life for Colin. She repeatedly said that she had no favourites among her children; favouritism was abhorrent to her. On these occasions André was seen to smile.

"Mother's gone to Colin," said Peronelle, as Rachell withdrew after a loving but hurried kiss, "she's scamped us." Peronelle spoke with no rancour, she was partial to Colin herself, but Jacqueline knew a stab of jealousy that almost made her forget her approaching end.

Colin, when his mother came to him, was already in a state of nature.

"Hullo, mother," he said, "feel my biceps."

Rachell felt them.

"I could knock you silly as easy as easy," he continued, "need I wash? Peronelle did my top before supper, and I did my own bottom yesterday."

"Show me your feet," said Rachell sternly.

Colin showed them, explaining that it was sunburn.

As she washed the filth of days off his toes Rachell knew a moment of exquisite happiness. After all, it was worth while. It was worth the years of struggle and child-bearing to be in this little whitewashed room at evening washing the curly toes of a little son. The candle flame on the magenta chest of drawers gave a sudden little leap, as though in assent, and Colin's shadow on the wall danced with it. The patchwork quilt was like a gay little flower-bed, and outside the uncurtained window the summer dusk was a deep and wonderful blue. The murmur of the sea was so faint to-night that it made no more sound than the little south wind that was stirring the leaves of the passion flowers.

Into her happiness, like a stone flung into a quiet pond, came suddenly the menacing sound of the distant foghorn. Though peace and homely beauty were in this room danger was on the sea. The happiness was gone. A moment of terror seized Rachell. She got up hastily and went to the window, as though to pull the curtain and shut out something that frightened her. At the window she stood still, looking out, her eyes dark with fear. At times Rachell had what the Scotch call "the two sights" and she had a "seeing" now. She saw Bon Repos as a little ark set in a waste of waters, surrounded by unimaginable dangers, a great darkness around and above it, hideous little waves licking its sides and fog wreathing around it. She knew quite certainly that her home, the cradle of her joys, was threatened. She put up her hand to her throat as she stood there in the safe little room. Then, not far from Bon Repos, she thought she saw through the fog the spars of a wreck, and from the wreck came a little boat with only one man in it. The man came to Bon Repos, and as he reached it it seemed that the waves licked and menaced it less cruelly, and that light shone through the fog. The light struck the man's face and she saw it clearly, a rugged ugly face, hard and self-contained, with a great scar across one cheek and an untidy thicket of grey beard emphasizing the look of wildness in the eyes. As his hand touched Bon Repos she knew that it was saved.

"Mother," said Colin, "what are you doing? I'm only half dry."

She drew the curtain and turned back from the window with a laugh. "Seeing things," she said.

The du Frocqs, when they told each other stories, which they did in season and out of season, always prefaced the yarn with the phrase, "I'm seeing things."

"Oh, mother, tell me," cried Colin excitedly, "did you see the King of the Auxcriniers? Is he out at sea to-night?"

The King of the Auxcriniers is a dreaded ocean ogre seen at sea only in times of danger.

"No, I didn't see him," said Rachell, and she finished Colin's toes and tucked him up.

"Well, I bet he's there," said Colin comfortably, "the fog's thick as hell and the foghorn going like mad."

"You mustn't say hell, Colin."

"Why not, when it's what the fog is thick as? Mother, I came home by the water-lane, and it was full of sarregousets[3] going backwards and forwards the way they do when there's death at sea. Do you think there'll be wrecks to-night?"

Rachell kissed him. "There are no sarregousets really, little son, they are only fairy tales."

"Oh, are they!" said Colin hotly, "then God's a fairy tale too."

"Colin!" cried Rachell, scandalized.

"Well, I've not seen God or the sarregousets with my outside eyes, but I've seen them both with my inside eyes, and if one isn't real the other isn't either," said Colin with finality. "Tell us a story, mother."

---

[3]Water fairies.

From downstairs came a voice calling "Rachell! Rachell!"

"I'll tell you the story in the morning," said Rachell.

"Right you are," said Colin, "you'd better run. That's father. I bet you anything he's jealous. Kiss me again. You did it all wrong before. You must look in at my windows and kiss me with your eyes."

Her face close to his Rachell looked deep into his eyes and then flickered her eyelashes all over his forehead.

"Rachell!"

Surely there was an unusual urgency in that cry? She got up and went quickly downstairs.

VII

André was standing in the kitchen doorway, his pipe in his mouth, his shoulders more bowed than usual.

"What an unconscionable time you do take putting that boy to bed," he complained.

Rachell smiled. She loved to hear that note of jealousy in his voice.

"He's always so dirty," she said, and slipping her arm through her husband's she drew him into the kitchen. They sat down together on the "jonquière." The oil lamp, burning low on the table, was reflected in the copper warming-pans and the dark oak of the table. All the willow pattern plates held a friendly gleam of light, and the old clock ticked companionably. The room was used to these two sitting there on the "jonquière" and talking, sometimes late into the night. It welcomed them and endeavoured to be helpful, the clock remarking monotonously that the nibbling seconds make an end of all things, even life, and the reflected lights replying warmly that there are certain things, seemingly unsubstantial, that cannot die, since their reflector is eternal. So full of ups and downs had the married life of André and Rachell been that this argument had gone on in their hearts and on their lips and in the room around them continually. The "jonquière" was quite dented by their nocturnal sittings.

André and Rachell had become engaged to each other at an age when they should still have been engrossed in the multiplication table, and they had married early, with a sublime contempt for ways and means that had cost them dear.

André was the second son of the chief doctor of the Island, a gentleman whose enormous opinion of himself had so impressed the Islanders that they had unhesitatingly laid their livers and lungs at his feet. The practice being so well established it had been decided that Jean, the eldest son, should also become a doctor, and have undisputed sway over those livers which his father could not find the time to grapple with. But Jean, though possessed of all those attributes desirable in a doctor, a warm heart, strong nerves, charming manners and an unshakeable faith in his own judgment, had suddenly and for no apparent reason gone to the bad, flung his stethoscope in his father's face and decamped to Australia, where he had completely disappeared.

André, many years younger, had been abruptly told on leaving school to pick up the fallen stethoscope and annex the livers originally destined for Jean. But André, always so gentle and pliable, refused. Dr. du Frocq ranted and stormed but still André refused. On being pressed to give reasons for his abominable obstinacy he replied that he did not like the human body. When in health it seemed to him ridiculous, sticking out in the wrong place and hampering the life of the soul at every turn, but in illness, when its works, badly arranged at the best of times in his opinion, went wrong, the thing became simply an unpleasant nuisance. Asked what the deuce he did like, he said he liked the earth and the corn that grew upon it, and the changing seasons that died and renewed themselves in beauty and dignity without making any fuss and bother. He further demanded that the old du Frocq farm of Bon Repos, which had been let for many years, should be given to him. He wanted to be a farmer, he said. Dr. du Frocq cursed and swore but André continued to say, gently but with obstinacy, that he wanted to be a farmer. So Bon Repos was given to him, along with a promise from Dr. du Frocq that as long as he was such a damn fool as to stay there he need expect no help from *him*.

It was at this point that André married Rachell, and the swearing of Dr. du Frocq when André decided to be a farmer was as nothing to the swearing of Rachell's father when Rachell decided to be a farmer's wife. At first he forbade the marriage, but Rachell made herself so consistently unpleasant in the home when thwarted that for the sake of peace he capitulated, stifling qualms of anxiety as to his daughter's future by giving her a handsome jointure and reflecting that Dr. du Frocq, the old scoundrel, was a warm man.

It could not be said that André as a farmer was a success. Filled with the artist's deep reverence for the earth he had, like all those who know nothing about it, romanticized the farmer's life, but when it came to the point he found that what he really wanted to do was to write about the earth, not grub in it. In his few odd moments he wrote, unknown even to Rachell, little essays and poems that were miracles of observation and beauty, but meanwhile the farm ceased to pay.

Nor could it be said, at first, that Rachell was a success on a farm either. She who had been the beauty of the Island, taking all ease and softness as her right, had been at first astonished and then outraged at the duties expected of her. For the first few weeks, in summer weather, in love with André, she had been upheld by her sense of her own nobility in marrying a poor farmer when she might have married the Lieutenant-Governor. But later, when she and André got up in the pitch-dark winter mornings and toiled all day in wet and cold, while the gales raged round Bon Repos and the sea thundered ceaselessly, Rachell was seized with black despair. André, this first winter, was so exhausted by unfamiliar toil that he never spoke, and Rachell was so exhausted that she never ceased speaking. . . . They came near to hating each other.

Then came the producing of children, which Rachell considered perfectly detestable from first to last. She agreed with André that the human body was badly arranged. She loved her babies but she wished she could hatch them out of eggs.

Somehow they battled through, they never quite knew why or how. It was as though they had entered into a whirlwind and after hideous battling had found themselves standing serenely in the core of peace at its centre. Rachell learnt the lesson of withdrawal into her own innermost tranquillity, André learnt that monotonous toil can be so used that it becomes the rhythm of thought, the pulsing background of the accompaniment that sets the notes of the violin winging to height beyond height. And both of them learnt that peace that is not threatened has no value, and thought that is not bought by pain no depth. There had flowered, too, as they clung together before the storm, a love for each other and their children and Bon Repos that almost terrified them by its intensity.

But meanwhile André, though his thoughts as he toiled were rare thoughts, did not become a more practical farmer, and Rachell, increasing in dignity and wisdom, saw her jointure grow less.

Rachell's father was dead now but Dr. du Frocq was still very much alive, though, owing to his passion for horse racing, reputed to be less warm.

"What is it, André?" said Rachell as they sat down together. Remembering her vision fear clutched at her.

André did not mince matters.

"For sixteen years, my dear, I've been making a fool of myself at Bon Repos, and now things have come to such a pass that we must clear out."

"Clear out?" Not until this moment had she realized how her life had twisted itself round Bon Repos. Torn from it she would surely die. Her feeling for it, hatred transmuted by endurance into love, had kept the same intensity all through. She could not speak, and for a full two minutes the ticking clock was the only sound in the room. Then André continued.

"We must sell. Bon Repos ought to fetch a good price."

"And then?" To Rachell her voice seemed to come from very far away, to come from that maimed woman of the future whose life had been torn from its resting place.

André moistened his lips and spoke in a voice devoid of all expression. It was one of the worst moments of his life. He knew himself to be pronouncing a death sentence, both on his own manhood and on Rachell's happiness.

"My father, foreseeing this, long ago offered to take us all in. While we stay here he will never help us, but once we own ourselves beaten he will be charitable . . . it amuses him to be charitable. . . . He would support us, I as his bottle-washer, you as his housekeeper. . . . He's fond of the children. . . . We'll accept that offer to-morrow."

It was said. He had pronounced himself a failure, a failure as man, husband and father. Mixed with the agony of bitterness that possessed him was a curious sense of relief that his sentence was past. From henceforth he would be known for what he was, a failure. The endurance of the world's eyes upon him would be a new test of his courage. It struck him suddenly that however low we sink we can never escape from that testing. Life pursues us, probing with his sword, testing in this way and that, hoping always to strike mettle. Would it ever be his fate to hear at last in his own life that ring of steel on steel? He was suddenly recalled to the kitchen of Bon Repos by Rachell, who had got the better of her stupefaction and fear, and was emptying the vials of her wrath upon him.

"Indeed, André, we will do nothing of the sort. Nothing will induce me to live with your father. I'd sooner we took to the roads with our worldly goods in the perambulator and the children in the workhouse!"

Rachell's eyes were blazing. She never had been able to do with her father-in-law. He was selfish and she loathed selfishness, he did not appreciate André and she hated those who did not appreciate André, he was an autocrat, and being something of an autocrat herself she disliked autocrats.

André steeled himself for argument.

"There is no help for it, my dearest. We are more or less ruined."

"There must be help for it. I'm not going to live with your father. How much have we left?"

"Only enough to carry us on for one more year."

"André!" Rachell was superb in her rage. "How dare you frighten me like this? If we've enough to carry us on for one more year then why move out now?"

"Would you not rather go now, with something in hand, than wait till we are destitute?"

"No, I would not. I'd rather be destitute in Bon Repos than luxurious anywhere else upon earth."

"I don't think you understand what destitution means."

"André, I ask you, is it sense to leave a home one loves for a home one will hate until one is driven to it? No, it's not, and I won't do it."

"It is common sense, Rachell, to look ahead and plan for the future."

"You are planning for a future of calamity, and that may be common sense, I daresay it is, mean, paltry, everyday sense; but there's such a thing as uncommon sense, a thing that plans for success and won't admit defeat."

"Not to admit defeat when it is upon you brings needless suffering on others. I am thinking of my creditors."

André twisted his hands together. Argument with Rachell was always extraordinarily difficult. He was unpractical enough, God knew, but she was even worse, and never, never, could she be made to see that she was wrong. The only things she could ever see were the appalling disasters that would result if her advice was not taken.

"Believe me, André, I am right. Am I not always right?"

There was triumph in her tone and André smiled. It was true that, unpractical as she was, she was more often right than not. Her decisions, made with the flashing of insight, seemed to pounce upon situations with such swiftness that they were twisted to her will.

"You are nearly always right, my dear, but once you made a disastrous mistake. You married me. You have got to face the consequences of that blunder."

Though he neither looked at her nor touched her Rachell was aware that inwardly he was agonizing over her. She pulled him fiercely to her.

"You dare say that, you dare, you dare!" she scolded. "Mistaken? Look at the riches my mistake has given me! Was ever woman so rich as I!"

She tried to hold him. Experience had taught her that with her arms round him she could generally do what she liked with him, but André quietly withdrew. He was extraordinarily obstinate to-night.

"What we are discussing is not your riches but your poverty," he reminded her, "sentiment won't help us now. We are faced with ruin if we stay here. We must think of the children."

"I am thinking of the children. If we leave Bon Repos their growth will be stunted. Let me explain, André— "

"It will be certainly stunted if we stay here and they have no bread and butter," interrupted André grimly.

Rachell raised her hands in a gesture lovely even in its impatience. "Be quiet, André, let me explain!"

André was despairingly silent while the clock ticked on inexorably and Rachell gathered her forces for what she felt was the greatest campaign of her life. It was always important to her to have her own way but never, she felt, so vital as now, when the foundations of their whole life seemed threatened.

"André, you can't create something and then destroy it. To abandon a lovely thing that is just beginning to flower out of suffering is sheer lunacy. Think back over our sixteen years at Bon Repos. Think of all the years of struggle and misery we had and then think of the lovely peaceful home that has come out of them. If we leave Bon Repos of what use were those years? Sheer waste."

"Life is mostly waste."

André, though he was no egotist, could not help his thoughts straying for a moment to all those unused talents paralysed within him.

"Nonsense!" cried Rachell, "only cowards know waste. Keep straight on along the path you've chosen and you'll not waste one single pang. Turn back and you'll waste the lot."

"What of the children?" asked André mildly, "must they suffer the pangs of hunger?"

"I'll not have the children rooted up from Bon Repos, hunger or no hunger," said Rachell firmly, "they are growing up in perfect surroundings, beautiful and peaceful, a house that courageous forefathers lived in, a home that you and I have made for them and steeped in our love. We've planted them in the right soil and I won't have the darlings transplanted to that horrid town house of your father's; stuffy, and basement kitchens with black beetles."

Rachell's impassioned eloquence dropped to more mundane misery as she had a sudden vision of the horrors of housekeeping in Grandpapa's abominable town house. Tears welled into her eyes and for the first time her voice trembled. She so seldom cried that André was terribly upset.

"What do you suggest, my angel?" he asked miserably.

"Stay on here till the last moment," whispered Rachell, "and something will happen to put everything right."

She put her handkerchief to her eyes and was distressed to find there were so few tears there. If only she could cry more often and with more water she would never have any trouble with André at all. Men always gave in to tears. . . . They made them feel embarrassed. . . . Make a man feel embarrassed and you can do what you like with him.

"What will happen to put everything right?" asked André.

"Something—I know it. Let me tell you, André. . . . I'm seeing things." She put her wet cheek against his and told him what she had seen upstairs in Colin's room. "Bon Repos was saved," she whispered when she had done.

André was entirely skeptical about the whole thing, but his wife's wet cheek moved him horribly. She had not cried since the birth of Colette—not for five years. God! What a cruel thing was love! A man for the sake of the love that he had for a woman took her to wife and thereby inflicted upon her pain after pain. "Alas, that love, so gentle in his view, should be so tyrannous and rough in proof." He caught Rachell to him.

"We'll wait another six months and see what happens," he whispered.

The clock, which always sided in all arguments with André the pessimist, gave a despairing whir—it needed oiling—but the willow pattern china and the warming-pans, optimists all, winked and gleamed at Rachell and she, lifting her head from André's shoulder, twinkled back at them, the lamplight turning the wet drops on her cheeks to diamonds. Once more in the du Frocq's kitchen faith had triumphed over caution.

Rachell's behaviour as a victor was entirely beyond reproach. From long practice she had reduced the graceful acceptance of victory to a fine art. She never triumphed over André. She never remarked that thank heaven he'd seen sense at last. She never even smirked. Instead, with gracefully drooping head and submissive murmurings, she suggested that she was a clinging vine to whose weakness his strength had stooped lest she should fall. His was the strong will, she suggested, not hers. If he yielded to her it was not through weakness but merely to indulge her whims. Sometimes, with consummate skill, she was able to convince him that the decision they had just come to was his, not hers.

"You are quite right, darling," she murmured low, "as you say, far better to wait another six months before we do anything drastic. By that time we shall know our position."

"We know that now," André was heard to remark, but she silenced him with, "You are so good to me, mon ange, I rely completely on your judgment."

They kissed each other while the clock struck the hour cynically, then put out the lamp, locked the front door and climbed the stone stairs slowly and wearily. They undressed in their candle-lit bedroom, under the picture of the Last Judgment, climbed into their big four-poster, and drew the crimson curtains to keep out the two Victorian ogres, night air and draught.

When she was in her husband's arms and there was no sound in the room but the sighing of the sea, Rachell whispered, "Promise," and André answered "Promise." She sighed happily. The long day with its work and its anxieties was over. One by one she laid down her burdens on the threshold of sleep and running, a little child again, was gathered in and pulled down, down, down, down into the very depths of tranquillity. Her last conscious thought was that Bon Repos for a little while longer—and Rachell, wise woman, never looked beyond the next step—was hers.

Chapter 2

I

IT was still early when Michelle awoke. She had been dreaming. She had dreamed that she lived alone in that little empty town by the sea-shore. All by herself she had paced slowly along a white terrace overlooking the sea; all by herself she had sat and dipped her feet into the cool little waves that creamed like flowers against the marble steps; all by herself she had watched the cypresses sway like an army of spearmen against the sky, and picked bunches of scarlet anemones and pale pink asphodel.

But she had not been lonely for her thoughts had been with her. She had known herself safe in a glorious solitude with them alone. Nothing, she knew, would come between her and them. She did not seem to think her thoughts. They seemed to come from outside her and to troop through her mind one by one, beautiful, true, luminous and satisfying. One by one she greeted them, and they her, one by one she looked at them, understood them and let them pass by, and as each came and went she knew herself the richer for their passing. It was as though each thought was a step that carried her higher up a staircase. She knew, with a quiet exaltation, that when she reached the top she would know something. What? As she floated from her dream towards wakefulness a line of Keats was singing in her mind. "At the tip-top there hangs by unseen film an orbed drop of light, and that is love." What was love? Was the answer to that question the final knowledge? When her questioning mind was one with that light would she be completely satisfied?

> ". . . . . In the end
> Melting into its radiance, we blend,
> Mingle, and so become a part of it,—
> Nor with aught else can our souls interknit

> So wingedly: when we combine therewith
> Life's self is nourished by its proper pith,
> And we are nurtured like a pelican brood."

Soon, soon, she would be one with it, only a few more steps and she would know what would satisfy her for ever—only a few more steps. . . . Her eyes unclosed and she saw her little pink washstand, her sponge squatting beside it like a hedgehog and her clothes in an untidy heap on the floor. . . . She was awake. . . . The little town had gone again. . . . She would never reach the top of the steps. . . . The knowledge that had been so near had been caught away from her. . . . Her feet, that had been cool with sea water, were sticky and hot with perspiration, her arms, that had held a bunch of asphodel, were clutching a sodden mass of nightgown. There were no cypresses to look at, only a sponge that looked like a hedgehog, there were no lovely clear thoughts trooping through her mind, leading her up step by step to a great light, only a confused mass of vague stupid speculations that led nowhere. In the bitterness of her spirit she rolled over and buried her face in her pillow. She must come back to the hateful life of the earth, the ugly life of the body. Ugly, that's what it was. Vulgar. She squirmed. There was a nasty taste in her mouth and her hair was a vile tangle over her eyes. Her abominable body could not even lie in bed for eight hours without getting hot and sticky and tangled. And now she must get up and wash it. Every day for years and years and years she would have to get up and wash the thing, and every year it would get uglier and uglier and nastier and nastier and require more and more attention, till she had none to spare at all for her mind, for that life of the little town. What, in that case, was the use of living at all?

She flung back the clothes, jumped out of bed and poured water savagely into her basin. As she sponged herself with the sponge that looked like a hedgehog she was suddenly cheered up by the thought that she was an extraordinarily original girl. She had not thought of this before and she found the idea pleasing. She smiled. She was sure no one else found the body such a nuisance and longed so passionately to live only in the mind. No. More ordinary people cared for the body. Peronelle, for instance, so fastidious over her clothes, and her mother with her black draperies and her rose in the belt—so stupid to want a rose in her belt at her age! She was quite sure they none of them thought the thoughts that she thought. Her mind must be quite original. Could she at this moment have seen into the mind of her father thirty years ago and seen how identical were his thoughts then with hers now she would have been astonished and slightly humiliated.

She dragged on her underclothes and her everyday dark blue cotton frock, pulling two buttons off her petticoat and tearing one of her stockings right across the knee. They were new stockings, and Rachell had given them to her. Rachell would be upset. She sighed and her self-satisfaction leaked away. Perhaps she wasn't original after all. Perhaps she was only a nasty, untidy little prig who couldn't think properly, or live an everyday life properly, a nasty hybrid creature, making the worst of two worlds. Much chastened, and carrying her shoes in her hand so as not to wake Colette, she tiptoed out of the room and down the stairs and into the garden.

Once outside she forgot herself in the strangeness of the morning. The sea fog was still there, but it was thinning, and an August sun, blazing behind it, gave it a strange luminous quality. There seemed to be colour and light in the white vapour, as though the sunshine and flowers hidden in it were bit by bit coming back to their own again, were calling out through the muffling pall that they were still unconquered.

"It's like mother's opal ring," Michelle thought delightedly.

Rachell had an opal ring that André had given her, and its misted colours always fascinated Michelle; she thought its reds and blues and greens, half hidden, half revealed, were more alluring than when they blazed out in the hard glory of rubies and sapphires and emeralds. Michelle had a mind that loved simile, and it struck her now that the world of her little town was like the colours in the opal and in the fog, all the more precious because of the mist that now and again hid it from her.

"If I had it always I shouldn't love it so much," she thought, and she went happily through the courtyard out into the lane. She was going to La Baie des Mouettes, the gulls' breeding place, an exciting place at all times, but most exciting of all in a sea fog.

The little lane ran seawards, getting narrower and narrower, until its stony surface turned into a sandy path and its stunted oak trees gave way to the gorse bushes of the cliff.

Michelle could hardly see the bushes in the fog but as she pushed by them they gave out little puffs of scent like hot peaches. She made her way through wet gorse, honeysuckle, foxgloves and tall grasses until she reached the cliff edge, when she dropped cautiously to her hands and knees. Here the cliff sloped steeply downwards to the sea and short turf and wild thyme took the place of the long grass and honeysuckle. On hot days this slope was as slippery as ice and the unwary one who lost his foothold was in danger of being dashed to pieces on the rocks below. Even to-day, when the turf was soaking wet and each regal head of purple thyme held a coronet of diamonds, Michelle crept downwards with the utmost caution, digging her toes firmly into crannies and searching with her fingertips for firm bits of rock to cling to.

The slope ended in a flat-topped rock and here Michelle lay down, her chin cupped in her lean brown hands, her feet in their shabby shoes kicking behind her. Below was a sheer and terrifying drop to the gulls' bay.

There was nothing to be seen as yet, but from the fog came weird cries and screeching and bursts of mocking laughter, and the beating of unseen wings. Michelle laughed aloud. In spite of their eeriness she loved the gulls, and this watchman's tower over their especial bay was her favourite haunt.

In the winter the gulls lived in the harbour, where they found shelter from the storms and food among the refuse, but in early February flocks of them migrated to La Baie des Mouettes. The males came first and when, waking in the early morning, the children at Bon Repos heard their screaming, they knew that spring was not far behind. Six weeks later the males were followed by the females and amid scenes of general rejoicings most edifying to behold they settled themselves to the business of nest building. Under the softening influences of domesticity the cries grew less harsh and soft crooning notes were heard amid the screams. When the first babies were hatched the gulls began to laugh, and their ha, ha, ha, ha, echoed among the rocks all the summer through.

This morning it seemed to Michelle that there was something vaguely terrifying in the screams and laughter and in the middle of her amusement she shivered a little. Had they screeched and laughed like that a year ago when La Bonne Espérance was wrecked in a fog on the rocks outside the bay and went down with all hands? Had there been a wreck last night and had they laughed? Horrible to hear such sounds for your last on earth . . . those and the sound of sucking waves.

It was a relief to Michelle when a sudden rent in the fog told her that the sun was conquering. She watched spellbound. Slowly, very slowly, the tops of jagged rocks appeared, then a stretch of green water, then a patch of early purple heather growing just below her, then a flurry of white wings as two quarrelling gulls flapped the fog away from them and appeared as though framed in a picture. Now trailing white scarves of mist drifted up to her, curled themselves round her rock and disappeared over the foxgloves, and now, quite suddenly, the sun was out and the whole bay below lay bright and clear and sparkling. Each little wet pebble on the beach shone like a diamond and the large flat rocks by the sea's edge were patched with bright green seaweed, as though the mermaids had flung rugs over them before they sat down to dabble their tails in the little ripples that whispered between them. The sea, where it lay over beds of seaweed, was wine-dark as the sea round Michelle's little town, while over the sand it was an intense blue-green. Michelle could even see the scarlet anemones in the pools and the yellow lichen staining the rocks below the heather clumps. And everywhere were the gulls. Soaring, dipping, swerving, diving, backwards and forwards, up and down, round and round. Their wings seemed to trace a pattern over the lovely scene, mist it over with a film of white feathers, seemed to gather all the colour together and make of it one lovely gleaming jewel.

"Mother's opal again," thought Michelle.

The thought of the opal brought her back to the thought of the two worlds and her own particular problem. How was she to live in two worlds at once and be happy in both? How could she reconcile her interior life with her outward life so that she did not immediately lose her temper when one impinged upon the other? It must be done somehow. She couldn't go through life alternating between ecstasy and bad temper, it was too exhausting and too trying for one's family. How was it to be done? She did not know. She would have to find out. She wondered if her father knew. But if he did know he wouldn't be able to help her very much. Everyone had to find out how to live for themselves—she had discovered that much already. Other people could point the way but one had to tread it for oneself. She sat up and stretched herself. Anyway, she could not lose her temper to-day, the world was much too beautiful. She was safe to be virtuous to-day. Beauty made her exquisitely happy and she was always good when she was happy.

She turned from the shimmering sea to look at the golden gorse and the regal foxgloves spiring up against the sky. Far up a lark sang, crazy with ecstasy, and, wonder of wonders, on a thistle nearby was a goldfinch singing his squeaky little song, twisting his slim body from side to side with the motion of a born coquette. He was mocking at the gorse bushes—telling them that his burnished helmet was as good as theirs any day. . . . How she loved these things! Each scrap and shred of beauty was a feather in wings that bore her soaring up and up towards the lark at heaven's gate. Keats began singing in her mind again.

> "Feel we these things?—that moment have we
> passed into a sort of oneness, and our state
> Is like a floating spirit's."
> . . . . "Glories infinite
> Haunt us, till they become a cheering light

Unto our souls, and bound to us so fast
That whether there be shine or gloom o'ercast
They always must be with us or we die."

Rocking herself backwards and forwards she began thinking, her thoughts slipping easily into her mind, without struggle or effort, as they had done in her dream. She was getting there . . . she was going to solve the problem . . . unity . . . oneness . . . she must be bound so fast to beauty that she had it with her both in the shine of the little town and the gloom of her bodily life. . . . But what *was* this winged beauty? . . . The sea and the gorse and the goldfinch were only feathers in her pinions. . . . What was she herself? . . . Beauty is truth. . . . Yet the orbed drop of light that hung at the top of the steps of thought in her dream had been love. . . . Were love and truth and beauty the same? . . . Just different facets of the orbed drop? . . . What was that drop of light and how could she melt into its radiance? . . . She realized with a pang that she had only come round in a circle to the earlier thoughts of the morning; she had got nowhere . . . not yet . . . but in a moment she would . . . just let her sit still for a moment longer. . . .

"Michelle! Michelle!"

Peronelle and Jacqueline were racing towards her, waving their arms above their heads, their black-stockinged legs twinkling as they bounded over tussocks of wild thyme. Peronelle, bursting with her usual attack of early morning exuberance, seized Michelle, dragged her up the slope on to level ground and swung her round. Jacqueline, with the best of intentions, pulled her pig-tail. Michelle wrenched herself free savagely. Idiots! Fools! How dare they seek her out in her special sanctum? Was there nowhere on earth where she could be by herself? Was even La Baie des Mouettes to be desecrated by her commonplace family? Her lovely train of thought had been leading her up and up, in a moment she would have got there, and now—it was all shattered. She felt sick with rage.

"Sals petits cochons! Why can't you leave me alone?" she stormed. "Sals petits cochons! You're never to follow me here again.

Do you hear? La Baie des Mouettes is mine, mine! I don't want you here. I don't want you!"

Peronelle, used as she was to Michelle's sudden rages, was completely taken aback. To have "sal petit cochon" hurled at your head was, for an Islander, an unforgivable insult. The remark was forbidden in the du Frocq family. She went a little white and felt as though a butterfly was fluttering in her stomach.

Jacqueline, always morbidly attracted by the seamy side of life, was pleasurably interested.

"Who taught you that?" she asked eagerly. "Did grandpapa? What does it mean, exactly? Why is it so insulting?"

Peronelle recovered herself and proceeded to lose her own temper thoroughly and enjoyably.

"Michelle, you're perfectly horrid. You want your mouth washed out with soap and water—that's what you want. Talking like that in front of Jacqueline! You're worse than grandpapa's coachman. And you, Jacqueline, wanting to know what it means, you've a nasty mind. Of course, she didn't learn it from grandpapa. He never uses bad language except at the coachman. She picked it up from Colin. She ought to be ashamed of learning bad habits from a boy like that. Come along home, both of you. I'm ashamed of you. Talking about dirty pigs on a lovely morning like this—" she paused for breath.

A lovely morning? Despair seized poor Michelle. Only a moment ago she had felt she was safe not to lose her temper in the midst of so much beauty. Beauty? It was around her but it wasn't in her. *She* wasn't beautiful, she who had wanted to be bound fast to beauty, she was a dirty, vulgar, ugly little prig. She began to sob.

"What's the matter now?" demanded Peronelle, exasperated, "and why have you got your everyday frock on? It's Sunday."

Glancing up through her tears Michelle noted miserably that her sisters were arrayed in all the starched superiority of Sunday. Their stiff white muslin frocks, gathered into toby frills at the neck and wrists, were worn over coloured sateen petticoats, Peronelle's pink and Jacqueline's buttercup yellow, and their curls were tied at the napes of their necks with large bows to match. The sight of them added to Michelle's misery. She had forgotten it was Sunday. She hated Sunday. She had to wear her best frock and she always felt a fool in her best frock. She had to go to church, and kneel on a hard wooden stool that hurt her bony knees and listen to a stupid sermon, when she might have been out on the cliffs in the sunshine. She had, in company with her starched family, to have Sunday dinner with grandpapa in his town house, and she hated both grandpapa and the sensations of fullness induced by his dinners of roast beef and Yorkshire pudding followed by apricot tart and Stilton cheese and plum cake. Above all, she hated the hypocrisy of the Victorian Sunday—grandpapa bending over in his pew and blowing piously into his top hat to impress his patients, when everyone knew he was as shocking an old heathen as ever lived—and people putting on their best clothes out of sheer vanity and then pretending it was all done to please God. If she were God she'd send a downpour of rain every single Sunday to take the starch out of their dresses and turn the roses in their bonnets to pulp.

Without a glance at her sisters she trailed miserably homewards, sobbing as she went.

Jacqueline followed, giving little hops and skips, and singing softly under her breath. It was one of her happy mornings—she *was* happy sometimes. She had woken up apparently healed of the tetanus and on such a lovely morning death and the grave seemed very far away. Moreover, she had her best frock on and she knew she looked sweet in her best frock. The Jacqueline she had seen in the glass this morning looked exactly like the Jacqueline she had created in her imagination. Pink cheeks and yellow and white frock. She had looked like sunlight and roses—much, much prettier than Peronelle, whose pale face pink did not really suit. She was undoubtedly the prettiest of the family. So utterly at peace with the world did her self-satisfaction make her that Michelle's sobs troubled her not at all—though she still wanted to know why "sal petit cochon" should be so insulting.

Peronelle, on the other hand, now that her anger had evaporated, was terribly troubled. She walked along with her golden eyes dark with sorrow and her heart heavy. At every heave of Michelle's thin shoulders she felt as though someone had stuck a dagger into her. It was no good asking Michelle what was the matter for Michelle could never explain her troubles. Michelle and Jacqueline were always suffering from mysterious griefs that Peronelle could not understand. Peronelle herself was always completely happy unless anyone she loved had a pain, when she was completely miserable. But what there was for anyone to be unhappy about if they hadn't got a pain Peronelle simply could not understand. The world, minus pain, seemed to her a completely delectable spot. Michelle, she supposed, had a pain in her soul. But why? Peronelle never had pains in her soul. They were to her wholly incomprehensible and rather silly. But she could not endure her darling Michelle to be unhappy and, greatly daring, for Michelle would box her ears as likely as not, she slipped up to her and put her arm round her waist.

But Michelle had had all the stuffing knocked out of her, and she did not box Peronelle's ears. Instead, she flung both arms round her and kissed her passionately on the left ear. By the time they reached the lane they were walking all three abreast, with arms entwined, singing "Onward Christian Soldiers" in three entirely different keys—none of the du Frocqs were musical.

The Christian soldiers, however, progressed no further than the third verse, for as they came to Bon Repos Colin shot out from the archway, with the speed of a stone from a catapult, shouting.

"There's been a wreck! Last night in the fog! Somewhere right out at sea. They're all drowned, as likely as not, Sophie says. There's not been a wreck for six months. Jupiter, what fun! A wreck, I tell you. A wreck, a wreck! Hurrah! Hurrah!"

II

It is necessary to go back an hour in this family chronicle in order to introduce Colette.

The closing of the door, as Michelle crept out, had awakened Colette. She found herself, on waking, right at the bottom of the bed with the blankets over her head. This, however, did not disturb her, for it was where she always found herself on waking. No matter how firmly she was placed at night with her head on the pillow, the clothes turned down to the level of her chest and her arms outside, by morning she had reached the bottom of the bed. How it was she did not die of asphyxiation has never been explained.

Finding herself awake and in the best of health she scrambled up the bed and emerged at the top like a chicken coming out of an egg. Her yellow curls, slightly damp from the night's immersion, increased her resemblance to a newly-hatched chicken.

She scaled her pillow and sat on top of it to rub the sleep out of her large goggle eyes with her fat fists. Then she laughed. Her laugh was not beautiful but as a mirth-provoker it was most effective. It started as a low rumble in her tummy, travelled up her throat with the sound of a soda-water syphon ejecting fluid, and arrived in her mouth as a series of shrill squeaks. . . . She had a habit of laughing when she was quite by herself which was most uncanny. This particular specimen brought Peronelle in from the next room. Peronelle was giggling. Everybody giggled when they heard Colette laugh.

It was Peronelle's morning duty to help Colette perform her toilet. They both enjoyed this enormously for both of them, young as they were, took the deepest interest in the adornment of their persons. They were very alike. Both had yellow hair and merry eyes, and the sunny disposition that came to them from Rachell, but while Peronelle was slim and dainty as a fairy, Colette was as circular as an apple dumpling. So stout was she that she had bracelets of fat round her wrists like a little baby, and rolls of it in the back of her neck like a young pig. . . . Her appetite was something startling.

In one thing only did she resemble her father and Michelle. She had, unperceived as yet, the gift of thought. But while in them thought was a rather torturing joy, a thing of conflict rather than rest, in her it was a gift of placid and happy wonder. She had another gift, peculiar to herself, the gift of piety. She was amazingly pious. Rachell was rather worried about it. None of her other children were pious—quite the contrary. Surely it was a bad thing to be too good too early? She feared a reaction would set in, and she preferred children to be bad first, at the spanking age, and good later, rather than good first and bad later. However, she consoled herself by reflecting that it would be difficult for any child as fat as Colette to be really bad—she had not the agility necessary for running away.

"May I get up, 'Nelle?" inquired Colette, bouncing solidly on her pillow. She never, good little angel, did anything without permission.

"You may, duckie," said Peronelle. She took Colette in her arms and, staggering and panting beneath the colossal weight, carried her to the washstand. Colette was perfectly able to walk everywhere by herself, and the exercise would have got her fat down, but Peronelle, intensely maternal, loved the feel of her little sister in her arms.

She pulled Colette's nightgown over her head and poured cold water into the basin. Warm water to wash in in the mornings was an unheard of luxury in the du Frocq household. They always washed in cold water, even in those rare winters when they had to break the ice in their jugs first.

Colette shrank a little as the cold sponge touched her warm satiny flesh, but she blew out her cheeks and screwed up her eyes and made no complaint. She was glad, however, when her ablutions were over and Peronelle had dressed her in her woollen vest, best frilly knickers and her white muslin dress over a blue petticoat. The dress was starched, and stuck out all round so that she measured more from side to side than she did from top to bottom.

Then Peronelle did Colette's hair, brushing the curls round her fingers so that they lay all over Colette's head like a lot of fat sausages.

When she was ready, all but her shoes, Colette trotted to her bed and knelt down to say her prayers. She bowed her head and covered her face, spreading out her fingers so that her hands resembled fat starfish. The soles of her pink feet, stuck out behind her, were turned up appealingly to heaven, and her toes wriggled ever so slightly with the fervency of her prayer.

What she prayed about Peronelle, standing at the window divided between mirth and reverence, could not imagine, but she went on muttering for some time. Then she got up and put on her shoes. . . . Colette, like the Mohammedans, never prayed in shoes.

"May I go out into the garden, 'Nelle?" she asked.

"Yes, darling, but don't get your frock dirty."

"No, I will not get my frock dirty, 'Nelle," said Colette, and made solidly for the door.

She went downstairs with the utmost caution, lowering herself always on to the right foot first and holding on to the banisters. . . . She had once fallen and it had hurt.

Then she took a little stool, her very own little stool, from the hall and ran across the courtyard and through the door in the wall into the garden.

The fog, though it still lay thickly over the sea, had left the garden now, and each petal and leaf glowed the brighter for the gift of moisture it had left them.

Colette planted her little stool in the middle of a moss-grown path beside a flower border, sat down and began to wonder. She wondered solidly for half an hour. Little arches covered with rambler roses spanned the path, and in the border beside her bloomed madonna lilies, Canterbury bells, phlox, and crown imperials. She looked at them all and wondered about them, and she wondered about the fat worm that was wriggling about under the little box hedge that bordered the path, and she wondered about God.

Only last week, on this very path, she had seen God, and she was still very excited about it. Her mother had told her about God long ago, of course, and read her stories about Him out of the red and gold Sunday Book, and she believed in Him just as she believed in Undine and Jack the Giant Killer, and all the people in the fairy-books. She had always said her prayers fervently because she had been told that little girls who said their prayers went to heaven, and she was very anxious to go to heaven because she wanted to see how the angels got their frocks on over their wings. This question of the angels' wings kept her wondering for hours. Did they have holes in the backs of their frocks through which they poked their wings when they dressed? Or were they born in their frocks and wear them always, never taking them off even when they went to bed? In which case how did they wash? Or were the wings attached to the frocks and not to the angels? This question did not torment her as it would have tormented Michelle; she just wondered placidly about it.

But though she had always accomplished her religious duties with thoroughness and precision it was not until last week that she had really seen God for herself. It had all begun by her wondering about the Canterbury bells. There were great masses of them in the border, pink and blue and white, and she began by wondering whether they ever rang chimes like the church bells did. She tapped one fat pink bell with her finger to see if it rang, but it didn't, it only fell off its stalk on to the path. She picked it up gently and stuck it on her finger and looked at it, and it struck her suddenly that it was pretty. It was the colour of Peronelle's best petticoat and it was shaped like the little silver ornaments that father hung on the Christmas tree on Christmas Day. She liked it. She turned it upside down and looked inside. It was just as nice inside as it was outside. "Pretty," she said. She got up and ran indoors to Rachell, who was making dumplings in the kitchen.

"Mother," she said, "the Canterbury bells are pretty. Did God make them?"

"Yes," said Rachell, sprinkling flour into her basin.

"Why?" asked Colette.

It was Monday morning and Rachell was really too busy to go into it.

"To please Colette," she answered. "Pass me the currants, Sophie."

Colette was quite satisfied with this answer—it had given her enough to wonder about, in all conscience—and she trotted back into the garden. Sitting on her stool she looked at the coloured world spread out around her, and for the first time noticed that it was very beautiful. A carpet of green moss under her feet, a canopy of blue sky over her head, flowers in their hundreds on either side of her, and all apparently let down from heaven, like a bale of coloured silk, for her delight.

She had not noticed beauty before. She had taken the gold-dusted whiteness of the lilies as much for granted as eggs for breakfast, but now she looked and looked, and wondered and wondered. The lilies were very tall and their flowers were shaped like bells too. "Bells." A nice word. Bells rang for happy things; they rang at midnight on Christmas night when Christ was born, and all the animals all over the Island knelt down in their stables to say their prayers; they rang halfway through Mass, just at that moment when all the heads were bowed down like corn before the wind, and God lifted the latch and walked in; they rang when gentlemen in top hats went to church and got married to beautiful ladies done up in a lot of white stuff like presents in tissue paper; they rang too when dinner was ready.

God must have made all the bells all the world over to make people happy, just as He had made the Canterbury bells to please her. It was very kind of Him and it must have taken Him a long time. She felt much obliged. What a lot of bells all round her, and all of them beautiful, white bells of the lilies with gold dust inside, yellow bells of the crown imperials with bulging drops of honey inside, blue and pink and white Canterbury bells, hundreds and hundreds of them. She gazed and gazed and quite suddenly all the bells began to ring. She listened open-mouthed. Yes, they really were. They were swinging slowly from side to side, the lilies, the crown imperials and the Canterbury bells, and chiming away like mad.

Why? It wasn't Christmas night; it wasn't that moment at Mass when the heads are bowed. . . . Then something began to chime inside her and, looking up, she saw God walking down the garden path.

Every day since that Monday morning she had sat herself on her little stool on the moss-grown path, but He did not come again. Every day the lilies and Canterbury bells spread their petals in the sun and shook out little gusts of perfume when the sea wind touched them in passing, but they did not chime again. There was a dull pain in Colette's heart because the bells did not ring any more. . . . Would they ever ring any more?

III

Breakfast was completely overshadowed by the wreck. Sophie had brought news of the disaster when she came that morning.

A boat coming from France to the Islands, while yet miles from port, had been wrecked on a hideous reef called La Catian Roque. As soon as the fog had lifted boats from the Island had set out to the rescue, but who knew what they would find when they got there? If the ship had been broken up, and the savagery of Catian rock was renowned, and there had been many on board, perhaps too many for the boats—what then?

"They expect the worst, m'sieur," said Sophie with relish, as she thumped the plate of boiled eggs down in front of André. "I knew last night there was death at sea. I looked out before I went to my bed, m'sieur, and there was the King of the Auxcriniers riding the fog, as plain as plain. I screamed right out, and my cousin Jacquemin Gossilin he called out to me, 'What ails you, girl? Is it a ghost that you have seen?' ''Tis death itself that I have seen,' I said, 'riding the fog like the man in the Bible astride the black horse. 'Tis hell itself,' I said."

"That will do, Sophie," said Rachell, "bring the coffee."

"*Tres bon*, m'dame," said Sophie, and departed, her broad peasant face wreathed in smiles, her black eyes snapping with excitement, her Sunday stays creaking.

"There were sarregousets in the water-lane last night, father," cried Colin, waving his egg-spoon in an ecstasy of delight, "lots and lots of sarregousets, backwards and forwards all the time. That means death when they can't keep still. I bet you all those people are drowned."

"Death is very terrible, Colin," said Rachell reprovingly.

"You told me last Sunday," said Colin, "that death was beautiful. You said it was—" (he searched in his mind for the phrase she had used) "a sleep whose awakening is in heaven."

Rachell sighed. The religious upbringing of children was really extraordinarily difficult. Short of keeping a notebook in which to record the various lies one had taught them, how was it possible to avoid inconsistency? André attempted to come to the rescue.

"Death is both, Colin," he said, "everything in life can be looked at from several angles. Every fact of existence is a thing of facets."

"Oh," said Colin, "may I have another egg?"

Michelle leant across the table eagerly. She adored teaching and had the gift of simplification, while her father, when he attempted to explain in speech (with a pen in his hand he was a marvel of clarity) merely made confusion worse.

"Facets are different sides of the same thing," she said, "now if you take a square box—"

"I don't want to," said Colin, "I want another egg."

"Oh, be quiet, 'Chelle," said Peronelle, "we aren't at school. It's Sunday."

Michelle stopped, flushing. There was so much that she knew, and she was always trying to impart it, but her wretched family never seemed to want to hear. Did they not want, as she did, to climb up and up? Apparently not. Self-satisfied, conceited fools! She glanced at her father, and he smiled secretly at her. She wondered if he too felt he had something in him to give, some gift that must be used or it would turn sour and bitter within him, poisoning his whole life. . . . That secret smile was balm to them both.

Sophie, panting and creaking, came back with the coffee. Sophie always panted dreadfully on a Sunday, for it was the only day when she wore stays. On weekdays her ample figure, clothed in blue sprigged print and a voluminous white apron, bulged in accordance with nature's whims, but on Sundays, with the assistance of her family and the bedpost, she confined her contours within a suit of whalebone armour inherited from a great aunt. The result, especially in church during the sermon, was a torture of breathlessness and sharp points that stuck in, but somehow the pain made her feel very religious, reminding her as it did of a picture she had once seen of St. Sebastian pierced by arrows and panting horribly. . . . Also she hoped that her Sunday curves would favourably impress her cousin, Jacquemin Gossilin, who was taking so long in making up his mind to range himself that she feared the sheets in her bottom drawer would have gone into holes in the folds before she had him safely between them. Sophie had a very economical mind, and the thought of those wasted sheets made her cry at night sometimes.

Breakfast over and cleared away the family fell into a flurry of preparation for church. Rachell went upstairs to unpack her husband's sacred top hat from its tissue paper shrine under the four-poster, André went to the stable to superintend the Sunday exodus of the tumbledown old landau, and the children went to their bedrooms to find their handkerchiefs and books and to brush their hair.

Punctually at ten o'clock Brovard, one of the farm men, brought round the landau with Lupin, the old grey horse, between the shafts, and André, after testing the dilapidated harness, rushed upstairs to change into his swallow tails.

No matter how early he got up he seemed never able to get the farm work done by church time, but if he did not go to church Rachell grieved, and he preferred any amount of rush and sleeplessness to a grieved Rachell. This morning, after days of torturing worry, the strain of last night's talk, a sleepless night of foreboding, and getting up at four, he was so tired that his fumbling fingers dropped everything he touched. On his knees looking for his stud, knocking his already aching head against the chest of drawers and the bedpost, he marvelled at the extraordinary stupidity of his life. He had no religion to speak of, and yet regularly once a week he dressed himself in garments unequalled for absurdity in the history of costume, and sat through a sermon that bored him, in order to do honour to a Deity in Whom he was not at all certain he believed. He hated his work and saw himself faced with ruin in it, and yet day after day, year after year, he forced his mind to it, adding the exhaustion of unwilling effort to the exhaustion of his toil. He had the gift of literary expression and day after day, year after year, he had to deny it life. He had not found the world sweet or easy, and yet he had chosen to bring five children into it, surely implying by that choice that the life he gave them was a gift worth having. Sham!

Sham! The whole thing was a hideous sham. . . . Where was that damned stud? . . . And yet, and yet—there were two sides to the thing. He had had great happiness at Bon Repos. He had learnt to love. He had learnt to think. At the heart of a life he hated he had found a sort of peace. His gift, if wasted, was nevertheless there, and his own. If only this forcing of a personality into unnatural channels were not so exhausting—so damnably exhausting. God! How tired he was.

"André, are you ready?"

It was Rachell calling below. He could visualize her standing in the coolness of the hall, gracious and beautiful in her black silk Sunday dress with the lace mantle, and her bonnet trimmed with purple pansies. He supposed it was for her sake he lived this sham of a life; for her he went to church in a top hat; for her and the children he sweated in the fields and stables; for her he stayed lingering on at Bon Repos faced with certain ruin; he had not sufficient strength of character, he supposed, to fight her. When he thought of last night he felt hot with shame. What sort of a man was he to be so easily swayed by the foolish whim of a woman? He hit his head violently against the washstand and, as pain stabbed him, cursed himself for a weak cowardly wastrel. But though he might curse he did not waste time in self pity, he was too humble a man for that. He had the humility to lay his failure at the door of his own character. If his life was a sham was it not his own fault? Surely only the weak found themselves pushed by circumstances in the wrong direction. Only the weak—but meanwhile Rachell was waiting in the hall.

"I can't find my stud," he shouted.

He heard the rustle of her silk dress as she came up the stairs, then she came in, swaying slightly like a poplar tree as she walked, bringing tranquillity with her. She found the stud—staring him in the face, of course—she helped him into his coat and brushed it, she found his prayer book for him and handed him his top hat, smoothing it once more lovingly as she did so. Finally, with amazing skill, with a mere smile and a touch, she smoothed out André himself. Then she led the way downstairs.

André followed her, completely cheered up. What a woman! And he had made her—he and the children, and Bon Repos, had made her. He remembered the wild untutored girl who had come here as his bride, and marvelled again. Strange that contact with one weak man, five squalling brats and an old farmhouse should have made of that girl this gracious courageous woman. He supposed the very weakness of what she had had to grapple with had developed her love and strength—in which case, perhaps, he need not count himself a failure after all. Thankfully, as he followed her down the stairs, he propped himself in spirit against her strength. Let her lead—he would follow her, however crazy the path she was following seemed to him. With her more direct, more tranquil nature, she could see more clearly than he could, divided and tormented in mind as he always was.

The children were already in the landau, Colin on the box seat, the girls behind, looking perfectly delicious in their Sunday finery. André, as he took his seat and gathered up the reins, glanced from one to another, his eyes lingering longest on Michelle, his favourite. Darlings! If life were but good to them! He wished he could pray for their safety, as Rachell did. He wished he could trust them confidently to life, as she did, but he had not got her faith in life. He was tortured sometimes by the thought of Peronelle's frail body in pain, of Jacqueline submerged by fear, of Michelle unable to her life's end to adjust herself to her own humanity, of Colette—but no, he never worried about Colette, her coating of fat and her sense of humour would surely be adequate protection against all fate's arrows. He was at ease about Colin, too. Anything as decided and impudent as Colin would surely always come out top.

The du Frocqs did not attend the Town Church behind the harbour, for that was Protestant, and the du Frocqs had for generations been Roman Catholics. The Island, in religion as in all else, was divided in allegiance between France and England. Of French blood, and yet subjects of Queen Victoria, the Islanders were curious hybrid creatures. A generation back the Island had been completely French, speaking the French language, turning to

France rather than to England for contact with the outside world. But now, in 1888, it was as though England had stretched out arms and was slowly gathering her child to her.

Rachell and André, who had talked French as children, now spoke English. Their children had never talked anything else. To converse always in English was now the sign of a superior education. . . . Only the peasants and the poorer shopkeepers kept the music of the old patois sighing and singing in the country lanes and up and down the narrow streets of St. Pierre.

The boys of the Island were no longer sent to school in France, the girls were no longer taught by the nuns in the old convent by the sea; instead the old boys' school was brought up-to-date and a new one for girls was built in St. Pierre, and spectacled men and women from England, with adenoids and degrees, braved one of the nastiest sea passages in the world to bring the horrors of modern education to the poor little savages of the Island.

Rachell, who had spent much of her girlhood in the convent, sitting in an austere sun-drenched room within sound of the sea, being taught by Soeur Monique to make lovely lace while Soeur Ursule read aloud the lives of the saints in exquisite French, was thrilled when Peronelle came out top of her form at mathematics and Michelle burnt her eyebrows off doing chemistry. It was all very wonderful, Rachell thought, and André agreed with her. The Island was developing marvellously. Education was making enormous strides. The children were having wonderful advantages which had been denied to their parents. Rachell thanked God for it—and yet—when she and André were too tired to sleep at night they would chatter to each other softly in the French of their childhood and be comforted, and when Rachell felt worried she would bring out her lace-pillow and the tap of the flying bobbins would bring a smile to her lips, while Soeur Ursule's stories of the saints, fluttering through her mind, would lift up her heart like a flight of butterflies. . . . To each generation the education it deserves. . . .

IV

But to return to the du Frocqs jolting along the lanes in their dilapidated landau.

Their progress was slow, for Lupin was very old, very fat, and very disinclined to take anybody anywhere. He advanced with a slow sideways motion, wheezing as he went, like an asthmatic crab. If he desired refreshment he stopped and partook of it, and if he desired to remove flies from the small of his back with his tail he stopped and gave his whole attention to it. But the du Frocqs bore it all with loving patience. They adored Lupin. They loved him even better than Maximilian and Marmalade, and that is saying a good deal.

On the outskirts of St. Pierre, just before the lane turned into a street and plunged frantically downhill, they stopped at a little inn and deposited Lupin and the landau in the stable. The task of getting Lupin up and down the steep streets of St. Pierre was never attempted by André. Here Lupin would remain, enjoying an excellent repast, until church and the weekly penance of Sunday dinner with grandpapa were at an end.

And now began the wonder and beauty of the Sunday Parade. André's top hat, which he could not wear in the landau for fear it should be dislodged by the bumps, and which had been reverently held by Colin throughout the drive, was adjusted upon his head. Rachell, having shaken out her skirts and inspected the children, took her husband's arm and erected the parasol, holding it well to the left, so that it gave her no shade whatever, but was safe from doing any injury to the top hat. The children fell into line behind them and the procession started down the street.

Owing to the extraordinary steepness of the hill and the way it had of turning into steps at unexpected moments, and the consequent necessity of climbing down rather than walking down, the procession was perhaps not as dignified as it might have been, but that was the fault of those who built St. Pierre up the side of a rocky cliff, and not of the du Frocqs.

At the bottom of the street they turned to the right, took a deep breath and proceeded to climb a long twisting flight of steps that wound up and up between grey walls. Right at the top was an old iron gate leading on to a flat rocky ledge and here were the little old Church of St. Raphael, and the Convent, built on the edge of a sheer precipice, with nothing below them but rocks and sea water.

So old and so weather-beaten were the Church and Convent that they looked like rocks themselves. It was hard to realize they had been built by man with blocks of stone, rather it seemed that unseen divine hands had hollowed out chambers in the solid cliff and that men, exhausted by the fury of winds and waves, had crept into them, had lit their little flickering candles in the dark corners and put their bunches of flowers where the shafts of sunlight fell, had said their prayers and swung their censers in trembling gratitude for safety and succour.

"I'm sure I don't know what we're to do about church when we're old, André," panted Rachell, clinging to the iron gate, "we'll never be able to get up these steps."

"We'll have to sit at home," said André, trying not to sound too jubilant. "I shan't have to wear my top hat," he added. This thought lit a sudden little candle in the dreary bleakness of old age.

The children, Colin in the rear, had now reached the iron gate.

"Mother, look at Colin," said Jacqueline, "he's simply filthy."

The whole of the front of Colin's white sailor suit, as well as his hands and face, were covered with dirt. All the way up the steps he had, in company with Joan of Arc, been scaling the walls of Rouen. The others had gone on ahead but Colin, his front pressed against the wall beside the steps, his fingers clinging to its grimy surface, had fought his way up, step by step, with Joan of Arc only just behind. The enemy were raining boiling lead on him from above, his scaling ladder was in imminent danger of giving way, he had a sword wound in his leg and an arrow in his shoulder, but still he fought on, up and up, bloody but undefeated, joyously facing death itself for the lilies of France and for the Maid.

"Good gracious, Colin," cried poor Rachell, "what on earth have you been doing?"

Colin smiled the sweet faint smile of an exhausted hero, weak from loss of blood.

"I fell, mother," he said, "six steps from the bottom I fell. Right down into the street again. On my front."

"Darling, you might have killed yourself!" Rachell, distracted, produced her handkerchief and rubbed his hands tenderly, "your poor little hands! André, brush him down the front."

"It hardly hurts at all now," said Colin bravely, as his parents ministered to his needs, "though it did at the time. I didn't call out for fear of frightening you."

"Good boy," said his father.

"Well, *I* didn't see all that dirt in the street," muttered Jacqueline, "he rubbed against the wall on purpose." Rachell and André did not hear, but Colin glared savagely.

"Come along now," said André. He offered his arm once more to Rachell, removed the top hat and led the way up the three worn steps, through the old porch and into the fragrant interior of the church. The children followed, Colin pausing to kick Jacqueline.

"Sneak," he said.

Tears welled into Jacqueline's eyes and her throat swelled. Before breakfast she had been happy but now she was miserable. She had done it again. She had sneaked. She was always sneaking. And yet she didn't want to or mean to. Why did she do it? The truth suddenly popped up its head out of her inside self and told her. She told tales of the others because telling them made her feel superior, and she adored feeling superior. But this her outside self would not admit for a moment. Jacqueline, the perfect Jacqueline, would never wish to feel superior. She smacked the truth on the head and sent it squirming back into her inside self. No, she had *not* sneaked. She never sneaked. She simply drew her mother's attention to truths about the others which it was desirable she should know. After all, what an awful thing it would have been if Colin had walked into church looking like Landoys the sweep. Of course, she was right.

She was always right. As she knelt in the du Frocq pew, with her head bent, she furtively wiped the tears out of her eyes with her white cotton gloves. When she sat back on the seat there were no signs of them and her face wore its usual smug expression of self-satisfaction, although her heart was swelling with misery. . . . Colin, sitting beside her, positively hated her.

What with one thing and another they were late for church, but so superb was the dignity with which Rachell sailed up the aisle that no one thought the worse of her for it. In fact, when Rachell was late, being late seemed to other people the perfect thing to be. It was impossible to put her in the wrong. If you put her in it it immediately became the right. The shimmer of her personality over hard facts took all the lateness out of being late and all the wrongness out of being wrong.

The little church, with its great walls four feet thick, and its little slats of windows, was dim and cool and musty. . . . The smell of incense and lilies and candle grease made one feel rather sleepy. . . . The Virgin on her pedestal, with the Babe in her arms and the candles flowering at her feet, seemed to be dreaming as she stood there so still in her blue cloak. . . . The Latin words sung by the nuns in their sweet treble voices sounded like a lullaby. . . . Perhaps all the du Frocqs except Rachell and Colette drowsed a little.

Rachell never drowsed in church. A woman with a husband and five children and cows and pigs and chickens and no money had far too much to pray about to waste any time in drowsing. It wasn't as though she had a great deal of time to spend in prayer when she wasn't in church. She had very little. She must make the most of that short time once a week when she knelt at the feet of the Virgin Mother on her pedestal.

To-day, after she had prayed for André and the children and even, with a great effort, for her father-in-law, she began to pray urgently that that decision of last night might be the right decision. . . . She had forced André to it. . . . She was responsible. . . . Desperately she prayed that their home might be saved. . . . Bon Repos. . . . "Harbour and good rest to those who enter here, courage to those who go forth. Let those who go and those who stay forget not God . . ." Trying to yield up her own will she prayed that she might have courage if she had to go forth. . . . Then all over again began to pray that she might stay in that restful harbour. . . . She could not go forth. . . . She could not. . . . The sanctus bell rang out very clear and sweet and she bowed her head as though a wind had swept the church, then lifted it again, conscious of some intense experience going on beside her. Her eyes were drawn irresistibly to Colette.

The church door had opened—Colin, the last to come in, had perhaps latched it carelessly—and Colette was gazing at the patch of sunshine on the threshold with an expression of such amazing welcoming beauty on her podgy little face that Rachell was positively scared. What in the world had the child seen? Colette withdrew her eyes from the door and began to laugh. Good heavens! That awful soda-water syphon laugh of Colette's! Just at the most sacred part of the service! Rachell stretched out a hand in alarm. But she need not have worried, the laugh did not develop as far as the squeaking stage, it was merely a bubble of delight ending in a smile at the Virgin, as though she and the Virgin shared some secret, before Colette buried her face in her starfish hands and began to pray. Rachell looked at her in increasing consternation. What on earth did the child pray about? Surely her behaviour was abnormal in so young a creature? An awful fear smote Rachell. What if the child should become a contemplative nun? How awful! How terrible! Her little Colette in a black habit with all her yellow curls shaved off! Hastily she prayed that Colette might not become a nun and then, ashamed of herself, hastily prayed a second prayer for forgiveness for the first, and then hastily prayed the first prayer over again.

The service was over at last and the little congregation filed out blinking into the sun. In the porch the du Frocqs squared their shoulders and prepared to face grandpapa.

Dr. du Frocq did not sit with his descendants in the family pew, he sat by himself in solitary glory on the other side of the aisle. He did not, he said, like being cluttered up with a lot of ill-behaved children. In reality, the children, excellently trained by Rachell, behaved a great deal better than grandpapa, whose demeanour left much to be desired. He never knelt down, he merely bent over, as has been stated, and blew into his top hat. He said "humph" loudly in the middle of all the prayers and always sat down three minutes before he had any business to and got up three minutes too late. At the beginning of the sermon he got out his watch, opened it, and placed it on the ledge in front of him. At the end of ten minutes—he considered ten minutes the utmost limit of length for a sermon—he shut it up with a snap and then opened it again, muttering under his breath "Fellow ought to be shot!" If the sermon continued in spite of his hints he spent the rest of it muttering and snapping his watch open and shut and blowing out his cheeks with a faint hissing sound. As soon as the priest had pronounced the last word of the final blessing he got up and stalked out, banging with his walking stick on the stone floor and eyeing the bowed heads of the congregation with profound distaste. Ridiculous bonnets the women wore! Damned ridiculous! And all the men bald. Ate too much, that's what it was. Dyspepsia. Made the hair come out. He'd told 'em so. He'd tell 'em again. Wouldn't listen, the damn fools. In the porch he stood and waited for his relations. An amazingly handsome old man; very upright, very tall, fine curly iron grey hair, a fierce projecting grey beard, choleric blue eyes snapping under beetling brows, a hard selfish mouth, wonderfully cut clothes, a silver-topped ebony walking stick and a top hat of exquisite beauty.

"Good morning, father." Rachell faced him with the coldly distant smile she kept for bestowal upon her parent-in-law only. Her eyes flickered in dislike from his choleric blue eyes to his selfish mouth. How *could* he be the father of André! How *could* he! André, of course, was like his poor mother. Rachell had never known her mother-in-law. Grandmamma had died many years ago.

"Good morning, Rachell." Grandpapa's voice was rich and deep, making one think of plum cake and port wine, and purple velvet smoking caps. "Those children fidget in the sermon. You should control 'em. André, you look yellow. Stomach. A bad business about this wreck. What? Bad business. A d-er-humph—bad business."

It should be said in grandpapa's favour that he tried really hard not to swear in front of the children.

"Any news?" asked André. "Have any boats come back yet?"

"Not a sign of 'em. Wreck's miles out, you know. Inferior seamanship, that's what it is. Never had all these wrecks when I was a boy. What? Steam, that's the trouble. A man was a sailor when he had to sail the seas in a windjammer. It took some skill to trim those sails, I can tell you. But now they stick a steam-engine in the hold, wind the damn thing up an' go an' drink whisky in the saloon. What can you expect? On the rocks in a twinkling and serve 'em right. What? In my young days ships were manned by sailors, now they're cluttered up by a lot of b-er-humph-ignorant mechanics."

He extended a hand each to Peronelle and Colette and led the way down the steps. Only for these two among his grandchildren did he feel any affection. Peronelle he liked for the simple reason that she had what a later and more decadent age calls sex appeal. In 1888 it was referred to as attraction for the opposite sex. Grandpapa considered that Peronelle was likely to Marry Well and do Credit to the Family. Marrying Well was the only way, in his opinion, in which a woman could do Credit to her Family. Colette he liked because she was stout. Grandpapa liked a well-covered woman and had the lowest opinion of Rachell's slender grace. He liked a bosom, and plenty of it, well upholstered.

Peronelle walked along in a silence that would have cast a chill on anyone but grandpapa, whose self-esteem was impervious to all the shafts of other people's dislike. Her hand in his was cold and unresponsive as a dead fish. She hated him. How dared he say that father was yellow! He wasn't. He was white because he had a headache. She knew he had a headache. And stomach! It was disgustingly insulting. As if father ate too much. The trouble was to get him to eat anything at all. He had a headache because he was tired. He was always tired. She wrenched her hand out of grandpapa's and ran back to her father. Her hand, that had been so cold, lay in her father's like a warm, pulsing little bird. In the shadows at the bottom of the steps, before they turned into the street, she pulled his hand up to her face and kissed it. Her face was white with rage. André, slightly embarrassed, patted her on the back and looked at her anxiously. What a passionate creature she was! How hot-tempered and how loving—and how thin! Would her body ever stand the strain of her personality? . . . He began to worry again.

Grandpapa bore the loss of Peronelle with equanimity. A pretty woman was allowed her whims. An impulsive child. Well, men liked that sort of thing. Should Marry Well. He smiled benignly on Colette, who beamed up at him. Colette loved him. Like a little dog she was quick to feel when other people liked her and responded with the gift of her whole heart, quite regardless of the moral character of the recipient.

At the bottom of the steps, slowly and with incomparable dignity, the Sunday Parade was continued.

V

Grandpapa, as was consistent with his dignity and his position as the only doctor worth calling a doctor on the Island—there were a few inferior persons who dealt with the diseases of the lower orders—lived in the principal street of St. Pierre. This street, called Le Paradis, was frequently referred to by grandpapa, with a wave of his ebony stick, as "the Park Lane of the Island." It was really no more like Park Lane than it was like Paradise, being a steep cobbled street twisting between tall dignified houses flanked by lovely gardens. It resembled Park Lane and Paradise only because the Best People lived there.

Grandpapa's house was halfway down. It was very imposing indeed, with a pink stucco front, an area leading down to the basements and lace curtains drawn across all the windows to hide the glories within from the inquisitive gaze of the vulgar populace. At the back of the house the curtains were drawn aside a little, so that you could see the garden and the glorious view of the harbour beyond.

Inside grandpapa's house was very magnificent and impressive, with thick carpets that stifled all sound, gilt-framed family portraits, mahogany furniture, luscious wax fruits under glass cases, shining damask and silver, and always a very great deal to eat and drink. Grandpapa, though frequently complaining that everyone ate too much, ate enormously himself. But his meals never seemed to do him any harm. It seemed that every portion of him, his interior organs as well as his heart and his soul, were made of hard, tough leather.

Grandpapa's material well-being was presided over by his English butler, Barker, and his housekeeper, Madame Gaboreau, a purple lady with an auburn front and sequins all over her chest. . . . She was simply horrid. She had under her iron hand several wretched underlings who led a scurrying life below stairs with the black beetles, and kept the house shining all over like polished glass.

"Fine day. What?" said grandpapa, plunging the knife into the sirloin. There was a squelching sound and a thin pink stream trickled out. . . . Grandpapa liked his beef underdone . . . Peronelle shuddered.

"It is one of the loveliest summers we have ever had," said Rachell, lifting her veil and wishing they could have a little window open. She began to talk charmingly about the weather. She always did her very best at grandpapa's. She felt it to be her duty.

André, whose headache made him feel a little sick, averted his eyes from the roast beef and smiled the patient smile that always exasperated his father beyond all words. His sons were a bitter humiliation to Dr. du Frocq. Jean, a wastrel, gone to the bad and lost sight of in Australia, and André, a stupid sentimental failure without even the ability to make the du Frocq farm pay. God knows where he'd be without his wife's money, and the devil alone knew how much there was left of that by this time. Well, he'd warned 'em. They needn't come whining to *him* for money—not unless they gave up that damned farm.

"Farm going well? What?" he asked pleasantly.

A steely glitter appeared in Rachell's eyes. Grandpapa, she knew, asked this question simply for the pleasure of thrusting a dagger into his son.

"Fairly well, I think," lied André.

"Good crop of tomatoes?" continued grandpapa. Rachell knew that he knew the tomatoes were diseased this year. Need he turn the dagger in the wound? She stretched out her foot under the table and touched André's boot very, very gently. . . . By her touch the dagger was subtly withdrawn.

Dinner passed somehow. Roast beef was followed by apricot tart, Stilton cheese—into which grandpapa poured a little port wine to increase its colony of tasty maggots—plum cake and dessert. Then they all went into the library and grandpapa and André smoked cigars, and they all gazed bleakly at the garden and the harbour through windows that were apparently hermetically sealed.

Rachell gripped her hands together and felt for the thousandth time that if she had to live here always she would go mad. Something must happen to prevent it. Something must, must happen to prevent it. But what? It seemed to her now, in the depression subsequent to overeating, that her vision and hopes of last night were just moonshine. She knew a moment of utter, black despair. The smoking of the cigars seemed interminable to her, but when at last nothing was left of them but evil-smelling wreaths twisting round the room like bad spells she suggested they should all go down to the harbour and see if there was any news about the wreck . . . André was getting whiter and whiter. . . . Cigars never suited him, but in grandpapa's opinion a man who could not smoke his cigar was a white livered nincompoop—and she feared that unless fresh air were administered promptly something really dreadful might occur.

"Shan't come with you," said grandpapa, "don't care if the beggars are drowned. Serve 'em right for taking to steam. Should have stuck to sail. Good-bye. See you next week. What?" And spreading his newspaper over his head he was snoring almost before they got out into the hall.

Thankfully, with the air of children let out of school, they went down the hill towards the harbour.

"Do you feel better, darling?" asked Rachell. "It was that cigar, only if you refuse it annoys him so."

André, taking great gulps of fresh air, nodded. The children ran on ahead and, though it was Sunday, were not rebuked. . . . Everyone's spirits rose.

At the very bottom of Le Paradis respectability left off suddenly with the turning to La Rue Clubin. Colin glanced up it but all its glory had been quenched by Sunday. The booths were gone, the gay jostling crowds were gone. Mère Tangrouille had gone, nothing was left of yesterday's delights but the mangy cats and a few dirty children playing in the gutter.

"Something ought to be done about that street," said Rachell, "it's a perfect disgrace, and they say the sweets they sell there are simply poison. Luckily the children never go near it."

André assented and Colin, overhearing, wore the expression of a seraph.

They passed the Town Church and came to the harbour. It was a glorious still hot day with a sea like smooth turquoise silk. Impossible to think that menace could lie hidden below that soft shimmering surface, yet the crowds that thronged the harbour wall bore witness that it was so.

"André," cried Rachell, "the boats are coming in! The children! I don't want the children to see!"

But it was too late. All the children but fat Colette, burrowing and squeezing, had already wormed their way through the crowds to the harbour wall, leaving their more ample parents hemmed in by stout perspiring Islanders in their Sunday best.

One by one the boats left the open sea, swung silently into the shelter of the harbour and glided across to the steps. Sympathetic hands were held out to help white-faced exhausted men and women up the steps to safety. The crowd, swaying a little with excitement, was silent except for little tense murmured ejaculations that ran hither and thither like darting flames in a stubble field.

"Ah, holy Virgin, poor souls, poor souls!" Rachell heard as she stood there clinging to André's arms. "All night on the open sea in the little boats, and always a swell round Catian Roque—" "'Tis the devil's own place, that reef. They say there's a demon hid in the caves below—" "I passed the reef once with my father. Black and scarred the rocks are, and the water round them always black like pitch, and makes a sucking sound that turns the blood cold in your veins—" "They were too many for the boats. A third of them was lost—" "They could see the dead floating on the water when the fog lifted—" "Yes, a third of them lost."

Some among the crowd, as each boat came in, were agonizedly scrutinizing the faces of the rescued, desperately hoping to see an expected face, for there had been Islanders on the wrecked ship. Now and then there was a snapping of self-control and a little burst of sobbing cut the hush like a whip. It was horrible. Rachell could hardly bear it. She caught sight of a woman's unconscious face as they lifted her from the boat. Why had she fainted? Had she seen her child dead on the water when the fog lifted? Rachell clutched Colette's hand tightly in hers and shut her eyes. She wished she could go home, but they could not move for the press, and where, oh where, were the children?

The three girls were jammed against the harbour wall but Colin, with his amazing genius for being where he wanted to be, was at the very top of a flight of steps, clinging to the rope handrail to prevent himself being pushed into the water by the crowd behind him. But he was not in the least alarmed. He was enjoying himself enormously. It was really better than the circus.

And now the very last boat had rounded the buoy at the harbour mouth and was skimming like a bird over the still water. . . . The last boat. . . . The crowd bent and swayed in an eerie silence. It was as though a sudden tempest rocked them, a hideous tempest that brought with it no familiar sound of wind-lashed trees but only a horrible deathlike hush. The boat drew up at the steps and the faces of those on board were clearly seen. There were one or two cries of welcome, so sharp with agonized relief that there was more pain than joy in them, but three or four tense figures turned abruptly and, pushing blindly against the crowd, stumbled away towards the town.

Colin, mad with excitement, was oblivious of either joy or agony. He gave a great whoop of joy. The boat was *his* boat. It was

Hélier Falliot's boat. In the bows stood Hélier himself with Guilbert beside him. Colin identified himself instantly with Hélier and Guilbert and felt himself the hero of the hour. It was *his* boat. *He* had toiled all the morning saving the shipwrecked. His heart swelled with vicarious pride. Sprawling down the slimy steps like a young crab, he was the first to lay steadying hands upon the gunnel. Here he remained, holding on like grim death, with men stepping over him, men kicking him, men prodding him and saying, "Damn you, boy, get out of the way," women above crying "Mind the child," and sea water washing over his best boots. It was *his* boat, and he was not to be detached from it until the last of those he had rescued was safely on shore. He crouched with his eyes shut, boots scraping his head and water splashing up into his face, but gradually as the commotion died he opened one eye and found himself looking at the last occupant of the boat, a grizzled man, his torn shirt and trousers dripping with sea water, who sat in the stern with his head in his hands.

"Found him clinging to a bit of wreckage," muttered Hélier to someone in his musical patois, "wouldn't be picked up till all the rest were safe. Only just room for him in the boat." He crossed to the stranger and tapped him on the shoulder. "M'sieur," he said gently, "nous sommes arrivés."

The man lifted his head, and he and Colin looked straight at each other. Colin had never seen so strange a creature. He had a rugged ugly face, hard and self-contained, and just now grey with exhaustion. He had a great scar across one cheek and an untidy thicket of grey beard that emphasized the look of wildness in his strange yellow eyes.

"C'est lîle. Venez, m'sieur." Hélier thrust his hands under the man's armpits and pulled him to his feet. Colin, drawn in some incomprehensible way by the stare of those yellow eyes, scrambled over the gunnel, went to him and seized hold of him frantically by his torn dripping shirt, as though he intended never to let him go. . . .

It was at this point that Rachell, for the first and last time in her dignified life, created a most deplorable disturbance.

She had been standing quietly by André, haunted by the thought of the unconscious woman she had seen lifted from the boat, and by those stricken figures who had crept away from the glaring, horrible sea, when she had opened her eyes suddenly as though someone had struck her a blow in the face. Through a sudden gap in the crowd she saw the boat at the harbour steps and her son Colin clinging to an ugly, rough-looking man with a torn shirt. She stared at the man's face. It was the man of her "seeing." . . .

All control fled from her. She became as a desperate creature fighting for life. Abandoning Colette she flung herself upon the crowd in front of her. Pushing, kicking, striking right and left with her parasol, she fought her way to the top of the steps. Hélier was just helping the man up them. She seized his arm.

"You are to bring him to Bon Repos," she cried, her voice rising almost to a scream. "To Bon Repos. Do you hear? As soon as he is recovered you are to bring him to me. Mrs. du Frocq. The farm called Bon Repos."

She shook Hélier's brawny arm savagely and gazed into his dumbfounded face like a mad thing.

"He is my friend. He must come to me. To Bon Repos." She stamped her foot in her urgency and shook the sailor again. The stranger, too exhausted to be conscious of her, stood swaying in Hélier's grip.

"Très bon, m'dame, presently we will bring him." Hélier's native courtesy conquered his astonishment. He made a gesture of politeness with one arm whilst heaving the stranger up the steps with the other. . . . Rachell stood back, panting a little, her hands at her breast. . . . Willing hands stretched down from above, and the man was borne off to the tavern just beyond the harbour wall.

Meanwhile André, with Colette sobbing with fright clutched beneath one arm, had arrived upon the scene of action.

"What in the world, Rachell," he demanded, "that ugly-looking vagabond! Are you mad?"

A crowd was surrounding them now, for Rachell was well known on the Island. Mrs. du Frocq of Bon Repos—the old doctor's beautiful daughter-in-law—hitherto a model of dignity and restraint . . . There was a certain pleasure in seeing her tumble off her pedestal and turn into an ordinary hysterical woman—the crowd pressed a little nearer. . . . They were terribly conspicuous. . . . Dreadful. . . . André had never before been so near losing his temper with his wife.

But with the same suddenness with which she had lost it Rachell recovered her self-control.

"André," she said, "we must go home and prepare for him. I will explain—"

With lovely gestures she gathered her family to her, settled her lace mantle, erected her parasol and took her husband's arm. The crowd fell back respectfully as she sailed through them with the motion of a superbly gliding swan. Other people might have left behind them an unfavourable impression, but, as usual, nothing was left in the wake of Rachell's magnificent exit but a sense of exquisite rightness.

Chapter 3

I

THE fogs of August writhed away behind the arched dome of the September sky, tipped like a shining bowl over an earth and sea clear and unsullied and bright as polished enamel. It never rained very much on the Island in summer, yet so richly stored with water was its earth that the wells were always brimful, and the water-lanes musical with their impatient little streams hurrying to the sea. Rich and lush was the grass around the wells and the ferns in the lanes were of an almost savage green, framing in their plumes patches of sky of so deep a blue that, gazing at it, one thought of the coolness of lake water rather than a limitless depth of sun-warmed space. Only on the cliff edge the short grass was dry and brown, panting for the autumn rains. Not so the heather. The little wiry stalks had crept and twisted everywhere, carrying a myriad purple bells over the cliff face and right down over the rocks almost to the sea. Dry and crisp and tiny were these little flowers of wind-swept space, giving out a faint almost metallic sound as the hand passed over them, with none of the caressing softness of more sheltered flowers yet pouring over the barren cliff a flood of opulent, almost blaring colour, triumphant as a trumpet blast.

Wherever one looked the heather colour was repeated. Out at sea purple cloud shadows striped jade green water and in the du Frocq's garden purple Michaelmas daisies bloomed above the spilled rose petals. The passion flowers round the windows were out, hiding their sacred sorrows under the green leaves.

Nature was perhaps aware of coming weariness, a little conscious that spring was a long time ago, but before the storms of winter overwhelmed her she was determined to flaunt a still vivid beauty before the eyes of men. If they could no longer revel in the cool blue and gold of her youth they should lower their eyes reverently before this regal purple of her age.

And the man who stood on the flat rock above La Baie des Mouettes did so, and sighed a little. It was very early and, in spite of a summer sky and sea, there was a cold nip in the air. "Autumn," he muttered and shivered. He had lived so long abroad, under a sun whose blazing warmth was a fact of existence to be counted on, that the thought of once more facing chill winds and driving sleet sent a little thrill of horror through him. He cursed himself for a fool under his breath. Assuredly he was a fool to stay and face an Island winter when all the warmth of the world was his for the taking. He would go. Nothing held him. He would be a fool to stay. He had been a fool to come. He had sailed from France to the Island intending to stay for one day only, simply to hear once more the Island patois singing in the lanes and the streams tinkling in the water-lanes, to see if the honeysuckle on the cliffs was as thick as it used to be, and if the little Church of St. Raphael still stood four-square to the great gales. Then he had meant to go back again to the hot countries where his life had passed from a riotously hopeful youth to a maturity scorched with bitterness.

Yet, perhaps there was more in it than that. Perhaps he had hoped that the pain of seeing the Island again would be sufficiently great to rise and submerge the searing flame of disappointment that ran backwards and forwards within him. To exchange one pain for another is sometimes as great a relief as cessation of pain. If that had been his wish it had not been granted him. Sometimes for a moment a pain that had its roots in his green youth rose like a well of water and promised refreshment, but while he was still taking great gasps of relief, like a parched man seeing a cup of water, it receded and he was left alone again with his scorching bitterness. He had come for one day, had found neither rest nor comfort, and yet had stayed a month. . . . He was a fool. . . . He turned his back abruptly and climbed up the grassy slope to the cliff top.

It was the same slope that Michelle had climbed a month ago but now it was slippery as glass, and only a man who had learnt in his youth how to negotiate it would have attempted it. . . . He climbed it with the carelessness of a reckless man.

At the top he turned and looked down again at the exquisite beauty of La Baie des Mouettes, and for a moment that little spring of refreshment rose in him. . . . The green and the blue and the purple. . . . The soft creaming of the waves round the rocks. . . . The gleam of wet pebbles. . . . After the scorching sands of the desert these things were good.

He raised his eyes to the gulls soaring, dipping, swerving, diving, backwards and forwards, up and down, round and round. Their wings were tracing a pattern, or a spell whose filaments were twisting round him and binding him to this blasted little Island. A spell? He smiled at the childish word, reminding him of the fairybooks of his childhood. Yet how else describe that power which Rachell and her children had over him? He had thought that no human being would ever again hold him, yet here he was, a wanderer, tethered against his will, and by a woman and a handful of commonplace children. . . . No, not commonplace . . . Michelle . . . Peronelle . . . Jacqueline . . . Colin . . . Colette. . . . These were each separate and unique strands in the spell that bound him.

He swung suddenly on his heel and walked away. He would have to stay. Something stronger than himself would keep him at Bon Repos. Their need of him? As this thought slipped abruptly into his mind he laughed out loud, and his laugh was as harsh and mocking as the gulls' own. Need? That was a word that he had never allowed admittance into his scheme of things. It had been his aim, always, that he should need nothing and that nothing should need him. Perfect freedom from all ties, absolute aloneness, had been his abiding ambition and he had pursued it with a ferocity that had the desired effect of keeping him isolated like a savage bonfire. What then? He could not admit for a moment that any weakening had come with age, and slewed abruptly away from his own thoughts.

Instead he went back in memory to that day a month ago when he had first become aware of Rachell and her tribe of children—that day of the wreck. It had been a hideous night, a hideous morning, and yet he had enjoyed it. Very few things stirred him in these days, yet the shuddering thrill that passed through the ship as she grated on the rocks had thrilled rather pleasantly in his soul—it had been a new experience to a man who thought he had drained the last dregs of experience. Then the night of activity—strapping lifebelts on the terrified women—lowering the boats—calming the children—it had all acted upon him as a narcotic and he had forgotten the ceaseless burden of his own disillusionment. When the bustle was over he had taken to the water with a sense of relief. There was no room for him in the boats and death seemed certain—he would be able to slip thankfully from a narcotic to extinction. Yet once in the sea he found himself automatically keeping himself afloat, and when the chance of clinging to some wreckage came to him he clung to it as though he were the ardent boy he had been forty years ago. Afterwards he had marvelled at this incident. There had been more in it than the natural instinct of self preservation. Perhaps the first filament of the spell had tightened round him then. When the fog had lifted and the boats from the Island had arrived he had been the last to be saved. He had waited cynically, not drawing attention to himself, still holding out a welcoming hand to death just round the corner, yet with the other still clinging to his spar. When Hélier's brawny hands had gripped him and hauled him into the boat he had spat out the sea water that filled his mouth and then laughed. . . . His laugh had not been pleasant to hear. . . . What sort of a fool was he? He had been near to complete freedom, without taking the path of obvious suicide and branding himself as a coward in men's eyes, and yet he had deliberately locked on the shackles again. . . . Savagely he shook off Hélier's ministering hands. . . . After that he had collapsed.

He had been vaguely aware of Colin's clinging hands at the harbour, and of Rachell's urgent voice, but he had seen nothing but a darkness shot with sparks until he had emerged angrily on the other side of a welter of whisky and blankets and rubbings, and a ceaseless flood of the Island patois he had so wanted to hear again. He had been almost too enraged to speak—enraged with himself, with fate, with the rough kindly hands that ministered to him and forced on him that human contact he hated. His silence was misinterpreted by the kindly ones who continued to rub and dose and croon under the impression that full consciousness had not returned to him. When he suddenly threw them off with a fierce gesture of both arms their astonishment had been pitiful. . . . He had been sorry then, and thanked them, but afterwards he had fallen into a sort of sullen stupor and let them do what they liked with him. Fate had saved him against his wish—had flung him ashore like a bit of driftwood—very well, then, let it fling him now where it would—he would be passive. . . . It had flung him into Bon Repos.

Marvelling, he had been led by Hélier across the familiar courtyard, under that French inscription over the door that he had so well by heart that he did not need even to glance up at it, into the old tiled kitchen and across to the hearth where stood Rachell and André.

Hélier had gone and he had looked long at Rachell, looked at her with an attention he had not condescended to bestow upon any human being for a great number of years. He had looked at her dark eyes under the strongly marked brows, the lids faintly shadowed with purple, at the coiled crown of her dark hair, at her tall figure, slender yet commanding. He noticed that she was dressed in black and that there was a maiden's blush rose tucked into her belt. Then she began to speak and her voice, low and vibrating, seemed to him in perfect keeping with her face.

She spoke slowly and charmingly, and with dignity, yet he was aware of a certain bewilderment and shrinking in her, and at the same time a desperate urgency. She was so sorry for him, she said, he was perhaps a visitor to the Island? . . . He nodded. . . . Ah, then she must offer him hospitality. She could not bear that he should go to common lodgings after the treatment he had received in their waters. La Catian Roque had done him a great injury, but the Island should make amends. He should not find the Island inhospitable. She had, unfortunately, no room in her house, but there was a room over the stable, intended for use in harvest time, when accommodation at the farmhouse was strained. . . . It was clean and comfortable.

. . . She had already prepared it. . . . Here she flushed, though her eyes, fixed on him, did not waver. He smiled rather unpleasantly. It struck him that the common lodgings might have been more comfortable. It struck him also that she was a past mistress of the great art of prevarication. The hospitable reason she gave was not her true reason for desiring his company with such urgency. He wondered what it was. She could not know who he was. He had never, to the best of his knowledge, seen her before. He did not even know that André had married. Why did she so desperately require him? His curiosity was more piqued than it had been for years. He gave an abrupt, rough little bow, with a slight memory of forgotten courtesy in it, and accepted her hospitable offer.

All this time he had not dared to look full at André, yet one fleeting glance had given him a very clear impression of this man whom he had last seen as a small boy. Yes, he had thought André would grow into just that sort of melancholy, sentimental idiot. The humble, hesitating manner, the sensitive mouth, the dreaming yet observant eyes, the kind rather apologetic smile, yes, they were all what he would have expected. The man looked too old for his years and his face had an exhausted look. . . . Did the old man stamp on him? Or was this beautiful woman too autocratic with him? Obviously André was completely in subjection to his wife. . . . He would be. . . . Weak fool.

"I am delighted. . . . Your name, monsieur?"

Rachell had quite recovered from her momentary embarrassment and was now the perfect hostess.

"Ranulph Mabier. I was born in Normandy, madame, but have spent all my life out East."

He jerked out the information in an abrupt way that forbade further questioning.

"You do not know the Island?"

"No, madame. I had heard of its beauties and intended to spend a short holiday here."

He shut his mouth like a trap and his queer light eyes seemed to Rachell to be boring right through her. . . . She felt that he could see right into that inner sanctuary where not even André might enter. . . . No, more, that he had come right into it, sullied its whiteness with his footprints and disturbed its harmony with his harsh voice. . . . In the midst of her triumph she felt suddenly terrified. . . . She swung round to André and he was astonished to find her fingers gripping him tensely, vibrating as though something discordant were jangling within her.

"André, take Monsieur Mabier to his room." Her voice was trembling a little. Having taken such infinite pains to secure the fellow she now seemed positively anxious to get rid of him.

As André led him across the courtyard towards the stable Ranulph was conscious that behind his polite gentleness his host was seething with a perfect whirlpool of dislike, dismay, bewilderment, anxiety and intense annoyance and resentment. . . . He smiled his rather nasty smile—an arrangement of the features that might have twisted the face of some Olympian god watching the sufferings of pigmy men from a far, far distance. The situation was intriguing in the extreme. A beautiful woman urgently desiring his presence for no known reason—a resentful and indignant host—a twist of fate flinging the prodigal son back to a home that did not remember him. . . . As Ranulph drifted into exhausted sleep that night he dreamed he could feel the filaments of a spell twisting around and around him, binding him, grappling him, lashing him irrevocably to Bon Repos.

II

But all that was a month ago and Ranulph Mabier was now an established fact in the du Frocq household. He had arranged his little room over the stables to his entire satisfaction and regularly paid André rent for it. The Islanders were of opinion that considering the deplorable state of their finances the du Frocqs were lucky to have grabbed a reliable paying guest out of the confusion of the wreck, even though the guest in question was one of the queerest devils ever spewed up out of the nether regions. He had become

Uncle Ranulph to the children who all, rather surprisingly, adored him. Rachell regarded him with a mixture of intense attraction, fear and trembling hope. . . . André simply hated him. . . . Maximilian and Marmalade had been seen to lick his boots in a passion of affection. It was all very queer and Ranulph, walking home to breakfast from La Baie des Mouettes, felt its queerness as much as anybody.

Behind a gorse bush beside the path he came upon Peronelle. It was Monday, and she was clothed in her dark blue school frock, a garment which she had long ago outgrown, but which even in its best days had not been designed to encourage grace in the female form. Her hair had been confined with such fierce determination in its Monday plait that it stuck out from her little head at an acute angle. Her long greeny-black stockings, from which her skimpy skirt withdrew in horror, were a marvellous example of the darner's art. Yet Peronelle, who all her life was to rise gaily above every misfortune, entirely transcended these disadvantages. Not even darned stockings and shrunken dresses could quench her magic.

She lay on her back, her legs kicking, a book held open upon her chest. Her face was pale and tense, her lips moving eagerly as she muttered to herself. Ranulph, his hands on his hips, looked down at her with amusement. She flickered an eyelash in his direction and, quite unembarrassed, continued to mutter. Ranulph laughed. He liked her. If he had admitted to himself that he was beginning, after years of aloofness, to take interest in human beings again, he might have admitted to himself that he loved the child. He bent down and callously twisted the book out of her grasp. . . . He loved rousing the du Frocq temper.

In a moment she was up and at him like a young fury. Lowering her head she butted at him with such passion that he staggered back, laughing and gasping. The young she-devil! But she had nearly winded him . . . her small head was as hard as a young goat's. He sat down on the grass to get his breath. . . . He looked quite white.

Peronelle was seized with one of the passions of remorse that attended her outbursts of anger like a shower upon a thunderclap.

How could she have done such a thing! She had behaved exactly like Ebenezer the goat! And Uncle Ranulph was old. Much older than father even. She flung herself down beside him, threw her arm round him and began to scold him passionately. She always scolded people she loved when they were hurt and those who knew her never resented it. They understood perfectly that her fury was not against them but against the pain that had dared to touch anything she cherished. . . . Her railing was far more comforting than other people's sentimental cooings.

"Ridiculous to be bowled over like that!" she stormed, "why didn't you get out of my way? . . . You're sure it doesn't hurt? . . . Ridiculous not to get out of my way! Of all the silly. . . . Oh, you're sure it doesn't hurt? . . . You're sure your ribs haven't gone into your lungs like Sophie's aunt's husband's when he fell off the hayrick?"

She continued to scold and hold him fiercely against her thin shoulder until sufficient breath returned to him to assure her that all his organs were in their proper places. Then they sat back, looked at each other and laughed. . . . Her eyes were like amber seen beneath clear brightly running water pierced with sunlight. Warm they were, and fresh, and of an entrancing purity. His eyes were faded and yellow, with the penetration of great experience yet dull with jaded appetite. Yet it might have been that once his eyes were exactly like hers. Looking at her he seemed to see his own boyhood in them, and the smile died from his face. . . . Her life must not go the way that his had gone. . . . It must not. . . . His thoughts twisted painfully, and turning abruptly from her he picked up the book that lay on the grass between them.

"Browning," he said, turning the leaves, "poetry, by gad! The perfect Robert. Such a good husband. Admirable in every way. Phew!"

There was mockery in his tone and Peronelle turned pink and pressed her palms together. If he laughed at Robert Browning she would have all the trouble in the world not to box his ears. She must remember that he was very, very old and that she loved him and that one did not, at least one did but one *ought* not, to box the ears of those one loved. Her eyes flashed dangerously, and raising herself slightly she slipped her hands beneath her and sat on them for safety.

She had quite lately gone down with a dreadful attack of Robert Browning which, with Michelle scarcely convalescent from Keats, her family found trying. The courageous optimism of that hale and bearded gentleman was completely in tune with Peronelle's mind, and his discovery was to her as soul-shattering as had been the discovery of the languorous beauty of Keats to Michelle. The book she had was an abridged copy of the poems out of the school library and she had read it over and over again, not cudgelling her mind over the passages she could not understand but fastening passionately upon those that were clear to her. The music of words meant nothing to her, what she cared for was the wisdom in them that could be put to practical use, and this she found in the shabby little book and absorbed hungrily into her vigorous mind.

This, she felt, was the way to love, this was the way to think. No shrinking away from things but a greeting of the unseen with a cheer. No useless wailing over suffering but a deliberate placing of it as the black background of white joy so that the shining was intensified. She had been reading that bit when Uncle Ranulph came upon her.

> "What's love, what's faith without a worst to dread?
> Lack-lustre jewelry! but faith and love
> With death behind them bidding do or die—
> Put such a foil at back, the sparkle's born!"

"I have read the fellow," said Uncle Ranulph, "and I can remember one line of his verse, it comes in *The Ring and the Book* I think, that entirely expressed my own feelings and has given me undying pleasure all through my life."

"Something lovely that has helped you? What is it?" breathed Peronelle, her eyes shining. Really, there was more hope for Uncle Ranulph than she had thought.

He eyed her solemnly.

"Matrimony, the profound mistake."

Peronelle was so angry that her hands shot out from underneath her and Ranulph's ears were in more danger than he knew. She jumped to her feet, seized her precious Browning out of his sacrilegious hands and marched towards Bon Repos, moving with that jerky motion which her family knew from painful experience denoted a mind seething with rage. . . . Ranulph followed humbly behind.

In the lane she paused and shot out a question at him.

"Have *you* ever been married, Uncle Ranulph?"

"Yes," replied Ranulph, "a profound mistake."

She turned with a swish of her skimpy skirt and marched on again, but gradually the jerkiness went out of her walk and its graceful gliding motion, so like her mother's, returned. Ranulph judged that gentler thoughts were coming to her. At the entrance to the courtyard she turned again and he saw, as he expected, that her eyes were melting with tenderness. He prepared himself to receive her sympathy.

"Well," she said, "I *am* sorry for your poor wife!"

III

Breakfast at Bon Repos on school days was at an appallingly early hour and much hurried, for the same farm cart that took Michelle, Peronelle, Jacqueline, and Colin to school had to take in the butter and eggs and vegetables to the market in St. Pierre.

They did not use the landau on weekdays, but a light cart with boards placed across it for seats on which the children sat, carefully tucking their feet under them so as not to bruise the vegetables beneath. Lupin was not used on weekdays either, or they would never have got to school in time, but a young ungainly coal-black creature called Gertrais, who pounded along the lanes as though he were himself in danger of being punished for unpunctuality.

Brovard, the farm-man, drove them, and Rachell always stood in the lane to wave to them till they were out of sight. . . . She hated seeing them go. . . . Those four frail little creatures bobbing about in the rough cart, entirely at the mercy of a rough peasant and a horse with legs like great ebony rolling-pins, one blow of whose hoofs, if they happened to get in the way, could maim them for life.

Particularly in the winter did she hate seeing them go, for on foggy mornings they started while it was still almost dark, bunched up to the eyes in coats and mufflers, their poor little noses scarlet with cold, their eyes still wistful and cloudy with sleep. When she saw them lurching off into the frosty mist, the hurricane lamp on the cart giving their faces a sickly pallor and accentuating the hollows round their eyes, she felt as though she had cast a shipload of loveless orphans out on to the great deep. . . . The moments when the darkness swallowed them up were the only moments when she wondered what right she and André had to launch these little bundles of shrinking nerves and trembling flesh on to the waves of a dark world. . . . She would run upstairs quickly and pray as she made the beds. "Calm the waters for them, oh God, all their lives long. Let no bitter waters overwhelm them," she whispered as she turned the mattresses. When she punched the pillows she said "Holy Mary, Mother of God, pray for us sinners." When she pulled the counterpanes up she felt better and said, "Goodness, I'm getting as silly as André."

But to-day the cart disappeared not into a lowering darkness but into a sunshine mellow with autumn richness and golden with warmth. The children, as they rolled off, were chattering like a nestful of wicked starlings. So radiant and safe seemed the morning that Rachell sang a naughty little French song as she made the beds and never prayed a single prayer.

Michelle, Peronelle, and Colin were as radiant as the morning, and talked at the tops of their voices the whole way into St. Pierre without pausing for a single instant and without hearing a single word that each other said. Their conversation surged backwards and forwards against Brovard's broad back like the sea against a rock and with no more effect upon its solidity.

St. Peter's College, the boys' school, and St. Mary's College, the girls' school, were on the outskirts of St. Pierre at the top of the hill, so Brovard could drop the children there before he dismounted and, clinging wildly to Gertrais's head, took the precious eggs and butter and vegetables skating down the cobbled streets to the market.

Colin was put down at some distance from St. Peter's and departed thither on foot. Nothing, he said, would induce him to arrive at his place of learning jumbled up in a cart with a lot of eggs and girls. Michelle, Peronelle, and Jacqueline were less particular, they let Brovard take them right up to the green painted door in the red brick wall that led into the day girls' cloakroom.

The turbulent din of that cloakroom, seething with blue-clad pig-tailed girls all shouting and yelling and hurling their shoes across the asphalt floor, was music in the ears of Michelle and Peronelle, and its smell of shoe polish and Windsor soap and yesterday's boiled cabbage was as incense in their nostrils. . . . Even fastidious Peronelle sniffed appreciatively as she entered. For Michelle and Peronelle adored school.

To Michelle it was the temple of learning, connected incongruously in her mind with her little white town by the sea-shore. Here she was taught to think. At every class she went to it seemed to her that her teacher's mind struck upon hers as steel clinks on flint and that from their contact a flame was born. As the day went on flame was added to flame till the whole world blazed with light and all the dark places seemed illumined. As she sat at her desk with her pale absorbed face tilted towards the teacher's desk, her eyes wide and her lips slightly parted in a most unbecoming way, she was determining in that tiny portion of her mind which was not engrossed by the business in hand that she would become a teacher. She would so train and discipline her mind that it became a thing of tempered steel, a thing fit to create flame. How marvellous to create light! Yet it was a miracle she could and would perform. She would light a thousand candles and a thousand eyes should look on beauty. Because of her those eyes should see how the gold woof of truth and beauty ran through the drab warp of life and would have their hearts lightened.

> "Yes, in spite of all
> Some shape of beauty moves away the pall
> From our dark spirits."

She muttered the words to herself as she hastily dragged on her indoor shoes and hung up her hat.

"You've burst the button off and that's my peg you've put your rotten hat on," said Jessie Lemezurier, a particularly objectionable red-haired girl whose pigeon-hole in the cloakroom was next to Michelle's.

"You ought to be pleased to have my nice hat on your loathsome peg," and putting her tongue out at Jessie, Michelle ran off. The first lesson was English literature and she wanted to get to her classroom in time to read over that last speech of Romeo's once more. How did it go?

> "How oft when men are at the point of death
> Have they been merry! which their keepers call
> A lightning before death: O, how may I
> Call this a lightning?"

and then, later on,

> "Shake the yoke of inauspicious stars
> From this world-wearied flesh. . . .
> . . . Here's to my love!"

If only the play could have ended there, at that perfect moment, instead of going on to that final welter of irritating relations. She could, she thought, have taught Shakespeare a thing or two.

Peronelle, though no less eager than Michelle, prepared herself for the pursuit of knowledge with a thoughtfulness and precision. She unplaited her already perfectly tidy hair, combed it and plaited it again. As she combed, her hair, electric and vivid as Peronelle herself, crackled and curled itself about her fingers as though imploring her to let it free, but she had no mercy on it. On Saturdays and Sundays she allowed it to fly loose, but on other days it must do as it was told. With her mouth closed in a firm determined line she dealt firmly with it, allowing no nonsense. Then she fastened her slippers carefully, hung her hat and coat on the right pegs, kissed Jacqueline good-bye—they were all three in different forms—and danced away to her math class. She liked lessons. She had a quick and eager mind, and it was a pleasure to her to use it. But what she loved best about school was being with the other girls. Of all Peronelle's gifts the greatest was her gift for human contact. People interested her more than anything else in the world and her chief study, now and always, was that of practical living. She wanted everyone to be happy, and her thoughts were always absorbed in deciding what different paths her different friends ought to pursue to attain to happiness, and having chosen their paths for them she used all her strength in propelling them kindly, but firmly, upon the right way. Like her mother she was perfectly convinced that the paths she chose were the right paths and that terrible disasters would befall those who did not follow her leading and, again like her mother, her instinct was so sure that she was nearly always right. Her thoughts were always directed outward towards others, and never inward towards herself. Except that her practical love of neatness and cleanliness led her to take pains over her appearance she never gave herself a thought. She never in all her life knew an introspective moment. Because of this there was no murky fog of self-consciousness between herself and others. She saw not her own disabilities but them and like unclouded sunshine her warmth and light were theirs without hindrance. No one was ever shy of Peronelle—she did not give them time to be shy. She looked at them, she loved them, and with one leap she had curled herself inside their hearts. When she grew up even the most reticent could tell their troubles to Peronelle simply because saying things to Peronelle was like saying things to God, one felt that she was already inside one, and knew it all already, so it did not matter if the tale were badly told; one stood hand in hand with her inside the tortured rubbish heap of one's soul and mourned with her over the mess there was, and then watched and marvelled as she tidied it all up. There was only one thing she could not understand—selfish morbidity. She could agonize over Jacqueline but she could not help her. A self-absorption like Jacqueline's was beyond her comprehension. Nor could she always quite understand Michelle, for she was too well-balanced to feel Michelle's hatred of the body. To her the body was a fair and lovely thing to be reverently tended and beautified. . . . Her own body carried her soul as a flower its perfume.

As she ran down the passage to the classroom she slipped her hands in her pockets to see if she still had safely a few things she had brought with her to solve the problems of her various friends. Marguerite Vesin's sister's boy was still as bald as an egg at four months, but she had found in a paper a recipe for making the loveliest curls appear upon an infant head, and had cut it out for Marguerite. Then she had a few of Rachell's cough lozenges done up in a screw of paper for Blanche Portier, and a tiny gold brooch of her own for Marie Lemezurier whose birthday it was. These things were in her pockets, but in her head she carried Browning's poem *Prospice* to repeat to Tonnette Laroche, who was scared of death, and Rachell's recipe for apricot pudding for Miss Jenkins the maths. mistress, who was engaged to be married and whose poor husband couldn't possibly spend all his time on the Asses' Bridge with nothing to eat. . . . Miss Jenkins' culinary knowledge was nil and Peronelle was very anxious indeed about her poor husband.

When the door swung joyously open and gave Peronelle to the maths. class it was to Miss Jenkins and the girls as though a blackbird sang in a lilac bush.

IV

And Jacqueline? Jacqueline had been silent all the way in to St. Pierre while the others chattered, and in the cloakroom, when Peronelle had kissed her and left her, she cried a little as she hung up her hat. School to her was slow torture. Nothing ever seemed to go right. She could never make friends and she was always at the bottom of her class. She felt it must look to other people as though she was both unlovable and stupid and she worked terribly hard to correct this impression. Between the classes, after desperate struggles with her shyness, she would go up to other girls and put her arm round their waists so as to show herself and them that she was not unpopular, and in the classes she would sit with her rapt gaze fixed on the teacher's face so that the others should see how clever she was. But somehow it never did any good. The girls she embraced simply shook her off and went on talking to someone else, and the teachers would say snappily, "Jacqueline, don't pretend to understand when you are not understanding." At the end of the day her head felt heavy and hot, and she couldn't remember anything she had been learning, her heart felt cold and empty with loneliness and she was so dreadfully tired that she felt quite sick.

To-day there was a special torment awaiting her—French translation. She opened her exercise book and there on the left-hand page was the English poem she had taken down from dictation three days ago, but opposite it, on the right-hand page, where she should have written the French translation of it, there was a virgin blank. It wasn't that she didn't know French, her mother had sung French songs to her when she had been a baby in her cradle and Sophie's patois echoed through Bon Repos all day, the trouble was that she did not understand the English poem and she had been too afraid of displaying her ignorance to ask Michelle or Peronelle or her mother to help her—she always pretended to her family that she knew everything. Mademoiselle Lebrun, when she had dictated it, had been afraid it might be too difficult for Jacqueline, the idiot of the class, and had said, "Now, Jacqueline, is it that you quite under-r-r-stand?" The eyes of every girl in the room had been turned upon Jacqueline, and a few had sniggered. Jacqueline was in agony. She did not understand the poem but if she had said so the others would think she was stupid. On the other hand if she said she did understand then nothing would be explained to her, she would not be able to translate the poem and there would be a dreadful scene three days later. She struggled with herself for a moment and then the thought came to her that in three days' time she would probably be dead—she had a sore throat that she was convinced was the beginning of diphtheria—so it would be best to appear clever to-day. She had looked up brightly and intelligently and said "Thank you, Mademoiselle, I understand perfectly."

But the sore throat had turned into an ordinary cold in the head, she had not died of diphtheria, and here she was on Monday morning with no French translation. She would be sent to the bottom of the class again. What on earth was she to do? Hot tears trickled out of the corners of her eyes and she rubbed them fiercely away with her knuckles. Well, anyway, French translation was the second class of the morning, drill came first. She would think what to do during drill. She gave a final dab to her eyes, put on her gym shoes, took her books to her classroom, and ran off to the school hall for drill.

In the middle of standing on one leg and swinging the other, with her arms stuck out at the side like a scarecrow's—this was Miss Brown's idea of training girls to be graceful—inspiration came to her. She would make her nose bleed, get excused from drill, go to the empty classroom and copy out the poem from someone else's book. The idea had the simplicity of genius. She couldn't think why she had not thought of it before. How thankful she was for her one great gift—the gift of making her nose bleed at will. It was a wonderful gift and she did not know how she had come by it. She had not inherited it from Rachell or André, it was peculiar to herself. She had only to blow her nose very violently, at the same time closing her mouth and gulping in a particular way, for the blood to gush forth. While Miss Brown was absorbed in crashing out some chords on the piano and the class was taking a half turn to the right she did this, and the result was entirely satisfactory. She turned to Miss Brown with a most convincing stain creeping over the handkerchief she had clapped to her nose.

"Please, Miss Brown, my nose is bleeding. Will you excuse me to go to the cloak room?"

The amiable Miss Brown glanced up over her spectacles.

"Yes, dear, certainly, try cold water and if that won't stop it go to matron."

As Jacqueline left the hall glances of envy and hatred pursued her. . . . The girls knew perfectly well that Jacqueline du Frocq made her nose bleed on purpose. . . . Underhand little beast.

In the cloak room Jacqueline checked the obliging flow by holding a spongeful of cold water to the bridge of her nose and dropping the key down her back. Then she ran to her classroom. It was as she had hoped, perfectly empty, and on Mademoiselle's desk was a pile of exercise books placed there for her to correct. At the very top was Julie Lefroy's. Julie was disgustingly clever and her work was always good. Jacqueline took the book and peeped in. . . . There was the translation. . . . She carried it to her own desk and copied it out in her book. . . . Then, for Mademoiselle would be coming to correct the books, she put hers with the others, went back to the cloak room and lay flat on the floor. There she was found by the girls when they came to change their gym shoes. They had a good deal to say, and said it rather nastily, but she did not care so much as usual for today, at least, she was safe not to be sent to the bottom of the class.

Mademoiselle was already at her desk when they entered, running her eye over the last of the exercise books. They went to their desks and sat down. Mademoiselle handed back the books one by one, with biting comments. Jacqueline sat with her ears getting pinker and pinker, and the palms of her hands wet with perspiration. . . . At last her turn came.

"Verie good, Jacqueline," said Mademoiselle, "très bon. It is not pairfeect—I do not expect pairfection from this so idiot class—but it is good. At least you have been tr-r-rying."

For the rest of the class Jacqueline sat in a glow of happiness. Mademoiselle, whenever she looked at her, smiled kindly, and the girls cast glances of surprise, even of admiration, in her direction. It was heaven. Jacqueline even felt that she had translated the poem by her own unaided efforts.

But, alas, retribution awaited her. After the second class of the morning there was a ten minutes break, and no sooner had

Mademoiselle's blue skirt swished round the door and disappeared than a heavy hand seized Jacqueline by her plait. . . . It was Julie Lefroy.

"Come along outside, Jacqueline," said Julie in a voice whose awfulness it is impossible to describe, "and you're to come too, all you girls."

The entire class, in a dreadful silence, trooped out into the garden and took up its position beneath the unsympathetic branches of a monkey puzzle.

Jacqueline felt as those condemned to death must feel when they stand blindfolded, awaiting the volley of bullets. She did not seem to see anything but she could hear sounds that seemed to come from hundreds of miles away, the tinkle of a piano, a bee buzzing in the dahlias, a girl singing, the sighing of a little wind in the monkey puzzle. Julie's voice broke the silence like the rip-rip of the bullets.

"I didn't go to drill this morning—I've twisted my ankle and Miss Brown excused me—I went into the garden. I looked through the window and there was Jacqueline du Frocq copying out my translation into her exercise book."

There was a little rippling murmur among the girls and then silence again. The condemned man would have been out of his torment by this time but poor Jacqueline was still alive. Julie, enjoying herself, continued:

"We knew Jacqueline was a sneak and a liar, but now we know she is a thief too. It's stealing to take someone else's translation. I shan't say anything to Mademoiselle—*I'm* not a sneak—but I thought it right that you girls should know."

Again there was that horrible murmur, threatening this time to grow into a hubbub, but Julie self-righteously quelled it.

"I don't want any of you to say anything, or to bully Jacqueline or anything like that, goodness knows she's a poor little worm and we don't want to crush her completely, but I do think that, for the honour of the school, Jacqueline ought to be sent to Coventry. Those in favour of sending Jacqueline to Coventry hold up their hands."

All the hands shot up into the monkey puzzle.

"Carried unanimously," said Julie. "Now you understand, all of you, that Jacqueline has been sent to Coventry. Not one of our form will speak to Jacqueline or have any dealings with her whatever for the rest of the term. . . . Now let's go and have some milk or the bell will be going."

They all followed Julie towards the dining-room and the eleven o'clock milk and biscuits, one or two of them pinching Jacqueline as they passed but most of them, obedient to Julie, the injured party, simply turning from her as though she were a bad smell.

Jacqueline stood perfectly still beneath the monkey puzzle. Anyone looking at her face would have thought that she had just been suffering the extreme of physical torture. Her body was cold as ice, but her mind was burning and filled to suffocation with two things, one the phrase "we knew she was a sneak and a liar, but now we know she is a thief too," the other the knowledge that what Julie had said was true. She had suffered too much in the last few moments to have the strength left to erect a barrier of self-deception between herself and the truth. For the first time in her life she quite clearly and definitely looked at herself and the result was a self-loathing so deadly that she would have liked to have died there and then under the monkey puzzle. But the bell rang and instead of dying she walked mechanically back to her classroom.

She sat through two more classes, grammar and English literature, without hearing a single word of either of them, she washed her hands and brushed her hair and then went in to school dinner with the others. After that she seemed to sit for hours and hours putting bits of boiled beef and suet pudding in her mouth, and swallowing them with an effort that seemed to wrench her whole body. When dinner was over she went quietly to the cloak room and was sick. The physical distress seemed to relieve the mental. She crawled to her pigeon hole, curled herself up in it and began to sob. Coventry! Not to be spoken to for the rest of the term. To live in complete and utter loneliness when loneliness was what she dreaded most of all in life. How could she bear it?

And she was a sneak, a liar, and a thief. Everybody hated her and she hated herself.

Here in her pigeon hole Peronelle found her, the most deplorable bundle of misery ever beheld.

"My stars!" cried Peronelle and locked her in her arms. But no amount of scolding, kissing, petting, or shaking, could get the story of her grief and shame out of Jacqueline. Her character had been revealed in all its horror to herself and her form but she was not going to show it to her family, no indeed, not if she knew it, she'd sooner die. Peronelle could get nothing out of her except that she had been sick, that her nose had bled, and that she did not like Julie Lefroy. . . . There was more in it than this, Peronelle knew.

"Let's go home to mother," said Peronelle at last, turning in despair to Rachell as the solvent of all difficulties.

"There's g-games and afternoon s-school," sobbed Jacqueline.

"We'll go to Miss Billing and get permission," said Peronelle, and gripping Jacqueline by the hand she marched her out of the cloakroom and down the passage to the head mistress's study.

Leaving her sister leaning against the wall, Peronelle, with the most perfunctory of knocks, flung open the door and entered the august presence.

"I'm taking Jacqueline home," she announced.

"Oh, indeed?" Miss Billing twinkled behind her glasses—she adored Peronelle. "Whose permission have you asked?"

"I'm asking yours now," said Peronelle, "thank you very much, Miss Billing. Good-bye."

"May I know the reason for my permission?" asked Miss Billing mildly.

For answer Peronelle fled into the passage and reappeared dragging Jacqueline.

"Look at that now," she said, "you can see for yourself I must take her to mother."

Miss Billing was really distressed at the appearance of Jacqueline.

"My dear," she cried, "what's the matter?" She drew Jacqueline to her and fondled her but Jacqueline was dumb as a post.

"It's no good you asking her," said Peronelle, "she won't tell me. She never will; I must take her to mother."

"She must go to the sick room and lie down first," said Miss Billing firmly.

"No, she mustn't," said Peronelle with equal firmness. "Something's happened at school to make her miserable and she won't be happy again till I've taken her right away from school."

Miss Billing had great faith in Peronelle's judgment. "Very well," she said.

"You'll tell Michelle we've gone," commanded Peronelle as she removed Jacqueline.

"Certainly, dear," said Miss Billing meekly.

The two girls took the same route home that Colin had taken a month ago—through the deep honeysuckle-scented lanes, past the cottage gardens with their dahlia clumps like bonfires in the sun, past the farms with their green ponds waiting for the dancing feet of the water fairies, and past the foxgloves down into the water-lane. Here, by the well, they paused.

"Let's sit down and rest," said Peronelle.

All the way home, with her arm round Jacqueline, she had been scolding gently, but now she fell silent through sheer bewilderment. If Jacqueline wouldn't tell her anything what *could* she do? Other people told her things, then why not Jacqueline? Was there something in the tie of blood that made it difficult for one to help one's own relations? Was one, perhaps, too near to them to be helpful? Was it necessary always to stand back a bit from things before one could see them clearly? She pondered a little sadly over this as they sat in the lovely deep grass beside the well.

Jacqueline, meanwhile, was struggling with a frightful longing to tell everything to Peronelle. Peronelle was so sweet, so warm, so comforting. But no, Peronelle would be so horrified if she knew what she had done that she would never speak to her again, and if she lost Peronelle's love she would be completely lost. She could never tell anyone who loved her because then they wouldn't love her any more.

Gradually the water-lane calmed them both. Peronelle was too practical and Jacqueline too self-absorbed to feel, as Colin had done, that there was something unearthly in the water-lane, but the nearness of a world other than their own had the effect of lifting them a little out of their slough of despond.

"Sophie says that there are always fairies in the water-lane," said Peronelle, dabbling her fingers in the cool water.

"There aren't any anywhere," said Jacqueline, miserably, "they are only make-believes. All the nice things are make-believes."

Peronelle had spoken idly, but the despairing note in Jacqueline's voice roused her. She always challenged anything in the least depressing.

"How do you know there aren't any fairies?" she demanded. "I expect there are heaps and heaps. I expect the world's brimful of worlds, world within world, that we don't know anything about. I think it's lovely to think that. If you think of the water-lane just packed with fairies, and all of them happy, you don't feel so unhappy yourself."

"Why not?" demanded Jacqueline gloomily.

"Because, silly, the bigger one thing is the smaller it makes another thing. The more you pile on the happiness heap the smaller the unhappiness heap looks in comparison."

"It may *look* smaller but it doesn't *feel* smaller," Jacqueline complained.

"Oh, come along to mother," said Peronelle.

When they had turned up into the second lane that led to Bon Repos a queer feeling of abeyance that had fallen on the water-lane when their unperceiving spirits entered it was lifted. It was once again filled with the soundless passing of Things that were not seen.

When they reached Bon Repos Rachell, André and Ranulph were having tea in the kitchen. At the sight of her mother Jacqueline's fountain of tears, which had mercifully been sealed up during the walk home, began to play again.

"Darling!" cried Rachell. She sank down on the "jonquière" and gathered Jacqueline into her arms. André, terribly distressed, stood by them stroking Jacqueline's wet cheek with his finger. Ranulph departed tactfully into the courtyard. Peronelle, worn out, sat down at the table and began to eat bread and butter. She was ravenous, simply ravenous; being sorry for people always made her dreadfully hungry.

"Darling! Darling! Tell me what's the matter. Tell mother all about it!" implored Rachell, but Jacqueline only sobbed and sobbed. André, stroking feverishly, felt near tears himself.

Peronelle took instant charge of the situation.

"Mother, take her upstairs and put her to bed," she said thickly through bread and butter. "She's been sick and her nose bled, but there's more in it than that. She won't say, though, so it's no good your asking her. When she's in bed father can tell her stories till she goes to sleep. As you go upstairs tell Uncle Ranulph he can come in again."

Rachell obediently departed, carrying Jacqueline and calling out to Ranulph as she passed. . . . Jacqueline sobbed all the way upstairs.

"Drought appears to have broken up," said Ranulph pleasantly as he returned and helped himself to cake.

"There's never drought for long with Jacqueline," said Peronelle. "Pass me the jam, please."

André thought they were both rather heartless. He drank cup after cup of tea but he couldn't eat anything. . . . Why did one bring children into the world?

Presently Rachell came down again.

"I've given her some milk and she's quiet now," she said, "but I can't get anything out of her. You go, André, you're better at comforting the children than I am."

"Father, tell her stories," prompted Peronelle, "tell her the one about the giant who had to carry his heart about in a paper bag. She likes that one."

André obediently departed.

"I'll call Sophie to clear away, I'm going to do my home lessons," said Peronelle. "Uncle Ranulph, take mother into the garden and turn her thoughts."

Sophie cleared away with the promptitude of a slave obeying her sultan, and Ranulph unquestioningly took Rachell into the garden.

V

Four Red Admirals, three Tortoiseshells and a Painted Lady were sunning their wings on the Michaelmas daisies. Rachell and Ranulph surveyed them in silence.

"I wonder why butterflies always choose the Michaelmas daisies to sit on?" said Rachell at last.

"Mauve is the proper setting for their colours," said Ranulph, "you'd hardly notice them on the dahlias. Natural things have a genius for finding their right environment. Not so humans. The longer I live the more idiotic I find the human race compared to, say, butterflies." He paused. "Jacqueline is hardly in her right environment in that blasted school."

"And I am idiotic to send her there?" inquired Rachell.

"Idiotic."

"I was to have my thoughts turned," she reminded him.

"You don't want your thoughts turned," said Ranulph, "you want me to help you over this problem of Jacqueline."

"I suppose I do," said Rachell slowly. It struck her suddenly that she was often turning to Ranulph for advice about the children.... It was almost as though there were some tie between him and the children.... He loved them, of course.... Hard though he tried to hide it she had discovered that much about him.

"It's idiocy to send a child like Jacqueline to a school like St. Mary's," said Ranulph, "you ought to have more sense. She's not the brains to profit by what they teach her there. Send her to the Convent." He spoke roughly, almost rudely, as André would never have spoken to her, but somehow she did not resent it.

"Why the Convent?" she asked.

"A child like that needs religion."

"I wonder why you say that," said Rachell, "you're not a religious man."

"No, but I'm aware of the psychological value of religion to a nature like Jacqueline's."

"The nuns at the Convent are very simple women," said Rachell, "I don't think their teaching is very up to date."

"I've already told you that Jacqueline has not got it in her to profit by up-to-date teaching. What she needs is to have religious truths applied very simply to her own torments."

Rachell gazed at him. "Torments." What a word to apply to a child's little troubles!

"Yes, torments," said Ranulph, as though reading her thoughts. "When we grow old we are apt to forget the torments of childhood."

"They have scripture lessons at school," said Rachell, "and I—I teach the children too."

"You've not sufficient simplicity to teach a child religion," said Ranulph rudely, "and as for school—all I ever learnt of religion there was that Abraham had six wives."

"He didn't. Aren't you thinking of Henry the Eighth?"

"I daresay. It's all one," said Ranulph gloomily.

"I must see what André says," said Rachell, "I am always guided by André."

"Indeed?" said Ranulph. There was an edge of irony in his voice, and Rachell flushed.

"But, of course, I always ask my husband's advice," she said, indignantly.

"I didn't say that you didn't *ask* it," said Ranulph.

They walked slowly down the garden till they came to the rampart of earth and stones and twisted trees that separated it from the cliff. There was a little gate here and they passed through it and picked their way over the hussocks of rough grass and wild thyme till they came to the cliff's edge. The sea lay sleek and shining under the long sun-rays that caressed it, and its murmur was infinitely still and peaceful. Rachell went back in memory to her days at the Convent. On just such quiet afternoons had she sat in the sun-drenched Convent parlour and listened to the sea as her lace bobbins tapped and danced on the pillow. The sea had worn just that sleek look on the day when Soeur Ursule read her the story of St. Christopher carrying the baby Christ across the water. She remembered she had looked out of the window half expecting to see St. Christopher struggling through the water gasping and straining under the great weight of the Christ who carried the sorrows of the world. . . . How to carry sorrow. . . . Could the nuns teach that to Jacqueline?

"Yes, I'll send Jacqueline to the Convent," she said suddenly.

"Subject, of course, to the approval of André," suggested Ranulph in a voice like silk.

"Of course," snapped Rachell. His little dig had broken a lovely moment that she had recaptured out of the past, and she felt annoyed with him. . . . Sometimes she was not quite sure that she liked him. . . . At other times she felt frighteningly attracted by him. . . . Often she wondered was he—a good man? . . . Had she done right to bring him to Bon Repos? . . . Looking back that queer clairvoyance that she had had about him seemed to her rather silly. . . . If he were—a bad man, might he not do some harm to the children?

With that uncanny gift he had for reading her thoughts he answered her.

"You must often wonder who and what I am," he said, "I'd like you to know that whatever I am, I could never, under any circumstances, do anything that could possibly hurt your children."

"Thank you," she said.

The mellow light of autumn, as evening drew on, seemed closing round them. The horizon lines were growing much softer and the colours of sea and earth and sky were less distinct, were melting each into the other. It was as though the walls of the world were slowly contracting and isolating the two of them in a great loneliness. . . . They felt very close to each other.

Rachell was conscious of a great struggle going on in the man beside her. . . . He wanted to tell her about himself and he found it amazingly difficult to begin. She had realized from the very first that he was a solitary, a man who prided himself upon his freedom from all ties and who had always been resolute to avoid them. She had realized also that as the weeks had gone by his resolution had been broken down. . . . The children had got him. . . . His capitulation had been all the greater because of his former pride. . . . But he would not own it yet. . . . She tried to help him out a little.

"Let's sit down," she said, "it's so lovely here. The others won't want me yet. . . . That story of the giant who kept his heart in a paper bag takes an age to tell and the children will never let André miss out one detail."

They sat down. Ranulph sat with his arms round his crossed knees, a little away from her, looking out to sea.

"It would be a good thing for André if he kept *his* heart in a paper bag and mislaid it occasionally," he said.

"You mean that André feels things too much?" said Rachell.

"André is a good man and the good men suffer—more fools they."

"You think it wise not to be good?" she asked smiling.

"I don't know. Life is a question of choice and one has experience only of the path one has chosen. You choose either martyrdom or hell and which is wisest who's to say?"

"Tell me what you mean." Rachell was almost afraid to encourage him. She knew it would ease him to speak out but she was terrified lest a slip on her part should shut him into himself again. But he went on.

"There's something within man—call it what you like—a core of personality—a flame—an indwelling spirit—to be true to it is to suffer a continual martyrdom of discipline and to be false to it is to burn in hell."

"And you chose the second course?"

"I have kept to it consistently from the start."

"How did you start?"

"I started with the laudable desire for freedom—kicked over the traces like many a young devil before me, and went to Australia."

"The young never understand freedom," said Rachell, "they always confuse it with chaos." Her thoughts surged agonizedly towards Colin—his passion for freedom always terrified her.

"Chaos exactly describes what I found in Australia," said Ranulph bitterly.

"What did you do in Australia?"

"Took to gold mining. There's no necessity to tell you about that. An exact inventory of all the furniture in hell wouldn't interest you. . . . Strangely enough I made money."

"And then?"

"Ever since then I've travelled out East trying to scorch out the really extraordinary bitterness that had silted down to the bottom of me."

"You couldn't?"

"No. It was a raging fire and yet at the same time it was solid metal. . . . It is a regrettable fact that what you have done never leaves you."

Rachell asked the question that burns on the tongue of every woman inquiring into a man's past.

"Did you ever marry?"

"Yes—in Australia. It seemed the easiest way to get my house cared for for nothing."

She recoiled at his tone and yet asked on.

"Did you—leave her?"

"Yes, I couldn't stand the shackles and she was a vile woman. . . . After I left her she was murdered," he added.

Rachell felt as though she had looked suddenly into the pit.

"Yes, it wasn't a nice place," he said, and then, after a long pause, "and now you know a bit about me. . . . Would you like me to leave Bon Repos?"

"No," she said.

They both got up, Rachell a little shakily. They looked at each other.

"So often during these last weeks I've turned to you for advice," she said, "and you've always given me good advice."

"Does that surprise you?"

"Yes. I thought it took a good man to give good advice."

"Sometimes those shut out from a garden can see the way about the paths more clearly through the bars of the gate than those inside," he said. "I daresay, if you asked him, you would find that Apollyon could direct you quite correctly through the lanes of heaven."

They were standing very close together and he gave her what she was always afterwards to call "his look of a fallen angel. . . ."

She turned and fled.

So ended Jacqueline's last day at St. Mary's.

Chapter 4

I

THE mellow September weather ended abruptly in days of wind and storming rain. It deluged. The gurgling of the water in the gutters and the swish as the javelins of the rain splintered into miniature rivers against the window-panes almost drowned the noise of the sou'wester out at sea. The courtyard and the farmyard seemed awash with water, and André and Ranulph, wading about in tarpaulins, seemed to the anxious eyes of the children in imminent danger of drowning.

"Look at it! There must be going to be another flood," said Peronelle, her face pressed so close to the kitchen window that the tip of her nose appeared to have turned into a flat white linen button. "Do you think Bon Repos will float like the ark?"

"Of course it won't," said Colin crossly, "it's glued on."

"Do you really think there's going to be a flood?" asked Jacqueline, fear stirring in her.

"Yes," said Peronelle excitedly, warming to the subject, "the water Things that live in the air are fighting the water Things that live in the earth and the sea. Each soldier in the army has been turned into a drop of water. We shan't know who gets the best of it because they'll have drowned us all long before the battle's over."

Jacqueline began to sob. A storm of any sort always frightened her. The noise it made seemed to be beating a tattoo with invisible little hammers all over her body, and the shivering and shrinking of her skin seemed to beget a shivering and shrinking within her.

"Oh, shut up, Jacqueline, you fool!" cried Michelle, who was sitting by the fire with her shoulders hunched up in the nastiest way possible.

The word "fool" applied to her always seemed to send a sword through Jacqueline. . . . She sobbed more than ever.

"Darling, you are the greatest idiot ever born," said Peronelle, and turning from the window she shook Jacqueline and then, penitent, promptly kissed her in the back of the neck.

"Children, if you can't behave yourselves I shall send you all to stay with grandpapa for a week," threatened Rachell from the hall. . . . There was instant silence.

The truth was that for two whole days it was so wet and stormy that the children could not go to school and had nothing to do but make themselves unspeakably disagreeable. Jacqueline, in particular, was enough to try the patience even of André. She wept the whole time because she could not go to her beloved Convent and her darling nuns. It was really too much. When she had been at St. Mary's she had cried the whole time and wanted to be at home, and now when she was at home she cried the whole time because she wanted to be at the Convent.

"She can't help it, poor darling," Peronelle explained, "she has a naturally watery nature just as I have a naturally dry one. One can't help one's disposition—it just has to be borne by one's family."

Michelle was consistently trying too. Her form had been in the middle of *King John* and she had come home on Wednesday not knowing whether Arthur was going to have his eyes put out or whether he wasn't going to have his eyes put out, and here it was Thursday and she couldn't get back to school, and apparently there wasn't a Shakespeare in the house.

"It's disgraceful for a—so-called—educated household not to possess Shakespeare," she said nastily.

"But we *have* a Shakespeare, darling," said Rachell, "it's just that I can't seem to lay my hands on it—it's got mislaid."

"Surely you've *read King John,*" said Michelle, "don't you *know* if Hubert put Arthur's eyes out?"

"Of course I've read *King John*, darling, but I can't quite remember now—it's so long ago—"

"I'm ashamed to own you for a mother," said Michelle and at this Colin went for her and it was all very dreadful.

But in the early hours of Saturday morning the gale dropped quite suddenly, as though a tap had been turned off, and the swish of the rain changed first to a gentle rustling sound, like wind sighing in a barley field, then to a little whispering farewell and then to small isolated drippings that accentuated the sudden deep silence. . . . They all woke up.

They were all, except Jacqueline, used to sleeping soundly through the uproar of a storm, but its sudden cessation was as disturbing as a thunderclap.

Jacqueline, opening her eyes, saw Peronelle sitting up in bed. Dawn was not very far away and the window was an opaque silver-white oblong patching the grey walls. Outside the raindrops dripped very softly among the leaves of the passion flower and away in the garden a robin twittered.

"Jacqueline," breathed Peronelle, "the gale's dropped."

Jacqueline sat up in bed with a sobbing breath of relief and pushed back her hair, heavy with the sweat of a feverish night, from her hot forehead. . . . It was over. . . . That horrible din, with its little hammers beating on her body and its terror writhing through her, was over . . . until next time.

"Are you happy now?" asked Peronelle.

"Yes," said Jacqueline.

There was such bliss in the tone that Peronelle, happy about her, turned over and went promptly to sleep again, but Jacqueline stayed awake revelling in the peace of the growing dawn. She fixed her eyes on the silver-white patch of the window and watched as its outlines grew clearer and clearer and the little flowers on the chintz window curtain bloomed in the dimness. . . . It was like watching spring come after the long blackness of the winter. . . . There was nothing she loved more than watching the dawn. She had an almost personal love for that white patch of window growing against the grey wall. She never slept very well and often had horrible dreams and she was frightened of the dark, so that the moment of sunrise was to her a moment of exquisite relief. . . . The greatest happiness she ever knew in these days was that of relief. . . . She lay quite still, breathing deeply, the slow relaxation of her tense nerves sending a lovely sense of well-being all over her body, so that she seemed to be swinging very softly in a hammock let down from heaven.

II

At breakfast the sun was blazing in a cloudless sky, and except for the glorious cool freshness in the air and the roar of the still agitated sea no one would have known there had even been a storm.

"Who is coming with me to market?" said Rachell.

There was a shout of joy from the children. Rachell always went to market on a Saturday and the children, for a great treat, sometimes went with her, for Saturday was always a whole holiday.

"We'll walk in," said Rachell, "and Brovard shall bring us back in the cart."

"I'll come with you to town but not to market," said Michelle, "I must go to the Free Library and find out about Hubert. . . . *They'll* have a Shakespeare," she added pointedly.

"I'll come with you wherever you go," said Ranulph.

Rachell smiled courteously, but her eyelids flickered a little, as they did when she was annoyed, and André, who was drinking coffee, left off drinking coffee, glanced at her, and then went on drinking coffee. . . . Sometimes she thought that Ranulph was with her a little too much. . . . It was because of the children, of course. . . . But the neighbours might talk. . . . And she was beginning to feel that André was growing a little jealous. . . . But how absurd. . . . She gave herself a mental shake. . . . Let the neighbours talk. . . . If one minded the neighbours all peace of mind would be at an end for ever.

"We'll start in half an hour," she said to Ranulph with her brilliant smile, but as she passed André in leaving the room she slipped her arm for a moment round his bowed shoulders. . . . He went to the pigsties completely happy.

They started—Rachell, Ranulph, Michelle, Peronelle, Jacqueline, Colin and Maximilian. Colette was left behind with Sophie. The walk was too much for her great weight and tender years.

They went through the water-lane and as they entered its leafy tunnel they all fell silent. They walked along, swinging their baskets rhythmically and treading delicately. Colin, wide-eyed, looked expectantly towards the shadows under the trees, and Maximilian, who was shepherding his family from the rear, lowered his tail. As they emerged again Rachell turned to Ranulph and laughed.

"Absurd, aren't we?" she said, "you know what Islanders think about water-lanes?"

"Fairies," said Ranulph, "I understand you are descended from them?"

"Why, don't you know about it?" cried Peronelle.

"Er—no," said Ranulph.

"Mother, he doesn't know the story. Tell him about it at once, for goodness sake."

"Tell us a story, mother," said Colin.

"I'm seeing things," began Rachell, and Ranulph, glancing with amusement at her face, saw that her eyes had grown strange and very clear, as though she looked right through the walls of this world into another.

"Once upon a time," she said, "hundreds of years ago, a very pretty girl called Oriane lived at Bon Repos."

"She was our umpteenth great aunt," Colin interrupted.

"Perhaps," said Rachell. "Well, one spring morning she thought she would like some gulls' eggs so she got up very early, just at dawn, and climbed right down to La Baie des Mouettes."

"A very dangerous climb. She should have known better," said Ranulph.

"Yes," said Rachell, "her mother had frequently forbidden her to do any such thing but she was a very headstrong girl—my children have unfortunately inherited that characteristic. Well, right down at the bottom of the rocks in La Baie des Mouettes is a very beautiful little cave which we call now le creux des faies."

"It's all green and yellow inside," interrupted Peronelle, "and it has pools in it filled with anemones, and the rocks round the pools are washed so smooth by the sea that they look like toadstools."

"Oriane had often been to this cave before," continued Rachell, "but never just at dawn. This particular morning that I am telling you about the tide was out and she climbed right down to the little beach in front of the cave. The sun was just shooting long, golden fingers out of the sea, feeling his way up the sky, the sea was smooth as shadowed silk, all the little pebbles sparkled like coloured jewels and the cave was filled with golden light. It was so beautiful that Oriane forgot all about the gulls' eggs and stood and stared. As her eyes grew accustomed to the sparkling light in the cave she suddenly gave a little jump and cried out in delight, for sitting on one of the rounded toadstool rocks and dabbling his feet in an anemone pool was a little man dressed all in green. He was very tiny, but he was very handsome and beautifully proportioned, and he had delicious pointed ears."

"Like Colin's?" asked Jacqueline.

"Yes, like Colin's," said Rachell.

Colin felt his ears and strutted in his walk like a turkey cock.

"When the little man heard Oriane cry out he turned round and looked at her, and when he saw her he cried out too and pulled his feet, all dripping with diamond drops, out of the pool, ran to her, reached up and kissed her. Now, no sooner had he kissed her than Oriane shut up like a telescope and became as small as he was himself. Then he kissed her again and she forgot all about her home and her relations, and the Island, and the gulls' eggs, and nothing existed in the world for her any more but the little green man. All day she sat with him in the cave and danced with him on the little beach and at evening, when the blue sky was dappled with gold clouds and the sea was mother-o'-pearl, she got with him into a little boat shaped like a seashell and sailed away with him to fairyland."

"Were her unfortunate relations distressed?" inquired Ranulph politely.

"Very," said Rachell, "they thought she had fallen and been drowned as she climbed down to La Baie des Mouettes. They cried for a year and a day but they had the consolation of feeling that they'd always told her so, and soon they felt better. Time passed on and she was forgotten, until one morning a man who was looking for gulls' eggs on the rocks above La Baie des Mouettes saw a host of little green men issuing, like bees, from le creux des faies and swarming up the rocks towards him. He stood his ground and asked them who they were and what they thought they were doing on the Island. They told him that charmed with the beauty and grace of Oriane, whom a cousin of theirs had brought to fairyland, they were determined to get themselves wives from the same country. The man said not if he knew it, threw his gulls' eggs at them and scrambled up the rocks to warn his countrymen. The Islanders, outraged and indignant, swarmed to the defence and there followed one of the worst battles the Island has ever witnessed. But, alas! what can poor mortals do against supernatural beings? What can the clumsy movements of flesh and blood avail against the flittings of ethereal bodies? The fairies drove them inland with lightning sword play and charges swift as the passage of the invisible wind and great and terrible was the carnage. The last stand was made at sunset near St. Pierre but, wearied and dispirited, the Islanders fell at last to their merciless enemies, who put every soul to the sword. The blood flowed down the steep streets of St. Pierre and tinged the waters of the harbour red—they are red at sunset to this day. The fairies then entered into quiet possession of the families and domains of the slain. The widows and orphans were at first annoyed and upset at the turn of events, but when the fairies had kissed them and their stature had been decreased and their memories erased, they were reconciled to their fairy lovers and the Island once more grew prosperous. But this happy state of things could not last for ever. The laws of fairyland will not allow their subjects to live among mortals for more than a certain number of years, and at last the fairies were obliged to say good-bye to the sea anemones and the heather and the water-lanes of the Island, and sail away from

La Baie des Mouettes in their fairy boats. They were very sorry to go and they cried so much that the little beach in La Baie des Mouettes and le creux des faies have, except at very low tide, been covered with water ever since. But since then no Island witch has ever needed a broomstick for her journeys, having inherited wings from her fairy ancestors, and the old people account for the small stature of many of our families by telling this story."

Rachell ceased talking and her eyes came back from far distances. The children sighed with delight and pride. Their fairy ancestry was a source of great satisfaction to them. It gave them, they felt, a pull over the children of the other Islands and over the children of England and France and Germany who, poor souls, were descended from apes, and looked it.

"Ah," said Ranulph profoundly, "now Peronelle is accounted for."

"Why her particularly?" asked Rachell, her eyes on Peronelle's legs twinkling along in front of them.

"She has a larger share of fairy bewitchment than the rest," said Ranulph, "she should Marry Well."

Rachell made a gurgle of annoyance in her throat.

"Really," she said, "there are moments when you remind me of my father-in-law."

"Oh?" said Ranulph, "is that a compliment?"

"No," said Rachell, and conversation languished until they came in sight of the market.

III

How describe the glories of the market? It was like a glorified—one might almost say a spiritualized—Rue Clubin on a Saturday night. Here was no narrow constricted street, no dirt and squalor, but a great domed building full of light and air and cleanliness. Here, too, were stalls piled with crabs and blue-black lobsters lying on beds of fresh seaweed, yet the stalls were bigger, the crabs seemed fatter and more imposing, the lobsters more sleekly and shiningly armoured. The market was confined to farm and garden produce and the harvest of the sea; it lacked the scarlet petticoats and yellow sunbonnets of La Rue Clubin, but it did not want for colour—the flower-stalls saw to that. Scarlet and yellow dahlias blazed everywhere, flanked by the great fat purple Michaelmas daisies and their little pale starry sisters, their yellow eyes fringed so delicately with innocent white lashes. Even though it was October there were still some bunches of hardy cabbage roses and the pink and white Island lilies still hung out a few slender trumpets on their grey-green stalks.

On the dairy stalls were slabs of butter, marigold colour, baskets of brown eggs and cans of buttermilk and curds. Beside the stalls sat the peasant women, most of them old and wrinkled, the grandmothers who were too old to work on the farms. Their brown wrinkled faces were framed in snow-white goffered sunbonnets, and white aprons covered their voluminous petticoats. They were all knitting and talking without pause and without cessation, and, apparently, without breath, the click of their needles keeping time to the rhythm of their patois.

There was a glorious smell in the market, combined of roses and seaweed and buttermilk and freshly ironed aprons, a deliciously invigorating smell that seemed the distillation of cleanliness. The sounds, too, were healing sounds. The great domed roof gathered up the click of the needles, the soft patois, the tinkle of the buttermilk as it poured foaming from the great cans, the rustle of the flowers as they passed bowing to their purchasers, mingled them to a soft fusion of sound and echo and handed back a lilting melody that stole into memory and stayed there when great symphonies were forgotten.

It was a lovely and lovable place, the Island market, yet to Colin it lacked thrill, and in his opinion could not hold a candle to La Rue Clubin. It was tediously respectable, connected in his mind with the restrictions that hedged his schoolboy existence, while La Rue Clubin stood to him for freedom and manhood and the limitless horizons of the sailor's life. He looked at Uncle Ranulph, listening politely as Rachell told him how curds were made, and noticed his beard and moustache leaning together to hide a yawn. Uncle Ranulph was also, it appeared, slightly bored with the market. . . . Colin formed the sudden daring project of taking Uncle Ranulph to La Rue Clubin. . . . Uncle Ranulph would understand its appeal. . . . He would not give him away.

In the middle of the market was the Bon Repos stall with old Madame Brovard, Brovard's mother, in charge of it. She smiled and nodded to them, but did not enter into conversation. . . . The families of gentlemen farmers, when they walked through the market, did not appear to own their stalls. . . . It would hardly be *comme il faut*. . . . Gentlemen were not in trade. Rachell paused just long enough to smile at Madame Brovard and notice how vastly superior was the Bon Repos butter to any other before she passed on to a stall positively groaning with crabs and lobsters and fish of all kinds. Here she purchased conger to make that particular Island delicacy, conger soup, and a fish never found anywhere but in the Island waters—a creature with green bones.

"You must taste all our Island dishes," she said to Ranulph, who had tasted them all before she was born. Then she paused, her purse in her hand, and meditated.

Peronelle went white. Horror of horrors. Mother was going to buy a crab!

Those who fancied crab bought him in the market still alive and kicking, carried him home in a basket with the library books on top to keep him in, and plunged him into boiling water still alive and kicking. . . . When the heat penetrated the chinks of his armour his claws seemed to clutch at the air in torment for a few moments, and then, except for an occasional twitch, were still. . . . To Peronelle this seemed a piece of hideous cruelty hard to beat. She could not understand how her family could perpetrate the horror, and above all how they could eat the poor crab after he was dead. Father, in particular, dear tender-hearted father, was devoted to crab and would sit poking the last remnants of tender flesh out of a dismembered claw with every appearance of enjoyment. . . . It very nearly made Peronelle sick. . . . Crab days were to her days of torment. Luckily they did not occur very often for crab was rather expensive.

Only one crab day did she remember with pleasure. They had brought the crab home, feebly waving his claws, placed him on the kitchen table for Sophie to deal with and gone to take off their hats. . . . But Sophie was attending to something else. . . . Coming downstairs again Peronelle beheld the crab walking across the hall. . . . Very feeble he was, only just able to drag his poor body over the hard stone floor, but he knew that somewhere, beyond this hideous parching land, was the sea. . . . Peronelle picked him up and ran. . . . Across the garden she went, across the cliff, down the path that led to the rocks below and there she stood and flung the crab back into the sea. Colin, in this situation, would have concocted a long and wonderful story to account for the disappearance of the crab. Not so Peronelle. She returned home, stood in the middle of the hall and shouted at the top of her voice, "I've put the crab back in the sea. Now there's nothing for supper. . . . Thank God."

But this was a long time ago and Rachell, if she remembered the incident, remembered it as one of Peronelle's outlandish escapades and not as an object lesson to herself. . . . She bought a crab. . . . He was placed in Jacqueline's basket. . . . Peronelle saw a claw raised once in protest before he was lost to view beneath a shower of apples poured on top of him to keep him down.

The fish with the green bones was given to Peronelle to carry, but she did not mind him. He was as dead as dead, and, anyway, a person who was eccentric enough to have green bones deserved to be eaten.

Rachell considered her lengthy shopping list and Colin slipped his hand into Ranulph's.

"I want to show you somewhere. Mother'll be ages."

Ranulph approached Rachell. "May we go off together? I'll see he gets home safely."

Rachell smiled and nodded. . . . She completely trusted Ranulph with the children.

IV

Colin dragged Ranulph out of the market into the arcaded main street of St. Pierre and down the hill towards the Town Church.

"There's a place where I go," he said, "it's lovely. You feel free there. All the sailors go there too. . . . You hear them talking. And there's a lady I'm fond of. . . . Mother doesn't know I go there. You won't tell her, will you?"

This was awkward for Ranulph, but he shook his head. . . . Colin had trusted him with his secret and he felt strangely elated. . . . Absurd!

"What's the name of the lady?" he asked lightly.

"Mère Tangrouille," said Colin.

Ranulph started very slightly. There had been a girl called Blanche Tangrouille, a wild black-eyed creature living in La Rue Clubin, whom he had known very well in his crazy young manhood. One of his most vivid memories was of walking up La Rue Clubin and of seeing the twisted chimneys of the house where she lodged black against a starlit sky. Then of stumbling up the two broken steps, pushing open the door with the creaking hinges, coming into the hot stuffy little room and looking with a sensuous pleasure at the tallow candles burning one on each side of the red geraniums on the windowsill. . . . Those geraniums had not been redder than Blanche Tangrouille's painted lips. Her hair had been dark as the night sky outside, her eyes wild as a trapped panther's, and her bosom warm with comfort. . . . Her presence had given him a sense of licence that was balm after his father's loveless discipline. . . . When his arms had been round her he had felt that he lived at last, and through her window he had been able to see the sea and the ships that sailed out into freedom . . . sailed as he longed to sail and could not.

He came back to the present to find Colin solemnly explaining Mère Tangrouille to him.

"She's large," said Colin, "very large, and when she's been drinking she doesn't talk very nicely. But you see she has to drink because it takes her mind off the spasms. She's very kind to me. I like her, but I don't think mother would, so I don't tell mother about her. . . . I don't tell mother I go to La Rue Clubin. . . . If one does things people wouldn't like I think it's best not to say anything about it, don't you?"

Loyalty to Rachell drove Ranulph, albeit stumblingly, along the path of the heavy uncle.

"I think," he said, "that you should never do anything of which your father and mother might disapprove," and he smiled sardonically into his beard.

"Oh, but I must," said Colin, "I must go off by myself—if I don't it hurts—here—as though there were a bird in me—"

Unable to express himself he clutched at the dark blue jersey that covered his thin chest. His face was alight with a sudden and extraordinary passion. Ranulph glanced at him, entirely comprehending. So that bug had bitten him! That longing for freedom, like beating imprisoned wings. . . . The boy might have been his son.

They turned up La Rue Clubin. . . . So Colin, too, so early, had found La Rue Clubin and Blanche Tangrouille. . . . Would it be the same Blanche? Ranulph felt—he didn't know what he felt. But the boy must be coped with. He was heading wrong. True, he had what Ranulph had never had, love and understanding behind him, but even so he was heading wrong. . . . What in the world to do with him? . . . Ranulph thanked his stars he had never had sons—a nephew was quite enough.

La Rue Clubin had not yet emerged into its Saturday afternoon wonder and glory, it was still in that state of confusion which precedes and follows glory. The stalls were being placed in position by cursing men continually getting entangled in the dogs and children that swarmed between their legs. The street was littered with baskets of crabs, boxes of gaudy underclothes, cats, refuse, and idle sailors with nothing to do, chewing tobacco and getting in the way. Everyone was swearing at everyone else, and the din was appalling.

Colin's eyes shone and he picked his way jauntily up the street.

"Isn't it jolly, Uncle Ranulph?" he said over his shoulder.

Ranulph, righting himself after stumbling over a cat, remembered that once he had thought that it was.

Mère Tangrouille had not yet begun to get her stall ready, but her front door was ajar and from inside the house her voice could be heard giving her candid opinion of her next-door neighbour. . . . Mère Tangrouille was nothing if not outspoken.

Colin hopped up the two broken steps, pushed open the creaking door and entered. . . . Ranulph followed as though in a dream. . . . The little room was hot and stuffy. . . . On the windowsill was a blaze of red geraniums. . . . Through it one could see the sea and the passing ships.

But Blanche Tangrouille? Ranulph, who for years had been as unresponsive to events as a block of wood, had quite lately, to his intense annoyance, re-developed a capacity for feeling. He felt now a sudden burning pain. This shapeless, hideous mass of humanity with its bloated, toothless face and shoulders bent as though with the last endurable ounce of weariness and self-loathing. . . . It was a sight so horrible to him that he receded a little. . . . Only her eyes were the same. . . . The eyes, dark, bold, and yet pathetic, with a bewildered, seeking look, were the eyes of Blanche Tangrouille whom he had once intensely loved. She had once been to him the symbol of what he wanted in life, the escape from martyrdom, now it seemed to him that she was the symbol of what he had found.

They came in. Ranulph was introduced. They sat down. Mère Tangrouille embraced Colin with passionate love. Ranulph noticed how gallantly, for the sake of his affection, Colin endured the embrace.

The room was scrupulously clean. In spite of age, drink, and spasms, Mère Tangrouille always managed somehow to keep herself and her room clean. If her neighbours commented upon this peculiarity she replied with pride that in her youth she had had to do with gentlemen, and gentlemen liked things just-so. To-day she was in one of her good moods and heaved about beaming with hospitality. She produced gin and glasses and she and Ranulph drank together. Colin was sternly forbidden by Ranulph to have any, but he did not mind very much. . . . It was all so exciting. . . . He was seeing life.

Presently, to his intense excitement, Guilbert Herode and Hélier Falliot came in, and there was delighted recognition. Hélier slapped Ranulph on the back and Ranulph slapped him on the back. . . . The one had saved the other from drowning and there was a bond between them. More drink was fetched from the pub down the street. More glasses were produced, and pipes were lit. To Colin's great surprise Uncle Ranulph began to talk in patois. . . . Uncle Ranulph *was* clever. . . . Fancy learning patois in two months.

The talk turned on the sea and ships. Colin could not understand all of it, the patois surged so swiftly, but it was all burningly exciting. . . . Talk of far lands where brilliant blue seas lay day after day under skies of brass, and where marvellous coloured fish glimmered along like rainbows, swinging their tails this way and that in the still water. . . . Talk of terrible storms, more fearful than anything they knew in the Island waters, when for day after day the sky was black like ink and all but a very few were battened down below, and those few had to crawl about the deck lashed on with ropes so that the great seas that swept the decks should not wash them away. . . . Talk of ports where one anchored amongst all the windjammers of the world, and gazed up to snowcapped peaks above feathery palms. . . . And outside the window Colin could see the ships passing, sailing away as he wanted to sail, as he *would* sail. . . . There in the stuffy little room he set his mouth and clenched his hands together. He would be free—free—free—nothing and nobody should stop him.

The talk grew shriller and louder, the smoke denser, and the smell of the drink was rather overpowering. Hélier, unperceived, had given Colin a sip out of his glass. . . . Colin began to nod a little. . . . He thought he was sailing out of the window into the harbour in a boat. . . . It had white sails and the wind was rippling in them. . . . The sails were straining forwards like white horses. . . . They were carrying him away and away. . . . Galloping over the rim of the world. . . . Ranulph's voice broke into his dream like a cracking whip.

"Colin, go home."

Colin was furious. He didn't know where he was or what he was doing exactly, but he did know that he was not going to be turned out of Paradise while Uncle Ranulph stayed behind surrounded by rainbow-coloured fish and white sails, and palm trees, and bottles of gin. He had a confused recollection of a lot of shouting and kicking, and himself biting Uncle Ranulph's hand hard, and then he found himself outside in La Rue Clubin all by himself. . . . Uncle Ranulph had simply chucked him out in the gutter, gone in again and shut the door. . . . It was too much. . . . Colin picked himself up, kicked Mère Tangrouille's door hard and, sobbing furiously, stumbled up the steps he had climbed so happily with Maximilian two months ago. . . . Where *was* Maximilian? . . . He stopped and glanced round miserably, and a wet nose was thrust against his bare knee. . . . Maximilian was here. He had followed them and waited patiently in La Rue Clubin all the time. Colin felt, not for the last time in his life, that dogs were vastly superior in all ways to human beings. He sat down, leant his aching head against the wall and gathered Maximilian into his arms. He was terribly unhappy. . . . Uncle Ranulph, he felt, had been cruel to him. . . . He had turned him out. . . . Why? . . . It wasn't fair. . . . He sobbed worse than ever. . . . Maximilian, covered with dirt and smelling horribly, nestled very close and licked Colin all over his face and neck. His tail wagged very fast with a circular motion it adopted when it was used by Maximilian to express deep and undying love. . . . Colin kissed Maximilian and felt a little comforted.

Ranulph, left behind in all the noise and confusion of Mère Tangrouille's parlour, had remained not because he was enjoying himself but because he had a debt to pay. Out of the past he owed this horrible woman courtesy and consideration. He stayed on, paying for the drinks, keeping her party alive for her amusement, telling her stories, treating her as other men would have treated a duchess. When Hélier and Guilbert had gone he lingered behind a moment to bow to her and wish her well. Mère Tangrouille rose swaying to her feet as he straightened himself. . . . All through the talk and the din she had been watching him, looking at his eyes, his hands, the shape of his head as she saw it outlined against the window, the way his hair grew—all those details about a man's body that a woman who has loved him never forgets. She had not drunk as much as usual, she had been too busy watching. She had known many men and forgotten most of them but she had remembered one very distinctly—the only one who had ever bowed to her.

"Jean du Frocq," she said hoarsely.

Ranulph started as though he had been shot.

"My name is Ranulph Mabier," he said coldly.

"Ah," she said, "I'll remember. You can trust Blanche."

To his horror he saw that the tears were running down her cheeks. . . . They made her look more hideous than ever. He stood, loathing the very sight of her, uncertain what to do. She took a few steps towards him and he, who had once thrilled to have her in his arms, felt his flesh shiver and contract with horror at her nearness.

"You'll come and see me sometimes, monsieur? To talk over old times?" she asked. She had come very near him and her aroma of gin and peppermint was in his nostrils. . . . He backed a little.

"Yes, Blanche, I will," he said, and bowed once more before he opened the door and fled.

Outside in the street he found himself staggering. The gin had been strong and he had had to drink a lot to please her. He wiped his forehead and gulped in the sweet cool October air, cool as spring water after the fetid stuffy atmosphere of Blanche's room. Here was another of them! Another tie binding him to the Island. . . . He felt trapped. . . . He would never escape from the Island alive. . . . Never. . . . A great longing for the rolling spaces of the desert came over him—those wind-ribbed sands that were born when Allah laughed. . . . He could not go back to Bon Repos just now. He turned down towards the harbour. Here at least one could feast one's eyes upon limitless distance. Here one could lash one's soul to a sea-going mast-top and watch her sail out and away.

V

Colin and Maximilian arrived home for dinner very late, very dirty, and very happy. Colin had quite recovered from his recent unhappiness. He loved Uncle Ranulph too deeply to feel resentment against him for very long. Moreover he was a sensible child and knew that grown-ups frequently had the best of motives for their incomprehensible and idiotic behaviour.

"Where have you been, Colin?" asked André.

"Uncle Ranulph and I," said Colin sweetly, "have been for a walk along the harbour wall. After that we went and said our prayers at St. Raphael's. Uncle Ranulph is still there."

"You'd better go and wash, Colin," said Rachell abruptly. Colin's account of his morning seemed to her extremely unlikely and not quite so inventive as usual, as though his mind was engrossed with something else and had no energy to spare for fabrication.

Colin washed and then devoted himself to hurriedly catching up with the others over the first course so that he should have a fair look in when it came to treacle tart. He never removed his eyes from his plate until, panting slightly, he swallowed his last mouthful of cold beef neck and neck with Peronelle. Then, still panting, he announced, "I'm going to be a sailor."

André and the girls received this announcement calmly, attaching no importance to it, but Rachell looked up sharply. There was a quiet steely note in Colin's voice that frightened her. . . . He meant it.

"No, Colin," she said.

"Why not?" demanded Colin sharply.

"Because it's a dangerous life and you are my only son."

Colin said no more but devoted himself to treacle tart in silence.

After dinner Rachell went up to her bedroom. She always went away by herself for a little at this time and woe betide anyone who dared to disturb her. She guarded this little oasis of peace in her busy day fiercely and jealously. At other times of the day work and servants and children were claiming her, and at night she was her husband's. This was the only time when she belonged to herself alone. . . . Sometimes she felt that these few moments kept her sane. Her family thought that she lay down on her bed and rested but she did not always do this. Sometimes she prayed, sometimes she read a little, but more often she sat quite still with her hands lying in her lap and her eyes closed. Sometimes she would murmur to herself as she sat, "Underneath you are the everlasting arms," and then she would feel her spirit sinking down and down through depths of tranquil light, that grew cooler and sweeter the further she sank, until she felt herself resting serenely against something, drawing in strength and peace through every fibre of her being. This lovely experience did not come to her always. It had come to her first one day when she had been in great physical pain that had almost wrenched her body and soul apart. . . . She had been frightened that first time and thought she had been dying. "It was as though my soul had come loose," she said to André afterwards. It came to her now whenever her life was very rigorously disciplined. At the slightest hint of self-indulgence, even in thought, it took wings and fled from her. Only ceaseless struggle could keep it with her, but she struggled; life without it was like a desert without wells.

But to-day she could not be quiet, could not concentrate. . . . Colin had said he would be a sailor. When she shut her eyes she saw his face floating on the water, grey like the face of the woman she had seen lifted out of the boat after the wreck. . . . In her ears was the sound of a great storm roaring.

An imperious hand was laid upon her arm and she opened her eyes to find Colin standing beside her. She was furious. No one, not even Colin, was allowed to disturb her quiet time. Her eyes blazed.

"Colin, how dare you!"

Colin was too angry himself to be abashed. "Mother," he said, "I *am* going to be a sailor."

"No."

"Yes."

They glared at each other.

Then the absurdity of it struck Rachell and she laughed. How ridiculous to get in such a state over a baby's chance remark! Next week he would probably be saying he wanted to be a dentist or the Archbishop of Canterbury. . . . Yet she knew in her heart he wouldn't. She put her arms round him and kissed him. Held against her heart he was deliciously warm, but flat and unresponsive as a hot water bottle.

"Darling," she said, "you can't be a sailor. I should never have a happy moment. Little son, you can't do that. Be an engine driver, sweetheart."

Colin kissed her right ear very politely above the little gold earring shaped like a seashell, but said nothing.

"Anyway you're too young for us to think about it now," she hedged, "now run along."

She released him and he went quietly from the room in dead silence. The back of his head expressed stony, unrelenting obstinacy.

Rachell, left alone, tried vainly to recapture her tranquillity, but in her ears was the sound of that great storm and before her eyes the waves were running and snarling like wolves.

VI

That same evening was memorable by reason of the first meeting of grandpapa and Ranulph. Grandpapa arrived first. He had lately taken a partner. After years of ill-treatment his patient stomach had begun to complain just a very little bit and grandpapa had come to the conclusion that it would be wiser to spend more time just sitting and quietly digesting, and less time in rushing round the Island after his patients. So he had imported a certain unfortunate young Englishman burdened with the name of Blenkinsop, into whose sufferings at the hands of grandpapa we need not go, since he is not important in the du Frocq history. But the importation of Blenkinsop had left grandpapa with a good deal of time on his hands, and he had taken to turning up unexpectedly at Bon Repos to see if Rachell was overfeeding the children. . . . He drove her perfectly frantic.

That evening, with supper and the children cleared out of the way, the lamp lighted and Ranulph not yet in, Rachell and André had settled down with sighs of relief to an hour's peace.

Rachell was sewing. She had abandoned her darning and was stitching at a lovely piece of embroidery, a strip of white satin with blue cornflowers and yellow poppies on it that she had begun in the leisure of her honeymoon and had not finished yet. She had not the slightest hope of ever finishing it, but just now and then she worked at it for a few moments because of the enjoyment that it gave her. Somehow the creation of a thing that was intended simply to be beautiful and nothing else gave her a feeling of spaciousness that was simply delicious.

"Why?" she asked André.

André, who was reading, removed his spectacles and thought about it.

"Because a thing that has no practical value but exists simply to be beautiful, a picture or a symphony, or yellow poppies enriching white satin, is a vision of reality."

"Why?" asked Rachell. "Shall I give this one orange petals or lemon?"

"A thing that's intended to be useful ties down your spirit to mundane things, but a thing that is simply beautiful opens a window and lets you go free—that's why you feel spacious. . . . That one must certainly have orange petals."

Rachell threaded lemon silk in her needle, and looked at her husband. His eyes had dropped to his book again and his face, usually so shadowed with worry, looked alight. He hardly ever had time to read and she was sorry, for a book was to him what her embroidery was to her.

"André," she murmured, "I wish you could go free more often."

He looked up at her for a moment and the light that had been in his face seemed to drain inwards, leaving it darkened. It did not return till he was once more absorbed in his book.

They sat together quietly, their bodies at peace, their spirits voyaging, their hearts attentive to and lovingly conscious of each other, while the clock ticked as though each little soft sound was a tap closing more and more firmly the door that shut out the noisy world. Into their peace came suddenly the sound of briskly tapping hooves, the creaking of a sharply applied brake and then a strident voice.

"Walk the horses, damn you. . . . Don't let them get cold. . . . Shan't be long."

The clock whirred complainingly, as though doors that had been closed flew open against its pressure. André dropped his book and Rachell ran her needle into her finger.

"Father," she said, with infinite resignation in her tone.

Grandpapa, in a voluminous many-caped cloak and with his beaver on the side of his head, stalked in. They rose and found him a chair, but he did not subside into it till he had stamped about the room examining it in minute detail. He ran his finger along the dresser shelf to see if it were dusty, he compared the clock with his own watch, he looked at the egg chart that hung on a hook by the fireplace, he picked some diseased tomatoes out of a basket and looked at them, and he fixed his eyeglass in his eye and stared for some minutes in complete silence at a damp stain on the wall. This behaviour he called "seeing to things at Bon Repos."

Rachell, praying for patience, commented on the state of the weather.

"What?" said grandpapa, "yes, damn chilly of an evening. October. Must expect it. . . . Your clock's wrong. Always is. . . . No eggs to speak of. . . . Tomatoes diseased. . . . You're a poor farmer, André. . . . Knew you would be. . . . Told you so. . . . No wonder the children are always ill if you live in such a damned unhealthy house. . . . What? . . . Look at that damp stain!"

"The children," said Rachell icily, "are perfectly healthy."

"Are they?" said grandpapa. "Three have died, haven't they? . . . Your own fault. . . . Would live in this hole against my wishes. . . . What?"

Rachell went white to the lips, and André leant forward with an exclamation. . . . Hardly ever even to each other did they mention those three dead children. . . . Grandpapa's voice grated on.

"Those you have left are too thin. Even Colette is fining down. . . . That's overeating of course."

"*Over*eating?" asked Rachell. She was crumpling her embroidery in her fingers, heartlessly crushing a yellow poppy against a blue cornflower in a way that took all the bloom off their petals.

"Overeating," reiterated grandpapa; "it's a well-known medical fact that if you overload a child's stomach it only has to get rid of it and the consequent wasting—" He paused. "Well, I'll say no more, but with that and this damned house you killed three of 'em."

It was at this point that Ranulph appeared in the doorway. Rachell looked up, and in spite of her sick rage she noticed that he swayed a little and that his eyes were bloodshot. . . . She gave a little despairing sigh. . . . It had happened once before. . . . So awkward with André the secretary of the Island temperance society.

Ranulph was quite sufficiently master of himself to take in the situation . . . Rachell was suffering. . . . That old devil had gripped her and André in his two hands and was twisting them. . . . Twisting their hearts from love of torture. . . . He came forward and, leaning on the table, faced Dr. du Frocq.

"Get out," he said.

"What! What! And who the devil are you?"

The veins swelled on grandpapa's forehead. He moved the lamp with a shaking hand so that he could see Ranulph's face better. . . . They stared at each other. . . . The clock ticked. . . . They were motionless for what seemed to Rachell a century. . . . Then Ranulph jerked his head back a little so that his face was in shadow.

"Get out," he said, "before I twist you as you twisted them." His voice, thick and low, was infinitely dangerous. André went up to him and touched his arm.

"Monsieur Mabier, this is my father. I would ask you to remember that this is also my house."

Ranulph turned and looked at André. His face was twisted as though by suffering and yet mocking at the same time.

"Father?" he said, "I beg your pardon." He went to the door and, forgetting to stoop, hit his head against the lintel with a sickening thud.

"André," cried Rachell, "go with him. He'll hurt himself."

André went. The two men, the one supporting the other, could be seen crossing the courtyard together. It was strange to Rachell to see them, who always seemed such poles apart, thus linked together as though in brotherhood.

There was complete silence in the kitchen until grandpapa's rage went off the boil sufficiently to allow him to speak.

"Is that drunken brute your paying guest?" he spluttered at last.

"Yes," said Rachell lifelessly. . . . Grandpapa had made her suffer so intensely for a few moments that she felt quite numb.

"Drunk as a lord," said grandpapa.

"I think not," said Rachell.

Grandpapa made a noise like the last half pint of water running out of the bath, "Don't pretend, my dear, that you're so innocent you don't know when a man is drunk."

"I didn't say he wasn't drunk," said Rachell tonelessly, "I merely did not consider him sufficiently drunk to be aristocratic. I thought him so slightly intoxicated as to be merely middle class—you saw, no doubt, that he showed a middle class capacity for noticing other people's feelings—but no, you're so aristocratic yourself that you probably didn't see that."

Grandpapa ignored this. "Do you intend to keep him here with the children? What? A fellow like that?" he asked.

"I do."

"What does André say to that? What?"

"André thinks as I do."

"Oh, does he?" said grandpapa nastily. "André, poor devil, always acts as you think or it would be the worse for him with a wife like you, but as for his thoughts, well, my dear, even a husband's thoughts are his own, let me tell you. . . . No, I won't stay, you're too damn touchy to-night."

He stalked out, muttering, and Rachell could hear him swearing at the coachman and puffing and blowing as he was heaved up into his seat, and then came the clip-clop of the horses' hooves and then silence.

But what a different silence to the one whose beauty grandpapa had broken. That one had held the stillness of a world narrowed to love and widened to eternity, yet shut to the clamour between. This one was dumb with the weight of hatred and grief. . . . When André came back he found Rachell in a heap on the floor, her head on the "jonquière," sobbing.

He crouched on the floor beside her, his arms round her, but for a long time she would not speak. Then she voiced a fear, implanted in her long ago by grandpapa, that had haunted her for years.

"André, André, did I really kill the children with overfeeding?"

"No! No! No!" Fiercely he kissed her hair, her neck, the hands that hid her face. Under his hands he could feel the beating of her heart and the labouring of her breast.

The lamp went out, and in the dim light, twined together, they seemed one body. The shadows gathered round them and their world narrowed again to each other and their love, so that grandpapa and Ranulph were forgotten, yet grief was not forgotten and its darkness, pressing in on them, shut them out from the far loveliness where they had been before. . . . Each tick of the clock seemed a tap that closed the door on them more firmly. . . . They were two children shut out in the night, crying together. . . . Grandpapa had a lot to answer for.

Chapter 5

I

PERONELLE'S passion for Browning, which had hitherto been nothing but a nuisance to her family, causing her to creep away by herself and read just when they were wanting her or else to stay and quote him by the hour together just when they didn't want her, became in the dark winter mornings a positive blessing. It caused her to get herself and the others out of bed in good time for school. Rachell in consequence had the highest opinion of Robert and had a good mind to write and tell him so. No longer had she to put on her dressing-gown while it was yet dark, and the draughts under the doors were cutting like knives, and go and drag the bedclothes off her protesting offspring—Peronelle saw to all that. Laziness and self-indulgence, Peronelle felt, were foreign to the mind of Robert. Promptitude, self-discipline, strong-mindedness, courage, these were all advocated by Robert, and getting out of one's warm bed on a dark, cold winter's morning gave one admirable training in all four. Peronelle could, in her mind's eye, see exactly how that wonderful family would have behaved on December mornings. The moment that they were called the nightcapped heads of Browning, Mrs. Browning and the little Browning would have been lifted from their pillows as by clockwork, and the instant that the curtains were drawn and the hot water cans put in the basins, their feet would have been upon the mat. They would have washed and dressed with the utmost thoroughness, going behind their ears and not missing out any of the buttons, and then, with calm but cheerful courage, they would have descended to take up the noble duties of the day. This programme Peronelle never failed to carry out herself, but getting the others to follow her example was very uphill work. However, she managed it. She was never known to fail in accomplishing any bit of work to which she put her hand.

At seven o'clock she would be awakened by Rachell tapping on the wall and at once, without giving herself time for thought, she would murmur, "I reach into the dark, feel what I cannot see and still faith stands," reach for and light her candle, and thrust her toes out into the bitter air. Then she would pour ice-cold water into her basin, calling out as she did so, "God's in His heaven, all's right with the world." Then she would drag the bedclothes off Jacqueline and leaving the poor exposed child curling up like a wood louse at the touch of winter's finger, she would march into Colin's room. He was a more difficult proposition, for as soon as he heard through the thin partition between their rooms the whereabouts of God and the state of the world he rolled himself completely up in his bedclothes and upon the entrance of Peronelle looked for all the world like an Egyptian mummy. However, she soon had him out of that. Seizing a hairbrush and casting herself on top of him she beat and pummelled and pinched and kicked until he yelled for mercy, and they both rolled on the floor with a resounding crash. With Michelle she tried oratory, for personal violence always made Michelle turn nasty.

> "Why comes temptation but for man to meet
> And master and make crouch beneath his feet,
> And so be pedestaled in triumph?"

she would demand of Michelle.

> "Lead us not into temptation, Lord!
> Yea, but, Oh Thou whose servants are the bold—"

But at this Michelle would shout, "Oh, shut up, I'm sick to death of you and your Robert," and arise. There was never any trouble with Colette. On the entrance of Peronelle the little cherub rolled to the floor with the suddenness of a rosy apple dropping into the orchard grass, and stayed there as placidly until picked up and washed.

On a particularly stormy and unpleasant morning at the beginning of December Colette plomped eagerly to the ground almost before Peronelle had got the door open, got to her feet, and, still heavy with sleep, staggered drunkenly towards the washstand before the candle was even lit. She was to spend the day with grandpapa. She was immensely excited.

Every now and again grandpapa, bored with himself and the Island and all the internal organs in him and it, demanded that Colette should spend the day with him. An entire day spent in the company of grandpapa would have seemed to anyone else purgatory or worse, but to Colette, who loved him, it was a delight. . . . Extraordinary the affection which the worst of men can inspire in the breasts of the very best of the opposite sex.

"I'm going to spend the day with grandpapa," she shouted, and had dragged her nightgown over her head before Peronelle had had time to pour the cold water into the basin.

In the intervals of eating an immense breakfast she chirped like a sparrow and later, driving into St. Pierre seated between Michelle and Peronelle, she sang hymns at the top of her voice—a sure sign with her of intense enjoyment.

II

Jacqueline and Colette were set down at the top of the hill while the others drove on to school. Grandpapa's was not very far from the Convent, and Jacqueline could take Colette there on her way.

They bobbed down the cobbled street hand in hand, blown about like puff balls by the tearing wind from the sea, their dark blue overcoats buttoned up to their chins and their scarlet tam-o'-shanters pulled well down over their ears. The damp had made their hair curlier than ever, and yellow and black kiss-me-quicks surrounded their faces and clung like tendrils to their tam-o'-shanters. Colette had her indoor shoes and a clean white pinafore done up in a brown paper parcel, and she swung it backwards and forwards as she walked with the ecstatic abandon of a puppy wagging its tail. . . . They looked perfectly adorable.

Jacqueline, standing on tiptoe, rang grandpapa's bell and waited beside Colette until she heard the door being unlatched on the inside, when she kissed Colette and ran off.

The door opened a crack and Madame Gaboreau's suspicious nose appeared at the aperture. But only for a moment. As soon as Madame Gaboreau's nose communicated to her brain that Colette was there the door swung wide open and the whole of Madame Gaboreau's substantial person, swelling and creaking with welcome, was exposed to view. Madame Gaboreau was not a nice person, but she liked Colette, and Colette, giving love for love, liked her. Kneeling down she pressed the little girl to the sequins on her bosom and received in exchange a warm, dewy kiss, full on her nasty, thin, rather cruel mouth.

Colette, on these occasions, did not see grandpapa till lunch time, for after breakfast he went out to see a few patients, and during breakfast his temper and language were so deplorable that he could not endure the presence of even Colette, and was obliged to swear at his eggs and bacon and curse into his coffee in complete privacy. Colette, however, was usually perfectly happy in Madame Gaboreau's sitting room, looking at photograph albums full of her horrible relations; or better still, she liked to go shopping with Madame Gaboreau, carrying the basket and scurrying along beside her like a yellow chicken bouncing after an old black hen. But to-day, no sooner had she arrived than a scurry of rain blew up with the wind and Madame Gaboreau decided that it was too stormy for her to go shopping.

"But I have two pairs of shoes," said Colette.

"No," said Madame Gaboreau, "children always walk in puddles out of mischief."

"I will not walk in any puddles, please M'dame Gaboreau," pleaded Colette, but Madame Gaboreau was adamant, and departed alone beneath an immense green umbrella, leaving Collette to the albums of relations.

She sat beside the fire in her white pinafore, on the very edge of a hard chair stuffed with horsehair and covered with shiny black cloth. Nasty hard horsehair prickles pushed their points through the cloth into the soft place behind her knees, that oasis between her socks and her knickers that all the gnats and prickles in the world always seemed to find. Open on her knee was an album and she turned the pages solemnly, one by one, giving polite attention to all the whiskered and crinolined Gaboreaus who confronted her. Usually this occupation, so different from anything she ever did at home, gave her a feeling of novelty and pleasure, and the Gaboreaus, most of them fat, and all of them self-satisfied, were so unlike mother and father that they interested her, but to-day, somehow, she did not feel quite happy. The rain, whispering down the window panes, did not seem quite happy either, and the wind in the chimney was definitely crying. The wallpaper and curtains of the room were of a mottled maroon and the mantelpiece was of black marble. There were no ornaments in the room except two funereal-looking vases filled with faded paper roses. The room, as the December storm thickened outside, was very dark. . . . Colette began to feel a little funny. She had inherited her mother's love of flowers and now, attracted by the pinkness of the roses in the dreary room, she slipped off her chair and ran across to look at them. She touched them with her finger, but they had none of the softness of the Bon Repos roses in June, they were prickly like the chairs, and they had a nasty dirty papery smell. . . . They were not what they seemed.

Until now Colette had thought the world a safe and happy place where everything that looked nice was as nice as it looked, but to-day she wondered. She had turned six last week and with every step that she took away from babyhood's downy nest a tiny little feeling of insecurity, that had been born in her when she fell downstairs for the first time, gathered strength.

Now, looking round this rather nasty room, the expression of Madame Gaboreau's personality, she felt afraid. She did not understand what she felt but she was, for the first time in her life, sensing that underworld of sin and misery that spreads its filth under the fair covering of outward things. This beautiful handsome house of grandpapa's, smooth and sleek as the green treacherous weeds on top of muddy ponds . . . what lay beneath its shining surface? She was too much of a baby consciously to ask this question, but that little feeling of insecurity inside her was voicelessly asking it of the long years of life that still lay before her. Colette's conscious mind only knew that she was frightened and that she would run down to the kitchen and stay with the maids until Madame Gaboreau came back.

She pushed open the door, glancing rather fearfully behind her as though she expected a sarregouset to jump out at her from behind the window curtains, and began to descend the stairs. She went down them with the utmost caution, lowering herself on to the right foot first and holding on to the banisters.

When she was halfway down the dining-room door opened and grandpapa came out on his way from breakfast to consult his case book in the library. He did not see Colette, so that the look of affection that his face always wore when she was there was absent from it. His eyes, unlit by the sight of her, were like cold pebbles set in the heavy pouches of his cheeks, his mouth was sagging at the corners in a bitter loose sort of way, and he was muttering to himself. . . . He looked nasty.

After the library door had closed behind him Colette stood quite still. Was this grandpapa? Kind, laughing grandpapa who told her stories and chucked her under the chin? No, it wasn't. There must be two grandpapas, and she was frightened of this other one. Abandoning caution she descended the rest of the stairs in a rush, and pushed open the green baize door at their foot that led to the back stairs.

Here it was very dark and smelly, for the kitchens were basement ones, and no light came to them except down the area in the front. Colette, groping in the dark, had to go down very, very slowly, and so she had time to hear the sounds that came up to her from below. There were all the usual sounds—cook carrying on cheerfully with the butcher, a kettle boiling, the cat mewing, the odd man whistling as he polished grandpapa's boots—but beside these there was something else, the sound of sobbing. She felt perfectly dreadful. She had, of course, heard people cry before. The others roared like bulls when they were in tempers, and she had herself wept drops the size of marbles when she hurt herself, and had been interested to find, when she licked them off the end of her nose, that they tasted salt, but it had been nothing like this. This was something quite different. The sobs did not make much noise and there was a short gasping interval between them, as though they were twisted out of a throat and breast almost too weak and tortured to give them passage. Every now and then they were drowned by the swish of water and the clatter of crockery. Colette realized that they came from the scullery on her right, on the opposite side of the passage from the kitchen. The door was ajar. She pushed it open and went in.

The scullery was very dark and more like a condemned cell than anything else—not one of the comfortable modern prison apartments but a cell of the Middle Ages. Its one little window was very high up and covered with wire netting, its walls, painted a dirty mud colour, were peeling with damp, and its stone floor, do what you would, was always wet, with little pools in the crevasses, as though it were a live thing weeping. At night it was absolutely alive with black beetles and even in the day they were not absent. The whole place smelt of damp and cabbages and defective drains, and was bitterly cold.

Colette, when she pushed open the door, found herself staring at the back of Toinette, the scullery maid, who was standing at the sink sobbing those terrible tearing sobs and washing up a perfect mountain of dirty dishes. Absorbed in her grief she did not hear the door open, and Colette had plenty of time to look at her back view.

It was a very thin back view. Toinette was even thinner than Peronelle and her shoulders were bowed in a way that Peronelle's were not, as though she had spent all her life in stooping and carrying things. A very skimpy, thin little print frock, covering apparently nothing in the way of warm petticoats, clung to her so tightly that it only accentuated her thinness and a dirty apron, two sizes too large, was wrapped round her like a winding sheet and secured at the back by a large black safety-pin. Her stockings lay in folds about her incredibly thin ankles, and her shoes had tramped so many miles on stone floors that the heels had given up in despair and fallen off. Her hair was twisted into a tight knot at the back of her head and secured with three hairpins the size of kitchen skewers.

Colette looked for a moment at the thin heaving shoulders and then ran forward to the sink.

"Toinette," she whispered.

Toinette started and looked down. The skin of her face was blue with cold and patchy with crying, and seemed stretched too tightly over her bones. Her eyelids were so swollen that Colette could hardly see her little black eyes, bewildered and desolate like a lost dog's.

"What do you 'ere, zen, Mamzelle Colette?" she asked hoarsely. She was a child of the Island and had only exchanged her patois for broken English when she took up her sojourn in grandpapa's house. Colette, standing solidly beside her at the sink, would have been none the wiser if she had been told that Toinette was a waif from La Rue Clubin. She knew nothing yet of the poverty and kicks and bruises in the midst of which Toinette's life had struggled into bud, nor of the toil and ill-treatment that had made flowering impossible, yet she felt the difference between them, and it made her feel bad.

"Toinette," she whispered, "must you wash all that?"

Toinette, taking another dish from the appalling pile, nodded and plunged it into the greasy water in the sink. She never paused for a single moment in her washing up, she went on and on as though she were a machine.

"There is t'ree days of it 'ere," she said, and her voice was caught up by another of those horrible sobs.

Colette's eyes grew round.

"Sophie," she said, "washes up every day."

"I 'ave been to my 'ome because my mother she died, Mamzelle," said Toinette, "and when I come back I find that they leave me t'ree days washing to do."

The atmosphere of tragedy in the scullery was so thick that Colette felt miserable. Then she remembered that people who died went to heaven, and felt happier again.

"Did you see your mother go to heaven, Toinette?" she asked, "did she have wings?"

Toinette stared bleakly.

"They put 'er in a black box an' buried 'er," she said. "Mère Tangrouille paid for ze coffin—mozzer an' I 'ad not ze money. She is good, Mère Tangrouille, très bonne. Ze gentleman zat come to see 'er gave 'er ze money."

A black box. Colette had always understood one went to heaven. She stared with her goggle eyes at the damp stains on the wall and felt worse and worse. What if they put mother in a black box?

"Toinette," she said suddenly, "your father has not gone to heaven, has he?"

"Never 'ad one," said Toinette, rubbing desperately at a dish whose egg stains were three days old and apparently immovable.

No father? Colette thought everyone had fathers. The uprising of pity in her chest was almost too much for her. She leant against Toinette and burrowed her head against her as she did against Rachell when Rachell had a headache.

"Do not do so, Mamzelle," gasped Toinette, "you 'ave 'urt my arm."

Colette raised her head and looked at Toinette's arm. It was all blue and bruised.

"Did you fall down the stairs?" she asked, painful memories coming to her.

Toinette dropped her voice even lower and glanced round with something like terror.

"M'dame Gaboreau," she said, "did it to me. She told me to wash ze dishes last night before I went to my bed but I could not, I 'ad ze 'eadache very bad. Zis morning, when she found I 'ad not washed, she—" A heavy step was heard on the stairs. Toinette stopped and the terror that had been in her glance flamed out all over her face in a way that was terrible to see. Her washing up became the feverish action of one desperately trying to placate the revengeful gods.

Madame Gaboreau pushed open the door and entered. Her face, before she saw Colette, wore an expression of cruelty that Colette had never seen before. Toinette's sobs, choked by terror, ceased.

"If those dishes are not done in half an hour," she began harshly, and then saw Colette. "Good heavens, child, what are you doing here?" She pounced on Colette, gripped her wrist and led her sternly from the room.

"If you can't get through your work, Toinette, you'll be dismissed," she called over her shoulder as she shut the door.

"Where will Toinette go if you send her away?" asked Colette as they climbed the stairs.

"Goodness knows," replied Madame Gaboreau indifferently.

"Her mother is dead," whispered Colette.

"Good riddance," said Madame Gaboreau. "You must not go to the kitchen, Colette. Your mother would have a fit if she could see you."

"Why?" asked Colette.

"You should not associate with the lower orders," said Madame Gaboreau. Colette did not know what she meant, but the word "lower" stuck in her mind. Upstairs in grandpapa's house everything was nice and comfy, but down below there were dark basements and people crying. Her lovely world had suddenly cracked at her feet and she had looked down into the crack and seen another hideous world below. Her baby mind recoiled. She wanted to go home to Rachell, but it was only the middle of the morning and she could not go home yet. She had to sit with Madame Gaboreau in her sitting room, full now of nameless terrors, and play spillikins with her. This had always been a delight before and Madame to-day was as kind to her as ever, but she kept thinking of the blue marks on Toinette's arm where Madame Gaboreau had hurt her, and she wondered whether, if she was very naughty, Madame Gaboreau would do the same to her. She was very frightened. She had never been frightened before. All her life long she was to remember this morning when fear was first born in her, and all her life long the word "underworld" was to give her a little feeling of sick horror.

At one o'clock things got better, for she was washed and brushed, and sent down to have lunch with grandpapa. When she came in at the dining-room door, her curls shining and her pinafore spotless, she was just a little frightened in case that other grandpapa whom she had seen in the hall should be there, but he wasn't. The man who picked her up and hugged her, pleasure and affection written large all over his face, was her very own grandpapa, not that other man. It was all right. The other one had gone away. In her delight at being with grandpapa she forgot all about him.

"Come to have lunch with the old man, has she?" chortled grandpapa, poking her in the ribs in a way that brought tears of delight to her eyes. "What? What? Bless my soul, what a dumpling! You eat too much, that's what it is. Image of your great aunt Augusta. Died of apoplexy. Barker, a chair for Mamzelle Colette. Now then, up with you."

Barker, grandpapa's English butler, heaved Colette up on to a chair piled with cushions and wheeled it in beside grandpapa's. Then he opened her napkin with a flourish and obligingly tucked it in beneath her chin, or rather chins, for she had three.

"Could your ladyship toy with a bit of chicken, what?" asked grandpapa.

Colette giggled. It was one of their jokes that grandpapa should treat her as a delicate lady of fashion with a fastidious appetite. Grandpapa, after placing a large slab of chicken on her plate, turned to Barker. "Give her ladyship a little vegetable," he said, "a mere soupçon. Just to tempt the jaded palate, what?"

Barker, twinkling, piled Colette's plate and the meal began.

Colette was too engrossed in slowly and solemnly absorbing her lovely food to talk very much, but grandpapa chatted away, telling her little stories about the funny things he had seen and done as he went about the Island, and she listened delightedly, every now and then, when he was particularly amusing, laying down her knife and fork and giving her soda-water syphon laugh. When she did this grandpapa felt as elated as a man at a dinner party who has won a smile from the reigning beauty.

Barker, standing behind grandpapa's chair, marvelled at the transformation wrought by Colette. "When that child is 'ere," he said later, to cook in the kitchen, "the old devil's a different creature. You'd hardly know 'im. Pity she don't come more often, that's what I say. It would be pleasanter for all."

"Ah," said cook darkly.

All through the chicken course Colette felt perfectly happy. This was the world she knew, the safe happy world where everyone was kind and loving. It was not till she was halfway through her helping of apple tart that she suddenly remembered the existence of that other world. She laid down her spoon and fork.

"What is it?" asked grandpapa, "full up to the back teeth? What?"

"Is Toinette having apple tart and cream?" asked Colette.

"Who the d—humph—and who is Toinette?" asked grandpapa.

"She lives downstairs where the black beetles are," said Colette.

Barker coughed discreetly. Grandpapa swung round on him. "Don't cough, speak out," he demanded.

"Toinette, sir," said Barker, "is the young person who assists cook. The scullery maid, sir."

"Scullery maid?" said grandpapa, "is the scullery maid having cream? Good God, no! Do you think I'm made of money?" His face became so congested that Barker hastily poured him out a glass of water.

"Her mother's dead," continued Colette, "they put her in a black box."

"What?" said grandpapa, "well, I can't help that. Humph. Course of nature."

Barker coughed again.

"Get out, Barker," said grandpapa. Barker got.

"Have you been in the kitchen with the servants, my young lady?" asked grandpapa rather sternly when Barker had gone.

"Yes," said Colette.

"What?" said grandpapa. "Well, you're not to do it again. Do you hear? Eh?"

"Why?" asked Colette.

"Not suitable," said grandpapa, "associating with the lower orders. Now finish up your pudding."

Colette finished it up, and the smoothness of the cream smoothed her bewildered feelings, but she did not for the rest of that day forget Toinette.

After lunch they went hand in hand into the library to have their forty winks. Colette did not really feel the necessity for taking forty winks, but she pretended that she did so that grandpapa should feel quite polite and happy about taking his. . . . Rachell had told her that this was the correct way to behave under the circumstances.

They sat down in two armchairs opposite each other. The chairs were so deep that Colette's legs stuck straight out in front of her as though she were in bed. Grandpapa placed his newspaper over his head and Colette, placing her handkerchief over hers, closed her eyes and folded her fat hands over her tummy in imitation of his attitude. Usually she stayed like this, quite still, and just quietly wondering about things, until grandpapa gave a snort and woke up again, but to-day, as soon as a series of rhythmical nasal sounds told her that grandpapa was asleep, she whipped the handkerchief off her head, scrambled off her chair, ran across the room and out into the hall. She had made up her mind, while she finished her apple tart, to give her coral necklace, her most precious possession, to Toinette to comfort her. By great good fortune Rachell had that morning clasped her coral necklace round her throat. It had been given her by grandpapa on her fourth birthday, and Rachell had thought it would please the old man to see her wearing it. . . . He hadn't even noticed it, so it hadn't. . . . So often are the kindly impulses of women rendered futile by their unobservant men.

She opened the baize door that led to the kitchen regions and stood wondering and uncertain. Dark steps led down to the black beetles of the basement, and more dark steps led up to the mice of the attics, but she did not know among which she would find Toinette, and she wanted to see Toinette alone. But the good luck or divine co-operation, call it what you will, that attends the charitable activities of the saints, was with her. As she stood waiting stumbling steps came up from below and she found herself looking down on the top of Toinette's soiled cap. The cap rose up from the nether regions, grew level with her toes, her knees, and finally overtopped her.

"Toinette," she whispered.

Toinette bounded to one side like a scared rabbit and her hand went to her side.

" 'Ow you frightened me, Mamzelle," she whispered.

Colette held out the coral necklace.

"It is for you," she said, "because you cried."

"Oo," said Toinette, and her eyes in their swollen lids held tiny sparkles of pleasure, dim as stars lost in deep waters. Then she drew back and rubbed her hands up and down her thighs.

"I couldn't take it, Mamzelle," she whispered, "I should be beat for taking your pretty t'ings."

"No one will know," said Colette, "please, Toinette."

She held up the necklace and the little globes of colour burned in the darkness like tiny lamps. Toinette held out her cold fingers hungrily and touched them. They were still warm from Colette's fat neck. She clutched them in a spasm of affection for the little giver and Colette let go and ran away. Toinette continued her stumbling progress towards the attics. Half-way she paused, and unhooking the high collar of her print dress fastened the corals round her neck underneath. The hard beads, pressed by her dress against her bony neck, hurt a little, but she endured the pain with the ecstasy of the pilgrim hobbling with peas in his shoes towards the shrine of his saint. But the love of the pilgrim for the saint was as nothing to the passionate adoration of Toinette for Colette, and the candles lit by him at the shrine in the sight of all men were neither so warm nor so bright as the little hidden red beads that rose and fell in darkness whenever Toinette breathed.

Colette scuttled noiselessly back to the library, scrambled into her chair, spread her handkerchief over her head, folded her hands over her tummy and, when grandpapa snorted and awoke, was resembling a quite immovable infant Buddha.

"Eh? What?" said grandpapa, "must have dropped off. Did you drop off?"

Colette, who never lied, smiled fatly and said nothing.

"You've a saintly disposition," grandpapa told her, "produced by sound teeth and excellent digestive organs. Mind you don't eat too much and admit the devil."

"No, grandpapa," said Colette.

"Good girl," said grandpapa, "now we'll play backgammon."

Colette was not really of an age to understand the intricacies of backgammon but grandpapa was always perfectly happy explaining the rudiments of the game to her, and making her moves as well as his own, while she stood by and rattled the dice, and the time passed very happily until Barker brought them afternoon tea.

Most Islanders had a very late and very large tea, between five and six o'clock, embellished by crab or shrimps, curds and goche, but Barker couldn't stand these heathen ways and had, after years of patient effort, succeeded in suggesting to the mind of grandpapa that this unseemly gorging was never indulged in by the Best People, and that tea and a little buttered toast at four o'clock was the height of culture. Grandpapa, though he felt he owed it to his professional position to be cultured, did not think much of its outward and visible sign. "Scorched bread and dish water," he called it, and kept a hidden supply of goche inside his safe for private consumption only.

But Colette thought afternoon tea lovely. The fragrant amber-coloured China tea, enlivened by four lumps of sugar, which grandpapa gave her in a Crown Derby teacup was very different from the milk and one lump of sugar in a blue mug dealt out to her at home by Rachell, and the little wafer squares of buttered toast, though they did not fill you up as satisfactorily as bread and jam and goche, were deliciously oily and crackly.

Colette, her inward grieving over the sorrows of the world eased by the gift of her necklace, felt happy and secure as she sipped her tea with loud sucking noises, and smeared butter all over her nose.

But after tea all her former terror returned with a rush. Madame Gaboreau, announcing that it was four-thirty and Jacqueline would be here to fetch her at any moment, appeared in the library and carried her off to be washed. Madame Gaboreau was now in a very bad temper. Toinette had broken two dishes, and her cringing way of lifting up both hands, like a dead mole, exasperated Madame Gaboreau beyond all reason.

She led Colette upstairs without a single word, and her grip on the fat wrist was like a bracelet of hard iron. Colette was terrified. Madame Gaboreau's cold grasp sent shivers of fear through her, and at every turn of the stairs she thought she saw thin weeping figures huddled in the shadows.

Upstairs in Madame Gaboreau's room, lit by only one candle, spluttering and wavering in the draught, she felt drowning in a sea of terror. The rain was tapping and scratching at the window like a mad creature trying to get in, and the crying wind of the morning had turned to a roaring tormented thing, beating imprisoned wings inside the chimney.

"Don't you know how to keep yourself clean when you eat? What a disgustingly dirty child you are!" said Madame Gaboreau, dabbing at Colette's buttery face with a cold, scratchy sponge, and giving her a little shake. To Colette's fear was added a sense of injustice. She knew she was *not* a dirty child. She was always as neat and clean as circumstances would allow, but sometimes circumstances were too much for her, and Barker, whose affection for her led him to use up at least half a pound of butter on her toast, was one of those circumstances. Two tears pricked behind her eyelids and then spilt over and trickled down her cheeks.

"What in the world are you crying about?" demanded Madame Gaboreau, "and where is your coral necklace?"

Colette, her lip trembling, made no answer.

"What have you done with your coral necklace? Answer me, child!"

Colette shook her curls. Her obstinacy acerbated Madame Gaboreau's already ruffled temper.

"I can't send you home to your mother without your coral necklace," she snapped, "if you don't tell me what you've done with it I shall slap you. You're a naughty, obstinate child."

But Colette, with the courage and truthfulness of the saints, would neither save herself with a lie nor deliver over Toinette to vengeance with the truth. She stood her ground and Madame Gaboreau slapped her hard.

It was the first time she had ever been struck, and the blow was like an earthquake that ripped open the ground at her feet. That morning she had peeped through a little crack and seen horror below, but now horror came leaping up through the great fissure and suffocated her. Cruelty and terror and grief and pain were leaping round the dim room like dancing devils and a pall of darkness was closing down on her and crushing her. Crazy with fright she ran from the room, and as she ran she heard again the mad creature scratching outside the window and the tormented thing beating its wings inside the chimney.

Helter-skelter she rushed down the stairs, the outraged Madame Gaboreau following more slowly with her hat and shoes, and fell headlong down the last six steps into the arms of grandpapa waiting at the bottom.

"Eh? What?" said grandpapa, "are the furies at your heels?"

They were, but she could not explain, she could only pant silently into grandpapa's beard.

"Taken fright at something," explained Madame Gaboreau, creaking down the last flight, "a queer child at times. A peculiar bringing up, if I may say so."

"Humph," said grandpapa, and he and Madame Gaboreau exchanged glances. They both had the lowest opinion of Rachell and all her works.

Colette stood quaking with fright while Madame Gaboreau put on her shoes and cap and coat, and, whenever possible, she clutched grandpapa for protection from the powers of evil that seemed to emanate from Madame Gaboreau. Once she glanced up at his face, and in the dim light it was once more the face of the man she had seen that morning, with pouches under the eyes and a mouth sagging at the corners, and she let go of his coat with another little spasm of fright, her last protection gone. And at that moment the bell rang. . . . It was Jacqueline.

Madame Gaboreau swung open the heavy door and there, standing under the lamp in the porch, like a visitant from another world, was Jacqueline. Her tam-o'-shanter was bright as a holly berry, her face had been whipped by the cold air to the colour of a red rose and her eyes were bright yet soft with the queer inward shining of a hidden joy. It was evident to even a casual observer that something wonderful must have happened to Jacqueline that day. She stood there smiling roguishly, sweetly, innocently, the personification of the love and cleanliness of Bon Repos, but she did not step over the lintel; that seemed a dividing line between her world and another. Behind her was the clean windy night and its fresh breath, blowing into the stuffy house, caught up Colette like a piece of thistledown and blew her across the lintel into Jacqueline's arms.

"Never said good-bye to her old grandfather, did you ever!" complained grandpapa. From the safety of the further side of the lintel Colette looked back into the hall and saw grandpapa and Madame Gaboreau standing there, no longer terrifying but infinitely old and pitiful, self-imprisoned creatures shut out from a world whose existence they did not even know of. With a rush of courage and affection Colette stepped back over the lintel, ran to them and hugged them, and then tore back to safety and Jacqueline.

Grandpapa and Madame Gaboreau stared at the shut door with a feeling of loss, yet aware that something of Colette's crystal clarity had been left behind in the murky house, piercing the vapours of evil thoughts, thinning them, driving them for the moment into dark corners. Then Madame Gaboreau sighed and moved towards the stairs. "Dear little thing," she said, "I wish she came more often. I'm afraid I may have been a little hasty with her. I've enough to try me, goodness knows." And at the thought of Toinette and her irritating incompetence Madame Goboreau's mouth snapped shut like a trap, and the evil thoughts looked out again from banishment.

Grandpapa grunted ungraciously, went back to his library and slammed the door. Seated in front of his fire he smoked a cigar and growled at the glowing coals. Somehow or other he had frightened Colette to-day. She had shrunk from him in the hall. Why? The memory of her shrinking lay heavy on his mind. He swore and jabbed at the coals with the poker. Was she to be alienated from him too? One by one they had shrunk from him and left him. His wife, Jean, André, his elder grandchildren, and now—would Colette go too? God knew he'd been a good enough husband, father, and grandfather. A bit of a disciplinarian perhaps, no patience with outlandish notions, but that, surely, was all to the good in the father of a family. Wild lads, such as Jean had been as a boy, needed the sting of the lash to break 'em in and useless imaginative notions, such as had flowered in André, must be nipped in the bud if the boy was not to grow up a sensitive ass. Was it his fault if the whip and rein had goaded one son to frenzy and driven the other into a morbid solitude? No, the fault was in them. They had inherited from their fool of a mother a passion for individual freedom in life and thought that had maddened him and been their own undoing. "Freedom." How often had his wife, Jean, and André used that detested word to him. He loathed it. How often had Jean demanded freedom to live his own life, André to think his own thoughts and his wife, puling wretch, complaining in season and out of season that her husband cruelly possessed her body, mind and soul, that she must be free to breathe a little, think a little, be herself once in a way, or she would die . . . and she had. . . . Fool! . . . At the thought of her grandpapa got up and paced the room with short, irritated strides. Life, to him, was an affair of disciplined striving for material welfare, in which mankind must be marshalled in the regularity and order of an army, captained by those, such as himself, whose cool judgment and strong character marked them out for leadership. From the led the leaders had the right to demand unquestioning obedience and complete sinking of individual personality, and loyal and admiring service. . . . Freedom. . . . Bosh. . . . . . That way led to chaos. . . . Each of his sons had gone his own way and where were they now? Jean, dead in a gambling house as likely as not and André, a sentimental failure, living on his wife's money. At the thought of his daughter-in-law grandpapa's thoughts became positively savage. She had all the qualities he most admired in a man, cool judgment, strong character and the gift of leadership, but in a woman they drove him demented. Women had no right to lead—they should be led. Their part was to follow meekly and obediently in the rear with the commissariat, not to seize banner and sword and spur to the forefront of the battle. Rachell, confound her, had set herself up as the leader and guardian of her family instead of relinquishing the post to her father-in-law, and just look at the disasters that had accrued! The whole turn-out on the verge of bankruptcy and his grandchildren alienated from him. Confound the woman! Women were at the bottom of all the trouble in the world. Look at his wife and daughter-in-law; between 'em they'd ruined his life.

Grandpapa's savage meditations ended suddenly in the desire for a drink. He stopped striding round the room and rang the bell violently. As he stood in front of the fire silently waiting for Barker he became unpleasantly aware of the wind and the rain—scratching at the window like a mad creature trying to come in, moaning and beating with imprisoned wings in the chimney—the inarticulate crying out of the weak crushed by the strong. He swore and piled logs on the fire so that the roaring flames might drown their plaint.

III

Colette's spirit, that day, had been voyaging for the first time into the darkness surrounding human life, but Jacqueline, to whom fear and pain had long been familiar, had voyaged even farther;

she had gone right through the circle of darkness into the circle of illimitable light beyond.

> "I saw eternity the other night
> Like a great ring of pure and endless light,"

wrote Vaughan, but to Jacqueline, when she had seen it that day, it had seemed more like the endless depth and length, and breadth and height of the sky, ringed only where it bent itself round the ball of darkness enclosing man, thrusting, probing, piercing with its spears of light to get through the darkness to him. And it had got through to Jacqueline. And, as always, it had used as the point of its spear the most trivial, common, even banal of happenings. Jacqueline had smashed a vase and so found God.

She had not done this all in one day, she had begun her voyaging when she first went to the Convent, but this December day of wind and rain had seen her sail her boat into harbour and let down the anchor. She never forgot this day as long as she lived—this day and the one when she first went to the Convent.

Rachell had been with her on that first day which now, so far had she travelled since, seemed hundreds of years ago. It had been a glorious September morning, warm yet with a delicious crisp edge of coolness to the warmth, and of a crystalline clearness. They had climbed together the steep steps leading to the Convent, Jacqueline palpitating with fright and clinging to Rachell's hand. They passed the old church porch and stood in front of the heavy grilled door of the Convent. Rachell, using both hands and all her strength, pulled the great iron bell that hung beside it. It clanged in a dreadful hollow way and Jacqueline thought of dungeons and rats and tortures and shook all over. Then the shutter behind the grill shook and rattled, and finally shot back, and Jacqueline saw an immense pair of spectacles gazing out. Behind the spectacles, and nearly obliterated by them, was an old face framed in white linen.

"Rachell, my dearest child," cried a shrill sweet voice from behind the spectacles, and the great door, after a creaking and grumbling of bolts, was opened, revealing the tiny black-habited figure of Soeur Ursule. Reaching up she folded the tall Rachell in her arms and kissed her on both cheeks, for of all the pupils whom Soeur Ursule had taught within the old Convent walls Rachell was the one who did her the most credit. Perhaps a little of Rachell's beauty of body and mind and spirit was due to heredity and up-bringing, but if so, Soeur Ursule had decided it was such a small part as to be entirely negligible; she took the whole credit to herself and Soeur Monique, though admitting, of course, that the blessing of God and the intercessions of the holy saints had been of assistance in their efforts.

Now, chattering like a small shrill little bird, she turned from Rachell to Jacqueline and gathered her too to her heart, commenting volubly as she did so upon Jacqueline's beauty, sweetness, clever forehead, and likeness to her dear, dear mother. Jacqueline's spirits rose. Not so had Miss Billing received her when she had been handed over to her for instruction at St. Mary's College. Here, obviously, was a woman who appreciated her worth, who realized that Jacqueline du Frocq was a quite exceptional creature, with brains and beauty far, far above the average. Clasping her arms round Soeur Ursule's neck she kissed her with an abandon of gratitude, and love unfolded his wings at their kiss with the suddenness of a scarlet pimpernel opening at the sun's touch.

But if Jacqueline's spirits rose Rachell's sank. Soeur Ursule, good woman, would, she felt, be the ruin of the child. For a little prinking, pruning peacock like Jacqueline, flattery was surely the worst thing possible. But here, strangely enough, she was mistaken. The Convent's appreciation was, in the long run, the salvation of Jacqueline.

"My dear Rachell," chattered Soeur Ursule, as she led them down a long stone passage and up a steep twisting flight of bare uncarpeted stairs, "I cannot say how much we are touched that you should entrust your precious flower to the care of your old teachers. It shows, dear Rachell," she added, turning on the stairs and wagging her finger solemnly, "that you realize education inspired by our Holy Church, and taking place within Convent walls, is the only education suitable for Catholic girlhood," and picking up her skirts and showing her elastic-sided boots, she turned round and climbed on again.

Rachell, feeling guiltily that only one of her four girls was to be educated at the Convent, and that one only after pressure from an unknown and possibly immoral man cast up at Bon Repos from a shipwreck, blushed hotly, and sailed up the stairs behind Soeur Ursule without speech.

"Is that not so, dear?" said Soeur Ursule suddenly at the top.

"I shall never forget all that I learnt here," said Rachell with perfect truthfulness. If she had learnt little that little had been precious beyond words.

Soeur Ursule opened a door at the top of the stairs and they were in the sun-drenched Convent parlour overlooking the sea. How well Rachell remembered it. In all these years it had not altered a tiny scrap. The same whitewashed walls. The same long ink-stained table with the same handful of pig-tailed girls in black Convent pinafores busy with copy books and old-fashioned grammars. The same lace pillows with the gay beaded bobbins laid out side by side on a form by the wall, waiting patiently for the afternoon's lace-making lesson. The same cracked blackboard. The same Crucifix on the wall with a vase of flowers on a bracket beneath. The same sea scintillating and murmuring outside the windows. The same placid peace flowing in, filling up, drowning the room under its sweet waters.

For a moment Rachell was lapped round with the old feeling of loving security that she had always known here, then she was jerked out of it by perceiving that the girls sitting at the long table were all tradesmen's children. In old days the children of gentlefolk had attended the Convent, now it seemed that with the coming of the new College the nuns' social and educational status had slipped downhill a little. Rachell was horrified. This would mean that Jacqueline, prone as she was to act the superior little cat, would feel herself set upon the pedestal of higher breeding and become quite intolerable. Rachell, outwardly gay and gracious as ever, said good-bye to

Jacqueline and Soeur Ursule and left the Convent heavy hearted.... The child would be ruined.... She should have been sent back to St. Mary's.... All the way home she wished Ranulph Mabier had never set foot on the Island and rated herself for an idiotic woman, running after Will-o'-the-Wisps of presentiments and fantasies with no more sense than the "faeu Bellengier[4]" himself.

Yet Rachell was wrong and Ranulph was right. The Convent was to Jacqueline the high road to happiness. All her conceited little ways, all her vain thoughts and ceaseless insincerities had grown out of her hidden unacknowledged sense of inferiority. At St. Mary's she must act the part of a girl she was not or own herself inferior, but here at the Convent the girl she was found favour. The simple lessons did not strain her mind, the affection of the uncritical nuns, proud to have her as their pupil, warmed her starved heart, and the admiration of the girls to whom, by reason of her birth and prettiness, she seemed set on a pedestal, was as balm to her. There was no more ceaseless striving to compel affection, no more struggle to attain to heights beyond her, no more exhausting playing of a part. Her strained nerves relaxed, and after a fortnight at the Convent she got so fat that Rachell had to let her waistband out. And yet, strangely enough, she grew less conceited, not more so. She was grateful for the love given her and gratitude goes hand in hand with humility, as health with normality. She had never known what it was to feel well, but now her placid life eased her body so much that she almost forgot about it. Living without strain and effort she was no longer so painfully aware of herself, and her horizon widened to take in thin Soeur Ursule, fat Soeur Monique, the other girls, the Convent kitten and the lace pillows and embroidery frames—above all, perhaps, the embroidery frames, for to her other joys was added the discovery of skill in herself. For Jacqueline, Soeur Monique discovered, had magic in her finger tips. She could toss and twist her lace bobbins and ply her needle with the skill of a busy little spider spinning a jewelled web—and she had never known it. She could

---

[4]Will-o'-the Wisp.

make a garden of crimson roses and golden lilies bloom upon white satin, and twist white threads into butterflies and daisies and white stars of Bethlehem—and she had never known till now that the power was in her.

"Child, did you never do embroidery at St. Mary's College?" asked fat Soeur Monique one afternoon as they sat in the parlour together embroidering a new banner—a marvellous affair of lilies and roses with the Virgin in the middle in a robe of startling blue.

"They taught us darning," said Jacqueline, breathless over a petal that she was shading from the deep colour of a clove carnation down to the flushed pink of a wild rose.

A contemptuous snort escaped from Soeur Monique's Roman nose—she was a large, downright, outspoken woman who snorted easily.

"Darning!" she said, "any idiot can darn—even the heathen do it, it is a natural gift, like eating, but the ability to embroider is a gift of God."

"Oh?" said Jacqueline, interested, and stopped working, her scarlet-threaded needle poised over her work like a dragon-fly.

"A gift of God," reiterated Soeur Monique, "and should have been discovered in you. They considered, I gather, that they educated you at St. Mary's College?"

"I think that was what the College was for," said Jacqueline, "they taught us everything there—geometry and algebra and literature and history and—"

Soeur Monique interrupted with another snort.

"They may have taught you, but they did not educate you," she said.

"Oh?" said Jacqueline.

Soeur Monique banged down her scissors on the table, adjusted her glasses, and launched herself on her favourite subject with vigorous enjoyment.

"The function of the educator," she declaimed, "is to discover in each individual child the gifts implanted in her by Almighty God and to develop and dedicate them to His service."

Soeur Ursule, seated near with her volume of the Lives of the Saints upon her knee, which she intended to read aloud whenever Soeur Monique condescended to leave off talking, put in a gentle word for St. Mary's.

"Sometimes, dear," she said, "it is very difficult indeed to discover what, if any, gifts *have* been implanted by Almighty God in a human creature. And when a school has such a large number of girls to deal with—"

"Women of discernment can discover a child's capacities at a glance," interrupted Soeur Monique, "Jacqueline had not been with me ten minutes before I saw from the shape of her hands that she could embroider. At St. Mary's, as far I can see, they discovered nothing about her except that she was a goose at geometry, algebra, literature, and history. Their discoveries were entirely negative, not positive, and negative discoveries are entirely useless in the service of God."

Jacqueline blushed hotly—it still hurt her to be called a goose.

"You needn't blush," said Soeur Monique tartly, "it is of no consequence whatsoever that you should be intellectually a goose. What is of importance is that the few gifts you *have* got should be used for God. . . . I've not seen you put that needle in for five minutes."

Jacqueline's poised needle darted down into the heart of the rose and Soeur Monique's wise words darted down into her mind.

"Then it doesn't matter if one isn't clever?" she asked.

"Matter? No, of course not. Why should it?" said Soeur Monique. "God needs you as He made you and not as He didn't make you. His purposes require us all to be differently gifted. An appalling thing it would be if we were all clever, there'd be no one left with the intelligence to boil an egg or look up a train in a time table."

All this was entirely new to Jacqueline and its healing ran like a fresh stream to all the parched sore places inside her.

"Am I to read about the holy St. Francis or am I not?" inquired Soeur Ursule with the slightest suspicion of asperity. "This is supposed to be the silent hour."

"Yes, dear, do," said Soeur Monique graciously, "I was merely talking while I waited for you to begin."

Soeur Ursule read about St. Francis and Jacqueline listened astounded. This ideal of poverty was also entirely new.

"Then it doesn't matter what you possess?" she asked when the reading was finished.

"Good heavens, no," said Soeur Monique, "why should it?"

"But you are not popular unless you have things," objected Jacqueline.

"What things?"

"Beauty or cleverness or money or nice clothes," said Jacqueline, "*something* to make people admire you."

Soeur Monique snorted.

"It doesn't matter two pins whether you are popular or not popular. . . . Why *should* you be popular?"

"It makes me happy to feel that people admire me," murmured Jacqueline, blushing hotly again.

"What does it matter whether you are happy or not happy?" demanded Soeur Monique, "nothing matters but the service of God. . . . Good gracious me, did no one ever teach you anything? You don't seem to know the rudiments of your religion."

Jacqueline went home that night with all her previous values hurtling about her ears. Indeed, the whole of her first month at the Convent was a time of mental change and readjustment, helped and eased by her physical well-being. It was a time of pulling down rather than of building up. It was not until her second month that she smashed the parlour vase, and the gates of vision opened.

The vase was a hideous object made in Birmingham, and for years and years it had stood on a bracket below the Crucifix in the parlour. Soeur Ursule thought it perfectly lovely; in the summer she kept it filled with fresh flowers, and in the winter with holly and dried sea lavender. It was the apple of her eye and no one was allowed to touch it but herself.

One morning at the beginning of November Jacqueline was sitting in the parlour with the others being instructed by Soeur

Monique in the rudiments of English grammar. It was a very simple lesson, well within her capacity, she was at the top of the class and she was enjoying herself. Indeed, they were all enjoying themselves except Soeur Monique, who hated English grammar and had never got, and never would get, beyond its rudiments. They were just in the thick of it when the door opened and Soeur Ursule appeared, her old face pink with excitement, and her arms full of chrysanthemums.

"Sent from the Lieutenant-Governor's own greenhouse," she gasped, "I always said there was more in that man than people thought. We shall be able to make the Chapel a bower. Soeur, may I have the girls to help arrange them?"

Soeur Monique adjusted her spectacles and looked at the clock. The grammar lesson should have lasted for another twenty minutes, but as her pupils already knew a good deal more than she knew herself, and she found the task of keeping up with them extremely exhausting, she was inclined to be lenient.

"You know that I don't like my classes interrupted, dear," she said severely to Soeur Ursule," but, of course, if you make a point of it—"

"It is so good for the girls to learn how to make the Chapel beautiful," pleaded Soeur Ursule," especially when I am pressed for time."

"Very well, just for this once," said Soeur Monique graciously, and the grammar class leapt to its feet with squeaks of pleasure. Jacqueline, her squeaks ended, glanced at the Birmingham vase. The frosts had come early that year and the tarnished Michaelmas daisies that filled it were quite unworthy to be placed at the foot of the Crucifix.

"May I bring the Birmingham vase and do it?" she asked.

Soeur Ursule hesitated. No hands but hers ever touched that precious treasure. Then she yielded. It would have been unkind to disappoint the child.

Jacqueline carried the hideous thing carefully to the little pantry where the Chapel vases were all laid out. There followed a hubbub of chattering girls and tinkling water and clattering cans, brooded over by the pungent lovely scent of great bronze and gold and lily-white chrysanthemums. Soeur Ursule followed after Jacqueline and the Birmingham vase with the frantic clucking of a hen whose duckling is making for the pond. Jacqueline felt slightly irritated. As if she couldn't be trusted to fill a vase with flowers without breaking it!

"Don't stand it in the sink, Jacqueline," implored Soeur Ursule, "you'll break it. Stand it on the wooden table and fill it from the can."

"Yes, Sister," said Jacqueline.

Now it happened that at the great moment of the filling of the vase Jacqueline was quite alone in the pantry with the kitten. She had taken a long time to choose her chrysanthemums, and the others were already staggering up the passage to the Chapel with their heavy vases, Soeur Ursule clacking after them. Jacqueline felt she must hurry. It was quickest to fill the vase at the sink. Better to disobey Soeur Ursule than to be called a slowcoach by the others. Jacqueline filled the vase at the sink, and just as the water brimmed over the top the kitten swarmed up her left leg and clung there, sharpening its claws on her knee. Jacqueline squeaked and staggered, the Birmingham vase crashed against the side of the sink and was shattered. . . .

The instinct to start everything with the supposition that whatever happened she was in the right, and things and events must be arranged to support that supposition, was still so strong in Jacqueline that before she realized what she was doing she had grouped all the objects in the pantry as witnesses to her virtue. She rescued the fragments of the Birmingham vase from the sink and arranged them on the table with the kitten placed in an attitude of contrition behind them, and herself on the floor searching for fragments, and was weeping genuine tears of sorrow over the iniquity of the feline race by the time Soeur Ursule returned from the Chapel.

"The kitten!" she sobbed, flinging herself into Soeur Ursule's arms, "the kitten knocked it over!"

Soeur Ursule kissed and comforted her, though tears of sorrow for the Birmingham vase were trickling from beneath her spectacles, and heartily agreed with her in attaching every scrap of blame to the kitten.

"You did no wrong, my cabbage," crooned Soeur Ursule, "you filled the vase on the table exactly as I told you. It was my fault. I should not have left the kitten in the pantry. There, there, do not grieve, my Jacqueline, the fault lay in myself and the kitten. Ah, it is bad, that one!"

The kitten, its tail erected like a banner of protest at a Hyde Park demonstration, and slightly twitching at the top, leaped to the floor and stalked out of the pantry with incomparable dignity.

For the rest of that day the Convent was plunged in gloom. Soeur Ursule had loved the Birmingham vase as a mother loves her only child. She had filled it with flowers and placed it beneath the Crucifix every day for forty-five years. She uttered no word of complaint, but she went about all day with red rims to her eyes, and every living creature in the Convent mourned with her. A very lovely Venetian vase, the colour of sea water, and fluted like a lily, was unearthed from a dark cupboard, filled with golden chrysanthemums and placed beneath the Crucifix, where it reared its beauty like a good deed in a naughty world, but Soeur Ursule was not comforted.... No one was comforted.... Jacqueline least of all.

Jacqueline, the victim of the kitten's sin, was the heroine of the day, a position which in the past had always given her exquisite pleasure, but, somehow, to-day there was no pleasure in it. Her power of seeing herself as she wanted to see herself had, to a certain extent, left her during the last month, and she was beginning to suffer a very little from that most humiliating and unpleasant capacity of seeing herself as she was. For the first time since she had started going to the Convent she went home miserable, and Rachell chose that very evening to burst upon her with the awful news that the nuns wished her to be prepared for Communion, and to make her first confession in December.

From that moment Jacqueline was plunged back once more into her old condition of morbid fear and misery. Only two words existed for her in the vocabulary—sin and confession. Only two facts in the wide world were clear to her—that her sins, especially the appalling lie of the Birmingham vase and the kitten, were the worst in the whole wide world, and that she could not, simply could not, confess them. It would be difficult to say what in the ordeal before her terrified her the most—the thought of having really, at last, to face herself as she was, the humiliation of letting another into the secret of her terrible crimes, or the fact that, in all probability, she would be made to tell Soeur Ursule what she had done and would lose Soeur Ursule's love. In all this one thing bulked large—was the last unbearable ounce in the load that crushed her—the Birmingham vase. Somehow this sin, the disobedience of it, the deceiving of Soeur Ursule, seemed more terrible than all her other sins and more impossible of confession. W. S. Gilbert suggested that the word "Basingstoke" could be a talisman to calm the nerves, but for the rest of her life the word "Birmingham" was sufficient to send Jacqueline into a perfect ague of remembered agitation.

Long nights of nervous terror were followed by long days of weary exhaustion, and Jacqueline grew so thin that her waistband had to be taken in again. Neither the sisters nor Rachell could discover what was the matter. They administered tonics and cream and kisses, and worried dreadfully, but nothing did any good. Only the kitten could have explained but the kitten, with the lowest opinion possible of the morals of the parlour, had stalked out of it forever and become a kitchen cat.

Only one gleam of hope lit up the darkness of Jacqueline's nights and days—the hope that she might be taken very ill before the awful day arrived. But, alas, on the day before *the* day—the day before Colette went to see grandpapa—she was perfectly well, without even a cold in the head. There was no hope now. No hope unless she did something really terrible, such as refusing to make her Confession with the others, or running away, or drowning herself. But somehow she did not want to do any of these things. Deep down in her was the conviction that if she could only go through with this thing it would be well with her. She was like the patient who shrinks in agony from the surgeon's knife yet knows that not to go through with the operation would be worse than to go through with it.

So, on this day before *the* day she stood at the parlour window looking out on a slate-grey sea speckled with feathery wisps of white waves, and knew that she would go through with it. Three other girls were in like case with her, yet they appeared quite unmoved. Rosy-cheeked and placid, they did their morning's work of sewing and copying as usual, and chattered as usual about their clothes, and their hair, and their relations. Only Jacqueline was silent, with a band of iron clamped round her throat and her fingers paralysed as though by cramp.

In the afternoon they had to go down to the Chapel where Father Lefevre, the priest who served St. Raphael's, was waiting to help them with their preparation.

Father Lefevre was very old and very wise, and very experienced in the handling of children. He spoke to them sweetly and simply. "God sees you as you are," he told them. "God knows all the secrets of your hearts already. Then why should you fear to tell them out loud to Him? Forget the priest sitting in the confessional. While he sits there he is no longer a man. He is but the channel of God's forgiveness flowing to you." The other girls were touched and encouraged, but Jacqueline thought it was all very well, it wasn't quite as simple as that. Certainly, Father Lefevre the priest would be the channel of God's forgiveness, but on the other hand, Father Lefevre the man, whom she loved and whose affection she prized, would by this time to-morrow know all about the Birmingham vase. . . . At the thought of to-morrow she gripped her hands together, and the perspiration trickled down her back.

Father Lefevre blessed them and left them in the Chapel with their pencils and paper. The other girls sucked the points of their pencils, pondered and searched their memories, every now and then brightening and scribbling, as they pounced gleefully on yet another peccadillo to add to the list, but Jacqueline wrote slowly and steadily with her cramped fingers. There was no need for her to search for her sins. During the last month they had been burning themselves upon her memory as though etched with a point of red hot steel. Her mind felt sore and full of pain. For the last month she had been looking steadily at Jacqueline du Frocq, and the humiliation of the sight was almost more than she could bear. Last upon her list was the sin of the Birmingham vase. There had come a terrible moment when she had been tempted to leave it out, but she had not yielded. . . . That would have been to damn her soul in hell indeed.

She went through the rest of the day's work mechanically, went home mechanically, went to bed mechanically, raising a cold cheek for the kisses of her solicitous family, and lay awake most of the night. She got up the next morning white and heavy eyed, but calm with the calmness that visits the condemned criminal on the day of execution. She felt like a sleepwalker, dazed and dreamy. Merciful nature had given her a draught of poppies.

It was, perhaps, fitting that this day of crisis in Jacqueline's life should be a day of storm. In the road where grandpapa lived it was comparatively sheltered, but as she climbed the steep steps to the Convent and the Church, the wind came screaming down to meet her, and she could hear the thundering of the waves on the rocks beyond the old grey walls. Usually wind terrified her but to-day, though it knocked all the breath out of her body and flung her reeling against the wall, she did not mind it. The thing she faced was so big to her that it dwarfed all minor trials.

The moment came quite early in the morning. The girls went, with Soeur Monique clucking beside them to give them courage, to St. Raphael's and knelt down in a pew near the confessional. The other girls, giggling a little, pushed Jacqueline to the end of the line so that she should be first. She submitted.

The old Church was very dark. The candles burning before the statue of the Virgin glimmered like fireflies in a dark forest and the flowers were dim and sweet in the shadows. Beyond the thick wall the gale was growling and snarling, but not a tremor shook the Church, not a flicker of draught touched the candle flames or the flower petals. Inside these walls was a peace and safety that nothing could shake.

Jacqueline knelt in her pew cold and rigid, with that band of iron clasped round her throat. As in a dream she saw Father Lefevre come in. As in a dream she got up, walked to the confessional and knelt down. Father Lefevre murmured some words she did not even hear and then waited for her to speak. But, horror of horrors, she could not. The band of iron was drawing tighter and tighter, constricting her throat so that no sound could come. For what seemed hours she struggled with it and then, quite suddenly, it was gone and she heard herself speaking fluently, calmly, with no effort. She seemed to be standing outside herself, marvelling at her own ease. And then she found it was over. Even the confession of the Birmingham vase incident was over, all in a few minutes, this dreadful ordeal that she had been dreading for months. It was over in the time it takes to tell one's beads and Father Lefevre was talking to her, quite calm and apparently unshattered by the recitation of her sins.

He was the perfect child's confessor, realizing children's acute power of suffering and aware of the, to them, enormous gravity of the little molehills that to their tiny stature seem such mountains, treating nothing lightly yet instilling courage and confidence into them. To-day Jacqueline heard hardly a word that he said, but in days to come she listened greedily.

Now she got up and groped her way back to her seat, dazed and unable to realize anything except that it was over, and ready to laugh hysterically that what she had dreaded for so long should be over so soon—and yet not quite over. Something commanded her, yet remained to be done and must be done at once while this new ease was yet with her. She got up from her knees, went out through the Church porch and in through the Convent door, and ran along to the pantry where Soeur Ursule was doing the flowers—that very same pantry where the crime had occurred.

Standing in the middle of the pantry floor she poured out the whole story to Soeur Ursule, and then watched in agony to see hatred and loathing spread themselves over Soeur Ursule's face. But they did not. Dismay and bewilderment were apparent upon the poor lady's countenance as she groped her way through this confusing narrative of kittens and chrysanthemums and vases and sinks, but when it was finished and the matter clear to her nothing was to be seen gleaming behind her spectacles but love. She clasped Jacqueline to her.

"Ah, my little cabbage," she crooned, "how glad I am that you have told me. How brave of you to tell me."

"I shouldn't have if Father Lefevre hadn't said I was to," said Jacqueline, determined now to be truthful or perish in the attempt.

"Ah, the so sweet little cabbage!" murmured Soeur Ursule, and renewed the kisses.

Her last trial over Jacqueline began to sob with relief. Soeur Ursule, sympathetic to a fault, began to sob also. Clasped in each other's arms they both sobbed. The kitten appeared in the doorway, surveyed them cynically, moved its whiskers contemptuously, sat down on the floor, stuck up one hind leg like the mast of a ship, and attended to the more personal parts of its toilet. Then it arose, moved its whiskers again with a further exhibition of contempt and departed, its tail stiffly raised and slightly twitching with the amused tolerance of an unbeliever.

For the rest of the morning Jacqueline felt nothing but a sense of exquisite relief and overwhelming fatigue. After dinner, while the others sat chatting round the refectory fire, she curled herself up in a corner of the armchair and fell deeply asleep. She slept for what seemed centuries, right down at the bottom of an ocean of sleep, with depth upon depth of cool peace around and above her. Very slowly at last she rose to the surface, floating up as though borne upon strong arms. Very gently the light pierced through the water and she opened her eyes. Good heavens! She was to have fetched Colette at half-past four and now it must be midnight! She glanced at the clock. It was three. She had only slept for an hour and a half. She sat up and rubbed her eyes. She was quite alone in the refectory but from the parlour overhead came a subdued hum. The others were having their sewing lesson, but good Soeur Monique must have left her to have her sleep out. She sat quite still. There was slowly growing within her a radiant happiness that was like a warm flame burning. She felt exhausted and yet alight. She almost expected to see the radiance that was within her lighting up the walls of the refectory, creeping over them as the crocus glow of March steals out over the winter turf. She looked out through the window and saw the tormented sea whipped to a white fury by the wind and the grey sky storm-twisted. Warm and glowing herself she felt sorry for them—all their blue glory eclipsed. Outside the refectory windows was a little narrow rock garden planted on a ledge of rock and protected by a wall. Jacqueline ran out of the refectory into the passage and out through the little door into the ledge of garden. The rain had left off for the moment and the sou'wester, wild and rough, was not cold. Jacqueline went to the wall, which reached nearly to her armpits, and clung there. As, this morning, the storm had had no terrors for her in her misery so now it had none for her in her happiness. Her joy was so huge that it bathed everything around her in its glory.

She clung to the wall and shut her eyes. The wind that buffeted her was so strong that she gasped for breath, yet so soft in its touch that it was like rose petals falling on her cheeks. Its roar in her ears was no longer terrible, but like a great organ swell of praise and triumph. And all the time that flame of happiness in her was glowing. Behind her closed eyelids she thought she could see its little crocus flames on the crest of each tortured wave, comforting the sea for its grey turmoil. Out from her streamed that lovely flame of comfort, into her streamed the touch and the sound of the wind. She and the storm were one and round them, uniting them, was a ring of pure and endless light, of a depth and height and breadth inconceivable, the same light that had lit the glow in her and set rolling the prelude of the storm. Clinging to her wall, her eyes tight shut, she slipped back again for a moment, as a child may, into the glory from which she had come, knew what cannot be held in the meshes of the mind and saw from behind closed lids what would have blinded open eyes. The gates of heaven were to shut again and bar her out but who that has seen ever forgets their opening, or ceases to watch for the crack of light under the door?

IV

Jacqueline and Colette, when grandpapa's door closed behind them, were caught by the wind and tossed up the street as though they were creatures borne upon wings. And, indeed, they felt like it. Ecstasy possessed them both. Jacqueline was still trailing clouds of glory and all Colette's fears were forgotten in the joy of escape. The storm that indoors had seemed part of the evil world she had just discovered seemed now to be a beautiful thing, one with Jacqueline and the lovely warmth she had brought with her. The feet of the rain, running along beside them, were the feet of a lover and the shouting gale that lifted and carried them was a gay and boisterous friend upon the way.

Running, bouncing, clinging together they blew up the hill, panting, chuckling, and laughing. It was not until they butted into her that they saw Rachell coming to meet them.

"Mother!" they shrieked, and clutched her wet black cloak.

Rachell, her slender figure swaying beneath the blows of the wind, her breath coming in gasps, seemed less able to stand up against the storm than her thistledown daughters, but she had come, it appeared, to their rescue.

"I came with Brovard in the cart to fetch you all," she panted, "the wind is getting worse and worse. I thought I could help you up the hill. You poor little darlings, blowing about in this!"

A huge gust nearly took her off her feet, and Jacqueline and Colette fastened themselves on to her, one on each side, to keep her down.

"Get under my cloak," she said.

They crept underneath and held it down round them. It was tremendous fun. The two little girls, reacting from fear and ecstasy, chortled and giggled as at the hugest joke. Rachell ached with love for them. Nestling under her cloak they seemed closer to her than they had seemed since she had carried them within her.

They got up the hill, blew round a corner into shelter and stood waiting under a lamp-post for the arrival of the cart with the other three.

Rachell looked down at her two little daughters. How strange their eyes were in the flickering lamp light, how deep and mysterious. Their lips were laughing and childish but their eyes held incommunicable secrets. Where had they been voyaging that day? Into what heights and depths where she could not follow their thought? Jacqueline, she knew, had had a great experience, Colette, perhaps, had had one too. But they would never be able to tell her about it. Children, she thought, with the dew of heaven scarcely dry upon their wings and eyes and ears that still can see and hear, tread sweet wild ways and have no words to tell of them. When they have learnt to pick and choose a telling word and a descriptive phrase the wings have fallen from their shoulders and the old ways are closed. Age has little left to tell of but memories and the trembling hope of returning one day to the old paths.

Chapter 6

I

CHRISTMAS day at Bon Repos was something terrific. The du Frocqs took the whole of December preparing for it and the whole of January recovering from it. From love of old association they kept up all the old Yuletide customs and to be abreast of the times they added to them the modern English customs, and to both they added strenuous religious observances. That they did not all collapse completely must be put down to the sustaining power of the Island air.

At the beginning of December Rachell and Sophie began to be frantically busy making puddings and pies and cakes, while the children, planted out in corners of rooms, behind sheltering barricades of furniture, made each other astounding presents in an atmosphere of secrecy and excitement thick enough to be cut with a knife.

The fever point of preparation was reached on the morning of Christmas Eve. Everyone was amazingly punctual at breakfast and amazingly anxious to get through with it and start decorating. The day before armfuls of holly had been cut from the hedges and put ready in an enormous pile on the hall floor, each smooth leaf and polished berry holding a gay reflection of sunlight in its gleaming little mirror. For the weather was obliging. A clear, sparkling, blue-washed sky and sea, winter trees purple in the shadows and a rosy brown where the sun touched them, tawny winter grass crested with white frost in the early morning and crystal drops at mid-day, and here and there, in sheltered folds of the cliff a few scattered flowers of the golden gorse. The rocks beside the little crisply breaking waves were quite warm to the touch and the rock sparrows, flitting from crimson seaweed-covered boulder to yellow-lichened cliff, were chattering as though it were spring. The robins were everywhere. There were three in the Bon Repos garden; hopping up and down the moss-grown path where the Canterbury bells grew in summer, chirping brazenly at the front door, cheeking the hens at the back door and boldly following Sophie into the kitchen to demand their Christmas largesse of crumbs and bacon rind. And they got it, for Sophie, like all Islanders, looked upon the robins as sacred birds. It was the robin who first brought fire to the Island. Flying across the sea with a torch in his beak he burnt his breast, but on he flew, undaunted, a little suffering speck of a bird lost between sea and sky. When he arrived at the Island, with his breast feathers burnt and raw and red, all the other birds were so sorry for him that they each gave him a feather, except the owl who, selfish creature, would not, and in consequence no longer dares show his face in the Island by day.

The decorating of the house with greenery and the wrapping up of all the presents kept Bon Repos in a hubbub all the morning. Rachell sailed serenely about her household duties, picking her way through balls of string, streamers of coloured paper, mountains of greenery, pots of paint required by Colin for some mysterious present he was making for his father, Maximilian running round in circles with his tongue out, and all the children tearing up and down stairs half crazy with excitement. Nothing seemed to disturb her tranquillity, but André and Ranulph had long since fled to the comparative peace of the farmyard. Colette, to be out of harm's way, was shut in the kitchen with Sophie, where she sat in a fat heap on the floor, breathing deeply and making dough babies with currant eyes, and gingerbread animals of no recognizable breed. Marmalade, the pagan creature, had gone mousing in the barn. She had no religious sense and the great festivals of the Church left her quite cold. In this she differed from Maximilian, who was a devout dog. He always went to the stable at midnight on Christmas Eve and knelt side by side in the sweet hay with the cattle and he listened very politely indeed, with his tongue out, when his family sang carols on Christmas Day.

Lunch consisted of cold meat and bread and all the remnants of last week's puddings heaped together in a dish and disguised beneath custard. This menu, resorted to by Sophie in moments of stress, usually produced an indignant outcry, but to-day, so great was the general goodwill, it was quite favourably received. Colin actually demanded a second helping of pudding and that though his first, beneath its yellow blanket, had contained a spoonful of tapioca—his particular detestation—a square inch of treacle tart, a slab of blancmange and the stones of three prunes now defunct.

After lunch hats and coats were put on and André brought round the landau, for they were all going in to St. Pierre. André, Rachell, Michelle, and Peronelle were going to confession, Sophie was going gallivanting with Jacquemin Gossilin, and Ranulph had promised to take the three younger children to look at the Christmas sights. The journey into St. Pierre took a long time for Lupin found the weight of the entire household, including Sophie in her stays and an electric blue coat and skirt and a scarlet hat, so preposterous that André, Ranulph, and Colin, had to get out and walk at every tiniest slope. But who minded? The air, sun-warmed yet cool and fresh as sea water, seemed to run through their veins like frosted fire, and all around them the world lay twinkling in a hushed expectancy of miracle, jewelled and glowing and palpitant, rich with stored treasure, yet held back by the fingers of the frost from the giving and the bursting and the shouting of the spring. Yet though the spring of the earth was far distant the spring of birth was in their hearts, and inwardly, beneath all the excitement and the fun, they adored and worshipped. Even Ranulph, who did not believe a word of the Christmas legend, and André, who was doubtful, caught the infection and for the moment were among the worshippers.

II

St. Pierre was reached at last and Lupin, heaving his flanks with relief, was unharnessed and established at his inn. His family bade him good-bye affectionately and pursued their way down the hill, separating at the foot of the steps leading to St. Raphael's. Sophie, her face purple from the tightness of her stays and the nip of the frost in the air, went to La Rue Clubin to find Jacquemin Gossilin and Ranulph, with Colette clinging to his hand, and Jacqueline and Colin dancing in front of him, went downhill to the town.

"Let's go to La Rue Clubin," chirped Colin.

"We are in charge of two fair ladies," Ranulph reminded him, "one doesn't take ladies to La Rue Clubin."

Colin looked over his shoulder and, meeting Ranulph's twinkling eyes, perceived dimly that men and women, inhabiting the same world for eleven hours in the day flee at the twelfth hour into a little jealously guarded haven of refreshment from each other.

"We'll go to the harbour till dark," said Ranulph, "and then we'll go to the market place and see the Christmas sights."

Down through the twisted streets they went, Colette riding on Ranulph's back, now and then, to rest her fat legs, Jacqueline and Colin chattering like magpies. Jacqueline, to whom her recent joys had come like the breaking through of spring to a little bird, seemed to have lost sight of all her fears and miseries, and chirped and hopped with an unself-consciousness akin to Peronelle's. Ranulph marvelled at her. Amazing that two silly old nuns could have worked such a change in so short a time. Well, Jacqueline owed this to him. He felt extremely puffed up.

They walked right out to the end of the pier and settled themselves in a sheltered corner where they could watch the ships. Here, out of the wind and full in the sun's eye, it was as warm as June. The Island could produce days of storm unrivalled for nastiness in any other part of the world, but she could also produce midwinter days of warmth and loveliness that were like gifts of unexpected joy in old age.

Ranulph, his eyes narrowed, looked from the sun-dappled waters of the harbour to the blue dome of the sky curved graciously over its glimmer, and was astounded to find himself glad to be alive. This sudden resurrection of happiness in his life was as surprising as this glowing day in the middle of winter. It was as though pink carnations had bloomed suddenly in the snow. He looked at the children grouped round him and his eyes caressed them. He owed this flowering to them. Well, he had repaid Jacqueline. He'd repay them all before he'd done. Here his old mocking habit caught him for a moment, and he jeered at himself for a sentimental fool. He had always fled sentiment. Was it to trip him up in his old age and make a prisoner of him? Well, let it. Sentiment might be as softening to the hard iron of character as warm rain to frost-bound earth, but green things, apparently, spring from its falling. He determined then and there to have a green, if silly, old age.

The children were equally happy. Jacqueline was jabbering about her Christmas presents. No one listened to her but she didn't mind. Her talk was only her deep-charged happiness bursting to the surface in a froth of bubbles. Colette, protected against possible cold by two flannel petticoats and an overcoat, looked as fat and sleepy as an overfed nestling. Bunched in her sunny corner she blinked at the sea and wondered about who knew what?

Colin looked at the shipping. He was capable of looking at shipping for hours without moving. Here at the pier head, swung out over the sea as though in the crow's nest of a ship, he could imagine himself sailing the ocean in a windjammer, and as he sat he swayed a little as though with its motion. Down in the harbour the ships were lazy, revelling in their Christmas rest. Sails were furled and no smoke twisted up from the funnels of the steamers. The little rowing boats along the harbour walls were empty and tethered like resting beasts in their stalls. There seemed not a soul on board any of them. The silence was absolute and wrapped in it Colin's spirit dipped and soared in his windjammer across the free spaces of the world; until his left foot went to sleep and the pain of it jerked him back into reality. He got up, stamped, and swore.

"Colin," rebuked Ranulph.

Colin smiled sheepishly.

"Why does it always make one feel better to swear?" he asked.

"Because you are forbidden to do it, and freedom is your desire. The human boy invariably suffers from the delusion that to wriggle himself free of fetters is to be free."

"Isn't it?" gaped Colin.

"No." Ranulph puffed at his pipe and frowned at the ocean. He had promised himself as long ago as his and Colin's visit to Mère Tangrouille to enlighten Colin as to the nature of freedom, lest Colin should tread the same path as he had trod and eat the same dead sea apple, but the part of an instructor of youth did not come easily to him.

"I *must* be free," said Colin suddenly and explosively, "and I *must* be a sailor."

"Is that a free life?" inquired Ranulph.

"Yes," said Colin, "of course."

"Why of course? Just think. What could be more restricted than life on a ship? A ship's not large, you know. I have known men on shipboard who felt like a hyena in a cage. I've felt that way myself."

"But one sails all round the world," objected Colin.

"In a cage," said Ranulph, "but be a sailor by all means. You want freedom, and the sailor is the perfect type of a free man."

"Er?" queried Colin, "but you've just said not."

"He imprisons himself that he may put a girdle round the earth. His walk is limited to the length and breadth of a narrow deck, yet he looks from horizon to horizon, and is on nodding terms with all the stars."

"Er?" Poor Colin, admiring Ranulph and having implicit faith in his judgment nevertheless found his arguments very difficult to follow.

"You can be sure of this, my son," said Ranulph, shooting out a lean forefinger, "whatever you want in life you must go for its opposite. If you want riches woo the lady poverty. If you want freedom chain your body and mind to discipline. Everything goes by opposites. Take this piece of advice from a man who hasn't done it, and who therefore knows."

Colin sighed. Ranulph continued, smiling sardonically at his own flights of fancy.

"Yes, it's a sighing matter, my son, and difficult of comprehension at your tender age. And it's no easy matter, if you long for light and glitter, to trample on the diamonds within easy reach and leap for the stars—it's so uncertain one'll get there. . . . But how explain? . . . Hopeless . . . I can only sow the seed. . . . In ten years' time ask your mother the meaning of the word paradox. It's an important word. Come to think of it the Christmas legend is a paradox, if ever there was one. Who'd have thought of looking for the courts of heaven in a stable? . . . And one day, mind you, ask your mother what your uncle Jean did and then don't do it."

Colin gave it up, but retired from argument with the impression that discipline was somehow good, and that Uncle Ranulph had no objection to his being a sailor. To these two facts his mind clung retentively.

But while they talked and wondered and brooded over the harbour warmth drained from the earth and the evening of Christmas Eve was upon them. A little flock of clouds had spread themselves in a fleecy network over the blue sky, and as the sun sank lower they turned pink while below them the sea, reflecting the diaper of pink and blue, turned lilac colour.

"Look! Look!" cried Jacqueline. They looked. It was an effect of light such as Ranulph, even in all his travels, had never seen. Brighter and brighter shone the pink and the blue, and deeper and deeper glowed the lavender until it was the colour of a purple iris. Ranulph gaped.

"The wine-dark seas of Greece," he murmured, "I never thought to see them round the Island."

Then quite suddenly the colours had gone. The sun, jealous for his treasure, would not leave them there for night to play with. He pulled them away with him over the rim of the sea, and the sky, robbed of the glory, grew pale and a little sad. The sea remembered that it was winter, and sighed a little at the sudden chill in the air. Along the harbour wall and up and down the streets of St. Pierre the lights pricked out the twilight like pinholes in a dusky curtain.

Ranulph leapt to his feet and pulled the children to theirs.

"It's the twenty-fourth of December," he reminded them, "and chestnuts are to be roasted in the market place for your pleasure."

Squeaking with delight they ran along the pier in front of him, the little girls' tam-o'-shanters alight like holly berries and Colin's substantial boots going clip-clop like the hooves of an impatient pony.

Along the harbour wall they went, away from the hushed sea into the crowded streets. St. Pierre was now like a town of the Arabian Nights. The shop windows were aglow with colour and the streets with holiday finery. Oranges and lemons, and pink hams, and coloured sweets. Rosy faces and sailors' blue blouses, and the red caps of children. Shops and crowds together threaded ribbons of colour in and out between the old grey houses, and up and down over the cobbled streets. And the houses and cobbles were not to be outdone this Christmas Eve. Lights lit behind crimson curtains and Christmas trees set in open windows were brilliant in their grey setting, and in the crannies of the cobbles frost-fires sparkled.

Like the glowing heart in a nest of coloured flame was the market place. A great bonfire was leaping and glowing in its centre, and all round it were booths loaded with oranges and apples. Hither and thither in the crowd went the chestnut men with their little red fires in iron braziers, and floating before and behind them went the delicious scent of roasting chestnuts. The crowd, laughing and joking and jostling to get to the chestnut men, was a kaleidoscope of colour, shifting and changing against the orange hues of leaping fire and the dim blue of the quiet night.

Ranulph, with Colette in his arms for safety, bought chestnuts for the children from a blue-bloused man with gold rings in his ears, who called down the blessing of heaven upon them and added an extra chestnut for Colette because her eyes were blue as the Virgin's mantle. After which acts of piety he swore horribly at a little thieving boy, and made for the public house across the way. Ranulph, at this, with Jacqueline's fingers clutching rather fearfully at his hand, thought it time to make for home and glanced round for Colin.

Not far from the bonfire, behind an immense pile of oranges, sat Mère Tangrouille, with Colin bowing politely before her and presenting her with a wooden mouse carved by himself from a piece of driftwood. It had pink ears cut out of pieces of sticking plaster and nailed on with large black nails. Its tail was of string. Colin had taken immense pains with it, and presented it to Mère Tangrouille as though he were Solomon laying spices at the foot of the Queen of Sheba. Mère Tangrouille took the gift in the spirit in which it was offered. It was a love gift, fashioned with care for her delight, and as such she accepted it. Her black bonnet trembled with delight as she kissed Colin, and her twinkling little eyes were moist. She swore that he was a cherub from above and that she would keep the mouse for ever. A mouse, she said, was exactly what she wanted. Her cat had killed all hers and home, she averred, was no home without a mouse. Colin withdrew from her embrace as soon as he decently could, clicked his heels together and bowed again. Ranulph, watching over the heads of the crowd, marvelled at the unself-conscious beauty of his politeness. These children, brought up in a farmhouse at the edge of the waves, companioned by birds and beasts and plants, proved that courtesy is ingrained in natural things. Even so would a wagtail bow or a dahlia pass the time of day with the wind. Imprisoned as he was in the chaste company of Jacqueline and Colette, Ranulph, to Colin's surprise, did not come and speak to Mère Tangrouille, but nodded to her kindly from a distance and called to Colin to come. Mère Tangrouille, nodding back, appeared to bear no ill will for this seeming rudeness. Had not the money for the rent, her Christmas present from the Jean du Frocq that was, reached her by that morning's post? But Colin did not know this, and as he trotted through the crowd at Ranulph's heels he felt a little puzzled. He felt that in courtesy Uncle Ranulph should have spoken to her. Was it because Jacqueline was there that he had not? Did even grown-up men sometimes hide their friendships from their womenkind? He wondered. He had wondered about it earlier in the afternoon when Uncle Ranulph would not take Jacqueline to La Rue Clubin. He wondered if all this had anything to do with Uncle Ranulph's confusing talk about freedom. Uncle Ranulph said that if you wanted anything very badly you had to look for it in the opposite direction from the natural one. It seemed natural to Colin to look for freedom in La Rue Clubin. But was he perhaps wrong? He felt hot in the head and gave it up, but a slight seed of doubt as to the desirableness of searching for freedom in La Rue Clubin was sown in him. Ranulph, had he known, would have slept easier that night.

The fun in the market place was only just beginning to rise to its height, and gather impetus for the raid on the public houses, when Ranulph sternly led his charges away. They must not keep their father and mother and Lupin waiting, he said, and they must go early to bed in preparation for the morrow. The children, their thoughts turning to their stockings, submitted with a good grace and followed him up the gay ribbons of the streets, in and out of the old grey brooding houses that had seen so many Christmas Eves come and go, over the old cobbles that had spread themselves through the centuries beneath the feet of so great a multitude of children. Overhead the stars shone frostily brilliant in a clear sky, just as they had shone when the Island was only a great grey rock set in the hungry sea and far away in Bethlehem a Child was born.

III

Sophie said good-bye to Jacquemin Gossilin when the fun in the market place was at its height, for she too wanted to get home to Bon Repos in good time. And also she was meditating a daring adventure on the way home. She had determined to pay a visit to the fairy well in the water-lane and find out once for all if she was destined to marry Jacquemin or if she was not. The peasants say that during the eight days before Christmas the supernatural powers are all active, fairies and demons as well as angels throng the lanes and the streams and the farmyards, and any girl who has the courage to look in a fairy well will see her fate looking back at her from the water, either the face of her husband or, if she is fated to die unmarried, a grinning death's head.

Sophie hurried up through the streets of St. Pierre and along the country roads towards the water-lane. Her legs were trembling with terror and her heart thumped and knocked like a threshing machine. This tampering with fairy magic on Christmas Eve was, she knew, dangerous, and looked upon with disfavour by the priests. There are so many angels about at Christmas time that the fairies and demons, jealous and vindictive, and ready to go to any lengths to show their power, are best left alone. Sophie, as she hurried along, glancing apprehensively at every dark bush and every moon-thrown shadow, was remembering all the stories of Christmas Eve disaster that she had ever heard. There was the man who, returning home late on one of the eight nights before Christmas, was led astray by the "faeu Bellengier" and instead of going to his own farm went to the edge of the cliff and fell over it to his death. Then there were those other men who found themselves followed or preceded by large black dogs which no threats could scare away and no blows could touch. And then, again, others who had found themselves beset by demons in the shape of white rabbits who went hopping along under their feet, tripping them up at every turn. Then there was the girl who, with mortal sin unconfessed upon her, went to the very well where Sophie was hurrying now and saw six skeletons grouped round it, gazing into the water. She had screamed and dropped dead as a door nail. At the thought of this last story Sophie stopped and pressed her hand against her stays on the left hand side. Her heart was thumping so with terror that she could not go another step. Then she glanced down at her best electric blue coat and skirt, the colour of shimmering water in the moonlight, and courage stole back to her. The sight of it made her feel herself to be a beautiful creature, as lovely as the deep velvety shadows under the trees and the frost stars glittering on the road, bound with them into a community of beauty by the encircling moonlight. This sense of comradeship buoyed her up and she went on again. She rounded the corner where the foxgloves grew in summer and entered the little round tunnel of the lane. It was inky black to-day, and plunged downhill as though it led to the nether regions. From far away below came the murmur of the sea against the rocks, sounding to Sophie's excited fancy like the moaning of souls in torment. It struck her that if she were to drop dead as a door nail at the fairy well—as might very well happen to her, meddling with magic on Christmas Eve as she was—her soul would join their number. She shivered, but her anxiety to know her fate drove her on. She could not wait for time to disclose it to her, she must do the forbidden thing and force the curtains apart from the future's face. A break in the close-knit branches of the trees over the well let through a moonbeam that lit up the smooth mirror of the water as though a lamp were hung over it. The ferns and grasses held it up to Sophie in delicate fingers. She knelt down and laid a silver piece in the grass—an offering to the fairy of the well. All around her, so it seemed, Things were passing backwards and forwards, following the tinkling stream down to the sea, coming up from the sea to the waters of the earth. Very populous the lane was to-night, full of the murmuring of unheard voices and the footfall of feet that left no print behind them. Sophie felt cold and clammy with terror, and there seemed a mist before her eyes so that though she was bending with her face over the water she could see nothing. Then the mist cleared and she saw the surface of the water, clear and smooth as polished ebony and reflecting a myriad of stars in its depths. It seemed to Sophie that the whole sky was there in miniature. All the scattered points of light seemed to have been picked out and gathered together in the well, it was a little tiny heaven of atom width lying under the immensity of sky, so small that she could span it with her arms yet holding eternity. Nearer and nearer she leaned, gazing at that depth of darkness and those crystal points of light, so fascinated by the beauty of it that she forgot all about Jacquemin Gossilin and the grinning death's head. The night breathed around her and the noiseless Things continued their passing and repassing behind and around her, and still she gazed and gazed, sinking as it were lower and lower into that mirrored heaven, her identity lost and submerged and drowning in it, so that time stopped and only eternity circled and wheeled round her. A little breeze, travelling up from the sea, ruffled the surface of the well. Little ripples broke across it and the stars were drowned. The Things, disturbed in their passing by that healthful current of air, seemed to have blown away into the shadows. Sophie was once more Sophie, sitting in the cold frosty grass in the water-lane gazing at a pool, with the night around her and the bare interlaced fingers of the trees patterning the sky over her head. She got up and, stumbling down the dark water-lane, turned to the right into the steep, waterless one. Here, away from the mysterious influences of the water, she came to herself. She felt very stiff and cold and extraordinarily silly. She supposed she had been mesmerized by gazing so long at the water—they said if you looked too long at anything bright it went to your head. Then a pang of disappointment went through her. She had not seen Jacquemin Gossilin in the water. But then neither had she seen the death's head. What *had* she seen? A heaven that she could span with her arms and infinity so presented to her that she could comprehend it. Was that her future? Well, it was a future that every soul could have for the taking and the only one that may be foretold with certainty. She felt disappointed, and yet at the same time amazingly reassured as she went up the lane and out into the road of stunted oaks that led to Bon Repos.

Black against the sky were the chimneys and the roof of the old farmhouse, friendly as the stars were the few lighted windows that linked hands with them to brighten night. Under the stable door a line of light showed. André, late as it was, must be busy there. Sophie remembered again that it was Christmas Eve when angels as well as demons are abroad. All stables are holy on Christmas Eve. It struck Sophie suddenly, as she looked at that line of light under the door, that they hold a heaven that can be clasped in the arms and an infinity so small that it can be seen and comprehended.

IV

A cow was sick and André was late in the stable that night. When he came out, leaving, according to the Island custom on Christmas Eve, fresh hay in the stalls and everything clean and sweet, he forbore to lock the door and left it just unlatched. This was so that Maximilian, when midnight struck and Christmas Day was born, could find his way in and kneel with the other animals. André laughed at himself as he pocketed the unused key, and wondered what on earth Ranulph would think of him if he knew. But he was not ashamed. He loved the Island legends; his mother had taught them to him, and whenever he could he reverenced and followed them. On his way to the house he noticed that Sophie had left Maximilian unchained in his kennel, and also that Maximilian was awake and waiting. His eyes in the darkness were like two bright stars. André patted him as he passed and Maximilian's tongue shot out like a long pink snake, and coiled itself for a moment damply and lovingly round André's finger. Marmalade was also awake and in the yard, but she was not waiting for anything. She was curvetting about, her green eyes like the lights of the "faeu Bellengier," and her tail twitching. Sometimes she would crouch on the ground watching something invisible, then she would leap at it, swerve aside from it, spit at it, and then tear round the yard as though chasing it. But whatever it was she liked it. There was an unholy glee in her face and the lights in her eyes were the wicked lights such as witches tie on the ends of their broomsticks. Whatever it was she was chasing André was quite sure it had no business in his yard on Christmas Eve. Had it not been that Maximilian was absorbed in the stable door André would hardly have liked to leave him alone with Marmalade and the thing she was playing with. But so engrossed was Maximilian with holy things that he seemed safe from the unholy. . . . André let himself into the house and went upstairs to Rachell.

Ranulph's little room over the stable had a window that commanded both the stable door and Maximilian's kennel. Ranulph, sleepless, was sitting and smoking at it as the night crept on. A little fire of vraic was burning in his grate but there was no other light. Only the moonbeams slid from wall to ceiling and mingled their silver with the golden glow of the vraic. It was Ranulph's first Christmas Eve in the Island since his young manhood, and he should have been thinking solemn thoughts. The past should have passed before him like a depressing pageant, and remorse and regret for a misspent life should have been with him in the room. But in reality he was trying to think of nothing at all except the peace and warmth of the room and his own sense of well-being. He preferred not to inquire into the cause of his satisfaction. He had no wish to admit to himself that he had utterly capitulated at last. All his life he had pursued complete independence as the highest good and now he had abruptly given up the chase and allowed himself to become hopelessly involved in place and person once again. He had no wish to look himself in the face and own up to his weakness. Sufficient that his captive state had brought him to this warm and peaceful room and to this dreamy pleasure and—freedom? Was it true that he felt, as he sat there, a free man? That corroding bitterness that his failure to find freedom had produced in him was now, to a large extent, gone. He was almost free of it and with it of his past life and all its horror. Was the paradox he had spoken of to Colin present in his own life? Had the acceptance of fetters unlocked the prison house? That eternal paradox! But he would not think and abruptly, as thoughts came, he turned from them to stir the fire or knock out his pipe. Thought was too confusing. He wanted only to enjoy with simplicity—a thing he had not done since his childhood's days. He began to think of his childhood and of the many Christmas Eves he had known in the old house in Le Paradis. While his mother lived Christmas had been Christmas, in spite of his father, whose tyranny brooded even over such things as Christmas trees and cakes and threatened to take the heart out of all rejoicing. He marvelled now to think how his mother must have fought and toiled to keep a little spontaneity in their common life. When she had died spontaneity had died with her. He and André had had no choice but to fit into an iron groove or cast themselves adrift. The thought of past Christmases made him think of the Island legends his mother had told them as they sat round the fire on Christmas Eve roasting their chestnuts. In imagination he could see the drawing-room at the Le Paradis house lit by the leaping flames of the fire and the starlight over the sea. His father was in the library, and they had dared to pull the curtains and open the window. His mother, her hand raised to keep the heat of the flames from her face, would sit on the floor by the fire, her dark maroon dress billowing out around her so that she looked like a dark rose flung down on the hearthrug, and tell the Christmas stories to him and baby André. It was so he liked best to remember her, for it was only when her husband was absent that she seemed truly herself—when he was there she was not allowed to sit on the floor and there seemed a constraint and heartbreaking sense of frustration about her. Watching the leaping flames of his own fire, seeing the stars through the window, he could hear her voice telling how at midnight on Christmas Eve the animals all knelt down to worship and the water was turned to wine. . . . A faint sound crept through the quiet of the room, hardly louder than the stir of the flames and the whisper of the sea. The bells were ringing. Down in St. Pierre the steeple of the Town Church and the squat little tower of St. Raphael's must be rocking and trembling with a cascade of sound, but up here at Bon Repos the chiming was so faint that it seemed unearthly. Ranulph glanced at his watch. Twelve o'clock. He looked out of the window. There was a line of light under the stable door. André, the idiot, must have left his lamp there when he went to tend the sick cow. As Ranulph watched he saw a dark shadow slip across the yard, push open the stable door and disappear. It was Maximilian. Ranulph suddenly decided that it was his duty to go and put out that light in the stable—no point in wasting oil. He was halfway across the room when he remembered his mother had told him as a small boy that no human being must set foot in the stables at midnight on Christmas Eve. It was the animals' hour. The poor ill-treated donkey, kicked and cuffed through the centuries, yet permitted to carry a King to Jerusalem; the cow, slaughtered for man's food yet giving its own sweet hay for a babe to lie on; the horse and the dog who bear so patiently with the folly of human kind, these are safe from man and may worship alone and at peace. Ranulph decided to leave the light alone and sat down again. As he did so he laughed and wondered what on earth André would think of him if he knew.

V

Colette, being the youngest of the family, was naturally the first to wake up on Christmas morning. She wriggled up from the bottom of her bed and popped her head out. It was still dark, but a faint greying where the window was gave promise of the dawn. It was very cold, and Colette, like a tortoise thinking better of it, withdrew her head and crept beneath her shell again. There in the warm darkness she remembered her stocking. Now that Jacqueline was growing up, Colette and Colin were the only ones of the family left to have stockings, for Rachell had decreed that those old enough to go to early Mass should lay aside such childish things as stockings. The sucking of pink sugar pigs in the early hours of Christmas morning was, so she said, for the consolation of those who had to be kept out of mischief until their elders returned from church. When she remembered her stocking Colette scrambled down to the bottom of the bed, dragged away the bedclothes, thrust her head out of the aperture and grabbed it. Then she retired under cover again, hugging its delicious hard bulkiness to her bosom. She did not want to wake up Peronelle by demanding a light, so, having satisfied herself by pinching that the sugar pig was there, and the orange and the apple, and the boiled sweets, and the doll, she fell asleep again, clasping it to her as a mother her babe. When she awoke it was to find Peronelle removing layers of bedclothes off the top of her head.

"A Merry Christmas, darling," cried Peronelle. "How it is you don't suffocate I don't know. And you've lain on your stocking. The doll will be all over pig."

Colette sat up and hugged Peronelle.

The candles were lighted, but day was faintly blue behind the curtains, and Peronelle was in her hat and coat ready to go to Mass.

Then began a frantic hubbub of Christmas hugs. Michelle and Jacqueline in their coats and hats came along to kiss and be kissed. Rachell in her best mantle, with her prayer book in her hand and every hair in place, sailed in to bless them. André, with his waistcoat inside out and his hair awry, rushed frantically everywhere looking for a lost stud. Colin in his white nightshirt played leapfrog over the beds, and down below the back door clicked as Sophie came back from an incredibly early Mass to get the breakfast and keep an eye on the youngest children while the others went to church.

At last the hubbub subsided and Colin and Colette hung out of the window to watch the landau drive off to church in the dim frosty dawn. Over the sea a star shone faintly in a brightening sky but night still clouded the land, and the landau, driving off under the trees with its swinging lamps, disappeared in a mysterious darkness. Colin stayed at the window watching the lights disappear and listening as the sound of the wheels died away. He felt awed. The darkness that had swallowed his family held the mysteries of religion that were yet unknown to him but known to them. Out of the darkness he felt fingers stretch and touch him, and something in him awoke and stirred a little.

Colette brought him back to reality by butting him in the back. "Look," she said, pointing, "is that *the* star?"

Colin looked. The star over the sea was still there, though the deep blue of the sky behind it was slowly changing to a dove-grey barred with pale lemon and lavender.

"It might be," said Colin, "but I don't think it's fat enough. The star in the Christmas pictures is always fat, with spokes."

"Perhaps they've fallen off," suggested Colette, "if the star was new when Jesus was born it must be very nearly worn out by this time."

"Stars," said Colin, "don't wear out. They are like God. Always as good as new."

"My stocking!" squeaked Colette suddenly and trundled rapidly back to her bed.

Following a time honoured custom in the du Frocq family they wrapped themselves in quilts and got into their parents' bed to open their stockings, drawing the curtains to form a sultan's tent, and sitting enthroned on the high pillows in great state. The stockings were all that could be desired. Each contained the essentials, the sugar pig, the orange, the apple, and the boiled sweets, and many delights besides, such as a doll and a miniature flat iron for Colette, a water pistol and a sailor's whistle for Colin. They had a lovely time. They ate all the boiled sweets except a few moist globules kept for the family, and all of the pigs except the hind quarters, kept for Rachell. Colette's pig, as Peronelle had predicted, had stuck to the doll, but it didn't really matter, and the paint from the doll's face that adhered to the flanks of the pig tasted quite nice. Colin filled his pistol with water and squirted at the picture of the Last Judgment, getting the angel with the trumpet full in the chest every time, and Colette, each time he hit the mark, blew the whistle. After an hour of this Sophie came up, took away the pistol and the whistle, mopped up the water and dressed them. Sophie seemed in an extremely good mood. She did not scold at all, even though the water was dripping down the Last Judgment and collecting in a pool on the floor, and she never smacked them once as she hustled them into their clothes. Her eyes were shining, her round red cheeks were redder than ever, and her stays creaked and popped like joyously tapping drums. Colette, quick to feel what others were feeling, sensed her joy.

"Have you had a sugar pig, Sophie?" she asked.

"Better than that," said Sophie, bursting to communicate her news, if only to the children. "I've had the offer of a husband. Holy Virgin! On Christmas morning, too!"

"Is that all?" said Colin, disappointed.

"Walking back from Mass he popped the question, as they say in England," said Sophie, "and there was I looking in the fairy well only last night and never saw a thing but the stars and the sky—just shows you there's nothing in these tales."

Colette, pleased but uncomprehending, put her arms as far round Sophie's waist as they would reach and kissed her.

"Who popped the question?" asked Colin.

"Jacquemin Gossilin," chattered Sophie. "It was that blue coat and skirt did it. All yesterday afternoon his eyes were on it."

Colin politely said nothing, but he was dismayed. How are the mighty fallen! He could not believe that his friend Jacquemin

Gossilin could be such an utter fool as to want to marry Sophie—he could not have seen Sophie with her hair curlers in.

But it was impossible to dwell long upon depressing topics on Christmas morning. Colin was soon racing round the garden pursuing Marmalade with the water pistol, while Colette trotted backwards and forwards from the scullery to the kitchen helping Sophie.

The breakfast was wonderful. Ham and boiled eggs and steaming coffee and jam and fresh rolls and, most marvellous of all, an Island speciality, the goche détremper, a milk cake always baked early on Christmas morning to appear on the breakfast table. Colette helped Sophie to open the oven door and take it out. Its exquisite milk-white freshness was faintly tinged with golden brown on top, and its lovely crisp smell filled the whole kitchen and floated out to greet the churchgoers as they drove into the courtyard, cold and famished.

Ranulph put in an appearance at breakfast time and ate more than his fair share of the goche détremper, which seemed hardly fair as he had done nothing either in the way of devotions or stocking-opening to warrant such an appetite.

No sooner was breakfast over than it was time for church again. André usually escaped from a second church-going on Christmas day on the plea of the farm, but to-day Ranulph, with a malicious twinkle in his eye, declared himself perfectly able to do all that was necessary on the farm in order that André might enjoy the felicity of accompanying his family. Rachell was grateful and delighted, and André went miserably upstairs to find his top hat.

With the family at church, and Sophie shut in the kitchen with the turkey, Ranulph spent an extremely profitable morning. Quick and efficient as he was he had done all that was necessary on the farm in half the time that it would have taken André. His work ended, he went into the little room adjoining the stables, half office and half outhouse, to enter the number of eggs he had collected in the egg book. He had only been here once or twice before, and that in the company of André, when politeness had forbidden a too great inquisitiveness. Now, closing the door behind him, he looked round with interest. The little narrow slip of a room, known to the family as the "corn bin" because the hens' food was kept there, was André's private sanctum. No one but himself and the hens had any interest in it. From certain signs it was obvious to Ranulph that André withdrew to it, as Rachell to her bedroom and Michelle to La Baie des Mouettes, to possess his soul. Ranulph went to the middle of the room, put his hands in his pockets and stared. He meant to go through this room thoroughly, as a thief the pockets of an unconscious man, and get to the bottom of André. He had no qualms of conscience about lifting the lid off another man's secrets. He had long ago dispensed with a conscience as a tiresome and hampering article, constantly interfering with desire.

There was nothing in this room at first sight to throw any light upon André. On one side of the little room stood the corn bins, opposite them was an old roll topped desk containing the farm account books and the egg book, with an almanack hanging over it, opposite the door was a window which looked out across a rough field towards a distant line of stunted trees and held to the left just a glimpse of the sea. Under this window was a table with a chair in front of it, and under the table was a roughly-made bookcase with a sacking curtain to protect the books. Now what books could André possibly want in the corn bin? The roll topped desk already contained a dictionary, and various noble tomes on manure, cows, bee-keeping, hens and mangelwurzels. What more could the man want? Ranulph dragged out the little bookcase, lifted the sacking curtain and looked. Plato, Shakespeare (Michelle had declared to him that there was apparently not a Shakespeare on the premises), Keats, Essays of Elia, Moby Dick, Molière, Euripides, Undine, the Arabian Nights (had André stolen these two from the children?) Dante, a book on pigs (this last evidently uneasy in its company), Goethe. An assorted lot. No wonder André was such a bad farmer. Obviously he withdrew to this sanctum to study pigs—the presence of the pigs between Dante and Goethe showed that an attempt on pigs was actually made—studied them for a couple of minutes and then turned to—what? To the cloudy splendours of Shakespeare—rainbow tinted mists of poetry wreathing and coiling over the still black tarns of insight; to the gentle calmly flowing stream of the Essays; to the sparkling waterfalls of French comedy. But did he only read? What was that table standing there? Ranulph turned abruptly from the books, went to the desk and began pulling out the drawers and ransacking their contents—but not to find the egg book—that he found at once and cast contemptuously aside. Account books and old bills and farm records and advertisements, these he cast from him like autumn leaves whirling before a north-easter—the desk was already so hopelessly untidy that André would never notice confusion had been worse confounded—until he found what he sought.

He lifted them out and carried them to the table—a handful of notebooks and school exercise books (filched from Colin?) filled with André's small neat writing. For André, so wildly untidy that his passage through a room was like the passing of a tornado, wrote neatly. These little books, filled apparently with poems and essays, were written with the loving care, neatness and beauty of an etching engraved on copper. The form was perfect, what of the substance? Ranulph drew up the rickety chair to the table and read. He read for an hour without stirring. There was no sound in the room but the occasional turning of a page and the scurry of a mouse as it pattered across the wooden floor. Outside the window, over the gorse-starred field, the sun rose to its glorious zenith and the line of the distant sea was molten gold. Then Ranulph closed the books. One, which had been at the bottom of the pile, he slipped into his pocket, the rest he carried reverently back to the drawer from which he had taken them, and closed it. He removed all traces of his presence, arranging the room exactly as he had found it, and went out, closing the door with the quietness of a doctor leaving a sick room. For assuredly André was a sick man. If he could write like that in his fugitive leisure moments, and bind his life to a wheel of toil that he must hate and loathe, the conflict in him must have exhausted his body and dragged his soul nearly in two. His life must be a veritable crucifixion, the upward surge of the artist crossed out, bound down always by the arms of necessity and frustration.

Ranulph went to his own room over the stable and sat down by the window and marvelled. Hitherto he had thought of his brother as a weak fool. Weak in practical ability and driving power he might be but as an artist he was supreme. His were not the lesser gifts of a retentive memory garnering the thoughts of others and dishing them up with a fresh sauce, nor yet of a quick wit ready to note and seize the humour and piquancy of contrast, but the greater gifts of the creator, born to endue passing things with immortality. He had too the passionate observation of the true lover of beauty. No procession of clouds, no fall of a leaf or flash of a bird's wing had passed by him unseen, and out of these moments of fugitive beauty, caught and held, he had created an enduring beauty. With perfect simplicity, with thoughts that were his own, clothed in phrases coined by himself, he had built of captured moments an unchanging monument to changing nature. Those particular sunsets and storms and unfoldings of spring had passed and gone, but in André's poems they were alive for ever. Ranulph got up and walked about the room. What was to be done about it? André in his harried life had only had time to produce that handful of poems and essays, and they, as far as Ranulph could see, unless something were done about it, were doomed to be thrown on the dustbin with the egg accounts. He was an example of the greatest tragedy of all, a life denied its true vocation. Some words frequently quoted by Peronelle when in the midst of the Browning epidemic seemed to say themselves in the room.

> "The honest instinct, pent and crossed through life,
> Let surge by death into a visible fire
> Of rapture; as the strangled thread of flame
> Painfully winds, annoying and annoyed,
> Malignant and maligned, thro' stone and ore,
> Till earth exclude the stranger: vented once
> It finds full play, is recognized atop
> Some mountain as no such abnormal birth,
> Fire for the mount, not streamlet for the vale!"

Ranulph swore suddenly and loudly. No! André should not wait for death to fulfil himself in this only life he had to live upon the earth. He should do it now. Who knew if there was any after death? Browning, with the easy optimism of a man with private means, seemed to think so, but Ranulph himself thought not. He began to walk round and round the room. His mind, hitherto occupied over the problems of Michelle, Jacqueline, and Colin, began to be busy over their father. He muttered as he walked. He would set André free before he died. The path was not clear to him yet, but he knew that he would do it. He, the failure, would keep his brother from following a like path.

André, Rachell, Michelle, Peronelle, Jacqueline, Colin, Colette. A rope of seven strands bound the advocate of independence, but he was so busy with his thoughts for them that morning that he had no time to notice how the touch of the rope had set him free from the fetters of his own obsession.

VI

To dine with grandpapa on Christmas Day was more than any one could bear, but since grandpapa could not possibly be expected to absorb turkey and plum pudding by himself at the festal season there was nothing for it but to bring him back to Bon Repos after church.

Ranulph, meditating in his own room, heard the spanking clip-clop of grandpapa's trotting horses mingling with the thump-thump of the ambling Lupin. Ten minutes later the dinner bell rang. Ranulph surveyed himself in the scrap of looking glass that hung on his wall. His hair was rumpled and his coat buttoned crooked, but he decided to leave them as they were. It would annoy the old man. It was not in his power to revenge himself for the blows his father had dealt him in the past, but little pin pricks of annoyance he could and would drive in. His untidiness would, unfortunately, annoy Rachell too, but never in this world can one aim a blow at another but some innocent victim catches the rebound. He strolled at his leisure into the kitchen. This also was intended as a pin prick. They were all waiting for him, and grandpapa was fuming.

"Didn't you hear the bell, sir?" he demanded.

"Certainly, sir," replied Ranulph, "otherwise I should not have been here. You will eat the more that I have kept you waiting."

Grandpapa blew out his cheeks and humphed. Their glances caught and held, like magnet and steel. It had been so at their first meeting. Ranulph wondered uneasily if it were possible that his father could recognize him. He wrenched his eyes from the old man's compelling, troubled gaze, and looked at his brother. André, irritated by his rudeness, was looking at him, and was astonished beyond measure to see admiration, reverence, and even affection in the older man's regard. There had always been a veiled hostility between them, born of their mutual love for Rachell and of André's jealousy, but now, for some reason unknown to André, it seemed gone. In spite of himself a movement of liking stirred in him and stretched out to meet Ranulph's affection. Rachell, intercepting their glances, blessed Yuletide the peace-maker.

The dinner was perfect and grandpapa, who had had the forethought to bring his own drinks with him, André, the fool, being a teetotaller, expressed himself as not too dissatisfied. The turkey, stuffed at one end with herbs and at the other with chestnuts, according to the Island custom, was browned to a turn and held out gallantly against the inroads of everybody's second helpings. The plum pudding, when carried in by a purple-faced Sophie, was seen even under its covering of blue flame to be of the colour of folded wallflower buds and stiff with fruit. . . . After a quarter of an hour there was none left.

"You're all eating too much," announced grandpapa, passing up his plate for more. "What? What? You all eat too much. You always have." He became aware that Colette was eating plum pudding, and his eyes nearly popped out of his head. "To give that child plum pudding," he told Rachell, "is equivalent to digging her grave. And don't say I haven't told you."

"It's only a thimblefull," Rachell pleaded.

"I never remember such heavenly weather at Christmas," said André nervously, terrified that grandpapa might revert to the topic of the dead children.

"What?" said grandpapa, "yes. Warm. Damned unseasonable. Well, as I was saying, if you overfill a child's stomach—"

Trouble was dawning in Rachell's face and Ranulph threw himself into the breach. Turning to grandpapa he began to talk as the du Frocqs had never heard him talk before. He talked as brilliantly as André wrote, and with the same creator's gift. Picking out the most gaily-coloured of his memories he built for them, bit by bit, the story of his travels, building up with skilful words an edifice of colour and scents and adventure that took their breath away. André listened spellbound and the children, reaching mechanically for nuts and oranges, never took their eyes off him. Rachell, her eyes slipping lovingly from face to face, was perhaps, more interested in their pleasure than in the story, but she gave Ranulph his due as a narrator. Even grandpapa seemed curiously interested in the tale, or perhaps, not so much by it as by the teller. He sat twisting his wine glass between his fingers and glancing every now and then quickly and sharply at Ranulph, at his eyes, at the shape of his head, his hands. But for the most part, he sat looking at the cloth and listening. Even so had he once sat in his library and listened while Jean his son, outside in the garden and unaware of him, had told some tale or other to the infant André. He had marvelled then at the boy's power of telling a story and he marvelled now at this man's power. They had told a tale in just the same way, with the same varied inflection of voice, stressing the lights and shadows of the story, the same power of painting pictures in the minds of their listeners, the same power of making a dead past live. Once more he raised his eyes sharply to Ranulph's face, and kept them there. Like the steel to the magnet, Ranulph's eyes slipped round to his, were held and gripped, and for the first time the story faltered. Grandpapa, strangely moved, got abruptly to his feet, spilling the dregs of his wine glass across the table.

"Are we to stay here all the afternoon stuffing ourselves?" he demanded fiercely and a little wildly. "Is it necessary because you live at a farm that you should ape the manners of the lower animals? Look at those children."

This was unfair, for though the children were eating nuts and the table was considerably littered with the debris there was nothing in the least piglike in their methods. You could not hear them eat and they did not slobber.

"We will go into the other room," said Rachell with dignity, and, rising, she swept into the parlour, followed by grandpapa and André. To her great relief Ranulph took himself off. When he and grandpapa were together the air was positively oppressive with a surcharge of electricity. The children scampered off on their various occupations. Michelle and Peronelle to help Sophie wash up, Jacqueline and Colin to mysterious private business. Only Colette trotted in the wake of her elders to the parlour.

Rachell sighed with relief as she established herself and her menfolk in chairs before the fire, with sleepy Colette on her lap. The sun-filled parlour, shut away from the clamour of dinner and washing up, was fragrant and peaceful as the inside of a flower. Part of the tronquet de Noel, the yule log, was burning in the grate and its blue and yellow flames, whispering sweetly, lit up with the sunlight the soft little gillyflowers and forget-me-nots on the curtains, the delicate fluted china, the Chinese dragons and the rosewood table. Rachell looked round on all her treasures and was comforted. André, worn out, was soon asleep, and Colette, overcome by an excess of food and joy, leant her head against her mother and slept too. Only grandpapa, though he spread his handkerchief over his head and folded his hands across his stomach, seemed unable to pop off. He was restless. He snorted and sighed, and shuffled with his feet. Rachell, her chin resting on top of Colette's head, considered him. He seemed upset about something. She felt sorry for him. He looked old to-day, and lonely. If his loneliness was his own fault it was none the less pitiful for that. He snorted again, gave up the chase of his forty winks, whipped the handkerchief from off his head and looked round the room. His eye travelled with disfavour over the soft pale colours of it, and he sniffed at the scent of pot-pourri and burning wood with obvious dislike.

"Draughty," he announced, "musty and washed-out looking. Damp. That's what it is, damp. I've always told you this house was damp."

Rachell smiled at him. Her pity this afternoon was stronger than her dislike.

"Don't you like my room?" she asked.

"High falutin,'" said grandpapa. "I suppose you call it artistic?"

"I think it is beautiful," admitted Rachell.

Grandpapa shifted his weight in his chair.

"Deuced uncomfortable furniture," he said, "beauty be damned, I like comfort. . . . No, you needn't 'ssh' me; the child's asleep."

He blew out his cheeks and his eyes travelled round the room again. They came to rest on the strips of Chinese embroideries sent home by a sailor du Frocq. He looked at them fixedly.

"Cousin Matthieu du Frocq gave them to me you know," Rachell said, smiling at her blue butterflies and golden dragons dancing on the wall.

"He was a great traveller," grandpapa announced. "Wild fellow too. Humph. Well. He's dead now. Sailors and travellers—there've been several of 'em in the family. There's a restless strain in us. That's what it is. Restless." He stared at the fire and Rachell wondered if he was thinking of his son Jean.

"Tell me about this fellow Mabier," he demanded suddenly. Rachell told him the little she could tell without betraying Ranulph's confidence.

"Humph," muttered grandpapa, "a queer fellow. Restless. A traveller. That's what it is, restless. . . . He told that story well; damn well."

"Yes," said Rachell.

"Story telling is a gift," grandpapa informed her, "my son Jean had it."

It was the first time he had ever mentioned his son to her, and she started. She supposed Ranulph's storytelling had recalled Jean to his father. She looked up and found the old man's eyes fixed on her. They were desolate. She made a little gesture of compassion towards him with her hand, but he ignored it.

"Often wondered if the fellow's dead or alive," he said gruffly.

"I think he must be dead," said Rachell gently. "If he had lived surely he would have come home again."

"Never expected him to do that," said grandpapa. "Hated me. Thought I'd killed his mother or some such damn nonsense. Bitter against me because I wouldn't let him be a sailor. Young fool! The young don't know what's good for them."

Abruptly he put his handkerchief over his head again and folded his hands across his stomach. Rachell dared say no more. The clock ticked on and there was perfect silence in the room. Grandpapa was quite still, but Rachell knew he was not asleep. His mind was voyaging savagely over the past, justifying all his actions for the thousandth time.

Rachell wished she could sleep a little before tea. There was a long evening of festivity to be got through first and she was very tired, but her arms and back were aching with Colette's weight and the pain kept her awake. She felt depressed. She distrusted for the hundredth time that "seeing" that had made her bring Ranulph to Bon Repos. She owed Jacqueline's happiness at the Convent to him, but except for that she could not see what good he had brought them. They were no nearer financial salvation. Faithful to their six months' compact, André had not so much as mentioned the word "money" to her, but she knew it was the five letters of that abominable word that were robbing him of his sleep and making him thinner and more bowed than ever. She looked at him as he sat in his chair. He looked ten years older than he was. Why, oh why, had she added to his burdens the continual friction of Ranulph's presence in his home? . . . She was weighed down by many things as she sat in her chair that afternoon, but the heaviest was the as yet unacknowledged fact that Ranulph loved her. . . . What would be the end of it all? She saw all their lives as a lot of strands hopelessly knotted and could see no way to unravel them. She looked round her pretty room for comfort. She looked at her French carpet, its pinks and blues faded to the colour of a dove's breast, at the miniatures over the mantelpiece and the French gilt mirror, at her tea-set patterned in blue and scarlet and gold, and at the stiff backed chairs that her grandfather had given her grandmother, and all these things stretched out fingers and touched her, whispering "wait." She was comforted. In spite of her aching arms she began to nod a little. The blue butterflies and the scarlet dragons, and the blue and yellow flames of the tronquet de Noel closed round her and began to pull her gently down and down, through depths of tranquil light that grew cooler and sweeter the farther she sank, until she found herself resting serenely against something, drawing in strength and peace through every fibre of her being.

VII

She was awakened by Peronelle, vibrating with excitement, rushing in to announce that tea was ready in the kitchen. Sophie had gone out to spend a blissful afternoon and evening with Jacquemin Gossilin and the refreshment of the inner man was now in the hands of Peronelle and Michelle. They had prepared a tea of a sumptuousness passing description. It was a proper Island tea, such as they indulged in on festival days, served at twilight and combining tea and supper, and the food of both. There were tea and coffee, ham and eggs, jams and jellies, and bread and biscuits, and, in the middle of the table the stupendous, mountainous, snow-white Christmas cake.

The major part of the tronquet de Noel blazed in the grate, and all the holly berries were awink, and the lamps were lighted. In front of the dresser stood the Christmas tree, glimmering with candles and golden and scarlet balls, and round its feet were piled the presents. The windows were uncurtained so that as night deepened they would be able to see the stars.

Tea till bedtime was to the children the best part of Christmas Day, and to grandpapa, Ranulph, Rachell, and André, vicariously young again, the hours passed with a chiming of bells that drowned the mutter of life surging past and towards them. Tea and presents and carol singing and games filled their evening brimful of delight. The sparkling kitchen shone like a glow-worm in the darkness of the world all round them. Out through the windows poured the laughter, and the singing, and the light, conquering a little and no more of the silence and the blackness.

Now and again, as the hours passed, there would come a knocking at the hall door and André would open it and find a little group of peasants standing outside, their figures grimly black against the stars. "Monsieur, alms in the name of Noel." Sometimes they asked it in halting English, sometimes in patois that sighed in the night like music. And André, though he had little to give, and had no business to give that little, never refused them.

This house to house begging was an old and reverenced custom, and he was glad too, this night of all nights, that the Bon Repos hospitality should shine far. . . . For it might be the last time.

As he bade God speed to one little group he stood for a moment in the darkness outside listening to the laughter and singing, and watching the long beam of light from the kitchen window stretching a caressing finger out across the courtyard, over the winter-bound garden, across the cliff almost to the cliff's edge. It seemed like a living thing, the radiance of something that he and Rachell had brought to life at Bon Repos. He turned abruptly on his heel and walked in. . . . The thought of that light quenched was intolerable.

VIII

Grandpapa had gone. The clip-clop of his horses' hooves had died away in the frosty night. Ranulph had gone. The children were in bed and asleep. The little lights on the Christmas tree had died with Christmas Day, and the lamps were turned low. Only the tronquet de Noel sent out a warm crimson glow from its falling ash. Rachell and André, moving with the slowness of exhaustion, were trying to bring a little order into the untidy room before they went to bed. Now that the children had gone they could hear again the mutter of life surging past and towards them, and the mutter was ominous. Where would they be next Christmas? They neither of them spoke, but the question was there in the room with them, pressing upon them intolerably. They finished their tidying, put out the lamps and crossed the room arm in arm, wearily. At the door Rachell paused. Through the windows she could see the light still shining in Ranulph's room, and at the sight of it her heart felt unaccountably lightened. She glanced round the room. The willow pattern china and the warming-pans, those incurable optimists, had each of them a little twinkling reflection of the tronquet de Noel. To Rachell's lightened heart each little friendly gleam seemed a promise of yet another Christmas to come, yet another Christmas at Bon Repos. In the doorway, under the mistletoe so thoughtfully placed there by Ranulph for the purpose, she turned and flung her arms round André.

"It will be all right, darling," she whispered, "it will be all right."

André, too, felt his heart lightened by what he considered her quite unreasonable optimism. They went upstairs hand in hand, undressed in their candle-lit bedroom under the picture of the Last Judgment, climbed into their big four-poster, and drew the crimson curtains. The last sound they heard as they fell asleep was the murmur of the sea.

Chapter 7

I

IT was only a fortnight or so after Christmas that Colette could not eat her breakfast. Everyone was astonished. Men might come and men might go, but Colette's appetite had always seemed one of the eternal verities. No one was more astonished than Colette herself. She gazed at her lovely brown egg and her eyes filled with tears. "I can't eat it," she said, in the tone of the great financier who says "I am bankrupt." Rachell put her to bed and sent for grandpapa. In startlingly quick time his horses were heard careering up the road. They arrived all in a lather, with the coachman crimson in the face, and grandpapa behind swearing at the whole turn-out for its abominable slowness.

"Eh, what? What's all this?" he demanded of Rachell as he stamped into the hall, casting his hat and coat from him, and hurling his bag on to the table. Rachell looked at it with dismay. It was large and black, and bulged, and struck terror to her heart. It was apparently chock full of instruments for cutting Colette in little pieces.

"It's nothing much. Just a little temperature and no appetite," she said soothingly, more to comfort herself than him, "she couldn't eat her breakfast."

Grandpapa was astounded. "What? Colette? Not eat her breakfast?" He hurried to the stairs. "Overeating, that's what it is," he said, as he stumped up them. "Giving the child plum pudding on Christmas Day! Ridiculous! I said so at the time. You must not overfill a child's stomach. If I've said so once I've said so a hundred times." He turned round and shot out a finger at Rachell. "Damp and overeating. That's what it is. Damp and overeating. I've told you so. You'll kill the lot before you've done." He turned and stumped on again, Rachell following with unreasoning terror clutching at her. How many times, when the three dead children had been ill, had she climbed these stairs behind Grandpapa's forbidding back. Looking up and seeing his broad shoulders outlined against the light from above, as she had seen them so many times, she swayed a little and clutched at the banisters.

"Well, young lady," said grandpapa, pushing his way into the little whitewashed room like a fat bumble-bee into a flower too small for it. "What's the matter with you? Overeating? Overeating on Christmas Day, that's what it is. Put your tongue out."

Colette lay under her patchwork quilt and looked at him with large bewildered eyes. She had never been in bed in the day before, and she didn't like it. It confused her. Her cheeks were very flushed, and her yellow curls were a little damp. Her head felt too big and her throat hurt her.

Grandpapa sat down on the bed and put his hand on her forehead. "Put your tongue out," he said. Colette, reassured by the touch of his hand, smiled sweetly, but kept her mouth shut.

"Put your tongue out, darling," prompted Rachell. Colette turned her limpid gaze upon her mother and folded her sweet lips firmly and tightly. She was not going to put her tongue out. Her pride was wounded. She had *not* overeaten on Christmas Day, and she was not going to show grandpapa a coated tongue and give him the opportunity of convicting her of greediness. She was *not* greedy. Coated her tongue might be but not through overeating. Anyhow, she was not going to put her tongue out.

"Open your mouth," said grandpapa. The corners of Colette's mouth turned upwards in the sweetest smile, but not a glimpse of pearly teeth was seen between her lips.

"Darling," pleaded Rachell.

"Get a spoon to hold her tongue down with," said grandpapa. "I want to look at her throat. I'll have that mouth open by the time you come back."

Rachell went. When she returned Colette was still smiling sweetly, but grandpapa's eyes were snapping angrily. He humphed.

"Might as well try and get a d—er—humph—dashed limpet off a rock," he growled, "a crowbar's what's needed here."

Rachell knelt by the bed and tried love and persuasion and explanation for ten minutes with no result whatsoever. Colette, her eyes on the silver spoon, refused to open her mouth. Rachell was puzzled. Colette had always been such a good child. This vein of obstinacy was as unexpected as it was disconcerting. Grandpapa stood at the bottom of the bed, his hands in his pockets, and blew out his cheeks.

"You go away," he said to Rachell, "leave the child to me. You're no use whatsoever. Not firm enough. She'll open her mouth for her old grandfather. Firmness is what's needed. That's what it is. Firmness."

Rachell went down to the hall and waited. A quarter of an hour later grandpapa reappeared, very red in the face, and with beads of perspiration on his forehead. He stumped down the stairs, across the hall, and out to his carriage without pausing for a moment in his irritated stride. Rachell had to run after him to hear the orders that he flung behind him as he stumped.

"Feverish attack of some sort. Can't get the mouth open, but probably due to overeating. Keep her quiet. I'll send up a bottle of medicine—though goodness knows how you're to get it down her throat. Never seen such damned obstinacy."

This brought him to his carriage, and the coachman heaved him in.

"It's nothing to worry about?" asked Rachell anxiously.

"How am I to know?" stormed grandpapa. "I can't get the child's mouth open. Why you can't control your children I don't know. Discipline is what's needed. Discipline. You're too weak."

"It's the du Frocq obstinacy coming out," said Rachell.

"Eh?" said grandpapa, "obstinacy? She don't get that from *my* side of the family, let me tell you. She gets it from yours. You're a hard, unyielding woman. I've had occasion to tell you so before."

"You've just accused me of weakness," murmured Rachell.

"Eh? What?" Grandpapa drew his fur rug over his knees and scowled at her. "Well, I can't sit here all the morning arguing over the characteristics of your fatiguing family. . . . Drive on, Lebrun."

The coachman whipped up the horses, and grandpapa, muttering to himself, departed to inspect more obedient tongues. Rachell went back to Colette. The first thing she saw, when she opened the bedroom door, was Colette's pink tongue hung out over her chin for all the world like a rug over a window sill. She gave her mother the benefit of it for some moments and then withdrew it.

"Darling, why wouldn't you let grandpapa see it?" asked Rachell.

"He said I ate too much on Christmas Day," said Colette. "I *didn't*. . . . Mummie, I'm thirsty."

II

Colette was very ill. For three weeks grandpapa came every day, and those three weeks aged him more than the ten years that had gone before. Rachell measured the seriousness of Colette's illness, and the depth of his love for her, by the rapid change in him.

The lovely Christmas weather had broken and outside the rain streamed down and the wind raced in from the sea, hurling itself against the house and breaking into whirling eddies that screamed and moaned round eaves and chimneys. Inside it seemed to be always night. The weight and gloom of darkness brooded over everything and dawns came and went unnoticed. No one slept very much or ate very much and only the wind and the rain seemed to have any strength or vigour. The life of the house halted, and its radiance seemed slowly dying.

Rachell spent all her time in Colette's room. For the moment her whole world was centred in Colette, and no one and nothing else mattered to her. Even Colin was forgotten. Desperate and tight-lipped she watched and fought, holding death at arm's length day after day, and night after night. Ranulph and Peronelle, the only ones who kept their heads, struggled valiantly to keep some sort of order in Bon Repos, the others either did no work at all or else did someone else's by mistake. Sophie could do nothing but cry, Michelle, Jacqueline, and Colin alternately cried and flew at each other's throats, and André, struggling about the farm, weak with grief and the violence of the weather, gave the pig wash to the hens and the horses' oats to the cows. Ranulph, striding after him in his tarpaulin and top boots, corrected his mistakes, paid the farm men, did the accounts, collected the eggs, and in the evening sat before the fire in the kitchen and told the children stories. Without him Peronelle, shouldering in the house the burdens he shouldered on the farm, would surely have collapsed, but with him she yoked herself to Bon Repos and, sharing the weight together, they pulled it through. It was during these terrible weeks that Ranulph, hitherto a stranger, intimate and beloved yet living always a little on the fringe of the family life, came right into its centre. They could none of them believe that there had ever been a time when they had not known him. He seemed one of them. They radiated from him as the spokes from the hub of the wheel. And he was the only one of the household who ever seemed to get through to Rachell. Though she seemed unaware of him he could yet make her eat or rest when necessity demanded, and afterwards she remembered that when he was with her strength had seemed to pour from his will into hers and courage to radiate from him.

The crisis came on a Saturday night. Grandpapa, abandoning all his other patients to the unfortunate Blenkinsop, had been at Bon Repos all day. There was not much he could do, but he hated to leave Colette for a moment. It was misery to him to look at her, once so fat and rosy, now thin and transparent as a little white moth, but the misery of going away and not looking at her was worse. It was tea time when he left Rachell with Colette and rambled down to the kitchen for tea. He didn't stump now, there was no more stump left in him, and he dragged his feet like a very old man. He sat down heavily in his chair and humphed feebly. Peronelle poured out his tea, and Ranulph cut him some bread and butter. All tension between him and Ranulph seemed gone and the jealousy that had once existed between Ranulph and André was as though it had never been. Grandpapa stirred his tea, and they all waited.

"Won't live through the night," he said at last, "she's unconscious now. We can't rouse her."

No one said anything. There didn't seem to be anything to say. André leant back in his chair for a moment and then crouched forward again as though the movement had hurt him. Something in the desolation of his attitude seemed to express what they all felt.

It was at this moment that Peronelle became aware of an insistent tapping sounding through the wind and the rain. Someone was knocking at the back door. Sophie had been sent out with Jacquemin Gossilin in the hopes that he might be able to quench her tears and instil a little sense into her. Peronelle, numb with misery, realized that she must go to the door. She got up and groped her way through the dim candle-lit scullery to the back door and opened it. At first, as the light shone out on the storm, she could see nothing but the silver spears of the rain streaking the whirling darkness, then she saw a hooded figure crouching against the wall. At first she had a moment of terror—Sophie had done nothing else for the last two days but see goblins, sarregousets and crows, forerunners of death, hopping round the house. Then her common sense came to the rescue, and she peered out into the darkness. "Who are you?" she asked.

"They say Sophie Lihou is to wed." The voice out of the storm was small and shaking. Peronelle was completely mystified.

"Yes, but why have you come? Who are you?" She stretched out a hand and pulled the figure towards her so that the light shone on it. An incredibly thin girl-child stood in front of her, wrapped in a dripping wet cloak. The face was almost unearthly in its haggard pallor, the hollows in the cheeks and round the eyes showed against the whiteness of the face like black patches and the eyes, black too, seemed without light or movement. Peronelle was almost frightened again. This creature was more like a goblin than a human being.

"They turned me out from Le Paradis t'ree weeks ago, Mamzelle," quavered the voice again. "I wasn't quick enough at my work. I've been near starvin.' Then I heard Sophie was to wed an' leave you, an' I thought you might 'ave m. . . . I'm strong." These last two words, so obviously untrue, were thrown out to the night like a challenge. Peronelle gaped.

"The little Mamzelle Colette was good to me," went on the voice. "I'd like to be with 'er. She'd say a word for me."

The mention of Colette, sending a throb of anguish through her, restored Peronelle to action. She seized the girl again and dragged her into the scullery. The candle light revealed the most pitiable object ever beheld. Peronelle's eyes travelled from the white goblin face, with stringy hair strained back and secured behind with three hairpins like kitchen skewers, to the bony scarred hands clutching the dripping cloak, the broken shoes and the stockings, three sizes too large, coiled in rolls round the thin ankles. Pity stirred in her. With characteristic energy she thrust her own trouble away out of sight and devoted herself to the matter in hand.

"Tell me all about it," she demanded. "How do you know my little sister?"

Falteringly Toinette told of the day when Colette came to Le Paradis and of the gift of the coral necklace. "M'dame Gaboreau turned me out, Mamzelle," she finished, "I thought per'aps you'd 'ave me. I can work 'ard if I'm not beaten. . . . I want to be with Mamzelle Colette."

"She's dying!" Peronelle shot out the words fiercely and her lips set in a hard line.

For a moment Toinette stared, then she shrank back as though she had been struck, and a pitiable little sound, like an animal's whine, came from her. She turned blindly towards the door and the storm again. Peronelle seized her arm. "Where are you going?"

Toinette wrenched her arm free, hit out at Peronelle savagely and blindly, and began stumbling away into the dark.

Obeying an impulse that came to her from she knew not where, Peronelle ran out after her, slipping and stumbling on the wet stones, the wind and rain lashing at her face and tearing at her hair. She caught up with Toinette at the farmyard gate. "Come back," she gasped.

The shock and her crazy run across the yard seemed to have exhausted Toinette. She came back dully and meekly. Peronelle, her face a mask of determination, banged the scullery door and pulled

Toinette's cloak off her. "You must come up and see Colette," she said fiercely, "you must make her come back. She'll come back for you."

Questioned about it afterwards Peronelle could never explain what it was that made her think Toinette could save Colette. She would say that she thought it must be the likeness in their names that had made her link them together in her mind, then she would say that she felt Toinette had some compelling power in her, then she would say she didn't know why she did it. Rachell would smile and say it was a "seeing." She had always known Peronelle had the two sights. She had in her eyes the little black specks that are the sign of its presence. Anyhow, Peronelle did it. She seized Toinette's cold hand in hers and marched her through the scullery, through the kitchen, across the hall, and up the stairs, Grandpapa and André and the others, sunk in their sorrow, had hardly realized her determined entrance before she had disappeared again. Ranulph half rose in his seat, but the others did not seem to take it in.

Peronelle knocked sharply and loudly on Colette's door. Rachell opened it. Her eyes, sunk in dark purple shadows, blazed in her white face.

"How dare you come knocking here!" she said to Peronelle. Her voice was harsh and rasping, stripped of all beauty.

Peronelle was not in the least abashed. Pushing her mother aside, and still gripping Toinette's hand, she marched in.

Colette lay flat under her little patchwork quilt patterned like a flower bed. She had become so thin that its surface was hardly raised at all. Her face was quite white and her eyes were closed. She seemed already in that coma whose awakening is beyond death.

Peronelle pushed Toinette to the bed. "Speak to her," she commanded, "make her come back." In her anxiety she twisted Toinette's fingers fiercely and almost cruelly. Toinette, though she was shaking all over like an aspen leaf, obeyed.

"Colette," she whispered hoarsely, bending over the bed, "Mamzelle Colette."

The attraction to each other of two spirits that seem as the poles apart—their coming together and the shaping of the bond between them—these things are as beyond comprehension as the affinity of the moon and the tides or the mating of the birds. With the gift of a coral necklace Toinette and Colette had somehow become a pair and their coming together, the mating of the moon and the tide, had given to one great power over the other. There was no explaining it. It was so. What the whole of Colette's adoring family could not do was accomplished by Toinette with a few whispered words. Slowly and with immense effort Colette opened her eyes. She looked straight into Toinette's goblin face, and to Rachell's fevered fancy it seemed as though ripples of light were passing over her face like waves of returning life. Her lips moved and she spoke for the first time for days. "Toinette," she said, "must have cream with her apple tart."

III

It was late on the evening of the next day that grandpapa crawled up the steps of his house and let himself in. He was extraordinarily tired. He had been up all the previous night nursing that tiny flicker of life in Colette. All day, though the flicker had steadied into a flame, he had not dared to leave her, but sat by her bed humphing and staring into the owlish eyes of, forsooth, his own ejected scullery maid. It was an absurd situation and had not grandpapa been so absorbed in Colette he would have been extremely annoyed. The idea of planting a dirty little waif from La Rue Clubin down beside the bed of his grand-daughter and declaring, as Rachell had declared, that she alone had saved the child, was sheer lunacy. What next? Rachell was mad. He'd always said so. Ridiculous woman. Well, no matter. The child was round the corner, thanks to his diagnosis and treatment. Funny little scrap! Grandpapa smiled at the remembrance of Colette as he had seen her last, peacefully asleep with a look of returning health just creeping into her face, and the tip of a pink tongue just showing between her lips. That tongue! If he could have got inside her mouth on the first day he could have found out sooner what was the matter with her. Obstinate little baggage! Just like her mother! He banged the front door and shouted for Barker.

"Mamzelle Colette's round the corner, Barker," he said as he flung his hat and stick at his admirable domestic. "I think she'll do now. Humph. Yes. She'll do. You can tell them below stairs."

Barker's face lit up. "Thank God, sir," he said, "and dinner is served."

Grandpapa stumped towards the dining-room. Barker noticed that he dragged his feet a little. He also noticed, as he served the soup, that his master's eyes were bloodshot.

"I'll have a bottle of claret," declared grandpapa. "What's there to follow?"

"Sole, sir. A bird. Sirloin. Soufflé. Angels on horseback. Dessert."

"I'll have the lot," said Grandpapa, "and bring up a bottle of port."

He finished his soup, leant back in his chair and sighed. He couldn't remember when he had felt so tired. He wasn't as young as he was. The whole affair had taken it out of him. That child! He was deuced fond of the snippet. What a kettle of fish if she'd died! He couldn't have borne it, damn, no! Well, he hoped the whole affair would be a lesson to Rachell. Overeating, that's what it was. The whole affair brought on by overeating. Barker entered with the fish and grandpapa looked round, his nostrils slightly quivering, to ascertain that the correct sauce was served with it. There was no trusting that fool of a cook. He attacked his sole. It was excellent. He had literally had no food the whole time he had been at Bon Repos, for no sane person could possibly describe the filth they stuffed into their mouths at Bon Repos as food. And as for drink, the whole time he had been there he had had nothing but Rachell's damned barley water and the soda stuff advocated by that fool André. "I'll have another glass of claret," he said to Barker, with his mouth full. By gad, but he was tired! He must get his strength up. By the time he had reached dessert he had eaten what would have sufficed to keep Toinette alive for a week, and drunk enough to drown the Duke of Clarence. Barker looked at him anxiously. The old man's face was very red and his hand, as he reached for the port for the twentieth time, shook alarmingly. Barker left the room and sought out Madame Gaboreau.

"You'd better go and see to the old man," he said, "I've never seen him get outside such a meal, and as for drink, I've been up and down the cellar stairs till my legs ache. It's my opinion the old boy's too tired to know what he's doing."

Madame Gaboreau, presuming on her years of service, knocked at the dining-room and entered. She was never frightened of grandpapa. She considered herself a match for him any day.

"You've had enough to drink, m'sieur," she told him, and dared to lay her hand on the decanter.

Grandpapa, already inflamed by his drinking, blazed out into such a fury that even Madame Gaboreau was taken aback. He swore at her like a trooper and his fury lit up an answering rage in her. For a few moments they blazed at each other, then Madame Gaboreau shrugged her shoulders and turned towards the door.

"You'll kill yourself, m'sieur," she warned him.

"Get out," said grandpapa. Madame Gaboreau got.

When she had gone grandpapa reached for the port for the last time. Had Madame Gaboreau let him alone he would have let it alone, but her interference had infuriated him. A pretty pass things were coming to if he could not be master in his own house. What? What? He had great difficulty this time in gripping the decanter—his fingers felt numb. Then he found it difficult to lift his glass to his lips. But he was not to be beaten either by Madame Gaboreau or his own weakness. Using every atom of strength and will power that he possessed he lifted his glass and drank. Then he leaned back in his chair and his thoughts slipped round again to Colette. The little baggage! He'd saved her. Rachell might babble nonsense about that little bitch of a scullery maid, but without his days and nights of care an army of scullery maids could not have saved that child. Yes, he had saved her. God, he was tired! A sudden vertigo seized him, and something between a groan and a cry broke from him. The whole world had turned red. He could see nothing but red. Red everywhere. A red world whirling round him. He pitched forward and clutched wildly at the tablecloth. He heard a crash of breaking glass before he fell sideways to the floor.

IV

Next morning Bon Repos was lapped in its habitual peace. The storm had cleared away in the night and great grey clouds, silver at their edges, were sailing across a sky of an intense and burning blue. Heavy with rain they sailed very near to the earth so that it and the sky seemed to be stretching towards each other like two friends who have quarrelled and then held out arms of reconciliation. For days the sky had pelted the earth pitilessly while the earth lay sullen beneath the blows, grey and dour, all her beauty quenched. Now the earth, yearning towards the sky, reflected its blue and silver in her pools, and the clouds reached down towards the tree tops. On every blade of beaten grass and every stripped twig the sky had hung rows of diamonds and the larks, dipping and soaring between earth and heaven, spun filaments of song between the two. There was a hint of spring in the air, a promise of renewal of life. Indoors, too, life surged joyously back and dawn and birdsong were noticed again. Those of the family who were not busy with Colette sat about in chairs and smiled weakly and stupidly at each other, immensely tired, but immensely happy, for had not Colette that morning absorbed an egg? A brown egg, laid for her on purpose with a great deal of fuss and clucking by an old hen who had not condescended to lay an egg for weeks. Colette had enjoyed the egg and asked for more.

Into the midst of this peace the news that grandpapa had had a seizure fell like a bombshell. It was a terrible shock to everyone but Sophie, who declared she'd known it all along.

"It's always the same, m'dame," she said to Rachell. "Again and again have I seen it. If death gives back one he takes another. So often have I seen it."

"But Dr. du Frocq is not dead, Sophie," said Rachell, "he may recover."

Sophie shook her head. "Between Christmas and Easter," she declared, "there is always one taken from every family. Death must be fed."

Rachell wondered for a moment from what old heathen cult, demanding its yearly sacrifice, this peasant superstition had survived. But she could not wonder for long about anything except the marvel of Colette restored to her. She could not even think very much about grandpapa, and André went off without her to see his father.

Ranulph seemed strangely moved by the news of grandpapa's illness. The family were surprised for what, after all, had it got to do with him? But though he was moved he seemed to entertain no doubts as to grandpapa's recovery.

"Tough old bird," he said as he went off to do André's work on the farm. "Nothing'll do for him. Selfishness is extremely strengthening, it's thought for others that's so fatiguing. . . . He's a permanency."

But Ranulph for once was wrong. Grandpapa's thought for Colette—the first piece of unselfishness in a lifetime—cost him dear. Three mornings later a message came from the agitated Blenkinsop that Monsieur and Madame du Frocq must come at once. André rushed out to harness Lupin and Rachell ran upstairs to find her bonnet. Colette was now so far on the high road to recovery that she could let her thoughts fly tenderly to the old man who had worked so hard to save her. When she came downstairs again to join André, Ranulph, hat in hand, came towards them from the stable.

"May I come with you?" he asked.

André and Rachell stared, astonished.

"I should like to come with you," he said. His request had the tone of a command and his queer light eyes, fixed on them, backed it compellingly.

"Certainly," said André.

Barker opened the door to them and Madame Gaboreau hovered behind him. Both had put on the correct expression and deportment of woe, but behind the assumed grief there was the hint of real regret. With the exception of Colette these two cared far more for grandpapa than his own family.

"The man Blenkinsop thinks he'll last out the night," Madame Gaboreau told them. "But I don't. He'll die this evening at the turn of the tide."

Barker took them to the library, where he had indicated grandpapa's condition by drawing the blinds half-way down, but not the whole way down, gave them the daily papers and left them. The three sat silent, Rachell and André grieving desperately because they were not grieving more, and Ranulph astonished to find himself sorry. Madame Gaboreau returned.

"Dr. du Frocq will see Madame du Frocq only," she announced.

Rachell was astonished. The old man had never liked her. Why this desire for her company? She followed Madame Gaboreau upstairs.

Grandpapa's room was over the library and looked seawards but the windows, double ones, were never opened. It was crowded with heavy and very valuable mahogany furniture, and had red velvet curtains. The four-poster was perfectly immense. Rachell, as she came in, thought suddenly of her mother-in-law. How awful to have to sleep with grandpapa in that great catafalque of a bed. How awful to have to die in this heavy, stuffy, oppressive room. Poor, poor woman! With a start of shame she recalled her thoughts to the one who had to die in this room now.

Grandpapa in the enormous bed looked almost small. He seemed to have shrunk since she saw him last. His eyes were bloodshot and his hands, lying on the quilt, were already the numbed useless hands of a dead man. Yet he defied pity. Pity in his extremity he would have considered an insult, and some lingering strength in him warded it off. Rachell did not kiss him—she knew better.

"Sit down," he said. His voice was thick and a little uncertain, but charged with more than its usual authority. Rachell sat.

"Colette," he said, "describe her condition."

Rachell smiled. So that was why he wanted her! Not for her own sake but that he might hear the latest news of Colette. She loved him for it. She untied her bonnet strings and embarked on a detailed account of Colette's food and drink, sleeping and waking, remarks and movements during the last four days. Grandpapa lay with his eyes shut but she knew that he heard every word.

"She laughed this morning," she finished, "the real old soda-water syphon kind."

"Humph," said grandpapa, "she'll do. Be careful with her convalescence. Don't be more of a fool than you can help. Don't overfeed her."

"Colette loved you," Rachell told him.

The old man opened one eye. "Humph," he said, "it wouldn't have lasted," and he closed the eye again.

There was silence for ten minutes, then grandpapa opened both eyes and fixed them on his daughter-in-law with intense dislike.

"What are you stopping here for?" he asked her, "I don't want you."

Rachell got up. "Would you like André?" she asked.

Grandpapa gave one of his old snorts. "No. The boy's a fool. Like his mother." He paused. "Is that fellow Mabier here?"

Rachell was astonished. What *was* this strange link between grandpapa and Ranulph? "Yes," she said.

"Then send him along," said grandpapa, and turning his head away from her he closed his eyes again, dismissing her. Rachell paused for a moment, gathering her courage to say what duty compelled her to say.

"Father," she said, "would you not like to see a priest?"

The furious blood mounted in a tide to grandpapa's forehead and he almost raised himself in bed in his indignation.

"No!" he snarled. "I've been a hypocrite in life, but I'm damned if I'll be one in death. Get out."

With incomparable dignity Rachell left the room, closed the door softly behind her and sailed down to the library.

"My father-in-law wishes to see you," she said to Ranulph. André looked up, astonished, but Ranulph left the room with no appearance of surprise. When he had gone Rachell remembered that she had not told him where to find grandpapa's room and she half rose. Then she heard his step overhead. . . . Evidently he had found it.

Ranulph stood at the bottom of the bed and looked at his father.

"Well, Jean?" said grandpapa.

Ranulph smiled his rather unpleasant smile, and drummed with his fingers on the bed rail.

"How did you know me?" he asked.

"I'm no fool," snapped grandpapa, "that story you told on Christmas Day—that gave you away—just your old way of telling lies—sit down."

Ranulph sat down, an odd flicker of affection in his yellow eyes. He was astonished to find, beneath what he thought was his hatred of his father, this substratum of affection. . . . The old man was so game.

With the entrance of his son a sudden recrudescence of strength seemed to have come to grandpapa. His voice was clearer. He did not look so ill. His eyes, fixed on Ranulph, were intense, as though he meant to get to the bottom of this enigma of his son before he died.

"A nice sort of a mess you've made of things," he told him, "a nice sort of a fool you've been—worse than André."

Ranulph smiled. "And yet you want to see me and not André," he said.

"Humph," said grandpapa, "always fonder of you than of André." He paused and then returned to the charge. "What made you turn such a damn fool?"

"Why go into it now?" asked Ranulph.

"Go on," said the old man.

Ranulph crossed one leg over the other. "You drove me to it. You wanted me to be bound by your will, but one cannot live out the will of another. I wanted to be a sailor. You wouldn't let me. You shut me in like a caged animal. Caged things always go mad sooner or later—go mad or die."

"Humph," said grandpapa and was silent. When he spoke again he was evidently following a train of thought suggested by Ranulph. "Your mother died."

"You killed her," said Ranulph.

"You liar." Grandpapa, roused to fury, spat out the words.

"A caged thing, worn out with beating against bars, has no strength to fight disease," said Ranulph bitterly, and could have killed himself for hatred of his own cruelty. What use in reproaching a dying man? His love for his mother, the strongest emotion in his life, and his grief at her death, were still so strong that they had betrayed him.

"It was after your mother died that you took to going to that bitch in La Rue Clubin," said grandpapa. Ranulph was startled. He had not known his father knew of this.

"Yes," he said. Grandpapa was silent again.

"One cannot," he said at last, "live out life again."

"No," said Ranulph, "pity."

Their eyes met and they looked at each other. Remorse, forgiveness mutually asked and given, a deep rooted affection surviving and reappearing after a lifetime of loss, were all expressed in their glance.

"You can stay here," said grandpapa.

"I'll stay," said Ranulph.

After that grandpapa slept and Ranulph sat perfectly still for what seemed to him hours. Madame Gaboreau fetched him once to have some food, but he went quickly back again. The sun, mounting higher, flooded the room with light. Through the windows he could see the sea and the ships passing. Once, overcome by the airlessness of the room, he must have dozed, for he thought it was his mother who lay dying in that hateful great bed and he was overwhelmed once again by that old agony of grief and horror. He awoke to find the sweat streaming down his face and his father's eyes fixed on him.

Grandpapa's voice was thick and weak again, but his mind seemed clear as ever, and was fixed on his grandchildren.

"Peronelle," he muttered, "should Marry Well."

"Certainly," said Ranulph, "fairy blood in her. She'll do Credit to the Family."

"Humph," said grandpapa, "taking little thing. Colette, too. Fat little baggage—thin now."

"It's surprising how she's blown out again these last two days," said Ranulph.

Grandpapa smiled. "If Colin wants to go to sea let him go his own way," he said.

"I'll see to it," Ranulph promised.

The sun passed its zenith and began to slip down the sky. The light in the room was less bright.

"You'll find I've left precious little," muttered grandpapa, "and that little to André. . . . Been improvident. . . . Horses. . . . André is a confounded fool. . . . Verge of bankruptcy."

There was intense anxiety in his voice. Ranulph's answer sprang quickly to allay it.

"I'll see to them all. I've money."

"Eh?" Grandpapa was startled into a last access of strength. He raised his head from his pillow and looked at his son. "*You've* money?"

"Yes. I'm what's called a warm man. I made a pretty penny goldmining." In spite of himself Ranulph could not help smiling at the astonishment and profound respect dawning in his father's eyes. It was almost comic.

"What? What? Good God!" said grandpapa, "and I called you a fool! . . . A warm man!"

Satisfaction beamed out all over his face, and was still there when he slipped off into a doze. Half an hour later a change in the quality of his stillness struck Ranulph. He got up and looked at him. The doze had become coma. Ranulph ran downstairs to fetch André and Rachell. There was another long wait while Rachell knelt beside the bed and prayed, and the two men stood at the window watching the first shadows of twilight dimming the sea.

At the turn of the tide grandpapa died.

Chapter 8

I

SPRING came early that year, and its breaking through seemed to Rachell more triumphant than ever. Or perhaps she only thought so because her own heart, dancing for joy at Colette's recovery, was more than usually in tune with the miracle of returning life.

She stood one morning outside the back door hanging up some washing. Sophie, who had always done such tasks for her, was now Madame Jacquemin Gossilin, and her mantle had fallen upon Toinette—a perfect marvel of incompetence. Rachell had to undertake half Toinette's work for her and even then the other half could hardly be described as done. Toinette's day's work was just a sketchy affair of blurred outlines, more a suggestion of what a day's work should be than an accomplished fact. Rachell, as she thought of Toinette, sighed. After Colette's illness she had, overwhelmed with gratitude, taken Toinette to her bosom and assured that waif that Bon Repos was her home for ever. Toinette had responded to kindness with the dedication of her whole self, stunted body, weak mind, undeveloped soul and all, to the service of the du Frocq family. A little bedroom was contrived for her in an attic boxroom and she settled into it, contented as a swallow under the eaves. It had all been very beautiful and very touching, and had carried them on a wave of rapture through the first trying weeks of Toinette's sojourn. But now the rapture had subsided, and Toinette's rather grubby methods of washing up and bed making had begun to pall a little upon everyone but Colette, whose soul was so linked to Toinette's that the weaknesses and failures of the body were of no importance. Rachell had even gone so far as to say to André, in the privacy of their four-poster, that her repentance for her bad deeds was never anything so deep as her repentance for her good deeds—and above all, for this good deed of the adoption of Toinette. "There are moments, André," she said, "when I could wish I was not a Christian."

"It does hamper one's style," agreed André.

"Were I a heathen I could turn the child out," sighed Rachell. But under the circumstances she and André were agreed that that was impossible. There was nothing for it but to accept Toinette as one would a stray mangy dog, feed her and love her, and expect nothing from her more practical than devotion. And Toinette herself, unaware of her own incompetence, was blissfully happy. Day and night she was safe from cruelty and day and night she lived under the same roof as Colette, and basked in her sunshine. Then, too, she had the bliss of feeling herself indispensable, for was she not the one and only domestic the establishment boasted? And the pride of regarding the whole family as chickens under her wing.

Rachell, to gather strength for her next encounter with Toinette, turned and looked at the scene before her. The back door faced inland across the farmyard, and before her stretched trees and fields and hills and dales. It was one of those early spring days when colour is riotously lovely. The farther trees were not yet green but burned beneath the sun with a warm ruby glow, deepening to amethyst when the cloud shadows swept over them. In the foreground the hawthorn trees shook out a transparent veil of little, crumpled bright green leaves, and beneath them a flurry of primroses starred grass that was still tawny from winter frosts. The sky, pale as harebells on the horizon, deepened overhead to hyacinth, and, threaded like a ribbon behind the rosy trees, was a streak of distance so deeply and unbelievably blue that it seemed a myriad bluebells, blooming before their time, had poured like a great wave over the distant hills. The birds sang madly. Thrushes, blackbirds, robins, chaffinches, linnets, goldfinches and the little shrill-voiced wrens; they all shouted together with such abandon that it was impossible to distinguish one from the other. In their ecstasy they seemed to have lost all fear. On a branch of lilac near Rachell sat a blackbird pouring out a cascade of song that filled and thrilled his throat nearly to bursting. She could have put out her hand and touched him, but he seemed not to know she was by. He was abandoned to his song as a saint to his contemplation. For a little Rachell looked and listened, sharing deeply in the ecstasy, drawing in strength, then she squared her shoulders and turned back to Toinette.

In the scullery, blinded by the light outside, she nearly fell over her, engaged in pouring buckets of water over the floor.

"I'm scrubbin' the floor, m'dame," Toinette told her jubilantly.

Rachell, lifting her skirts above the flood, remarked that she saw it was so.

"It's like a river in spate," she said, "*must* you use quite so much water, Toinette? Are you able to swim?"

"You must always use water for washin,' dear m'dame," Toinette told her gently and patiently.

Rachell felt rebuked. Whenever she was betrayed into impatience or sarcasm with Toinette the child's patience with her failings made her ashamed. She carried the potatoes into the kitchen—it was impossible to stand ankle deep in water in the scullery—and began to peel them.

"Where is Mademoiselle Colette?" she called through the swish of the water.

"Down the garden with 'er playmates, m'dame," called back Toinette. Rachell's heart stood still. These playmates were a new development. With the others at school, and her mother struggling to keep the house going without Sophie's help, Colette in her convalescence had been lonely and had produced from her imagination three invisible playmates to amuse her. That, at least, was how the situation was described by Colette's family; she herself did not consider her playmates invisible, and was firmly convinced that they came not from her imagination but from behind the trees at the bottom of the orchard. They lived there, she told her mother, and came to her when she called them. Asked what they looked like she shook her head and smiled a very secret smile.

II

They had first appeared on the very first morning that she had been allowed to go and play in the garden alone. It had been a fine day in late February, warm and soft, and full of little whispers. Only the snowdrops and aconites were in bloom, and the trees were still bare, but the damp earth was speared all over the place with sharp, green points and the bare twigs were thickened and flushed with life. Colette, in her two flannel petticoats, her overcoat, her goloshes and her tam-o'-shanter, ran across the courtyard and into the garden. She stood and looked round her. She had not been here by herself for weeks and she felt she had to get to know the garden all over again. She went slowly down the moss-grown path where the Canterbury bells grew in summer. There were snowdrops everywhere, little white bells veined in green drooping on slender, pale stalks that seemed too weak to hold them up. Colette wondered if they would ring, but they didn't. They seemed too busy spearing up through the black dampness of the garden to have any energy left for music. Colette felt that the garden was not paying much attention to her, it was too busy fighting its way back to life after the death of the winter. This was not very nice of the garden, she felt, for she was doing exactly the same herself, and it should have had a fellow feeling for her. She turned her back on it and ran on into the little orchard. Here, growing in the tawny grass under the thickening twigs, were the aconites. There were hundreds of them, spilled all over the orchard like fairy gold, each pale gold disk framed in a green toby frill. Sophie had often told her how the fairies hid their treasure in the cromlechs, but how mortals could never find it because when they entered the cromlechs it turned to shells. Colette herself, when once Peronelle had taken her inside a cromlech, had found a pile of tiny little shells lying in a corner and had picked them up, thrilled to feel herself handling fairy coinage. To-day she wondered if the aconites were not fairy sovereigns too. There was certainly something unearthly about them. She tried to talk to them but they were not in the least conversational. They had none of the cheeky friendliness of golden crocuses. The paleness of their faces made them look a little reserved, and the frills round their necks, like the boa of a lady of fashion, kept one in one's place.

It may have been her own lack of bodily vigour that made Colette feel depressed, or it may have been that the garden was really too engrossed in its preparation for the spring resurrection to be friendly, but whatever the reason she felt lonely.

She turned her back on the orchard and went on to the rampart of earth crowned with twisted oak trees that separated the orchard from the cliff beyond. These trees had always fascinated her. The winter storms had twisted their trunks and branches into the most extraordinary fantastic shapes, so that they looked like queer rheumatic old men holding up bony arms and outspread knotted fingers against the sky. On the landward side their branches were black, but on the seaward side they were covered with grey lichen. They had almost the appearance of white-haired negroes. They were quite certainly alive, not only with the universal life that was shared by all the other growing things but with an individual life of their own. Colette loved them and, in spite of their ugliness, was not in the least afraid of them. She knew they felt friendly towards her, and not only towards her but towards the whole little world of Bon Repos that lay stretched at their feet. For did they not protect it? Year after year they stood on top of their bank holding out their arms to shelter the house and garden from the wild tearing wind from the sea. The full violence of the storms beat upon them, twisting them and spoiling their beauty, but never vanquishing them. All the years that they had stood there not a single tree had been uprooted and not a single branch broken off. In the blackness of midnight storms, on the rare occasions when the tumult awakened her, Colette would think of them standing out there in the darkness, bending, creaking, straining, lashing back at the wind with their tortured arms but never yielding for one moment. . . . They were invincible.

To-day there was not a breath of wind and they were resting in a rare peace. They stood up black as ebony against the tranquil silver sky spread behind them. Their knotted old hands were resting on each other's shoulders, and their hoary heads lolled a little. There was not a single swelling bud to be seen upon them. They never achieved much in the way of foliage, the few leaves that did put in an appearance arrived upon the scene very late and fell off very early, blackened and nipped by the salt in the wind. Colette was quite glad to find they were not, as yet, giving the spring a thought; they would, perhaps, have a little attention left to spare for her. But they hadn't much. They greeted her kindly and even, in spite of the windlessness of the day, tapped her gently on the shoulder as she ran along beneath them, but they were really too tired after the rigours of the winter to do more than pass the time of day. They knew they had a good deal more in the way of spring storms to face and they were resting and gathering strength. Colette quite understood, but at the same time she really did feel extremely bored. If no one would play with her, what on earth was she to do with herself? Her old habit of placid wonder seemed to have left her. Her illness had left her feeling weak and yet restless. She wanted to be amused. . . . It was then that the miracle happened.

She was standing looking at her friends the trees. Behind them spread that lovely silver sky, and the air was filled with the murmur of the sea. The brightness of the sky behind the black branches was dazzling, and she blinked and shut her eyes for a moment. When she opened them again she saw that three heads had popped up from behind the bank, and that three pairs of eyes were looking at her from between the trunks of the trees. Just at first, with that brilliant silver light behind them and shining round each head like a nimbus, she could not see their faces, but after a moment she saw that they were children and that they were smiling at her. She was delighted. "Come on," she cried.

They scrambled over the bank between the trunks of the trees and came to her. They were extraordinarily jolly children, two boys and a girl. Thinking about them afterwards she was surprised to find that she did not know in the least how old they were. They didn't seem to have any age. They were just children. But they were evidently Island children for they knew all the Island games and songs and nursery rhymes. Colette had a perfectly glorious morning playing with them. They played the pebble game, singing its rhyme as they played.

> "Mon toussebelet va demandant,
> Ma fausse vieille va quérant,
> Sur lequel prends tu, bon enfant?"

And they played the cushion game that, brought by an Islander to England centuries before, had so delighted Charles the Second. And they played the lovely dancing game, careering round and round over the aconites in the orchard and singing the refrain as they danced, "Saluez, Messieurs et Dames. Ah! mon beau lau-ri-er!" And when Colette was tired she sat down on the bank under the oak trees and the children sang nursery rhymes to her. They sang all Colette's favourites, the Island shoeing song, "Ferre, ferre la pouliche," and "L'alouette, l'alouette, qui vole en haut," and the cradle song, "Dindon Bolilin, quatre éfants dans la bain de Madame." Their voices, sweet and shrill, floated, across the orchard and the garden, but strangely enough, Colette found afterwards that no one in the house seemed to have heard them singing. When the dinner bell rang the children popped over the bank and disappeared. As they went one of the boys said something that puzzled Colette. "You very nearly came to us," he said, "wouldn't it have been fun if you had?" But he had gone before she could ask him what he meant. "Come back to-morrow," she shouted to the empty bank. "Yes, coming back to-morrow;" the words, called by three young voices, sounded like silver bells tolling very far away.

III

"How long has Mademoiselle Colette been in the garden?" asked Rachell of Toinette.

"Ten minutes," said Toinette, "she took 'er goloshes. She said she must 'urry. They were waiting for 'er."

"The—the—her imaginary playmates?" stammered Rachell. Somehow the mention of these children of Colette's made her heart beat twice as fast as usual.

"What an' 'ead that child have for romancin,'" giggled Toinette lovingly, "she told me their names to-day."

"What are their names?" Rachell could hardly get the words out.

"Martin, Matthieu and Renouvette," said Toinette.

The kitchen seemed whirling round Rachell. She dropped the potatoes she was peeling and groped her way out to the front door, Toinette staring after her with goggle eyes. Clinging to the lintel of the door she tried to look across the courtyard to the garden but there seemed a mist in front of her eyes. . . . Martin, Matthieu and Renouvette. . . . Her three dead children. Had Colette heard the names and attached them to her three imaginary playmates? . . . Or had—or was—? Rachell's thoughts seemed reeling. With her hands in front of her, as though she were groping in darkness, she crossed the courtyard and came to the entrance to the garden. In front of her stretched the moss-grown path, bordered now by a blaze of golden crocuses. Colette, her back to her mother, was running down the path. Each of her hands was held out as though holding the hands of two children running one on each side of her and every now and then she laughed back over her shoulder as though at a third. Rachell watched till Colette disappeared behind the trees of the orchard and still she stood at the garden door, watching and straining, but she could not see what Colette saw. For a long time she stood there, breathing deeply, a great joy glowing all through her, then she turned and went, treading on air, back to the kitchen and her potatoes. She had not seen with her eyes—the dead are the dead, and the living are the living, and only a child may pass without harm from one world to another—but conviction was hers. She was gloriously, radiantly happy. She was as happy as the blackbird who had sung on the lilac bush. Martin, Matthieu, and Renouvette were out there in the garden, dancing between the crocuses and in and out of the apple trees. . . . Martin, Matthieu and Renouvette. . . . They were still at Bon Repos. The light of their lives was still part of its radiance. Nothing, she knew now, could put out that light and nothing, she vowed to herself, nothing in all the world, could make her leave this home where it shone.

IV

It was a half-holiday, and after dinner all the children offered to help wash up. Gone were the happy days when Rachell could go to her room and leave the washing up to Sophie. Anything left to Toinette was never finished till midnight. The function of a helper being primarily to get in the way, Rachell sighed a little, but she marshalled them out to the scullery and dealt round dish cloths. It was bad for their characters to have their generous impulses quenched. Toinette squeaked with delight. There was nothing she liked better than to have the whole of her beloved family with her in the scullery, where she could gaze with admiring eyes into each face in turn and do no work at all. Michelle and Peronelle splashed about in two tubs of hot water, and the rest stood round in a semicircle and dried. Everyone talked at once and Colette, who should have been lying on her bed, sat on top of the copper and laughed her soda-water syphon laugh. Then, as is the way of children, they suddenly began to make portentous announcements. Colette began it. A propos of nothing at all she suddenly stopped laughing and announced, "I shall get married and have ten babies."

They all laughed except Rachell, who was silent with intense relief. Her fear that Colette might become a nun had been strengthened by the morning's events. . . . The child seemed to have such a gift for the supernatural. . . . But if, even at six years old, her mind was already bent on domesticity Rachell felt she might be more at ease.

"I shall marry," said Peronelle, flinging her dish cloth like a lassoo round Colin's neck, "if I can find a man with no beard who never has a cold in the head. But I shan't have ten children. Five's enough. Don't you find five quite enough, mother?"

"I wouldn't be without one of you," declared Rachell, "but, yes, I think five's enough."

"I shall teach," said Michelle primly.

"What else *can* you do with a face like yours?" asked Colin rudely. "You're a prig. Men don't marry prigs." He didn't like washing up, and he had been annoyed by Peronelle's damp dish cloth coiling round his neck, and he felt suddenly, as he often felt, that there were too many women in the world.

"You beast, Colin!" said Peronelle hotly, and dropped a plate.

"If he likes to make vulgar remarks, let him," said Michelle with increased primness, "they hurt no one but himself." The atmosphere became a little tense.

"What are *you* going to be, Colin?" asked Rachell, to lighten it.

Colin did not answer, but the eyes he flashed angrily round on her were an intense sea blue—tinged, perhaps, by his future. . . . His mother's heart sank.

"Can't you answer when mother speaks to you?" demanded Peronelle, fuming. "You're a rude, vulgar, nasty little toad, and you've made me smash this plate!"

Colin lowered his head and butted. Peronelle, with great skill, ducked and seized him round the legs. Rachell pushed them, locked in a death grip, out into the yard and shut the door on them. She sighed. She always found it very tiring to be helped by the children.

"I've done this lot," said Michelle, "I think I shall go and read Plato. You can call me if you want me, mother."

"Very well, dear," said Rachell meekly, and Michelle walked from the scullery with chilly dignity.

Peace now descended. Toinette splashed greasily by herself in one tub, and Rachell and Jacqueline tackled the other. Colette, singing a little song to herself on top of the copper, seemed to have forgotten all about them.

"Mother," announced Jacqueline, "I'm going to take the veil like St. Theresa."

Rachell dropped a dish cover. Toinette emitted a squeak of joy and then thrust her knuckles into her mouth. That Madame should break something after scolding her, Toinette, day in and day out for her smashings, was really too delicious. Jacqueline stooped to pick up the pieces and her mother looked down at the top of her head with bewildered astonishment. She had been afraid of Colette's desires turning in that direction, but not Jacqueline's. She had always thought of Jacqueline as an empty-headed rather frivolous little creature. Well, one never knew. Jacqueline's eyes, as she rose up from the floor with the broken dish cover in her hands, held the same look as Colin's had done when he announced that he must be a sailor. . . . She meant what she said.

"You see, mother," Jacqueline continued solemnly, "I'm not clever with people like Peronelle is. I can't make them laugh and tell me things. And I've no brains so I can't teach them like Michelle's going to do. But Soeur Monique says that however much of a goose you may be you can always pray for them. That's what I shall do. I shall pray like St. Theresa's Carmelites, and my unseen influence will be immense." She ended on a note whose loftiness, borrowed from Soeur Monique, was quite overwhelming. Toinette, overwhelmed, dropped a butter dish. Rachell was both astonished and horrified. Astonished that Jacqueline should admit her own shortcomings—she who could never in the past be brought to admit anything against herself—horrified at the priggishness of her remarks. Really, it was quite enough to have Michelle prigging about the place, to have Jacqueline as well would be too much. Then she remembered that priggishness is an inevitable stage in spiritual development, and was ashamed of herself. But, nevertheless, you could have knocked her down with a feather. As soon as the washing up was finished she staggered off to the corn bin to find André. She knew he was there doing accounts. When she came in he was sitting at the table in the window writing. He slipped his blotting paper over the scattered pages to hide them. Rachell sat down on a sack of meal and sketched his children's futures to him.

"I can't let Colin be a sailor, it's too dangerous a life, and I can't let Jacqueline take the veil—her hair's so pretty," she wailed.

"Let them do what they like," said André. He paused, sketching arabesques on the blotting paper with his pen. "I often think," he said sombrely, "that looking for happiness through work is like tunnelling through the solid rock for gold. One needs to put driving power, the whole force and drive of one's nature, behind one's tunnelling if one is to get through. How can one do that if one's heart is not in one's work? Let them do what they want to do."

He turned his back on Rachell, pushing some pages that still peeped out farther under the sheltering blotting paper. Rachell wondered why he was so anxious to hide the farm accounts from her, and why he was doing them on loose pages instead of in the usual account book.

"Let the children choose their own work," André went on. "I want them to enjoy it. They'll have to work hard—and soon."

"Soon?" There was a hard edge to his voice that frightened Rachell. He swung round and looked at her.

"The six months is more than up," he said. "We agreed, if you remember, to stay on for six months more at Bon Repos and then see how we stood." His eyes looked a little desperate, like a trapped animal's, and his voice, as always when he was deeply moved, was dull and flat.

"How *do* we stand?" Rachell gripped the sack on each side of her and felt cold. The lovely spring day seemed to darken.

"It's very simple," said André. "Our money—*your* money—is finished. We had hoped my father would have had something substantial to leave. Well, he hadn't. He left debts, as you know. . . . Those miserable horses."

"He left a little," pleaded Rachell.

"Enough to help us move from Bon Repos and settle in some little house while I look about for a clerkship."

"You—my husband—a clerk!" Rachell could hardly speak for indignation.

"My handwriting," said André cynically, "is beautiful."

Rachell got up and shook the dust from her black skirts. She had been very tired after the washing up and her native strength and determination had for the moment forsaken her. Now they flowed back. She stood in front of André, dominating him. The door had swung open, and behind her he could see the lovely world of Bon

Repos—the cobbled courtyard with the doves strutting in the sun, the doorway crowned with its huge old lintel, the front door of the house with its French inscription over it and the fuchsias on either side, the little diamond paned windows with the passion flower creeping round them. In front of it all stood Rachell like a tigress defending her young.

"The money that father left," she told André, "will keep us here for four months longer."

"And then it, too, will be gone and there will be nothing left to start us in a new way of life."

André's voice was harsh with obstinacy. Rachell saw she was going to have a harder tussle with him than she had had before, but over against his weak obstinacy she set her real strength and knew that she would win.

"We are going to stay here until the last possible moment," she said.

"You are normally a clear-headed woman; why are you so amazingly unreasonable on this one point? You know quite well that I cannot make this farm pay."

"Since Ranulph Mabier came here and helped you things have been better."

André winced, and the angry blood surged to his forehead. Her thrust was cruel but true. In a thousand unobtrusive ways Ranulph, practical, competent and clear-headed, had eased the situation on the farm. André swallowed down his humiliation. "Mabier is a better farmer than I am, but even with his help this farm still does not pay—and I do not like accepting his help."

"Nevertheless, we will not go till we are driven." Behind her Rachell could hear the cooing of the doves and the rustling of the wind in the budding fuchsia bushes. In her mind's eye she could see her parlour with the yellow flames of the driftwood fire touching with fingers of light the Chinese dragons and the gillyflowers, the butterflies and the forget-me-nots. She could move her treasures to another house—to the hideous modern villa of a jobbing clerk—but the spirit of Bon Repos that infused them with life would be dead and about them there would be the scent and horror of corruption. And the children—the living children—here they had the strength and beauty of fishes in the sea, but what would they be like taken out of their home? Breathless, suffocating things. And the dead children? There was no power, anywhere, that could tear her from this garden where they played. She raised her arms for a moment as though to protect the little world behind her.

"Once again, Rachell," said André harshly, "what makes you so crazily unreasonable?"

"Do you remember what I said before?" said Rachell. "You can't create a thing and then destroy it. That is murder. You and I have created something here. We have brought to life a living spirit in Bon Repos. It is a real thing; it fills the house and everything in it, and gives them life. It is like a light shining out. You must not, cannot put it out."

She felt what he had felt on Christmas night when he watched the long beam of light from the kitchen window stretching out across the courtyard to the garden and the cliff beyond. He started, and his will was a little shaken. When he spoke again it was more weakly.

"Don't you realize that the longer we put off the crash the greater it will be when it comes?"

"It will never come. Something will happen to prevent it."

He gave an exclamation of impatience. "You said that before."

"And I say it again. It is true. I know that it is true."

Rachell's faith in her own vision, so often wavering, grew stronger the more he opposed her, and as the flame of it burnt up she bent her will more and more strongly to oppose him. There was no softness in her now, no shadow of yielding. She did not, as she had done before, melt him with tears. She was too desperate to cry. She bore him down with the solid rock of her opposition. For a little while longer they argued, and then the interview ended abruptly in the usual complete rout of André. But it did not end happily. For, perhaps, the first time in their married life Rachell's gifts of loving finesse and persuasion were lost in her driving strength. She did not leave André feeling that the decision come to was his. She left him feeling a beaten and humbled creature. The argument over, he swung round in his chair, his back towards her, and bent over his papers. Turning to go she looked at him and was pierced to the heart by his attitude.

"André," she said, "let me help you with those miserable accounts."

"They are not accounts," he said.

"Then what are you doing?"

"I am writing. I am keeping myself sane by the exercise of my art," he said, and turned his back on her once more.

Rachell felt as though he had struck her a blow between the eyes. He wrote—and he had never told her. He had a secret life, and he had kept her out of it. She thought she had his whole confidence, and she had not. All these years he should have been putting his whole driving power into the farm, their means of livelihood, and instead of that he had frittered away his strength on what was probably nonsense. She had devoted her whole life to him, given him all that she had, and how had he rewarded her? He had lost all the money she had given him and brought her and her children to the verge of ruin. She went back across the courtyard, across the hall, and upstairs to her bedroom. Her heart was very hard towards him. She threw herself face downwards on her bed.

V

But the trials of that day were by no means over, the chief of them was yet to come. The children had gone down to the beach for a picnic. Rachell, André, and Ranulph had an early and very silent tea together. André's distress of mind issued in an exceeding crossness. It was most unusual for André to be cross, but Rachell had humiliated him and his heart, for once in a way, was bitter towards her. His bitterness increased hers. Ranulph raised his eyebrows humorously and looked from one to the other. His humour, seeming as it did to drive a little wedge between himself and Rachell, exasperated André's already rasped temper. He got abruptly to his feet, leaving his tea unfinished.

"I'm going down to St. Pierre on business," he said sharply, and looked at Rachell. His eyes had steel in them. She wondered if he was going to make secret inquiries about that clerkship and that horrible modern villa.

"Certainly," she said coldly, and he went. She was left with Ranulph.

She leant back and sighed. After the scene with André she felt horribly tired. Once again she had fought her husband and wrested the leadership of the family from him, but this time she was so tired that she felt hardly able to shoulder the load. She almost wished she hadn't done it. Moreover she had been so unskilful that she had made André antagonistic. Of what use to stay on at Bon Repos staggering under a burden too heavy for her, and losing André's love? A thrill of panic went through her. If their love failed then the spirit of Bon Repos would indeed be dead and the three children in the garden would go away. A disagreement with André was so rare that it made her feel the end of the world had come, and the reaction from her output of strength made her feel horribly weak. . . . She wished André were a strong man. . . . If only she had someone strong to lean on what heaven it would be.

"Come out into the garden," said Ranulph suddenly.

"I haven't time," she said. Some instinctive shrinking shot out the words almost without her knowledge.

"You've all the time there is," said Ranulph. "I happen to know that Peronelle has done the ironing for you, and as for the supper, it's cold and in the larder. I saw it with my own eyes. Come out. You want air."

He dominated her. In her present mood of weakness it was almost pleasant to be dominated. Together they went across the courtyard and into the garden. The day was brilliant as ever and all its brightness seemed to Rachell to be centred in the crocuses. She remembered how she had seen Colette, hands outstretched, running down the path that morning between the golden borders.

"And its streets were paved with gold." The words made her heart ache. The heavenly country was so near, in her soul and all around her, yet now, in her bodily weakness, she could not enter in.

Ranulph, aware of the weakness and melting softness in her, judged this a good moment to open a campaign he had long meditated.

"Cheeky fellows, these crocuses," he said, "they remind me of Colin."

"You're very fond of Colin," said Rachell.

"Stuff in him," said Ranulph, "I'd like to see him a sailor."

"Why?" she asked sharply.

"Because he wants to be."

"Is that a good reason?" Rachell's voice was more weary than defiant. There was no more fight left in her.

"It's like this," said Ranulph, "happiness is hidden in life like gold in the rock, and there are many different ways of tunnelling down to it. A child's instinct will tell him which way is best for himself to tackle. Try and make him tackle the tunnelling a different way and he'll run amok—lay a fuse and blow up the whole thing, himself, and the gold, and all."

"Did André tell you to say that?" demanded Rachell.

"No. Why?"

"Because he said practically the same thing himself this afternoon and used the same metaphor. . . . I do find metaphors so fatiguing."

"Fatiguing but useful," said Ranulph. "Don't you think one grasps a truth best in the form of a picture? One does not even know a soul is there unless the thing is draped in a body. . . . It looks as though André and I had seen that boy alike."

Rachell was silent.

"It's difficult to say what's most disastrous," mused Ranulph, "an unloving and autocratic father or a loving and autocratic mother. I suffered from the first. I lit a fuse and blew up myself and the gold. Colin suffers from the second. He may do the same."

"I wonder," said Rachell, "why I let you say these things to me? No one else would dare interfere between me and Colin."

"You let me because the poor devil means well."

They crossed the garden in silence. Though Rachell said nothing Ranulph was aware of a yielding in her silence. He judged himself a victor.

They came to the orchard. The leaves of the apple trees, crinkled, jade green and spear shaped, were just unfolding and beneath them the primroses were thrusting up through the grass. Colette's hoary old trees, still bare of leaves, twisted intricate black tracery against the sky. Great grey clouds, edged with silver, were sailing up out of the sea. The birds, now that the shadows were lengthening, sang less riotously but with a heart-piercing sweetness.

"What loveliness!" said Rachell, "lovely and yet mocking. Nature can be very hard. When you are happy she laughs with you, but when you are miserable she mocks."

"Tell me why she is mocking now," demanded Ranulph. Again he dominated her, and against her will she told him.

"You are right," he said, "you must stay here. Stick to it."

"But I have no practical reason for my certainty that all will come right," she murmured miserably. "It is only an intuition. On the face of it, it is André who is right and I who am wrong—crazily wrong."

"It is you who are right. The kind of certainty that you have, based on no practical reason, is the only certain certainty, Irish as it may sound."

"But why?"

"Practical reasons are as brittle as the material facts they are based on, but intuition is the pressure of fate upon you—the future that ought to be taking your hand."

"That ought to be?" she repeated.

"That will be," he said. There was something forceful in the way he spoke and she looked at him. His queer light eyes seemed to be looking through her. She felt, as she had felt on the night when he first came, that he had come right into the inner sanctuary of her, had sullied its whiteness with his footprints and disturbed its harmony with his harsh voice. She felt, as she had felt then, terrified, and turned quickly away through the little gate that led to the cliff. He followed her. On the farther side of the gate one of the old trees—was it on purpose?—had pushed a root out. She caught her foot in it and gave a little cry, feeling herself falling. Ranulph caught her, lifted her free of the roots, and carried her a few steps over the rough grass. They stood caught between the frieze of the old fantastic trees and the blue sheet of the sea. The world of Bon Repos was hidden from them by the trees and the horizon line of the sea was lost in a soft haze. As once before, evening was melting the colours of earth and sea and sky, and the walls of the world were contracting. They were shut away together.

Ranulph's arms, that had slackened, suddenly tightened round Rachell. His passion flamed out and he kissed her bent neck and the coils of her dark hair. She raised her face with her eyes closed, and he kissed her lips. His arms round her were strong as iron and seemed to her to be lifting her up above the sea of trouble that had been drowning her. She felt like a spent swimmer buoyed up by a flung lifebelt. Warmth and courage came to her from his strength. She leant against him in an ecstasy and time stopped. Then once more she lifted her face, her eyes wide open, and looked at him. Passion was alight and blazing in his face, transforming it, and the transformation was ugly. . . . And she had let him, this creature, walk right into her soul, defiling it. . . . She twisted agonizedly in his arms. "Let go of me," she whispered. For a moment he gripped her more fiercely and looking up at him, terrified, she saw a hideous struggle going on in his face, then, with the suddenness of a spent body falling from life to death, his arms fell from her. She turned and fled.

VI

Ranulph, left alone, paced the narrow strip of turf between trees and sea with the savagery of a leopard behind bars. The evil that was in him, caged so long, had got out and paced with him, unsatisfied, snarling. Striding backwards and forwards he fought it.

The melting evening light had become sunset before he had got the thing caged again. He sat down under the trees. From the pinnacle of their great age, desire dead in them, they looked down at him pitifully. The warm day was closing with a hint of thunder and the sunset had a yellow tinge. The grey clouds edged with silver had become buff colour tipped with gold and the sea was muddy.

"Sulphurous," said Ranulph, and a harsh humour twisted his face. What in the world had come over him? What in the world had he done? Ever since he came to Bon Repos his love for Rachell had been growing but he had felt secure in his own power of self mastery. He had never intended, never for one moment expected, that the thing would become unmanageable. His natural recoil from all ties should surely have protected him from such an exhibition as this. What in the world had tripped him up? He thought it must have been the unexpected yieldingness, almost weakness, of her mood that afternoon. When with her he had grown accustomed to facing a strength that equalled his own, he had been like a man leaning against a strong wind. It had been suddenly withdrawn and he had fallen. Was that it? Or was it that his acceptance of human ties, after so many years of freedom from them, had made him subject to human frailty again? He had once more opened the doors to the sweetness of intimacy and the abusing of intimacy, once practised by him and so long dormant, had come alive again. His past, upon which he thought he had turned his back, had found him out and tripped him up. Well, whatever the reason, his momentary madness had landed him in a pretty mess. How was he now to carry out his plans for Bon Repos? He had seen himself, with his wealth behind him, taking over the management of the farm and freeing André, giving to Rachell comfort and ease, and helping the children to their life's work. He had foreseen for them all a happy life together. Yet all this entailed his bodily presence at Bon Repos and that, now, would be difficult. For how account to Rachell for his behaviour without telling her that he loved her and how, with that knowledge between them, could they tolerate life together? Moreover the incident had possessed him of a piece of self-knowledge. He loved this woman more than he knew. The load was going to be one uncommonly difficult to carry. What was to be done? He supposed there was nothing to be done but to go on pursuing his self-appointed ends and hoping for the best. He got up heavily. It was evening now and he was stiff and cold, and slightly rheumatic. Rubbing his knees he looked up at the old twisted trees. They looked rheumatic too, and extremely mocking. Their attitudes suggested that at his age he should have had more sense than to have made such an exhibition of himself. As he went through the orchard he was cursing his folly in having returned to this blasted little Island. It had always played havoc with his emotions. His love for his mother and his grief at her death—his love for Blanche Tangrouille—his struggle with his father—his crazy young manhood, the result of all four—and now this love for his brother's wife—the Island had seen them all, had, he felt, caused them all. There was something about this Island, its beauty, its magic, that made it impossible to chew the cud in torpor; one was obliged to think and feel. . . . A great mistake. . . . He wished he'd never come back to the wretched place.

He came through the trees of the orchard into the crocus-bordered path. Through the door that led into the courtyard he could see the open front door of Bon Repos. The lights in the house were already lighted and a long orange finger stretched from the front door across the courtyard and right down the garden path to his feet. It seemed like something alive, the spirit of the house made visible, stretching out to him and touching him, claiming him. He belonged to it. There was no escaping from that now. He belonged. He quite suddenly changed his mind and, in spite of difficulty and suffering to come, was glad he had returned to his wretched little Island.

Then, standing on the garden path, tethered as it were, by that long finger of light, he began to wonder about Rachell. She had yielded to him. She had clung to him. It was not until their mutual passion was a little spent that fright had seized her. . . . Why? . . . Her love for André was, he felt, one of the unshakeable facts of nature. . . . Then why? . . . There was, of course, love and love. . . . That finger of light pulling him he began to walk slowly towards the house.

VII

Rachell, when she left Ranulph, fled for the second time that day to her bedroom. But she did not lie on her bed this time. She paced, as Ranulph had done, backwards and forwards, fighting this sudden flaring up of passion in her. It was not until dusk fell and the silver-fringed clouds were gold-tipped that some measure of tranquillity was restored to her. What in the world had come over her? How could she, Rachell, who for sixteen years had been dedicated, body and mind, to her husband, have behaved in this appalling manner? What to another woman would have seemed a pleasant interlude in a drab life seemed to Rachell treachery of the deepest dye. The memory of her yielding, of her kiss voluntarily and passionately given, filled her with self-loathing. Desperately she tried to understand herself and to look the thing in the face. First and foremost there had been her own weakness. The day's doings, above all the tussle with André, had exhausted her. Then there had been her rare bitterness towards André. That, she knew, had come from her own sense of failure. She had been unskilful in her handling of him and, human like, had chosen to be exasperated with him instead of with herself. Bitterness between her and André was so rare that it had about it the quality of an earthquake. It was disintegrating. Feeling herself weak and in pieces she had cried out for something to prop and bind her, and had found it in Ranulph. That was it. She had always felt the man had a great strength in him, a great power of binding up and re-organizing the broken and the chaotic. But that was not all. She had not only been the weak woman yielding to strength. She had given as well as yielded. What then? Did she love him? This made her stop in her pacing and stand still at her window. For a long time she stood, then she sighed and turned away, groping for a chair. She sat down weakly. She did love him. The love she had for André, a thing of use and wont, and of many years' growth, was unshakeable. This other thing was something entirely different. There was more of passion in it than of actual love. She was so utterly weary after years of hard work and struggle that the man's strength had touched her. She felt towards him as a child feels towards arms that pick her up and carry her through a storm. And then, too, Ranulph was in his queer way picturesque, almost romantic. He brought with him the flavour of adventure and something of the excitement of worldliness. She was a beautiful woman who for years had had no homage paid to her beauty. She had had to fight hard, in the old days, to batten down her longing for pleasure and for admiration. She supposed now that her imprisoned vanity was revenged on her. It had come out of its cage, clamouring for food. Yes, that was it. This love of hers and Ranulph's was based on weakness and on the clamouring of imprisoned things—a despicable thing and to be treated as such. . . . One more thing to fight. . . . The supper bell rang. . . . She got up and slowly washed her hands and prepared herself for supper. . . . One more thing to fight. . . . She had heard of this happening to other women, but never had she thought it could possibly happen to herself. . . . Well, there it was. . . . One never knew. She took some primroses from a vase on her dressing table and tucked them into her belt. She put a smile upon her lips, drew herself erect and sailed down to supper.

They were all there and waiting for her, André, Ranulph and the children. "Am I late? I'm so sorry."

Her eyes swept over them all, resting caressingly on each child, meeting Ranulph's glance fearlessly, looking long and searchingly at André. He returned her glance and smiled. The cloud that had been between them lifted and was gone, and they were back again on the old footing. Rachell sighed a little with relief. If things were as ever between her and André she felt secure to tackle this new and puzzling relationship.

Supper passed as usual, the children went to bed, and André to some job about the farm. Toinette cleared the table, and Rachell and Ranulph were alone. Any other Victorian woman, Ranulph thought, would have taken very good care not to be left alone with him again, but not so Rachell. She crossed to the "jonquière" and sat down, her hands folded in her lap, her eyes fixed on him. Ranulph, his arms folded, stood in front of the fire and looked at her. He gave a short laugh. "Well?" he said.

Rachell smiled a little. It was, she thought, characteristic of him to offer no word of apology.

"I am in a predicament," she said. "I would like to ask you to leave Bon Repos, but yet, somehow, I feel you are necessary to it."

He raised his eyebrows and shot out his hands in a French gesture that he used now and then. "I am," he said, "and I have no intention of leaving here."

"Why is it that we both feel you are necessary?" asked Rachell a little tartly. "You have done nothing, that I can see, to justify that feeling."

"Wait," said Ranulph, "fate, weaving the pattern of Bon Repos, introduced a new colour when she cast me up here. When she's finished with the colour we'll see its place in the pattern. Let us trust our intuition—the pressure of fate upon us."

"I wish," said Rachell impatiently, "that you wouldn't always talk in metaphor."

"It amuses me," said Ranulph.

Rachell flushed with sudden anger. "I suppose your behaviour this afternoon amused you?"

"No," said Ranulph, "I can't say I was amused. My little exhibition of passion was quite genuine. . . . So was yours."

He raised one eyebrow and looked at her mockingly. At the thrust Rachel's flush disappeared and she went quite white.

"I love you," said Ranulph, "but it was never my intention to make the matter quite so obvious. . . . I was certainly very crude. . . . Something caged in me got out."

"As did my vanity," said Rachell.

"Oh?" queried Ranulph, "caged vanity? I daresay it did you good to let it out for a moment. I am glad to have done obeisance to your beauty."

"Well, please don't do it again." She got up and faced him. "I hope what you said just now was no more than a sop to my vanity?"

Ranulph smiled. "Love? No, it was the truth. The thing is between us. On your side as well as mine."

Rachell flushed again. "How dare you—"

"Oh, a mere molehill to my mountain and capable of being crushed by circumstances. We will ignore it. Most things die if ignored. What was it Benvolio and Romeo said? 'In love—out—of love.' The passage from one to the other can be accomplished with a little good will." He smiled, bitterly, and she was touched.

"I am so sorry. Will you find it hard?" she asked. Her voice was soft and her whole figure seemed melting a little. Ranulph's face hardened.

"With your sympathy—yes; without it—perhaps not."

She drew herself up. "Then you shall not have it," she said. "Good-night."

"Good-night."

She walked to the door, but he called to her a little urgently.

"Rachell."

She paused. "Yes?"

"Human relationships are queer things. No single one is like any other one. I think yours and mine is quite unique, and not altogether despicable."

She turned and looked at him. To her horror she saw he was trembling as with an ague, and that his eyes were alight with a feeling whose depth his words had hardly hinted at. She had not realized it had gone so far with him. . . . In a minute it was gone.

"Well, that's finished with," he said lightly, "and don't reproach yourself. The thing is not despicable."

"No," she said, and smiled. Then she went out and shut the door, leaving him alone.

Chapter 9

I

GOOD FRIDAY and Holy Saturday of that year were long remembered on the Island, the one for its beauty and the other for its storm and shipwreck. By the du Frocqs they were remembered as marking the beginning and the end of an epoch. To both, the Island and the family, those two days together seemed to bring home the twin facts of life and death with a rather terrible force.

As Easter approached Toinette began to suffer from what the Islanders call "avertissements"—warnings of evil to come. She heard queer noises about the house, bumps when there was nothing to bump, steps going up and down stairs when everyone was in bed, the crowing of cocks at unusual hours, the howling of dogs and hooting of owls. She came down every morning goggle-eyed and full of it, and Rachell had the greatest difficulty in making her keep her avertissements more or less to herself.

"You'll see, madame, you'll see," she said, "something terrible will 'appen."

"Be quiet, Toinette," said Rachell. But it was no good. Strong minded as the du Frocqs were Toinette's avertissements sent a little shiver of uneasiness through them all.

Even Ranulph, on Good Friday morning, felt the least bit disturbed. He was standing at his window looking across the farmyard to the meadow beyond. There were ladies-smocks now in the meadow grass, and along the hedge was a line of budding bluebells. His gaze, dreamily appraising the blue and the silver, wind-rippled, suddenly became fixed. A familiar bearded figure was walking across the meadow. The face turned towards him and he saw quite clearly the man's queer tawny eyes and a great scar across one cheek. He knew the fellow. He was puzzled at first to think who it was, then he realized it was himself. He recoiled and there flashed through his memory the peasant superstition that the dying sometimes see their own wraith before their death. Then he recovered himself and looked out of the window again. . . . There was nothing there. . . . Laughing at his own stupidity he turned back into the room and reached for his cap. . . . He was going to take the children down to L'Autel beach to roast limpets, according to the quite outrageous custom of the Island on Good Friday.

II

This Good Friday was perhaps more vividly remembered by Michelle than by anyone else. She began the morning by having one of her customary moments of clear and lovely thinking and she went on from that to have one of her equally customary violent falls from virtue. But after that, with the help of Ranulph, she got nearer than she had ever got before to reconciling the two.

She awoke at dawn. She had been dreaming, she didn't quite know why, of wings. All night they had been rustling and flapping round her. For the most part they had been the familiar wings that she knew, the serene slow flappings of the gulls, the soft whir of Rachell's doves, the little flip-flaps of the robins and the wrens, but every now and then there would come a beating and a violent rushing, and something terrible would sweep like a great wind through the gentle sounds. Whenever this happened she would wake up suddenly with a feeling of terror, realize it was only a dream and go to sleep again.

When she awoke finally it was to find a wind blowing, not a gale but the fresh south-westerly wind that sometimes precedes a gale. She thought perhaps the sound of it, penetrating her sleep, had made her dream of all those wings. But it was a gay, jolly wind, it didn't account for that terrible flapping thing. . . . She thought of Toinette's avertissements and shivered a little.

Then she jumped out of bed, ran to the window and pulled the curtain. She gasped at what she saw. It had been raining in the night, but now there was a dawn beautiful beyond anything she had ever seen. It had a naked, rather terrible beauty, wind-swept and amazingly clear. The sky, a cold intense blue-green, was scattered all over with little windy wisps of cloud of a burning gold, flecking larger, steadier clouds, pale hued, almost invisible, that had not yet caught the sun. Down on the horizon, over the sea, were bars of cloud of a rich blood-red. From where she stood she could see, over the courtyard wall, the garden and the orchard, and the twisted oak trees. Easter was late that year, and the apple blossom was already out and at the mercy of the wind. White petals were drifting like blown sea spray at every gust of wind and the fat coral buds, terrified, were clinging, limpet-like, to the brown twigs. Below the apple trees the bluebells and ladies-smocks were dancing and shifting and, down the garden path, on each side, the stolid spires of hyacinths and the wallflower buds, black with folded colour, were bowing and swaying. The air was so amazingly clear that Michelle felt she could almost see each individual petal and crinkled leaf. Such a clearness, and such a vivid sky, were ominous. She looked beyond to the row of old oak trees. Yes, they were tossing their arms already, black and rather alarming against those red streaks of cloud.

But Michelle was not afraid of storms and she passed quickly from foreboding to amazement at the morning's beauty. Those tossed little plumes of cloud made her think of the ruffled feathers of a dove's breast. Her mind full of birds it seemed to her that the farther clouds beyond them, sailing more steadily before the wind, were like widespread slowly beating wings. It was years later that a poet[5], seeing, perhaps, such a sunrise as this, was to write:

> ". . . though the last lights off the black west went
> Oh, morning, at the brown brink eastwards springs—
> Because the Holy Ghost over the bent
> World broods with warm breast and with ah!
> bright wings."

---

[5]Gerard Hopkins.

If Michelle could have read those words she would have pounced on them joyously as expressing perfectly the feeling in her that was trying to find expression, but as it was she had to grope about in her own mind for the words she wanted, for words she must have; she and the sunrise had met and from all union there is birth.

She remembered how last summer, out at La Baie des Mouettes, she had thought of beauty as a bird and of all the scraps and shreds of beauty that make up that shining whole as feathers in her wings. And then she had thought of love and truth and beauty as being the same, just different facets of the orbed drop. She had realized that the problem of life is one of unity. The orbed drop of light, the winged beauty, is there, but how melt into its radiance and become one with it? But she had got no farther than that, for Peronelle and Jacqueline had interrupted her and she had immediately behaved abominably. But now, so early in the morning, with no one to disturb her, here was a further chance of getting somewhere. Reality, she knew, is beyond knowledge, and only to be apprehended a little in the form of pictures. The picture of the dove was presented to her now and she fixed her thoughts upon it. The warm brooding golden breast and the wings above stretching farther than she could see, almost invisible. The one turned earthwards and the others beating in heaven. Earth and heaven united by that great gleaming spirit. For yes, a bird was the symbol of spirit as well as the symbol of beauty, and love and truth and beauty were different facets of that orbed drop of light that hangs at the tip-top and must be—spirit. Then if spirit were the shining whole of beauty every scrap and shred of beauty must be spirit too. Spirit must be not only a great dove brooding over the world but also a mysterious something indwelling created things. It must be like the candle set in a coloured lantern that gives unearthly beauty to what without it is only a dull affair of paint and glass. Michelle thought again. Was it in her? She knew that she could love, that she could on rare, very rare, occasions, think clear thoughts and say sweet things. That must be spirit. The same spirit that made a bluebell a lovely thing and set magic in a blackbird's song, the same spirit that brooded winged over the world; and she must learn how to link the spirit in her to all those other effluences of spirit. But how? How? Did anyone ever find out? Did nuns in their convents know, or those hermits who had gone away to live in caves, alone with day and night and silence? She felt that if she looked for a little longer at that great dove in the sky she would begin to know. Propping her elbows on the window sill and her chin in her hands she gazed and gazed. She could feel, as Jacqueline had felt in the Convent rock garden, something in her stretching out to join something in the beauty outside her, but it was only a sensation and it did not satisfy her as it had satisfied Jacqueline. It was not enough to feel; feeling, she realized, was fleeting and not always to be trusted, she wanted to *be*. She wanted something permanent, some union that could be held and kept with her always. If she waited patiently perhaps—perhaps. . . .

It was at this moment that Colette, full of the best intentions, awoke, perceived Michelle, and running across the room butted her in the back. A starving, homeless beggar who has tramped for miles uphill in bitter weather to gain a promised meal at a warm fireside, and then has the door shut in his face, could not have been more crazily, heartbrokenly, savagely outraged than Michelle at this moment. She leapt to her feet with whirlwind fury and boxed Colette on the ears. Now Colette had never suffered this outrage at the hands of anyone but Madame Gaboreau, and to have it presented to her in the bosom of her own family was simply more than she could stand. She was normally a placid, sweet tempered creature, but the blow, bringing back as it did the memory of the terror of that day at grandpapa's, and rewarding with cruelty her excellent intentions, completely bowled her over. She howled. She roared. She screamed. She stamped. She kicked. The row brought Peronelle rushing in, slipperless, her nightgown flying behind her.

"What in the world are you doing to Colette?" she demanded fiercely.

"She butted me in the back—horrid little thing—I boxed her ears." Michelle had a considerable temper of her own and it was now thoroughly roused. Her cheeks flamed and her heart within her grew harder and harder.

"You—boxed Colette's ears? *Colette?* And she's just been ill." Peronelle flung back her head and each separate golden hair stood straight out, quivering with rage.

"She's perfectly well now," said Michelle sullenly, "quite well enough to have her ears boxed. She's been spoilt, that's what it is. She thinks she can do what she likes—nasty little beast."

The red flag of battle was now flying in Peronelle's cheeks too. She swung her long slender arms and the box on the ears she gave Michelle had about it the overwhelming strength of a righteous cause. Michelle yelled. Colin, charging joyously in in his nightshirt, and not knowing on which side to ally himself, tilted at each in turn to be on the safe side. Jacqueline, clinging to the door knob in terror, sobbed. Colette roared. The uproar brought in Rachell in her nightgown and André in his nightshirt. It took twenty minutes of hard work, and a spanking for Colin, to restore anything like order, and even then the backwash of sobs echoed through the house till breakfast time.

It was a silent meal. Rachell looked round her family with despair. Where did they get these awful tempers from? Colin and Jacqueline, before the riot was quelled, had also been in tempers of sorts. Even now she felt it was by no means over. Peronelle and Colin, whose tempers were of the firework variety, were themselves again and eating hugely, but Michelle was silent, sullen and hard, and ate nothing. She would, Rachell felt, be quite likely to set them all off again before the day was over. Michelle, she thought, was very, very difficult. Unquestionably the most difficult of the children. There seemed no reason for her appalling outbursts. She seemed to fall into them suddenly like a man tumbling down a precipice. . . . From what heights did she fall? . . . And then, having fallen, she did not recover, she remained apparently stunned for hours and hours, stupid and dull and sullen, and quite impossible to live with.

"André," said Rachell suddenly, "it's Good Friday. I shall take the children to church this morning." That would, she thought, keep them quiet and out of mischief.

"You can't, dear," said André mildly, "Lupin's gone lame and I want Gertrais on the farm."

Rachell gave an exclamation of annoyance. . . . It was just like André to make difficulties. . . . To walk both ways would be too much for the children. . . . Her eyes flashed. . . . Ranulph, looking at her, thought it was easy to see where the children got their tempers from. He had been watching the scene with his customary rather irritating expression of humour, now he smiled broadly. Rachell, guessing why, shot arrows at him out of her eyes. . . . He smiled yet more broadly.

"It's Good Friday," he said, "since, owing to equine engagements and disabilities, we can't be Christians we'll be heathens. I'll take the children to roast limpets on the shore. That, I believe, is the heathen custom of this Island?"

"It's extremely kind of you, Mabier," said André gratefully, "It'll be a comfort," he added darkly, "to get the children out of the way."

He did not usually speak like this, but it had been an exhausting morning and spanking Colin on an empty stomach always wearied him. Michelle, stung to the quick by his tone, sank yet deeper into the mud that engulfed her.

"Very well, then," said Ranulph, with an irritating brightness, "we'll go to L'Autel beach. We'll start in an hour and take our lunch."

"Not Colette," said Rachell. "It'll be too far for her."

Colette, now quite restored, smiled fatly. She didn't mind not going. She would be able to play in the garden with those other three who never, never boxed her ears.

"I'm sure we don't want her," said Michelle acidly. Peronelle jumped to her feet, the red flag running up again. "Hold your tongue!" she shouted. "You're a loathsome toad, you're a—"

Rachell arose in majesty. "If I hear a single word more from any of you," she stormed, "you shall all be locked in the stable for the day."

"I think," said Ranulph, "that we will go to L'Autel beach as soon as ever the lunch is cut."

III

They went. It was quite a long walk and the exercise and fresh air, making as they did little punctures in the balloons of temper and letting out the gas, proved beneficial. They hadn't gone half a mile before everyone but Michelle had recovered. She, nasty thing, walked half a pace behind the rest and glowered. Ranulph, fond of her, felt that a knot needed untying here and his fingers itched to be at it.

L'Autel beach was on the flat side of the Island and they walked downhill all the way through narrow corkscrew lanes. In no other part of the world, thought Ranulph, could you find lanes quite like these. On each side a rampart of earth and stones was crowned by a thick matted hedge of twisted honeysuckle, veronica, fuchsias and escallonia. Behind these stunted oak trees bent over to form a roof. Most lanes, if they were not actually water-lanes, had a little trickle of a stream running down one side, edged by vivid luxuriant fern. In summer the scent of mingled honeysuckle and escallonia was overpoweringly lovely but Ranulph, when in Africa he had been choking in dust storms, had always thought of the pungent spring scent of the lanes; wet earth and ferns and moss, primroses and bluebells and the wind from the sea laden with salt.

To-day the lanes were almost startlingly vivid. The double clearness of rain past and storm to come gave to each primrose and buttercup petal, and to each patch of blue sky seen between bright green leaves, the brilliance and hardness of mosaic. There was no distance. The leaves and flowers at the bottom of a lane seemed, as you walked down, to be crowding up to meet you and weaving a brilliant flat pattern just in front of your eyes, a pattern that receded as you walked, and seemed to be luring you on into the very heart of beauty.

"Where are we going?" asked Ranulph.

"To L'Autel beach," said Peronelle, surprised.

"Are we?" said Ranulph. "Colour seems crowding in on us to such an extent that it seems to me we are walking right through it to the other side."

"What is it like on the other side of colour?" asked Peronelle politely.

"Quite white," said Ranulph.

"My stars!" said Colin, "has anybody got matches? We'll want to light a fire to roast the limpets."

The agitated and finally successful searching of Ranulph's pockets turned the attention of everyone but Michelle away from Ranulph's curious remarks. Only Michelle, as she trailed disagreeably in the others' wake, wondered what he meant by saying that whiteness is on the other side of colour.

They came down the last lane on to a flat white road winding across a stretch of common, and in front of them was the sea. This side of the Island was so entirely different from the Bon Repos side that it seemed a different country. Here there were no cliffs. Stretches of sand and grass, seal holly and feathery fennel, ran level with the beach. Little low whitewashed cottages edged the road, their gardens full of veronica and tamarisk trees, and low rocks of rose-pink granite ran out into a sea of an intense blue. Nowhere else round the Island was the sea quite so blue as it was at L'Autel beach. Ranulph stopped, caught his breath and stared. Until to-day he had been too lazy to come to L'Autel. He had forgotten its magic. He had forgotten that any sea, anywhere in the world, could be so blue. He remembered now that L'Autel beach, though perhaps not so grandly beautiful as the rocky coast at Bon Repos, with its chasms and precipices and caverns, had an unearthly beauty that had about it the quality of a dream. One was always afraid it might suddenly melt away. Its colours, except for that vivid sea, were the pale colours of the rainbow, and seemed as fragile. The soft yellow green of the tamarisk trees, the blue-green of the sea holly, the pearly white of the cottages, the mauve of the veronica, the pale pink of the rocks echoed in summer by the diaphanous pink of the tamarisk flowers, all these were the colours of enchantment. Only that brilliant slash of blue, encircling them, seemed to keep them from fading away beyond human sight.

"I tell you what it is," said Ranulph, "if that sea were not there, keeping L'Autel in the curve of a rainbow, keeping it visible colour, it would dissolve into thin air and let one through to the other side. It's tranquillity, that's what it is; tranquillity and acceptance."

Only Michelle heard what he said. The others had gone racing down to the beach. Michelle was far too bad tempered to bother at the moment, but she saved up his remark for future reference.

They set to work collecting limpets, all except Peronelle who couldn't really take to this limpet roasting custom. In spite of repeated assurances to the contrary she was always so dreadfully afraid that perhaps the limpets didn't like it.

"They don't feel a thing, you idiot," Colin assured her, "do they, Uncle Ranulph?"

"A limpet," said Ranulph, struggling with one, "is nothing but jellified obstinacy."

"Well, anyhow, I'll collect the stuff for the fire," said Peronelle, and removed herself.

The limpets, when collected, were laid shell uppermost on a flat rock and covered with dry sticks and furze. This was set on fire, and a glorious sheet of flame covered the rock and made a savage note of colour against the pale greens and pinks of L'Autel. Michelle turned her back, but the others danced round the fire, Colin every now and then leaping over it. They had seen the peasants doing this round the bonfires lit on the first Sunday in Lent, "le Dimanche des Brandons." These fire dances had, Ranulph knew, their origin in a heathen cult driven underground centuries ago. Watching the growing absorption of the children and their almost trance-like movements he suddenly got up and stopped them.... They did not know what they were doing.... It seemed to him that with their dancing something evil stirred for a moment in the heart of L'Autel, something it was better to let alone.

When the flames had died down to glowing ash, and the limpets were done to a turn, Peronelle unpacked the bread and butter, the hard-boiled eggs and the milk, and they settled down to an immense meal. Ranulph, watching limpet after limpet disappearing down the throats of Michelle, Jacqueline and Colin—Peronelle somehow couldn't fancy them—marvelled at the digestive powers of children. If only this cast iron interior could be preserved through life there would, Ranulph thought, be much less crime in the world.

When everything that could be eaten had been eaten Colin took off Peronelle and Jacqueline to play a game known as "murder and assassination," a very noisy game which entailed a great deal of screaming and rushing over the rocks.

"Come too, 'Chelle," pleaded Peronelle, but Michelle wouldn't budge, she stayed sitting beside Ranulph looking very white and staring out to sea. The wind was rising steadily and white horses were rollicking in at their feet.

"By this time to-morrow," said Ranulph, "it'll be blowing great guns."

"Mm," said Michelle, "I think I'm going to be sick."

"By all means," said Ranulph pleasantly, "come back to me when you've finished."

When she came back, cold and miserable and crosser than ever, he had put a little tin cup in the embers and was warming milk in it. He gave her the milk, wrapped his coat round her and took her to sit in a sheltered cranny of the rocks. Here in the sun, with Ranulph's coat round her and a solid wall of rose-pink granite between her and the wind, Michelle began to feel warm and comforted.

"I beg your pardon," she said.

"Don't mention it," said Ranulph politely, lighting his pipe, "it was inevitable. Exaltation followed by temper followed by limpets was bound to end in physical distress." He cocked his eye at her, "I hope the stomachic disturbance has eased the spiritual one?"

Michelle smiled. The crossness was beginning to ooze out of her. She felt weak and tired, and very peaceful.

"If you mean am I less cross," she said, "well, yes, I am. It's funny, but I feel quite seraphic now."

"Be careful," warned Ranulph, "that is a particular stage of deep fatigue and is followed, as the fatigue grows less, by a condition of extreme irritability equally trying to the sufferer and his friends."

"Why's that?" asked Michelle.

"I don't know. I once had some small experience as a doctor but not as a psychologist—though the latter study has always interested me enormously."

"What is it exactly?"

Ranulph felt her curiosity was a healthy sign of mental recovery and smiled at her encouragingly.

"Psychology? The study of the mind. Put more simply a psychologist employs himself by finding out where people are being fools and why."

"Does it interest you to see where people are being fools, Uncle Ranulph?"

"Enormously," said Ranulph. "I like to get human beings under the microscope. I like the feeling of Olympian detachment which it gives me, and it is a delight to find that, idiotic as I am myself, others are frequently more so."

Michelle, interested, sat up and cupped her chin in her hands. Her eyes, so dull all the morning, began to look alive again.

"Are we all idiots?" she asked.

"We are all quite, quite mad," said Ranulph solemnly, "some of us more so and some of us less so. The more so get shut up, the others, unfortunately, do not. It's just a question of degree."

"It's a pity, isn't it?" said Michelle.

"What can you expect? In most people you have the soul and body constantly at war with one another and the mind refereeing them and getting battered in the process. Is it any wonder if the poor thing gets permanently warped?"

Michelle heaved a great sigh. Ranulph, glancing at her, realized he had put a finger on her problem.

"One lives in two worlds," she said slowly, hesitatingly.

"Exactly," Ranulph encouraged.

"And when the—the—everyday world comes in on top of the other and shuts it out one gets in a frightful temper—at least I do."

"Very disturbing for all concerned," murmured Ranulph.

"Yes, but what can one do about it?"

"Why ask me?"

"But you understand things. . . . How did you know I'd been—what you called exalted this morning?"

"The extreme violence of your reaction led me to infer that there had been something to react from."

"What can I do about it?" she pleaded, "I can't go through life getting in tempers and making other people miserable and I can't, *can't,* give up that other world—the world of the little white town."

"What little white town?"

"It's built of white marble—by the seaside. 'And, little town, thy streets for evermore will silent be—' "

Ranulph smiled. "Oh, *that* one? Yes, it would be a pity to give that up."

He puffed out smoke thoughtfully. Then he looked at her, twinkling. How desperately earnest she was over the old problem, so old that it was almost stale.

"The problem," he said, "is one of unity. The two worlds must be linked together and you yourself, your spirit, must be linked to what is behind all this—" he circled his pipe stem towards the sea and the rocks and the tamarisk trees—"to the whiteness behind colour."

"Yes, I know," she said impatiently, "but how, how? It's all very well to talk like that, but one never seems to get any farther."

"Most of us don't. We just talk. But one in a thousand does."

"Yes?" She was almost panting in her eagerness, and again he looked at her with amusement.

"I once met a man who said he had. He was a German—they are apt to be mystical, something to do with eating sausage and pickled cabbage."

Michelle snorted. "I don't want to know what he *ate,* I want to know what he *said.*"

"Ah, but you needn't snort. The two are very intimately connected. What you eat has a very great effect upon what you feel, just as what you feel can very often affect what you eat—or have eaten—as you've just experienced."

Tears of vexation stood in Michelle's eyes. Ranulph, penitent, composed his features, knocked out his pipe, and started again.

"He said—the German—and he hadn't eaten anything for hours but dates—we were travelling through the desert together—that in the process of unity there are three stages. First, you have your vision of reality—spirit—call it what you will—we'll call it your little white town, the thing that you want to be one with—which comes to you invariably, though few seemed to realize it, through your body and the unfortunate despised everyday world."

"Oh?" said Michelle, startled, "but one seems to fight against the other."

"Only because we make them fight. Our minds, the poor battered referees, are usually so stupid that they set one against the other instead of reconciling them. . . . Give the poor material world a chance. . . . Would you ever have seen your little white town if the man Keats had not written about it with, probably, a battered quill pen on the back of an unpaid bill, and if a rackety printing press had not bound his words into a book, and if the book had not come across from England to this Island in a filthy steamer so that your bodily eyes—give the poor body a chance—could scan the printed page and give a vision to your soul?"

"Oh—yes—" said Michelle.

"Stupid, weren't you? Well, now we've seen the necessity of one world to another we've more or less linked them together in a friendly way and we can go on to my German's second stage of unity—the stage where you always come a cropper."

"Well, go on." Ranulph was getting just a little bored and Michelle had to prod him.

"My German said it was a stage of tranquillity and acceptance. Having realized the necessity of everyday life to vision you then proceeded, instead of getting into a temper with it, to accept it with tranquillity and let it break down barriers in you—those barriers which separate your spirit from the spirit behind and in all created things, that Thing that you want to be one with."

"Keats' orbed drop of light," said Michelle. "But how can one let everyday life break down barriers?"

But Ranulph, though anxious to help her, was now getting really bored—morality always bored him. He had failed so utterly in that direction himself and one's personal failure, he thought, is always extremely boring. But he blew smoke patiently through his nose and continued.

"My German said it was a case of taking each event of life as a piece of discipline, as an opportunity for exercising courage, purity, or whatever virtue seemed to you most unpleasant and stupid at the moment. In that way, he said, you could get rid of all the sin and what-not that clog you up like a lot of fat. In that way, so he said, each trivial event in life acted like the blow of hammer and chisel in the carving of a statue—it knocked away extraneous matter and let free the form of the thing, the spirit of it. Once your spirit is, so to speak, freed, it can link itself with spirit immanent and transcendant."

"Then goodness is the thing that frees a spirit," said Michelle primly. Her tone was so like Miss Billing's that Ranulph nearly yelled.

"Don't mention the word good to me," he exploded, "it's a vile word. It's not the right word at all. It—it—stinks of Victorian hypocrisy and top hats, and flannel petticoats, it—" He stopped, fuming.

"What *is* the right word then?" said Michelle crossly. Not so did Miss Billing receive her pious remarks.

"There is no word. How can there be in these days when virtue is the fashion and crawling worms of human beings, posturing as eagles, take all the eagle words, apply them to themselves and smother them in mud?" He snorted. "In any case, what word is there to describe a chiselled, liberated human spirit? It's as impossible to describe as the charioteer of Delphi."

"What's he like?" asked Michelle.

"Like?" Ranulph snorted again and waved his pipe. "Like? He's a statue—you'll see him one day. He's the victor in a terrific struggle. . . . And now it's over. . . . He's simply standing there, very upright, very tranquil, and with that ease that's the reverse of indolence.

And the dignity of his simplicity is amazing. . . . He's come through something that has left him stripped of everything that doesn't matter. . . . And now he's waiting for his laurel wreath."

There was a silence.

"You haven't talked about your German's third stage," said Michelle at last. Ranulph seemed soothed by the thought of his charioteer and she felt it was possible to question him again.

"The laurel wreath. . . . The consummation of unity. . . . The whiteness behind colour. . . . How do you expect me to talk about it when I know nothing of it? Even my German, who did, could find no words. . . . They never can. You can describe the symbols or visions with which in your first stage of union the Thing you desired seemed clothed, but when it comes to union with the Thing itself you are dumb—so said my German. You'd better go and see the charioteer of Delphi, he can tell you about it—but he uses no words."

Ranulph got up abruptly. His face had become grim and a little bad tempered again. Michelle felt rather frightened of him. What had she done?

"You didn't mind telling me all that?" she asked timidly.

"Mind?" said Ranulph crossly, "of course I minded. Do you think it's pleasant to describe a delectable country at second hand?" He began to walk savagely across the beach, Michelle running after, trying to catch the flying fragments of talk that he dropped behind him.

"Why are we born blind as kittens and deaf as adders? . . . Fools! . . . Only one life and that spent in running in the wrong direction, blind and deaf. . . . And the thing is written in the visible world and shouts in invisible sound. . . . Fools! . . . And the devil's own torture that at last one sees clearly from outside the gate."

Michelle, scared, couldn't think what on earth he was talking about, but she felt she had disturbed him horribly. She was sorry, but at the same time tingling with the things he had said . . . gloriously tingling. When she'd had time to sort them out she felt she really would at last get somewhere.

Ranulph stopped where the path to the little village of L'Autel led from the beach across the grass and the sea holly. "It's cold," he snapped, "time to be getting home." He yelled like a braying donkey for the others, still murdering and assassinating round and round the rocks. Michelle, puffing and blowing, came up with him. They stood together looking round at L'Autel, at its pale pinks and green and pearly whites whipped by the rising wind.

"Now I know what you were thinking of as we came down," said Michelle triumphantly, "you were thinking of your German."

Ranulph, though still inclined to growl, smiled a little and began to shoot out disjointed sentences again. "Stage one, the lanes; vivid colour, irresistible beauty luring you on. . . . Stage two, L'Autel; pale rainbow colours. Tranquillity and acceptance born of storm. . . . Stage three. Unity. Merged colour. Just the whiteness of light. . . . Good luck to your hunting, Michelle."

IV

So strangely are destinies intertwined that one human being, standing merely as a link between one soul and another, changes the whole current of a life. That unknown German gentleman, who had years before expounded his philosophy to a bored Ranulph in the heat of a desert march, reaching out through another gave an impetus to Michelle's life that carried it far. Often in later years she wondered how far she would have got along her road if it had not been for that windy, lovely Good Friday. The days slip by, one after another, uncounted beads, but now and then comes one, rounded like other days with dawn and sunset, yet bright with the significance of a lamp set at a crossroads. This Good Friday was so illumined not only for Michelle but for André too, for one Charles Blenkinsop, an elderly English publisher with asthma, was able that day, through Ranulph, to remake André's life.

The day that had unfurled itself with a spreading of dove's wings above a brooding breast was closing with the beat and clamour of an eagle's flying. The wind had risen almost to gale force and wild shreds and tatters of cloud were flying across the sky like torn feathers; grey they were, trailing here and there an angry red-blood streak. There was a roaring in the air, a hint of battle and tumult. Ranulph, hunting round the farm for André with a letter in his hand, felt oppressed and laboured, as though he too were fighting. . . . Fighting for what? . . . Life? . . . He didn't know. He only knew he wished this storm were over. Spring storms could be nasty. He wished it were over.

He found André ministering to the pigs. "I want to talk to you," he shouted above the wind. "When you've tucked them up and kissed them come to my room." Then he abruptly turned his back and disappeared. He loathed the pigs. The monotony of their conversation and the inadequacy of their legs revolted him. André, scowling, watched him go, his slight figure leaning up against the wind, the letter in his hand gleaming white. He had a good mind not to obey the command. The friendship that he and Ranulph had achieved during Colette's illness had now entirely disappeared. . . . He loathed the fellow. . . . The blame lay at the door of Rachell.

Suffering the pangs of an over-active conscience Rachell, with a stupidity extraordinary in so wise a woman, had told André all about the affair with Ranulph. When the curtains of their four-poster had enclosed her and André in that little intimate twilit world that was all their own she had felt her extraordinary behaviour rising up like a barrier between them. . . . She could not bear it. . . . For sixteen years she had kept nothing from André except the methods which she employed in dealing with him. . . . She blurted the whole thing out. . . . As soon as she had done it she felt immensely relieved and comforted, but the effect upon André had been quite disastrous.

He had kissed and comforted Rachell, explaining her behaviour to her as the effect of the extraordinary magnetism of the man. An unhealthy magnetism, he averred, compelling, queer. André himself had felt it. And grandpapa. Look how extraordinary had been the power of Mabier over grandpapa. And the children. They scampered at his heels like the rats after the Pied Piper. Something odd about the man.

"A fallen angel," murmured Rachell to her pillows.

"What?" said André.

"That's why he has such power," said Rachell. "The giants, even though they fall from heaven, keep their stature."

"What?" said André.

"Even though they take the wrong turning they still tower over pygmy men. And they see farther too. Even if they have barred themselves out from Paradise they can still see which way the paths run there, and how the fountains play, and suffer in proportion to their vision."

"What?" said André.

"Good-night, darling," said Rachell, and, relieved of her burden, slept.

But André did not. His feelings towards Ranulph, as the days went on, crystallized into something like hatred. The man had come between him and his father on his deathbed. Between him and his children, taking their confidence. Worst of all, he threatened to come between him and his wife. . . . Who and what was he?

André, washing the pigs off himself in the scullery, had a good mind not to obey Ranulph's summons. Why should he? Then he remembered that letter, showing up so whitely. Somehow it drew him. He put on his coat again and went out into the windy twilight. He went up the stone steps built, French fashion, on the outside of the stable wall, and knocked at Ranulph's door. It opened at once and he went in. He had not been in this room since Ranulph's occupation and he looked round him curiously. The room, facing landwards away from the storm, was hushed and peaceful. A fire of vraic was burning and outside, through the window, André could just distinguish in the twilight the whiteness of the ladies-smocks in the meadow beyond the farmyard and the dim horizon of the bluebells. The room was very bare. Ranulph had added nothing to its simple furnishings but a writing table and a bookcase, but yet it seemed to André to be very much alive. The colour of the vraic flames was deeper, he thought, and the shadows darker and more shifting here than in other rooms. A great bowl of primroses stood on the table in the window—André wondered with a stab of jealousy if Rachell had given them to Ranulph—and the smell of the flowers, mingled with the scent of tobacco smoke and burning vraic, was to come back vividly to André, again and again, for the rest of his life.

"Sit down," said Ranulph curtly.

"Thanks," said André, and remained standing.

"I've a letter from a friend of mine, a man I met once out in Egypt, Charles Blenkinsop, a publisher. I'd like you to read it."

"Blenkinsop, of Blenkinsop and Garland?" asked André. He spoke the great names of a leading English publishing firm with the breathless reverence of all unpublished authors for the gods upon Olympus. He took the letter in a hand that trembled a little—though why he could not conceive—and carried it to the window.

Ranulph, standing in front of the fire, his hands in his pockets, watched him. In spite of the dim light he could see André's face go dead white and see how his hands trembled. He turned his back on him and lit the candles on the mantelpiece. When he turned round again it was to find André fixing him with eyes blazing with anger. The mixture of emotions in his face, fury and bewilderment with joy struggling somewhere behind them, was so comic that Ranulph laughed. The laugh added fuel to André's rage.

"Did you—dare—to take my papers from my desk and read them?" he stuttered.

Ranulph laughed again. "Come, come, man, it didn't take all that courage. You're not as formidable as all that."

André scented contempt, and flushed hotly. "It was unpardonable," he said.

"Oh, quite," said Ranulph dryly, "most of the things I do are. It was your own fault though. You let me loose on the farm on Christmas morning. I naturally ransacked your room. What else would you expect?"

André choked and Ranulph went gaily on. "Having found what I considered works of genius I naturally sent an example of them to an expert for his opinion. I always refer everything to experts. It saves trouble in the end. I was flattered to find his opinion coincides with my own." He flicked the letter in André's hands with his finger, and André looked down again at the sentences that seemed burning themselves into his brain. . . . "miracles of loveliness. Both poems and essays have a luminous beauty that is most arresting. . . . The power of deep thinking linked with both beauty and simplicity of expression is rare. . . . It is difficult to launch an unknown poet, but nevertheless at whatever risk to myself this one must be launched. . . . I hope you will be able to send me the rest of his work to consider. . . . I shall congratulate myself upon having the opportunity. . . . . I shall be happy to meet—"

Ranulph's voice cut across the butter-smooth sentences. "One more bit of evidence for the superiority of my judgment over other people's—yours for instance. I gather, since you apparently did nothing with them, that you thought nothing of your own work?"

André moistened his dry lips with his tongue. An intense palpitating joy was slowly creeping in and eating up his anger.

"I sent it to one or two publishers; they thought nothing of it," he said hoarsely.

"And you sat down under their opinion? You aided and abetted them in hiding your light under a bushel? How like you! How like your crawling subservient humility!"

Again there was a tiny lash of contempt in Ranulph's voice. André's anger flickered back again at its touch.

"You have, I believe, done me an immeasurable service. . . . But yet you had no right—"

"None at all," said Ranulph easily, "my behaviour was quite unprincipled, but then, luckily for you, I have no principles. . . . Sometimes, André, I wonder what measure of success would ever come to the children of light if they had not got the children of this world to boost them." He smiled and filled his pipe. "Yes, that's it. Every successful child of light is surrounded by a little group of worldly children who take the bushel off the flame, shout about its brilliance, tell lies about its heat, blow out, when possible, rival flames, haggle for terms and generally advertise heaven by the methods of hell."

He laughed and André, trembling, groped for the chair beside the fire. "Yes, André, there's money to be made out of you and Blenkinsop, aided by me, will make it. Trust Blenkinsop. That's all bunkum about the difficulty of launching unknown poets. Blenkinsop wouldn't be gurgling about the cost to himself of publishing your work unless he thought it was a loss likely to be repaid a thousandfold. Yes, André, you're rare. Didn't you know you were rare?"

He spoke suddenly very gently, drew up a chair opposite to André and sat down, looking at him.

"No." André, looking up, saw the queer tawny eyes, alight and eager, fixed on him. It struck him, irrelevantly, that in their eagerness and colour they were like Peronelle's. But he was too stunned to follow out the idea. Ranulph leant back in his chair and began to talk, quietly and appreciatively and with deep insight, of André's work. He seemed not to have forgotten a single word of the poems and essays he had read. He quoted whole lines of them and all the thought in them he seemed to have made his own. As he talked André felt all anger melt out of him, its place taken by a sensitive shrinking. . . . Those poems had been self-revealing and now this man, a stranger whom he disliked, had, in reading what he had written, read him too. Ranulph talked on and gradually this sensitiveness receded. So great was the man's understanding that he felt something of the relief of a penitent who has shared the burden of self-knowledge with his confessor, followed in its turn by almost a feeling of affection for this man who knew his secrets. Then all other feeling was swamped in a flood of joy, a joy that as yet he could not quite analyse. He felt liberated. He felt, in anticipation, fulfilled. He felt alive and growing. Skilfully Ranulph turned the talk from André's writing to himself. He spoke with admiration of André's toil and with sympathy of his frustration. Letting loose his story-teller's gifts he built a rosy picture of André's future as a writer. Warming to his subject he leaned forward in his chair, waving his pipe and gesticulating. . . . André was reminded suddenly of an elder brother telling him stories in the garden at Le Paradis. . . . He began to smile at the other's vehemence.

"And what of the farm?" he asked.

"You must get a good bailiff. You must waste no more time over the farm. It is a criminal, damnable shame that your talents should be wasted. . . . Waste. . . . There's nothing worse in this world and nothing more tragic than the right man in the wrong place. Stay on at Bon Repos by all means, it's your home and you and Rachell have created its spirit, but waste no more time on pig wash. Get a good bailiff."

"And how am I to pay him?" smiled André. "If, as you think, a writer's career is before me it will yet be some time before my earning powers can support bailiffs."

"Get a bailiff with money of his own who will throw in his lot with yours and leave you his money when he dies," said Ranulph.

André laughed out loud.

"This is not midsummer eve," he said, "I shall not find such a rare bird under a rose bush at midnight."

"It is Good Friday and you will find him on the other side of the hearth," said Ranulph.

André stared and the laughter went out of his face. "You?"

"Yes," said Ranulph, "I. I've been a wanderer all my life and I'd like to anchor at Bon Repos. I love the place, every stick and stone of it. I ask nothing better than to stay here. I'm a good farmer—I've given you proof of that—and I have money—plenty of it. I'll put it into the farm. If I die first all that I have will be yours."

André did not answer. Ranulph saw that all joy, amusement, gratitude and affection were draining away from his face, leaving it like stone. He realized, bitterly, that hidden under all surface emotions André had a fundamental dislike of him. . . . He did not want him at Bon Repos.

"I could not let you do that," said André harshly.

"Why not?"

"It's fantastic and I should not wish to give up all control of my own farm."

"It would not be necessary for you to do that, or to give up all the work even. A little practical work is necessary to thought, I know—the rhythm of it. We would work together, but you would be free of all anxiety, able to come and go as you wished."

"I could not possibly accept all that service from a stranger. It is strange to me that you should offer it. . . . What makes you?"

"Love of Bon Repos."

"You talk more like a crazy idealist than like the practical man of affairs that you are. You know as well as I do that these compacts between strangers end badly."

"I am no stranger." He spoke seriously and André feared that he had wounded him.

"No," he said generously, "you have been and are an amazingly good friend. I have no words to thank you. But there is no tie of blood between us—"

"Yes." The word seemed to rip across the quietness of the room as though a curtain were torn from top to bottom. André looked up startled, and found the other man's eyes fixed on him piercingly. He felt, as Rachell had felt, that Ranulph had come right into him, had taken possession of him. He felt almost a little thrill of fear and was aware again of the far away moaning of the wind, coming like a traveller from far distances, beating with its clamour about Bon Repos, sweeping on again into invisible space. This man in front of him, he felt, had something of the quality of a storm about him, something mysterious and restless, fierce and clamorous. He had felt this power often in the sailors and Island born men whom he had known—this strength of the sea and surge of the tides active in a man's blood. He leant forward, gazing at Ranulph, afraid, yet drawn irresistibly to him.

Ranulph smiled. "André, to think that you wrote those amazing poems and then thought so little of them that you knuckled under to the opinion of two beggarly publishers! And to hide them away even from Rachell. What an instance of your appalling self-depreciation! Even as a baby you were like that—the result of our father's bullying. We were both driven to loneliness by it, both of us. I rebelled and went off by myself, you hid. . . . Well, we've come together again now."

The room was whirling round André. The faint noise of the wind seemed to have risen to a great roar in his ears and the vraic flames were sheets of fire in front of his eyes. Through it all he was aware that he had got up and gripped Ranulph's hand. He heard strange sounds which seemed to be himself trying to speak and then from very far away came Ranulph's voice saying, "Let's have a drink. We need it," and from even farther away came the clinking of glasses. Emotion swept over them and even Ranulph was submerged.

It seemed days later that, restored, they were sitting in their chairs and rising to the surface again after hours of talk.

"Why did you not tell me? Why did you not tell me?" reiterated André like a parrot.

"Independence. I did not want to admit the claims of family. I thought they would bore me. Then the children laid siege and my defences gradually came down. . . . The children did it."

"And Rachell?" Ranulph fancied there was a touch of hardness in his brother's voice. He looked him full in the eyes, challenging it.

"Yes, and Rachell. . . . And the discovery through your poems of the stuff of which you are made. . . . And the old man's death. . . . They all took me captive."

"The old man knew you? That was why he wanted you when he was dying?"

"Yes. He did not need telling. . . . Why did you think he wanted me?"

"He took strange fancies for people. It would have been like him to want a stranger at his deathbed rather than his own son. We saw nothing strange in that, Rachell and I. And you are compelling. Rachell considers you of giant stature, a fallen angel."

Ranulph got up. "I think I put that idea into her head," he murmured. "I told her once that Apollyon, from outside the gate, could direct you correctly through the lanes of heaven. . . . Shall we go to her? Shall we tell her? I'd like her to know to-night."

Twilight had deepened into night, and it was pitch dark as they went down the steps. The wind had risen higher and came leaping at them over the garden wall. It pounced on them, tearing at them, trying to drag them apart. André, he did not know why, suddenly gripped his brother's arm as though to keep him at Bon Repos. Afterwards he remembered this little action.

V

By the afternoon of Saturday, as Ranulph had foreseen, it was blowing great guns. All night the wind increased and by morning there were floods of rain and a sou'wester that nearly lifted the roof off. The farm men, fighting their way in at Bon Repos gateway, declared that they had never known so sudden a spring storm. "Bad work on the sea to-night," they muttered to each other ominously, and went about their work in silence. And, indeed, everyone was silent. Used as they were to storms they found something unusually oppressive in this one. The roar and the deluge, coming crash in the middle of an unusually lovely spring, seemed almost cruelly destructive, as though the gods, unpropitiated, had vowed to make men's pleasure in peace and sunshine a brief thing.

In the afternoon, when the rain slackened a very little, Ranulph struggled out to the cliffs above La Baie des Mouettes. It seemed a crazy thing to do for the force of the wind was terrific at the cliff's edge and he could hardly stand, but life indoors to-day was intolerable. In the farmhouse he was pressed upon by the bewildered and, he felt, rather forced ecstasy of the family to whom he had declared himself uncle and brother, and in his own room he was a prey to fears and forebodings. Only outside, where every thought and nerve were needed to fight the storm, could he find relief. Clinging to a rock above the bay he looked down through flying spray to the scene beneath him. The water boiled and seethed as though a great cauldron had been set on hell fires and the gulls, tossed along on the wind, screamed despairingly. Beyond the bay the great waves came riding in with the majesty of a cavalry charge, curled themselves to the height of a man's head and crashed sickeningly on to the jagged rocks, whose javelins, destroying their huge curves, made of them a welter of spent foam and sent them back screaming over the shingle. Les Barbées, the reef of rocks beyond La Baie des Mouettes, was almost lost to sight in towers and pinnacles of hissing spray. For a long time Ranulph clung there, with the wind snarling and tearing at him like a pack of wolves and the rain and the spray dashing against his oilskins and running down him in rivulets. He was happier than he had been all day. Indoors the noise of the storm, setting his nerves on edge, had seemed to make other things weigh more heavily on him, but out here in the thick of it the fury was so majestic that it filled his whole consciousness. He stayed clinging to his rock until dusk came and his hands were so cold that they had lost all feeling, then he struggled reluctantly back to Bon Repos. The lights were lighted in the kitchen and they were having tea, he could see the children's bright heads through the window. He stood outside in the courtyard looking at them, then he turned away. He did not want to go in to them. He had said he would have supper in his own room. Standing on the stone steps leading up to it he turned back and looked again. He could no longer see the children but he could see the light shining out from the window. It did not reach far to-night, splintered by the rain it only made little blurred mirrors of the cobbles in the courtyard, but in his imagination he made of it a great light that lit up the whole world of Bon Repos; the old house with the passion flowers and the fuchsias growing against it, the courtyard with the strutting doves, the garden full of wallflowers and hyacinths, the orchard and the twisting oak trees, the farmyard and the byres and the meadow where the ladies-smocks and bluebells grew. Inwardly he looked round upon them all and then went into his room and shut the door.

He lit the lamp and poked up the fire and drew the curtains, got into dry clothes, lit his pipe and sat down in front of the fire. Then, with his usual courage, he looked events straight in the face. A dead man had come back to life and, as usual, the resurrection could hardly be called an unqualified success. He looked back over the happenings of last night and this morning. Last night he and André had gone to Rachell and told her. At least André had told her and Ranulph had watched her as shock, incredulity, bewilderment, dismay, and finally a marvellously simulated delight chased over her face. Then Ranulph's plans for future partnership in the farm were revealed to her—not the history and hope of André's writing, that, almost too precious to be spoken of, he kept for the four-poster—and her delight was so wonderfully natural that only Ranulph's keen eye could have detected simulation. They talked far into the night, a loving, joyous, excited talk, with an undercurrent of strain that was like a distant menace of thunder on a summer evening. The grandfather clock had struck twelve gloomily when Rachell began to tell Ranulph about her "seeing."

"I was right," she said, "you see, you have saved Bon Repos." She turned to smile at André. "I was right. You see? You have only to trust me. And I'm not saying 'I told you so.'"

They sat for a little longer laughing and talking, but the undercurrent of strain was still there, and both men were secretly glad when Rachell kissed them and went up to bed. They smoked in front of the fire till one o'clock, but they were tired, and the talk halted. Their silences were filled by the wind thudding at the window and the sound, they knew not why, depressed them. At last André got up and knocked his pipe out.

"I'll go up," he said, "the writing; I want to tell her."

His voice, as they discussed plans for the farm, had been dragging wearily, but now it thrilled. Ranulph, getting up, smiled. Here at least, in this liberation of André, was a certain fount of joy. The two men gripped hands.

"The writing," said André haltingly. "I can hardly realize it, the more I realize it the fewer words shall I have with which to thank you—a dumb fool—you cannot possibly understand what you have done for me."

But Ranulph thought he could. André, all other things for the moment forgotten, looked a new man. As the prison doors swung open the fresh air of the mountains that he would scale seemed already blowing upon him. Breathing it he looked taller, younger, stronger. Here, at least, thought Ranulph again, was success. He returned André's almost painful grip and was nearer to him than he had ever been, so near that their union was somehow exhausting. Words seemed stupid. They smiled in silence and André left the room and went upstairs. Ranulph dropped into a chair. He felt, after that moment with André, drained of strength. It struck him that he was going to find domestic bliss exhausting. His spirit, used to loneliness, was not going to find union easy. He and André, for one short moment, had achieved the sort of unity about which he had been holding forth so tediously to Michelle, and it had done him up. . . . He felt depressed. . . . Loneliness was easy, any fool could put out his tongue at his fellow man and turn his back, but worthwhile union was, he could see, hard work. . . . He sighed. . . . Overhead came a murmur of voices. . . . He could imagine the scene in the four-poster. Rachell, when she discovered exactly how much had been kept from her by both André and Ranulph, would hold forth at some length and her righteous indignation would be very stimulating—Ranulph wished he was there to see it—but gradually her love for André would get the better of her rage, and her joy and pride would mount so high that it was unlikely either she or André would get a wink of sleep that night. . . . Ranulph smiled to himself and leant back in his chair. . . . How he had come to love them both. . . . But could he, out of practice as he was, live with them successfully till the end of his days? And could he keep his love for Rachell within reasonable proportions? And why had the resurrection of Jean du Frocq been, somehow, not quite successful? . . . He leant forward again and looked at the fire, frowning. He sat tortured by these questions until the flames died to grey ash and he grew cold. Then he got up, went out into the courtyard and across to his room. But in bed the questions chased round and round in his mind and assumed the proportions of a nightmare. Such sleep as he got was more tiring than wakefulness. He got up the next morning so tired that he felt quite unprepared to be the uncle of five brats.

And the children, told by Rachell before breakfast that Uncle Ranulph was really and truly Uncle Jean, were decidedly odd. They were wildly excited. They yelled and shouted and hopped and bounced, till Ranulph's already aching head seemed splitting, but they one and all seemed anxious not to be left alone with him. Behind the excitement they were shy, a thing they had never before been with him. He supposed that by turning himself into a real uncle he had robbed himself of some of his fairy tale quality. He was no longer a shipwrecked romantic stranger, he was that dull thing, an uncle. By turning himself into a relation he had ceased to be an exciting rebel, like themselves, and had allied himself with the armies of law and order. Was that it? He didn't know. He only knew that there was something wrong with this resurrection of an uncle this morning just as there had been something wrong with the resurrection of a brother the night before.

Now, this stormy night of Holy Saturday, sitting in front of his fire, he tried to turn conjecture and confused feeling into certainty. He tried to discover exactly why it was that he was oppressed by this sense of failure. He had the whole evening before him. He had said that he would not have supper with them. Surely that in itself was significant? Why did he feel that Jean du Frocq, who had just been resuscitated, must be removed from his family for a little? His family! It was there, he saw suddenly, that the difficulty lay. They were his family and yet not his family. He had in his youth deliberately cut himself adrift from them, he had died, and the ranks had closed behind him, how could he expect now that they should open naturally and take him in? . . . The dead, he knew, should not return. . . . True, when Colette was ill they had taken him to the very centre of their life, but that was under stress of great emotion, they would have done the same to any kind doctor or nurse who had helped them. It was a state of affairs that could not last. And then the family was the father and mother and the children, a trinity, and the admitting of a fourth to that three was, he knew, in nine cases out of ten, disastrous. . . . No. . . . As Ranulph Mabier, a temporary paying guest, he was all very well, though André had found him excessively tiresome, but as Jean du Frocq, a rather disreputable relation forcing himself in upon them, he saw that he would not do. . . . And then there was André. Would even a liberated André, intent on his own work, like seeing Ranulph succeeding on the farm where he had failed? Would he not be happier with a paid bailiff? . . . And then there was Rachell. . . . He loved her. . . . He had told her that love could die of a little neglect, but his had not done so. That moment on the cliff edge had set a flame burning that he could not put out. . . . And the children. . . . He loved them as though they were his own, but they were not his own. He wanted this woman and these children for his and André, he thought, knew that he did. That would be between them always.

He got up and began tramping the room. He cursed that moment of infatuation under the oak trees. But for it he doubted if Rachell would have realized her own feeling for him, and but for it his own feeling for her might not have grown into this torturing thing, maddening him, threatening to escape his control. It came to him suddenly that in his life he had only loved two women with this tormenting love. Blanche Tangrouille and Rachell du Frocq. He smiled bitterly. What a contrast! But both Island women. The Island again! He felt, as he had felt before, that there was something about the Island that forced feeling upon him. In no other part of the world had he loved and suffered as he had loved and suffered on this Island, both in his boyhood and now in his age. Looking back now over his past life he saw those two periods stand out vividly; all the rest, in spite of the toil and money-getting and sin and horror and boredom that he had known in it, seemed to have faded into insignificance. It was the Island that mattered. Detachment and egotism and hardness of heart had been possible in other parts of the world, but not here. The Island, with her exquisite vivid beauty and the wildness of her storms, had forced joy and pain upon him again, had made the dead man live. . . . Had made the dead man live. . . . Yes, the dead had come back. He had lived again and living he had saved Bon Repos. But now he wished that he could fade out once more. Yet if hè went back to the East his wealth would go with him, travel was expensive, and Bon Repos needed his wealth.

Standing by the window he opened it and looked out into the night. The wind was still high, though lessening a little, and the sky covered with cloud. He could see nothing in the rushing, groaning, pitch black darkness but in front of him, he knew, was the meadow with the ladies-smocks and bluebells where he had seen himself. He drew back, slammed down the window and pulled the curtains. . . . The "avertissement." . . . There were more ways of fading out than one, and the death of his body would solve all difficulties. . . . Suddenly he abandoned all his problems. He would wait and see what the morrow brought forth. Meanwhile, released from thought, he spent a very pleasant evening. He made an excellent supper off the bread and ham and coffee he always kept in his cupboard. Then he lit his pipe and sat in front of his fire reading *Undine*, which he had stolen from André's bookshelf in the corn bin. He read it with delight. Undine the water fairy made him think of the water-lanes and sarregousets of the Island. As he read, his beloved Island, personified in the person of Undine, seemed almost present with him in the room. He read right on to the end of the lovely, magical, tragic story and then he sat and smoked and thought. . . . So she had gone back to the water. . . . She had tried to live in a human family but she, the solitary from another world, was not made for human union. Gifts and wealth she could bring from her world to the other for the use of her beloveds, but she herself brought them only jealousy and grief. . . . And she went back to the water.

Ranulph got up and knocked his pipe out. He would find some way by which the gifts and wealth he had brought to Bon Repos should remain while he and jealousy and pain went back to the water.

He went to bed and slept soundly.

VI

His waking dream was one of wings. Hundreds of unseen little fledgelings were rustling and flapping and whispering round him, and far off he was aware of the powerful beat of larger wings, an eagle or swan. Nearer and nearer they came, cleaving the air with a rushing sound that grew into a roar, and Ranulph in his dream ducked and cowered in fear. Still nearer, and he realized in terror that this was no swan but some terrible winged creature of night, some demon of death bent on his destruction. The paralysis of nightmare was on him and he could not move, he could only wait while the sound swelled into the scream of an oncoming wave, and the wind of the beating wings was on his face. Then with a crash the thing was on him, and he shrieked and woke. For a moment he lay still, trembling and sweating and still bound by that dreadful immobility of his dream. Then he realized that he was awake and that the first pale hint of dawn was outside the window. He sat up. The gale had dropped in the night and the sound of the wind in his room was hardly louder than the rustling of little birds' wings. But the uproar had not left the sea. The waves not half a mile from him were surging in with the rush and roar of the wings of his dream. The room was filled with growing and then receding waves of sound. Ranulph listened. What was the crash or report that had wakened him? The sound of another incoming wave filled the room, and just at the height of its roar the report came again—a shot fired not a mile away. . . . Two shots with three minutes interval. . . . Shipwreck. . . . With a bound Ranulph was on the floor and dragging on his clothes.

Just beyond La Baie des Mouettes was a little sandy cove, Breton Bay, with a little village of fishermen's cottages nestling in a hollow of the cliffs just above it. Here lived Sophie with her Jacquemin, and Hélier Falliot and Guilbert Herode and their wives. Down in the little cove were their fishing boats, drawn up high and dry on the beach in dirty weather, but left floating on the sheltered water of the bay when the sea was calm. Accidents were frequent at Breton Bay, for just outside was the terrible reef of rocks, Les Barbées, and the currents ran swiftly around it. Bathers were always getting into trouble, and those double-dyed imbeciles, the visitors from England, though always told not to sail a boat anywhere near Les Barbées, always thought they knew better, did it and came to grief. A gun was kept on the cliffs above the bay and fired twice as a signal for the rescue of fools in distress.

Ranulph, hurling himself into his clothes, wondered what was up this time. It was no mere sailing boat in trouble. At dawn after a night of severe wind it could only mean a wreck. He pulled on his boots, raced to the door and dragged at the handle. Then a sudden thought struck him. He turned back, went to his writing table and rummaged in its drawer. He pulled out a long envelope and laid it on the table in a conspicuous position. It was his will, leaving a small legacy to Blanche Tangrouille, and all the rest that he died possessed of to André du Frocq. Then he went out, closed the door softly behind him and ran down the steps into the courtyard and across to the house. As he expected, Bon Repos was up and doing. As he got to the hall door André came running downstairs struggling into his coat, which had somehow got inside out in the process of dressing. On his right foot he had one of his farm boots and on his left foot was one of his Sunday ones. The girls were running about upstairs in their nightgowns squeaking, and Rachell in the kitchen, calm and dignified, was poking up the fire and putting kettles on. Whatever went wrong, whether it was birth, or death, or shipwreck, Rachell put on kettles. Hot water, she was apt to say ghoulishly, both to wash the dead and make tea for the living, was the chief necessity in all distress. Ranulph had just time to notice and love her calm competence before the incompetent André joined him. Rachell in the kitchen turned round, and her eyes, dark with fear, went to her husband. "For heaven's sake be careful," she said hoarsely, "don't run into danger needlessly," and her eyes seemed to bore right through him as though trying to impress every detail of him upon her mind. For Ranulph in the doorway she had not a glance or a thought. It was as though he were not there. . . . He felt a sudden terrible pang. . . . Then André seized his arm and they were running together across the courtyard, down the lane and along the cliffs towards Breton Bay.

VII

A little figure clothed in a blue jersey and knickers thrust on pell-mell over his nightshirt, so that his stern bulged like a balloon, had slipped down the stairs behind André. Like a wraith he crossed the hall, well in his father's shadow. If Rachell had not turned round at that moment he would have got out and away. But she did turn round, and like a tiger she pounced. "Colin!" she said, and grabbed him by the slack of his jersey as he whisked out of the door. Colin twisted and turned, but Rachell seemed for once to have a man's strength. With one hand she dragged him backwards, and with the other she slammed the front door. "Not *yet*, Colin," she said fiercely, "not *yet*," and Colin, for the first and last time in his life, kicked his mother. Rachell gave a little cry and staggered, but she had the presence of mind to stagger between Colin and the door handle. Colin rushed upstairs to his room and slammed the door. From behind it he could be heard roaring like a hundred bulls.

Rachell, limping a little, went back to the kitchen and her kettles. Presently, Michelle, Peronelle and Jacqueline, sobered and dressed, came down and helped her. Colette, they said, when the gun went off had arisen and said her prayers but was now back in bed again singing a quite dreadful comic song.

"Very low and vulgar," said Peronelle, "goodness knows where she learnt it, but it's cheering up Toinette—Toinette's been crying."

Rachell and her daughters, having put on all the kettles there were, got breakfast ready and then sat down and waited. The girls got up now and then and moved restlessly to the courtyard and back, but Rachell sat perfectly immovable upon the "jonquière."

"Can't we go out to the cliff and *do* something?" asked Peronelle impatiently, but Rachell shook her head.

"Women are only in the way," she said, and her voice grated harshly. Peronelle, sitting down beside her, knew she was suffering and longed to hug her, but did not dare, she was so aloof and stern. Peronelle did wish that when people were suffering they wouldn't build stone walls up round themselves so that the people outside couldn't get at them. . . . It was so dreadful for the people outside. . . . It was horrible waiting like this. Simply horrible. She did hope father would be all right. Father, the darling, was so dreadfully silly. If he *could* step backwards off a boat into the sea he always did. . . . It was dreadful to love anyone as much as mother loved father. Quite dreadful. She began to pray inside her for André's safety, and then realized suddenly, with a start, that she had forgotten all about Uncle Ranulph.

"Mother!" she said out loud, "did anyone say good-bye to Uncle Ranulph?—I mean Uncle Jean?"

"Ranulph? Jean?" said Rachell confusedly, and then she looked at Peronelle in horror. "No!" Her mind had been so full of André that she had forgotten all about him. She had not even given him a glance as he went off to face danger, perhaps death, on that awful sea. Ranulph—no, Jean—who had saved Bon Repos for her. And she had thought not so long ago that she loved him a little. Well—that just showed. Beside her love for André, the father of her children, it was just the flicker of a farthing dip to the flame of a bonfire. And yet, she supposed, if she had been a society woman with nothing better to do she might have wrecked André's home for that flicker. But all the same her heart reproached her. She felt wretched and sick with foreboding. "No," she said again, "not one of us said a word to him."

Peronelle suddenly began to sob—a most unusual proceeding with her. "Poor Uncle Ranulph—I mean Jean—how horribly lonely for him. What if he dies thinking we don't love him?"

At the mere suggestion Jacqueline began to sob too and Michelle, as always when moved, began to scold. "Ridiculous nonsense! Idiots! Talking as though father and Uncle Ranulph were going to be drowned when they've only gone to see what's happened."

"That's all. Just to see what's happened," said Rachell cheerfully, but she did not smile and still sat there as though she were turned to stone.

"Mother, what did you mean by saying, 'Not yet Colin, not yet?' " asked Jacqueline tactlessly, through sobs. "I heard you from upstairs."

Rachell swallowed and moistened her lips. "Colin wants to be a sailor. I meant that when he is a man I shall have to let the sea take him, but not yet. He is still only a little boy."

"But I thought you weren't going to let him be a sailor?" pursued Jacqueline, "you've always said not—Peronelle, what are you kicking me for?"

"I shall let Colin be a sailor if he wants to be," said Rachell tonelessly, and she seemed to herself to be saying the words to Ranulph. . . . Could he hear?

Silence fell again. Colin's roars had subsided, and there was no sound but the distant crash and drag of the waves. Outside the wet, sullen dawn spread over the garden.

VIII

Ranulph, as he ran up the lane and along the cliff with André, found himself confused in thought and feeling yet vividly aware of passing sensation. It was still raining and the sting of it against his face, and the wet cliff grass drenching him as he ran made him feel as though he were already plunging through solid water. . . . Water. . . . Water. . . . He would go back to the water. . . . He remembered that moment of hideous pain when Rachell's eyes passed over him without seeing him. He no longer felt the pain, but he remembered it as a man remembers a signpost pointing him along his road. Feeling as he did Bon Repos was no place for him. . . . A swirling and rushing of wings was round them. . . . La Baie des Mouettes. . . . He remembered Peronelle lying on the turf reading Browning, and his thoughts raced confusedly back to her and to the other children and their mother. . . . He'd saved their home for them.

"Nearly there," panted André.

Ranulph turned for a moment and looked at him and André, meeting the look, smiled. They were locked once more into a moment of sudden and intense union. . . . The one-time prisoner and the man who had set him free. . . . What greater bond could there be between two men, thought Ranulph. . . . Then the moment passed and he was only conscious again of the rain and soaking grass and his own laboured breathing.

The little path they were following swerved away from the sea and downhill, taking the curve of Breton Bay. A high hedge of blackberry bushes and sloe trees hid the bay from them but they could hear shouts from below. They plunged downwards, pushing their way through the bushes and grass, and slipping and slithering on the wet ledges of rock that thrust themselves up through the ground. The path reached the level of the bay and ended abruptly in a tumbled mass of seaweed-covered boulders. A landsman would have slipped and broken his leg at the first attempt at crossing those treacherous rocks, but André and Ranulph, Islanders both, leapt and clung like cats until they reached the firm sand of the bay.

A handful of fishermen, with Jacquemin, Hélier and Guilbert among them, were already dragging down their boats to the water's edge, but they were few for the task in front of them and hailed the appearance of two more pair of hands with a shout. Down on this lovely little curving sandy bay there was hardly a stir of wind and the waves, with the tide going out, were negotiable, but outside the bay a huge sea was still running and Ranulph, looking at it, realized with exhilaration that they were all quite mad. . . . The madness ran in his veins like fire and he could have shouted with delight. He remembered nothing now but the excitement of the moment.

"Where?" he demanded of Guilbert as he took his place beside him and heaved at a boat with the rest.

"Les Barbées," said Guilbert briefly.

Ranulph looked out to sea, to the left of the bay. Fountains of spray now hid, now revealed, the rocks at the western edge of Les Barbées. . . . Hideous rocks. . . . Wedged between them he could dimly see a ship.

"Looks like a yacht," he muttered, "who on earth?"

"English," said Guilbert, and spat contemptuously.

"How do you know?" demanded Ranulph.

"Only the English sail yachts round the Island in spring weather," said Guilbert savagely, and spat again.

"Fools!" said Ranulph, but was grateful to them. Not for anything would he have missed this glorious exhilaration that was lifting him upon a peak of ecstasy. There was no more speech for they were off and every ounce of strength was needed for the oars. Even in the comparative calm of the bay it was hard work, and Ranulph wondered for a moment what it would be like when they were out beyond the sheltering cliffs. He soon knew. It was like being pitched suddenly into a mill race. The raging wilderness of water seized and caught them, and it took every ounce of strength in the bodies of the men manning the boats to keep their craft head-on to the wreck. Progress seemed impossible. “Hold her! Hold her!” Ranulph heard himself gasping, but his voice was lost in the rush of the waves and the screaming of the gulls. Then, as though by superhuman strength, they held and steadied, and began slowly, slowly, inch by inch, to creep forward. The current was against them and it seemed to Ranulph that with each straining effort unseen forces were pushing the boat back and back. He felt as though one moment’s relaxation would send them hurtling backwards over an abyss. The spray was dashing over them, blinding and choking them but, thank God, the wind had dropped. To Ranulph, out of practice as he was, the effort of rowing was colossal. He wondered how André in another boat was faring, but remembered that André, though the weaker man of the two, was in better practice. Soon all sense of exhilaration was lost in the agony of his physical distress. A ton weight seemed fastened on the end of his oar, and with the effort of pulling it through his lungs seemed bursting and every muscle in his body dragged out to torture point. The sound of the blood drumming in his ears seemed to drown even the sound of the waves. He could see nothing. A crimson curtain seemed let down in front of his eyes.

“All right going back,” a voice seemed saying, “the current with us then. Just got to get there.” Get there! But how to get there? How to endure long enough? The drumming in his ears turned to a roaring and his body seemed tearing into little pieces. It seemed to go on for a hundred years. At every stroke it seemed as though the breaking point were reached, and yet at every stroke his will thrust it a little further on—a stroke further on. . . . A shout tore across his consciousness. . . . They were there. . . . Guilbert, the best seaman in the Islands, who knew the surface of the sea as a palmist reads an outstretched hand, had brought them round to the far side of the wreck, out of the current. Ranulph, conscious that the others could hold her now, fell forward over his oar and the red curtain in front of his eyes turned black. A hand dragging at his shoulder roused him again. He looked up and saw the yacht looming up through the spray. . . . There were those fools to be got off her. . . . Only a handful, thank God. . . . He could see them up there, a few blue clad sailors, a woman with a child, and a man clothed in what had once been white ducks. Obviously the imbecile owner. Guilbert was on his feet and throwing a rope. Ranulph tried to get up, but found he could not. Damn! His usefulness was over. Well, he'd helped to get them there. He could see André on his feet grappling with a rope in one of the other boats. André had weathered the gruelling passage better than he—obviously more strength in the man than he had thought.

The rescue of the yacht's crew was arduous. The waves were still boiling so wildly round the wreck that it was impossible to come near to her. The Island men could only fling ropes and shout to the others to fasten them round them and jump. But except for the white-duck lunatic, his wife and child, the men on the yacht were sailors, and somehow the miracle—and the awestruck Island swore later in the day that it was a miracle—was accomplished. A joyous yell from Jacquemin, rising triumphantly above the sound of the waves curling hungrily round those terrible rocks, announced that one more feat of Island daring was accomplished on the sea. Ranulph, strength rushing into him from that shout, raised his head and saw a little drenched half-unconscious morsel of humanity lying across his feet. It was the child from the wreck. For one awful moment, so astray were his wits, he thought it was Colette. . . . Then her father—and Ranulph was not too exhausted to notice that he was obviously English and a fool—picked her up, and at Guilbert's shout they bent to their oars again. Ranulph, gripping his oar with hands that seemed now numb and nerveless, wondered if he would get back alive. . . . Well, he knew his time to die had come—he'd known it yesterday. The return journey, with the current in their favour, should be easy, but he had not now one drop left of the strength that had brought him out. Yet he went on rowing, pushing the moment of collapse always one stroke further off, and still one stroke further. He heard again the surge of the blood in his ears and then clear above it Guilbert's voice shouting "In the bay!" And suddenly, at that triumphant cry, he came to the end of his surface strength and tapped that supply of hidden power that only the using up of the last drop of surface energy brings into play. Life seemed to flow back again. The ghastly hammering and bursting of his heart and lungs lessened. He drove his oar through the water with a stronger stroke and the crimson curtain lifted from before his eyes. He looked up and saw, with the clearness and yet remoteness of a vision, a vivid magical picture of the Island. In a moment of time he seemed to see it all, down to the tiniest detail. The rain had stopped and patches of fragile blue were showing through rents in the clouds that were now thinning into blown wisps of grey gauze. There was a hint of coming sunlight and the little bay, with the waves flinging white flowery half-moons of creaming foam across its smooth sand, shone brilliantly gold and silver against the sombre cliffs. Up above the purple and indigo of caves and rocky caverns the young spring bracken and hawthorn trees frothed vividly green between sea and sky, and above them again blue spirals of smoke from the pink and white fishermen's cottages streamed away landwards on the wind. For a moment it seemed to Ranulph that the Island, a living presence, slipped between him and this actual scene and showed him all her glories in a moment of time. He saw Bon Repos and the doves dreaming under a hot summer sun, the cobbled streets of St. Pierre and the waters of the harbour lilac under a sunset sky, the round green tunnels of the water-lanes, the market with its fruit and vegetables and curds, the old Church of St. Raphael standing four square to the winds, and the pink rocks and tamarisk trees of L'Autel. The Island! An Undine spirit of earth and water, a sweet, magical, tempestuous thing that had given him life and would rob him of it. Even as his queer moment of vision passed there was a warning shout from Guilbert.

They were entering the bay and a little careless from exhaustion and victory they had come too close to the rocks that stretched out into the sea from the cliffs at its northern side. A great wave, pouring over the rocks from the heavy sea beyond, hit them just as the calmer waters of the bay had made them relax their vigilance. The boat heeled over, a cold sheet of water drenched and blinded them, and the white-duck Englishman, either from the natural imbecility of his disposition or from shock, let go of the child. She was overboard in an instant and carried swiftly away from the boat by the wash of the wave. Her little wet yellow head seemed to Ranulph to be Colette's. Before the boat had righted itself he was out of it and after her, so swiftly that with half a dozen strokes he had reached and caught her. But the act was the last of Ranulph's life. Even as he grabbed her the dreaded cramp seized him. Keeping her head above water, and drifting with every moment farther from the boat, he fought it and watched with anguish the figure of Guilbert, who had plunged after him and was swimming towards him. Would he be in time? He kept his eyes on Guilbert's arm, curving over his head, cleaving the water with a steady, unhurried stroke, curving over his head again, and with his last effort of will pushed the moment of collapse one stroke further off, and still one stroke further off. . . . Guilbert reached him. . . . "I'm all right," he said, "take the child."

One more moment of sight was his. He could see the sailors struggling to right the swamped boat and get her out of the danger zone, he could see Guilbert, swimming strongly, taking the child towards them, he could see the yellow bay with that flowery crescent of foam thrown across it, and then he deliberately abandoned effort and sank like a stone.

IX

It was some five hours later that André, rested and fed, and with dry clothes on, stood alone at the kitchen window looking out across the courtyard. He and Rachell were alone in the house with Ranulph's dead body. When Jacquemin had come running to Bon Repos with the news of the disaster Rachell had sent all the children out for a walk. She would not let even Peronelle stay and help her though Peronelle, indignant, begged and prayed to stay. They had never seen death. A terrible thing it would be, she said to André afterwards, if Ranulph, who had saved Bon Repos for the children, should, carried in dead, give them their first moment of real horror. . . . He'd never forgive her. . . . So she packed them out of the way.

André at the window looked out on a vivid blue-green world. Every vestige of the storm had disappeared. There was nothing left of it now but a glorious freshness in the air and the scent of bruised flowers and wet earth. The sky cupped over the scented, shimmering world was blue and cloudless, the shadows in the courtyard and the smoke curling up from the kitchen chimney were blue, and through the garden door could be seen the green sheaves of the hyacinth leaves and the blue scented spikes of the flowers. But André didn't see it. His eyes, wide and a little haunted, saw nothing but the sands of Breton Bay with his brother's dead body lying on them and the crescent of waves, so rhythmically and callously flung, fretting at the dead man's feet. . . . Those hateful little waves. . . . They were like the paws of an animal that has killed its victim and then toys with it.

It had all happened so quickly that even now it seemed to André that he looked out upon a dream whose memory would pass from him as the sun rose higher. In their exhaustion, the confusion of the child's rescue and the righting of the water-logged boat, it had been a few minutes before any of them realized that Ranulph had disappeared. It had been André and Jacquemin in the second boat who had found him at last, and got him ashore—but too late. For nearly an hour, in Sophie's little cottage above the bay, they had tried to bring back life, and failed. A wreck at sea had brought Ranulph to the Island and a wreck had taken him away again. André sent Jacquemin on to warn Rachell, but he himself waited to walk behind the hurdle on which Guilbert and Hélier carried Ranulph back to Bon Repos. As they climbed slowly with their burden up the steep path from the bay to the cliff top, and then along past La Baie des Mouettes and down the lane to the farmhouse, the day passed more and more jubilantly from storm to sunshine. The birds were singing madly in the bushes and the pattern of the gulls' wings, woven across blue sky and torn grey cloud, and white-flecked jade green sea, was one not of fear but of joy. The world had passed from death to life, and the passage through it of the dead body seemed somehow incongruous; something from a dead past lingering too long into the present. In spite of his grief and exhaustion André, walking through the growing glory of the morning, felt suddenly that for him and for Bon Repos this was a day of birth. The years of struggle and fear and suppression were over and a new life was beginning. . . . His eyes went back to the body carried in front of him. . . . A new epoch rooted, as always, in death. "Except a grain of wheat fall into the ground and die." The truth of that rule of life came flashing through the bright morning and pierced André like a sword.

And now he stood at the kitchen window calmly and quietly, as though nothing had happened, while upstairs over his head Rachell's footsteps went backwards and forwards. She was up there by herself laying out the body. He shivered a little. He hated to think of her performing that terrible task alone. But she would do it. She would not allow anyone else to help her. He understood how she felt. She was filled, as he was, by a passion of regret and remorse. This man had saved them and had wanted to be one with them and they, who owed everything to him, had not wanted him.

There was silence upstairs. He could imagine Ranulph lying in their four-poster beneath the picture of the Last Judgment with Rachell kneeling praying by his side and just for a moment, in spite of his grief, he wondered just how much these two had meant to each other. . . . Then, as he heard Rachell coming downstairs, he put the thought from him with shame. She came in and putting her arm through his looked with him at the scene outside. "How lovely," she said, "and all ours for ever. . . . And your real life beginning at last. . . . And the children. . . . We'll never know how much he did for them. . . . And then we didn't want him here."

"Thank God he didn't know that," said André.

"Of course he knew it," said Rachell, "he knew everything. That's what made him a little uncanny. I think it was because he always saw through us all that we didn't really want him as one of the family. Families, however many friends they have, want their own inner privacy, don't they? Just like individuals. Even a beloved outsider in their sanctuary seems to violate it. Father and mother and children. A fourth upsets the balance of the trinity, disturbs relationships.... Ranulph nearly upset yours and mine.... Families must work out their own salvation. We'll work out ours."

But André was not to be comforted. "The salvation that he brought to us," he said.

"And to himself," said Rachell. "Was there ever such a rank individualist as that man when he came to us? Yet in less than a year he had no thought but the salvation of a family and he died saving a child.... It was the Island did it."

"The Island?" asked André.

Rachell slipped her arm round his neck. "You can't be an individualist on our Island," she said, "there's so much magic packed into so small a space. With the sea flung round us and holding us so tightly we are all thrown into each other's arms—souls and seasons and birds and flowers, and running water. People understand unity who live on an Island. And peace. Unity is such peace. Ranulph found peace on the Island I think."

So she talked on and André was at last comforted. They sat together on the "jonquière" and watched the sun mount higher and higher until the patter of feet took them out to the courtyard. The children were returning laden with flowers. Bluebells and ladies-smocks and ragged robins and buttercups were cascading from their arms. Colette was almost staggering under her load.

"I thought they'd better all *do* something," said Peronelle the practical, "so I offered twelve doubles out of the housekeeping money for the best bunch of flowers.... Colette's won."

Colette held up her great bunch towards the sky, offering it apparently to the sunshine, or to the unseen spirit of the place.

"Why!" said Peronelle suddenly, "we'd all forgotten—it's Easter Day!"